STALKED

ALSO BY BRIAN FREEMAN

Stripped

Immoral

STALKED

BRIAN FREEMAN

**Doubleday Large Print
Home Library Edition**

ST. MARTIN'S MINOTAUR
NEW YORK

**This Large Print Book carries the
Seal of Approval of N.A.V.H.**

For Marcia

Where the dead red leaves of the
   years lie rotten,
The cold old crimes and the deeds
   thrown by,
The misconceived and the misbegot-
   ten,
I would find a sin to do ere I die.

> —Algernon Charles Swinburne,
> "The Triumph of Time"

PROLOGUE

The prisoner squinted at the threatening ebony sky through the steel mesh that made up the cage in the rear of the patrol car. He knew he should be afraid, but he was dead inside. His heart was black. All he could do was watch the big wind come and hope it would scoop him up into its twisting, churning middle.

Five seconds later, the storm howled down upon them.

"Oh, mother of God," the cop who was driving squealed. She was a rookie and heavyset, with squat fingers clutching the wheel. Sweat dripped down her cheeks from under her butch dark hair. The ferocity of the wind lifted the front wheels of the speeding vehicle off the highway, and rain like a deluge sheeted across the glass. The driver did the only thing she could do; she stopped, because she was blind. The car danced, doing a shimmy on its tires.

"Keep going," her partner told her.

"Are you fucking crazy? The storm shifted, you stupid son of a bitch, it's coming right at us."

They were stopped askew on a rural section of highway, surrounded by deserted farmland. All the residents had left, headed north, abandoning their homes to the wind and water.

"We're thirty miles from Holman," the other cop repeated. His voice was scratchy, like quarry dust. "We need to get this sack of shit back behind the walls. Keep going."

Debris hammered the car windows: rocks, tree branches as large as his thigh, roof shingles, dead birds.

"No way, man, no way. We have to get inside right now."

"Inside ain't going to make any difference," the other cop replied. The inmates called him Deet, because he trailed a sweet smell of insect repellent to drive away the Alabama mosquitoes. That was the only sweet thing about him. He was short and lean, but he was a beast. He wore steel-toed boots and liked to break shinbones with a swift jab of his toe.

"I saw a farmhouse," the driver said. "I'm going back."

She wheeled around in her seat as she backed up. The prisoner stared into her eyes, which were wild with animal panic. She was petrified, close to soiling herself. The smell of her fear awakened something familiar and arousing inside him.

The pavement gave way to gravel, and she stopped.

"I see it!" she said, as lightning lit up a battered farmhouse.

Deet jerked a thumb at the backseat. "What about him?"

"We can't leave him in the middle of the storm."

"We *ain't* letting that guy out of the cage," Deet growled.

The prisoner leaned forward, his hard face against the mesh, and spoke to the two cops. "Leave me here, I don't give a shit."

He didn't care. Dying here was better than going back to Holman.

For weeks, he had anticipated the road trip to Tuscaloosa, so that he could inhale the river stench of the Black Warrior again and eye the street girls in their halters. There was nothing they could offer him for his testimony; he was a lifer. All he wanted was a taste of the city grit on his tongue and a vibe off the street. One more bite of the life that had been stolen away from him ten years ago.

Ten years ago. He remembered that smug bitch watching from the back row of the courthouse as he was sentenced. She had tracked him across the south and tipped off the Alabama cops, and he went down for murdering a competitor, his life erased over a nobody who deserved what he got because he was skimming the merchandise. He wished he could have had another half hour with her, to wipe that fucking grin away like sand, before they buried him inside the walls.

Being outside again only made it worse to go back. The few minutes in court—in a suit without the cuffs or the leg irons—were a hoax, like a steak dinner before they slipped you the needle. It made the years ahead—in an overcrowded, stinking cell, seeing gray

cement and steel every minute of your life—
seem unbearable. Getting sucked up by the
storm would be a blessing.

"Where the hell can he run?" the woman
screamed at Deet. "Come on, we have to go
now!"

Deet cursed and flung open the car door.
The wind ripped it out of his hand, and the
metal groaned. The noise of the storm
roared like a train. Deet pulled his gun and
pointed it at the prisoner's head.

"You give me any trouble, you're dead!" he
shouted. He unlocked the rear door.

The prisoner got tangled up in the chains
and fell to the ground as he tried to plant his
feet in the dirt. He felt Deet's hand on his
shirt collar, pulling him up. He spit out mud
from his mouth.

"Let's go!" the woman yelled. She waved
an emergency radio and slammed the trunk
of the squad car shut.

Rain buffeted the prisoner, like ice picks
jabbing at his face. He struggled to walk in
miniature steps up the driveway, which was
a rushing river now. When he stumbled, his
feet hobbled by the leg irons, he felt the barrel of Deet's gun on his neck, pushing him
forward. They reached the front porch of the

two-story farmhouse, but the door to the home was barricaded by plywood nailed to the frame. The woman cop put down the radio and clawed at the boards to tear them away. Her fingers bled.

He wondered how far he would get if he tried disappearing in the storm. Deet read his mind. He eyed the prisoner and cocked his gun. "You want to run? Go ahead. It'll save—"

Deet stopped talking. When the prisoner narrowed his eyes against the driving rain, he saw that Deet didn't have a head anymore. Right above Deet's body, a yellow highway sign with a dripping, bloodred fringe bobbed in the side of the house where it had flown like a guillotine and become impaled. Something like a soccer ball rolled down the porch and then was picked up by a gust and whisked away. Deet's head.

He heard the other cop wail, an awful noise, primal and terrified. Deet's body collapsed in a heap, gushing watery blood that spilled down the wooden steps like paint. He dove for the gun, but so did the other cop, and she was surprisingly fast for a big woman. She kicked him backwards off the porch and drew her own weapon. She grabbed Deet's gun and shoved it in her belt and, not taking her eyes off the prisoner lying prostrate in the blood and mud, she squatted and threw up over Deet's body.

"Get up!" she screamed, wiping her mouth.

She got the front door open and waved him in ahead of her with a flick of her gun. He pretended to limp. The frame of the house rattled like aluminum cans, and the wooden beams under his feet shuddered as if their nails were about to pop. It was black inside, and the cop switched on the radio and its emergency beacon. Angry static crackled between the walls, and every two seconds, the room flashed with red light.

"Downstairs," she instructed, pointing to an open door.

"Unlock me."

"Bullshit."

"I can't take stairs in these chains," he insisted, keeping the desire out of his eyes. *Do it, do it, do it.*

"No way."

"I'll break my fucking neck, you stupid bitch. I can't see in the dark."

"Move."

"Shoot me if you want, I'm not going anywhere like this."

She swore and threw a set of keys at his feet. He kept a tired mask on his face as he freed himself and stretched his numb limbs. He took stock of the cop, who held her gun with unsteady hands. Her uniform was wet and painted on her skin, and water dripped from her hair. She danced with impatience.

"Downstairs," she repeated, her voice cracking.

The uncarpeted steps shrieked as his foot landed on each one. She was right behind him, but she was young and she stayed too close, the gun jabbing into the small of his back. He tripped, and she froze. His hand snaked back, and in an instant, he yanked her wrist, pulling her past him and uprooting her down the steps. She screamed as she tumbled, breaking her legs and collarbone, landing in a fleshy heap on the concrete floor. The radio shattered into plastic pieces. He was on her immediately, stripping away both guns, dragging her by the scruff of her shirt into the center of the basement.

She moaned in agony. Blood spat out of her mouth. *"You bastard!"*

He fed on her fear. Seeing her at his feet, helpless and desperate, made him feel like a reptile sloughing off an old, unwanted skin.

He was reborn out of ten years in hell, a new man.

With a great crash, the half-window notched into the concrete wall of the cellar erupted inward, and water poured through in waves. The smell was fetid and moldy. The cop screamed as dirty water puddled around her. "Oh, Jesus, the river's flooding. We've got to get out of here."

He laughed at her. "We?"

"You can't leave me here, for God's sake. I can't get up."

Three inches of water swirled around his feet and grew steadily deeper. He watched as the cop pulled herself up and then splashed back as her splintered bones gave way. She flailed at the water and shouted for help, but her voice was a whisper as the storm assaulted the house.

"Please," she begged him. "Please."

He became physically aroused watching her. He rubbed himself through his jeans and listened to the sounds of her pain. She went under for the first time when the water was up to his thighs. She came up again, coughing and gagging, and then swallowed as the water closed back over her head. Each time she rose up, she screamed obscenities now, railing at him because he was the one in control of her fate, he was the one with absolute power, he was the rock-hard instrument of life and death. There was no escape.

A metamorphosis took place before his eyes. He no longer saw her face. Instead, he saw the face of the bitch who had taunted him like a devil for ten years, and he knew there would be no escape for her now, too.

"That's the thing about floods," he told the cop, the last time her face broke free of the dank river water. "They wash away your sins."

PART ONE

I KNOW WHO IT IS

1

Maggie awoke with a start, dreaming about sex. She wondered if she had dreamed the gunshot, too.

She lay tangled in the black sheets, her skin moist with a sheen of sweat. As she blinked, her brain tried to stutter out of the dreamworld, but the nightmare held her in its grip. Her eyes were open, but she was blind. She felt impossibly strong hands on her body, holding her down. A stench of dead fish overwhelmed her nostrils and made her want to vomit, but her mouth was clamped shut. She thumped against his flesh with her fists, but it was as if she were a fly tapping against a glass window, trying to get out and getting nowhere. He laughed at her, a mean rumble of pleasure. She screamed.

Her eyes snapped open. She was awake. Except she wasn't.

Stride was sitting on her bed. She heard herself say, "Hey, boss," making it sound seductive, which it wasn't. He was smiling at her, his eyes maddeningly dark and ironic. She opened her arms wide, and he came into them, and she was ready to taste his kiss when he crumbled into sand.

That was when she heard it. Muffled and distant. *Bang.*

Maggie sat up in bed. Her breaths pounded in and out of her chest. She looked at the clock on her nightstand and saw that it was three in the morning. She had been asleep for two hours, although it wasn't sleep so much as a drunken unconsciousness filled with strange dreams. That was all they had been—dreams.

Except she wondered about the gunshot. Something had awakened her. Maybe it was Eric, moving around restlessly downstairs. Or maybe it was the violent wind outside, making the timbers groan. She sat in bed silently, her ears pricked up. Snow had begun—she could see the white rain through the window—and tiny flakes of ice hissed like whispers on the glass. She listened for footsteps, but she heard nothing.

She remembered what Stride always told her. Never listen to worries that come to you in the middle of the night.

Maggie realized she was cold. The bedroom was drafty, and her skin was damp. Even in January, she slept only in panties, not liking the confines of clothes under the blankets, but it meant she often woke up freezing. She got out of bed and scrambled to the thermostat, bumping it up several degrees. Down in the bowels of the house, the furnace rumbled to life, breathing warm air into the room.

She went to her closet to grab a robe. There was a full-length mirror on the door, and Maggie stopped to look at herself in the moonlit shadows. She had spent years finding things wrong with her body. She was too short, not even five feet tall, and too skinny, with bony limbs and breasts that were like twin bunny slopes. Like a doll in her mid-thirties. Her black hair was cut as it always was, in straight bangs across her forehead. She was pretty—everyone told her that. She didn't see it. Her nose was small and pert, but her cheeks were too round. Her almond-shaped Asian eyes were so dark as to be almost black, with a few yellow flecks in an irregular pattern. Her features were too symmetrical. She could make her face do amazing things, twisting it into sarcastic expressions, making her mouth into a tiny O rimmed with cherry-red lips, like a fish gulping for air. But pretty? She didn't think so.

She held up a forearm. There were goose bumps on her honey-colored skin. She took a hand and laid it on her bare, flat stomach and watched herself in the mirror as she rubbed her abdomen in slow circles. Her vision blurred as she began to cry. She opened the door so she didn't have to look at herself anymore and slipped a silk robe off a hanger. She shrugged it on and tied it with a tight knot.

Maggie turned away, sniffled, and wiped her eyes. She felt dwarfed by the huge master bedroom and its massive mahogany furniture. On the far wall was a burgundy dresser, taller than she was; she had to stand on tiptoes to see inside the top drawer. Four hand-carved wooden posts loomed on each corner of the great empty stretch of the king-sized bed. It was too much bed for her by herself, which was how it had been for weeks. She hated even being near it.

She took a step and her head spun. She still felt the effects of the wine she had drunk in the park. She steadied herself with a hand on her nightstand. When she looked down, she saw her shield and felt all the complex emotions that came with ten years on the job. She hadn't expected to be working now, but there was a part of her that couldn't leave the Detective Bureau, that wanted and needed to be with Stride. Or maybe it was because, step-by-step, the rest of her life had become a horror in the past year, and being on the job was a way to forget.

She stared down at the nightstand again and felt unease worm its way into her stomach. Something was wrong. She mentally retraced her steps, what she had done, where she had gone, hoping she had simply made a drunken error. But she hadn't. She had come upstairs and dropped her shield, her wallet, her gun, her keys, on the nightstand by the clock.

Now her gun wasn't there.

It had been an ugly Wednesday night. Bitter cold, the way January always was. By ten o'clock, Eric hadn't come home. Maggie had ginned up the courage to talk to him, but when he didn't show up, she felt herself growing angry. He had been secretive and withdrawn in the week since the holidays. She couldn't blame him for that. They had been strangers for weeks, arguing constantly. It was her fault. She was the one who had closed herself off, who had shut him out, because she couldn't deal with everything that had happened to her.

She grew sick of waiting for him and left the house. She took a bottle of chardonnay and a corkscrew. She bundled up in her Russian sable coat, a wedding gift that she didn't wear often, but it was warm and made her feel like royalty. The snow hadn't started yet, and the streets were clear. She drove down into the city, which was still festive with holiday lights, and then north along the shoreline drive until she came to a turnoff by the lake. It was deserted. She parked and opened the wine. When she got out of the truck, the wind blasted her face, but she ignored it as she followed a snowy trail to the dark, moving mass of Lake Superior. The stars winked down at her, undimmed by the glow of lights from the city to the south. The branches on the evergreens drooped with snow. Her boots sank into the drifts. Her coat hung to her mid-thighs, and between the fur and her boots, the cold slashed at her legs.

There was no ice growing from the shore here; the water moved too fast. Only in the worst stretches of winter was the cold powerful enough to send a tentative sheet of ice a few hundred feet into the lake. Instead, there was nothing but angry midnight swells now, frigid whitecaps breaking on the rocks and undulating hills of water that looked like sea monsters wriggling toward the beach.

She tipped the wine bottle to her lips and drank. It was chilled and dry. She had skipped dinner, and the wine went straight to her head. She felt sorry for herself, but with each swig of wine, she cared less and less. She stayed there for an hour, until the wine was gone and her limbs were numb. She threw the empty bottle end-over-end into the fierce waves. She thought about lying down in the snow and not getting up.

Take off her clothes. Die of exposure.

But no. Even though she had nothing to go home to, she knew it was time to go. She climbed unsteadily back to the parking lot and sat, thawing, inside the truck. Her mouth felt stiff. Her face was pale, and her hair was crusted with snow. She was like the Tin Man, rusted over, needing oil.

She drove home slowly, feeling the effects of the wine. Her street was dark and quiet at one in the morning. Everyone had turned off the lights in their big houses and crawled under their goose down comforters. When she opened the garage, she saw that Eric was home, too. He would be sleeping in his office. She thought about waking him up and doing what she had planned to do, but it could wait until morning.

She stripped off her fur coat in the hallway, not even turning on a light. There was an antique chest near the door, underneath a brass mirror. Something was sitting on the varnished wood. Eric had left it behind when he came in. It was a black ceramic coffee mug, and under it, a small folded note with her name scrawled on it in Eric's handwriting. The mug still had remnants of coffee grounds in it.

She unfolded the paper. Even in the dim light, she could make out the words:

I know who it is.

Maggie stared at the note long and hard. It was the same old song, the same tired accusation. She was angry that he still didn't trust her. She crumpled the note into a tiny ball, shoved it into her pocket, and went upstairs to sleep.

Where was her gun?

She could think of only one explanation. Eric had taken it. He had come into their room and taken it off her nightstand. She had not dreamed the gunshot. Except it made no sense at all. Eric was not suicidal; he was a life force, energetic, passionate, pushing his limits. And hers.

Maggie saw a cone of white light shoot through the bedroom. Instinctively, she crouched, then crawled to the picture window that overlooked the lake. She stood up, out of sight, and edged her face against the cold glass until she could see. The blackness in the room kept her hidden. She saw headlights on a car parked fifty yards away, and as she watched, the car accelerated, its wheels spinning in slushy snow as it did a U-turn and vanished. She couldn't see its make or color.

She waited, watching the street. Snow was falling outside, big wet flakes streaking the window. She stared straight down and saw footprints in the white dust, leaving a track down her driveway to the street. Already the wind and snow were making the indentations fade.

Maggie ran for the bedroom door. Turning the knob, she hesitated, then threw it open. The hall was filled with vast shadows. She took a chance and said quietly, "Eric?" She said it again, louder.

"Eric!"

She heard only the oppressive silence of the house. She smelled the air and caught the stale odor of beef she had made for a dinner that went uneaten. Maggie kept close to the wall as she went downstairs. She glanced in the living room and dining room and found them empty. Her feet were bare, and the floors were cold. She tugged the robe tighter and crept up on the open door to Eric's office. She wished she had a weapon.

Near the doorway, she heard dripping. Slow and steady. Drops falling into a pool. Her stomach lurched. She reached around the doorway and clicked on the light, squinting as the brightness dazzled her eyes. From inside, the noise kept on: *drip, drip, drip.* There was a new smell, too, one with which she was very familiar.

When she went into the office, Eric was there, limbs sprawled, blood forming creeks down his face, soaking the sheets, and splattering into red puddles on the slick floor. A gunshot wound burrowed into his fore-head. She didn't run to her husband. There was no point—he was already gone. He was one more body in the hundreds she had seen over the years. Her eyes studied the room by instinct, a detective hunting for answers. She found none, only a terrible mystery—her gun, which had been on her nightstand when she went to sleep, was now in the middle of the floor. Smoke mingled with the mineral stench of blood.

Maggie wished she could cry. More than anything, she wanted to crumple to her knees and weep and ask God how this could have happened. But when she looked inside herself, she had nothing left. She bit her lip, stared at the man she had once loved, and knew that as bad as her life had been in the past year, it was about to get worse.

2

_____

No footprints in the snow, Jonathan Stride thought. That was going to be a problem.

Footprints didn't last long in this weather. Looking down at the front yard, he could see the harsh wind already erasing his own boot prints, which he had left seconds earlier. Even so, he would have felt better if he could have used his camera phone to take a photograph to prove that the tracks had been there.

The tracks of an intruder. Someone other than Maggie.

He hated thinking like that, but he knew how the investigation would go. Maggie knew it, too; she had described the scene to him on the phone. She would be the prime suspect. They had solved murders together for more than a decade, and it was almost an immutable law. If a husband got killed at home, the wife did it. And vice versa. It didn't matter if you were a preacher, a Christian, a politician, a family man, a saint, or a cop. Your spouse gets murdered at home, you did it.

Stride brushed snow off his heavy, black leather jacket and his jeans. He was tall, almost six feet two, and lean. He ran a hand back through his wet, wavy hair, and the silver streaks glistened amid the black. He didn't need to ring the doorbell; it opened while he waited on the porch. Maggie stood in the doorway, looking tiny in a red silk robe. He searched her face for tearstains and didn't see any.

"Hey, boss," she said.

He looked at her, at a loss for words. "I'll leave my boots outside," he said finally. He slipped off his boots and took his coat off, too, and left them in a corner of the porch. As he stepped over the threshold, he bent down to study the lock on the door.

"It wasn't picked," Maggie told him. "I checked."

"Don't try to run the scene yourself, Mags."

"I know whether a lock has been picked," she sniped at him. She bit her lower lip, and then, as if to apologize, she hugged him. She was small but strong, and she spent long seconds embracing him. "Sorry," she murmured. "Thanks for coming."

"Why didn't you call 911?" he asked, not liking the accusation in his voice.

Maggie backed up and folded her arms together. "I *know* what's coming. Cops tramping through the house. Hours of interrogations. Newspapers. Television. I didn't want to deal with it, not right away."

"This is a murder investigation. Minutes count."

She scoffed. "Investigation? This is going to be a witch-hunt. Let's not sugarcoat it. I'm in big trouble."

He didn't disagree with her. "Did you search the house?" he asked.

"No."

"All right, let me look around."

"I told you, he's gone."

"He?"

"I'm assuming it was a he. Then again, we're talking about Eric, so I shouldn't assume." She gave a sour laugh.

Stride frowned. "I'm going to tell you something as a friend, Mags. Not as a cop. You should *not* say things like that. Okay? You should shut up."

Maggie kicked at an imaginary piece of dust on the floor. "Yeah, but I don't want to shut up. I want to get mad. I want to scream at someone."

"That won't help."

"No? It'll sure make me feel better." She saw his face and softened. "I know, I know, you're right. Look, you shouldn't be here. If you want to leave, that's okay."

He didn't reply, but it was true. He was on thin ice being here, because this wasn't going to be his case. He and Maggie had been partners and friends for more than a decade, and as a result, he would be walled off from the investigation. He was the lieutenant in charge of the Detective Bureau that investigated major crimes in Duluth, at the southwestern corner of Lake Superior, where the lake narrowed like a knife point plunging into the city's heart. Duluth was small enough that Stride played a lead role in most of the serious cases himself, but this homicide would wind up in the hands of one of his senior sergeants.

He knew that was why Maggie wanted him here before the others arrived. She wanted him to see the scene, to talk to her, to form his own opinions. She was drafting him onto her team.

"Make us both some coffee, okay?" he said. "I'll check out the house."

Maggie screwed up her face. "You know I don't drink coffee."

"You do now," Stride told her. He added, "I could smell the alcohol on your breath when you opened the door."

Her face blanched as she turned away.

Stride began in Eric's office, but he stayed at the threshold and didn't go inside. He saw the single gunshot wound in Eric's forehead. His muscular body was stretched out on a burgundy leather sofa, a white blanket draped over his legs and stomach. His hairless chest was bare. His head and its long mane of blond hair lay propped on a pillow, which now cradled blood like a punch bowl. The gun was in the middle of the floor, at least ten feet away from the body. Too far to be a suicide. He looked for dirty water on the floor that might have been left by snowy boots, but whoever had done this had been careful. He had probably left his boots in the entryway where everyone else did and then crept through the house in stockinged feet.

Assuming anyone had been in the house at all.

He felt nothing looking at Eric's body—he had deadened himself to that kind of emotion years ago. Even so, he knew Eric well. Eric and Maggie had been married for more than three years, and Stride had been to their house many times. It was awkward for all of them. Stride and Maggie had a long history before Eric entered the picture. For years, Maggie had indulged a quiet crush on Stride, and he wasn't sure it had entirely gone away. Eric knew it.

Stride went room to room on all three levels. It took him nearly half an hour. The house was huge and ghostly for two people, full of cubbyholes with strange slanted ceilings, and secret spaces where cold breezes sneaked through the walls. It was in a neighborhood of vintage estates, clustered together a few blocks west of the north-south highway near Twenty-fourth Avenue. Once this had been an old money enclave, and now it was dominated by city professionals and entrepreneurs. Eric had owned the house for more than a decade. He was an ex-Olympic swimmer who had built a lucrative international sporting supply business, mostly serving athletes in the Winter Games. It was his kind of house, like a European castle, full of social aspiration. The outside was weathered tan brick and gables, an imposing monster from the street. Maggie hated it. When Eric went on business trips to Norway and Germany, she sometimes came down to Stride's house on the lake and stayed with him and Serena.

When he returned downstairs, he found Maggie in the kitchen, staring into her coffee cup. The empty stretch of azure marble counter behind her was wiped clean. "I didn't find anything," he told her.

She nodded as if this wasn't news.

"Go over it for me again," he said. "Like you did on the phone. Tell me what happened."

Maggie recited the events of the evening in a monotone. She told him about waking up, hearing the shot, seeing the car outside, and then finding Eric downstairs. She didn't mention getting drunk, and Stride wondered what else she was leaving out.

"How did the killer get in?" Stride asked.

"I've been thinking about that," Maggie said. "He could have been waiting outside and slipped into the garage when I came home. We don't lock the door from the garage to the house."

"And your gun?"

"Let's just say it wouldn't have been hard for him to come into the bedroom without waking me up."

"Has Eric been having problems with any-one?"

"Not that I know of."

"How's his business going?"

"As far as I know, great."

"As far as you know?"

"I don't ask. I have no idea how much money he has. The bills get paid. I assume he makes more than I do, even on a cop's lavish salary."

Stride smiled thinly. "Where was Eric today?"

"I don't know. He was in the Cities over the weekend. He got back on Monday, but I barely saw him. He didn't come home for dinner tonight."

"How were things between the two of you?"

She shrugged. "Fine." Her voice wasn't convincing.

Stride waited to see if she would say

something more, but she didn't. "Is there any-thing else you want to tell me?" he asked.

"No."

"Can you think of anyone who would want to kill him?"

"You mean, other than me?" she asked sharply. "I *didn't* do this. I need to know you believe that."

"I do."

"But?" Maggie was smart. She could see that he still had questions.

"You haven't been yourself for weeks," he said. "Why?"

Maggie's face reddened with anger. "That has nothing to do with this."

"Are you sure?"

"Drop it, boss. It's none of your business."

"I thought we didn't have secrets from each other."

"Stop treating me like a child." She stood up, and her robe slipped. He saw more of her chest than was appropriate, but she made no effort to fix it. "I should get dressed. We better call in the dogs."

"You know what they're going to ask you," he said.

She nodded. "Why wasn't Eric sleeping in the bedroom with me."

"So?"

Maggie shoved her hands in the pockets of her robe. "Eric had trouble sleeping. He'd go down to his office and work, and when he got tired, he'd crash out on the sofa."

She didn't meet his eyes as she left the room. He knew she was lying.

3

Stride sat outside in his Ford Bronco, watching the crime scene investigation unfold around him. His window was rolled down, and he was smoking a cigarette. He allowed himself one a day, sometimes two. This was his third. The snow continued to fall, sticking in wet sheets to his windshield and blowing into the truck. The icy flakes landed like mosquito bites on his cheek.

He didn't like being shut out of the police activity, but he had already recused himself. When several cops came his way for instructions, he shrugged and pointed them inside Maggie's house to find Abel Teitscher. None of them was happy to realize Teitscher was in charge. That included Stride.

His cell phone rang. He felt as if he could take the pulse of his life by the country song playing on his phone. For a while, he had used "Restless" by Sara Evans as his ring tone. He had been away from Duluth then, on a brief, strange detour to Las Vegas. Now he was back home, but he had never been able to relax, no matter where he was, and he didn't know why. So he put Alabama's "I'm in a Hurry" on his phone. As the song said, all he really needed to do with his life was live and die.

It was Serena on the other end of the phone. He and Serena shared a house and a bed, but they spent so much time with Maggie that they sometimes felt like a threesome.

"How is she?" Serena asked.

"She's hiding something," Stride said.

"You don't think she did it, do you?"

"No, but she's not being honest. That's going to hurt her."

"Who's running the investigation?"

"I talked to K-2," Stride said, using the department's nickname for Deputy Chief Kyle Kinnick. "He handed it off to Teitscher."

"Shit."

"Yeah, he wouldn't have been my choice."

"Can you help her?"

"Not much. I'm between a rock and a hard place."

"I'm not," Serena said.

"That's true, you can do whatever you want."

"Keep me posted."

Stride closed the phone.

He had been given a second chance after the death of his first wife, Cindy, five years ago. Serena was a former homicide detective from Las Vegas. They had worked a case that had roots in both cities and wound up as lovers. When the case came to an ugly end, he followed Serena back to Las Vegas, but it was obvious after only a few months that Stride was a fish out of water there. When he had a chance to get his old job back in Duluth, he jumped at it and asked Serena to come with him. She didn't offer any promises or guarantees; she was worried that she would be as much an outcast in Duluth as Stride had been in Vegas. But she had been with him here for more than a year now.

Stride glanced at the stone steps leading

to Maggie's front door and saw Abel Teitscher heading his way. Strangely, he had Teitscher to thank for the opportunity to come back to Duluth. When Stride left the city, Teitscher had applied for and won the job as lieutenant overseeing the Detective Bureau. He was a solid investigator, dogged and thorough, and he had the gray hair for the job. Teitscher, in his mid-fifties, was almost a decade older than Stride, but he was a stubborn loner with no gift for leadership. The detectives on the force launched a near rebellion after a few months with Teitscher in charge, and K-2 was forced to rescind Teitscher's promotion. He used the opportunity to lure Stride back from Las Vegas to lead the squad again.

Teitscher still carried the grudge.

The older detective came around to the passenger side of Stride's Bronco and squeezed his long legs inside without being asked. They eyed each other with strained politeness.

"Hello, Abel," Stride said.

Teitscher nodded. "Lieutenant."

The older detective carried all of his years in his face. He was tall and lean, with white skin and a spider's web of wrinkles carved into his narrow cheeks. His hair was gray, clipped in a military crew cut that neatly matched his trimmed Hitler mustache. He was an obsessive runner, without an ounce of fat on his body, but he wound up looking skeletal and unhealthy, with jutting cheekbones and a protruding jawline. His wire-rimmed glasses were too large for his face.

"Have you lost your mind, Lieutenant?" Teitscher asked.

"Meaning what?"

"You contaminated a crime scene."

Stride shook his head. "I did no such thing."

"You were here for an hour with the body and the suspect before you called the police."

"I am the police," Stride reminded him.

"Not on this case. You knew damn well K-2 would yank you. What the hell were you thinking?"

"This is Maggie we're talking about. She didn't do it."

"No? You're not looking at the evidence, Lieutenant."

Stride didn't want to get into a fight, not here, not now. "Look, Abel, Maggie called me first. We've worked side-by-side for ten years. I came and talked to her. I made sure there was no one else in the house. Then I rallied the troops. End of story."

"You're a witness now. I have to interrogate you."

"Go ahead."

Teitscher shook his head. "Not now. But I want a report from you of everything that went on while you were alone in the house with her. This is on the record."

"Fine," Stride said.

"I want it by noon."

Teitscher opened the truck door, and Stride clapped a hand on his shoulder. "You're a good cop, Abel, but sometimes you get so focused on what's in front of you that you don't see the big picture."

"What does that mean?"

"This is Maggie. If she says she didn't do it, you can take that to the bank. Something else is going on here."

Teitscher leaned in close, and Stride winced at the musk of his cologne. "I'll tell you what's going on. I've got a woman inside with a dead husband and her gun on the floor. And she's lying to me. You think I can't tell?"

"If she's hiding something, it's not about the murder."

"Listen to yourself, Lieutenant," Teitscher said scornfully. "If this were anyone else, you'd practically have her in cuffs by now."

Stride knew he was right, but he also knew that Abel had his own bias, too. "Are we talking about Maggie here, or are we talking about Nicole?"

Teitscher flushed. "That was years ago."

"That's right. Years ago, it was *your* partner with a dead husband on the floor. You trusted Nicole, and you were wrong. So now you're poisoned against Maggie."

"You should have learned the same lesson that I did," Teitscher snapped. He thrust his long legs out of the Bronco, then stuck his head and shoulders back through the door. He wore a trench coat that wasn't suited for the cold, and it billowed behind him like a cape. "You can't trust anyone, Stride. Instead of covering for Maggie, maybe you should ask yourself how well you really know her."

Stride thought about Teitscher's words as he drove home. How well did he really know Maggie? The answer was, better than almost anyone else on the planet.

She was nothing like the quiet, conservative Chinese girl he had first met more than a decade ago. She had grown up in Shanghai and gone to the University of Minnesota at age eighteen to study criminology. When she became enmeshed in political activism on campus following the uprising in Tiananmen Square, she found herself on the wrong side of the Chinese government and decided to stay in Minnesota after graduating, rather than risk prison back home.

Stride hired her for her near-photographic memory and her razor-sharp ability to size up a crime scene. She was smarter than most cops who had been on the job for years, but she was blunt and serious, much more Chinese than American. She didn't care about fashion or makeup, and she didn't crack jokes. Her face never moved. When Stride teased her, she thought she had done something wrong.

But times changed, and so did Maggie.

A decade in the United States had transformed her. She was stylish and hip today, with a closet full of leather and spiked heels. Most of the time, she shopped in the girls' department because she was so small, and she was as well turned-out as any trendy teen. In her mid-thirties, she managed to look twenty-five and pull it off. Her round bowl haircut was oddly old-fashioned, as if that were her one concession to her Chinese roots. But otherwise she was carefully made-up, right down to the diamond stud she had added last year to her thimble of a nose. Hurt like hell, she said, but she loved the glint of the jewel on her face.

She had grown into a sexy woman, but Stride had never seen her as anything but a daughter, of whom he was fiercely protective and proud. Maybe it was because he had first met her when she was barely out of her teens, at a time when he was happily married to Cindy. He mentored Maggie and watched her blossom, and soon, she fell in love with him. Cindy warned him about the huge crush that Maggie was developing, but he pretended that the attraction wasn't there, and eventually, Maggie did the same. It was still the elephant in the room between them—invisible but something they always had to dance around.

She didn't carry much of her past with her anymore. She was bubbly, sarcastic, funny, sharp-tongued, and foul-mouthed. It had taken years for all her rough edges to blend together. She was more like a machine in her early days, not revealing any trace of her emotions, because she thought cops didn't do that. But Stride knew that you needed emotion to succeed in this job. You couldn't divorce yourself from your feelings, and you couldn't let them dominate you. It was a delicate balancing act.

He still remembered the investigation where Maggie took the first big leap, becoming someone new and whole. It was the kind of case detectives hate, the kind that haunts them. That was something Maggie didn't understand. She was accustomed to solving cases. She figured she was smart enough that if she simply brought enough brainpower to bear, and studied all the details, she would dig her way to the truth. Usually she was right. But not always.

She and Stride had been working together for more than a year when a girl's body was found one late August morning on the dewy grass of the golf course near Enger Park. She was nude, and the rape kit came back positive. Her head and hands had been hacked off and were never found. The coroner concluded that she was about seventeen years old, and from the bruises on what remained of her neck, she had been strangled. The only identifying marks on her body were a collage of tattoos from rock bands and video games, like Bon Jovi, Mortal Kombat, Aerosmith, and Virtua Fighter.

They tried everything to solve the case, but in the end, they weren't even able to find out who the girl was. They reviewed thousands of missing person reports from the entire Midwest. They ran DNA from the semen found in the girl's body and came back with nothing. They worked with a local psychiatrist on a profile that got them nowhere. They contacted hundreds of tattoo parlors. They checked video game fan clubs. They got in touch with each of the bands. Weeks went by, and the case got cold.

She was simply the Enger Park Girl, and that was who she was going to stay.

He remembered Maggie pacing back and forth in a City Hall conference room a month after they had found the body. She kept rerunning everything they had tried, looking for something they had missed, or some other angle they could pursue. Finally, her face serious and confused, she looked at Stride and asked him how they were going to solve the case. As if he had been deliberately holding back the answer.

He had to tell her the truth. Unless someone came forward with new information, they weren't going to solve it. A murderer was going to walk away free. A young girl wasn't going to get justice. Sometimes that was how the world worked.

It was as if the idea had never occurred to Maggie before.

She dropped down in a chair, looked him dead in the eye, puffed out her cheeks in frustration, and said without a trace of an accent, "That really sucks, boss."

At that moment, Stride knew she had become an American. And a cop.

4

Stride and Serena lived in an area of Duluth known as Park Point, a narrow finger of land that separated the churning waters of Lake Superior from the ports where the giant cargo boats loaded and unloaded shipments of coal, taconite, and grain. They lived on the lake side, steps from the beach. He arrived home before dawn on Thursday morning, and in the windy darkness, he heard the roar of waves like an invading army on the other side of the dune. He followed the snowy trail behind their 1890s-era cottage up the slope toward the shoreline, where he was face-to-face with the muddy waves rolling onto the sand. There wasn't much beach to be seen now, just a gray sheet of ice stretched over the sand like a boardwalk. Stripped, bare tree trunks littered the shore, washed up after months of floating with the waves.

The wild rye grass on top of the slope formed a wavy auburn wall. Snow and wet sand mingled at his feet like melted marshmallow running over chocolate ice cream. He sucked in cold, fresh air. To the west, he could see the fog-ringed lights of Duluth climbing sharply up the hillside from the lake. On his right, the Point peninsula stretched for another mile, and on the other side of the open water, a gauzy lighthouse beam circled from the Wisconsin shore. The sun would be dawning soon, but the clouds were so thick over the city that he would have to take it on faith that the sun was still up there, giving warmth.

He couldn't escape a feeling of loss and loneliness when he came here. All of the important people from his past were long gone. He had grown up on the North Shore and in the course of his life had lost his parents and then his wife of twenty years here. He had never missed having children while Cindy was alive, but there were days when he regretted that he had no reminders of her other than fading memories. Staring at the angry waves, he thought of his father, too, who had lost his life to the lake when Stride was a teenager. He often imagined his father's ore boat, shouldering through the deep, cold troughs, out of sight of land. You just never knew when a rogue wave could reach up and snatch someone away. They never recovered his body.

He wondered if it was true that you couldn't go home again. That was what he was trying to do. For years, he had lived on the Point with Cindy, but he had moved away after his second marriage and always regretted it. That marriage lasted only three years and was a mistake from the beginning, which he realized when he met and fell in love with Serena. When she came back to Duluth with him from Las Vegas last year, they bought a house out on the Point again, and he was back where he had spent most of his life. He felt renewed, but his only worry was that he would spend too much of his time living in the past.

He heard the crunch of snow behind him and turned to see Serena climbing the slope. Her black hair was loose and uncombed. She had a grace and beauty about her even when her body was buried in a heavy coat and her long legs were up to their knees in drifts. She joined him without saying anything, and they stood watching the lake and feeling the brittle morning air make its way under their skin. The cold made her face flush pink. She wasn't wearing makeup.

"I know you don't want to hear this," Serena told him quietly, "but Maggie could have done it."

Stride's face hardened into a mask, and he kicked his boots in the wet sand. "No way."

"I'm not saying she did do it, but she's been on an emotional roller coaster for a year. Everyone has a breaking point."

"I know all that, but she says she's innocent."

"What does Abel think?"

"Teitscher? He's already got a target painted on her chest. I'm worried what he'll find when he starts digging."

"Like what?"

"I think Maggie and Eric were having big problems."

Serena showed no surprise. "She's had three miscarriages in eighteen months, Jonny. You don't think that plays hell with your emotions?"

"I know it does, but if their marriage was in

trouble, it gives her a motive. Particularly because of Eric's money." He added, "Abel also thinks that Maggie is hiding something, and I think he's right."

"Do you know what it is?"

"No."

Serena slung her arm through his. "Listen, Maggie asked me something a couple of months ago. I don't know if it means anything."

"What?"

She hesitated. "Do you really want to know? I don't want you to feel like you have to feed all this back to Teitscher. We're pushing the box pretty far here."

Stride grimaced. Driving over to Maggie's in the middle of the night, he knew instinctively that he was walking into an ethical gray area, where he had no road map. His principles were about to be stretched like elastic, and he wondered when they would snap. "Tell me."

"She asked if you and I had ever done anything strange."

Stride raised an eyebrow.

"Sexually," Serena clarified.

"Did you tell her about the garden hose?"

Serena punched him. "I'm serious. It sounded like Eric was pushing her to do some weird stuff."

"Like what?"

Serena shrugged. "She didn't say."

Stride chewed on this idea and didn't reply. He didn't like where any of this was going.

"But officially, you don't know about this, okay?" Serena repeated. "Maggie didn't want me to tell you."

He nodded. "She could use your help, Serena. She's going to need someone to investigate her side of what happened, and it can't be me. I can't be seen giving her any special treatment."

"I'll do what I can."

Serena hadn't joined the police force in Duluth. Stride supervised the city's detectives, and the employment lawyers frowned on nepotism. Instead, she had obtained her state license as a private investigator and begun struggling to find work. So far, her projects mostly involved plowing through trade journals and attending industry conventions to unearth competitive intelligence for a few Duluth-based start-ups. He knew the assignments left her bored and restless. She was a cop at heart, and she missed the street.

"I've got a new client meeting today," Serena added.

"Oh?"

"Dan Erickson wants to hire me."

"*Dan?*" Stride retorted. "Why the hell does he want you?"

Serena arched her eyebrows in offense. "Excuse me?"

"You know what I mean."

"He said my police background was a plus," Serena said.

"Except you live with me. That should be a big minus for Dan."

Dan Erickson was the county attorney and chief prosecutor for the region. He blamed Stride for the media fallout over a botched trial that had cost him a statewide election as attorney general. He was now widely considered damaged goods in Minnesota politics, and it was an open secret that he resented being stuck in the north woods of Duluth and was looking for a way out.

"You might want to think twice about this, Serena," he cautioned her.

"I can't say no. This is a big break for me."

He heard the stubborn resolve in her voice and knew her mind was already made up.

"You can't trust him."

Serena shrugged. "Dan can open doors

for me all over the state." She added, "Besides, I don't trust any of my clients."

"Do you know what he wants?" Stride asked.

"No, he wouldn't talk about it on the phone. He asked me not to tell you anything about it."

"But you're telling me anyway."

"It's in the box."

They had struggled to find a way to work through the secrets they both had to share, without creating personal or professional problems for either of them. The reality was that they needed each other. Stride wanted her input on investigations because she was one of the most experienced detectives in the city, but her contributions had to be confidential and unofficial. Serena in turn wanted to get Stride's bounce on her own assignments, without worrying that anything she told him would wind up in a police file. So they invented the box. When they wanted to share information privately with each other, it went in the box.

"He'll make a pass at you," Stride added, smiling.

"He makes a pass at everyone."

"That's Dan."

"Why does Lauren put up with it? She's the one with the money."

"Dan and Lauren are all about power, not sex. If Lauren cared about Dan's affairs, she'd have cut him loose long ago."

"Spoken like a man," Serena said. "So what do you think Dan wants?"

"He probably needs to dig up dirt on a political opponent."

"Yeah, that was my guess. The legislature is back in session soon."

"Just make sure he doesn't hang you out to dry," Stride said. "For Dan, everyone around him is expendable. I've been there."

"I can take care of myself."

Serena closed her eyes and lifted her chin to let the icy wind strike her face. When she did that, you didn't argue with her.

Stride knew she had survived a long time on her own and was fiercely determined to make it here without his help. He didn't bother warning her that Duluth could be as extreme and cruel in its own way as Las Vegas. All he needed to do was look at the great expanse of the lake to remember that one person alone was pretty small in this part of the world. No matter how strong you were, there were things around here that were stronger.

5

Serena climbed the steps toward the county courthouse for her meeting with Dan Erickson and felt an odd sensation dogging her again, as it had for weeks. Uneasiness settled over her, and she stopped dead in her tracks. The feeling blinked out of the gray morning like a neon sign in her head, broadcasting the same word.

Danger.

She waited on the top step of the garden with her back to the courthouse, studying the comings and goings in the government plaza. A stony-eyed statue of a centurion towered behind her, guarding the three historic buildings clustered around the park. City Hall, where Jonny worked, was on her left. The federal building was directly opposite, on her right. All three government buildings were austere monuments from the 1920s, built of sand-colored granite blocks. Cars were parked in the slush around the circular driveway, and people hurried up the sidewalk, tramping through the cold in their winter coats. No one looked at her. She surveyed the windows in the neighboring media buildings one by one, then examined the street, her eyes moving from car to car.

A television truck with a satellite dish on its roof. A purple van from a computer repair shop. A delivery truck from Twin Ports Catering. A police car.

Nothing out of the ordinary.

Serena shrugged off the feeling and blamed it on the ugliness of January. It wasn't the cold that she found hardest to get used to living in Duluth. It was the deathly pallor of the city at this time of year. Days would go by, sometimes weeks, with only the same charcoal mass of clouds overhead. Winter felt like a long, cheerless twilight, full of somber faces and ominous skies. Those were the times when she felt a sharp pang of longing for the desert with its sunshine and energy.

But for all that, she liked it here.

Her old home was barren compared to this ever-changing landscape. The Duluth summer had been cool and glorious. The fall, with its palette of reds and yellows stretching for miles on the trees, had awakened a strange, uplifting sadness in her when she passed through the rain of dying leaves. Even the winter was beautiful, with something spiritual about the severity of cold and clouds that made her live inside her mind.

She liked that she stood out in this city. She was tall and athletic, with full, highlighted raven hair. In Las Vegas, she had regularly been mistaken for a showgirl, but statuesque beauties were a dime a dozen in that city. Not in Duluth. She enjoyed the stares. She liked watching men melt. It empowered her and gave her the confidence that she was up to the challenge of making a new life for herself in a new place.

She liked what being here did for Jonny, too. He was home, in a cold place, in the shadow of the lake. Serena found that her love for him had deepened and matured this past year, as she got to know him in a more intimate way. Their attraction had been electric and physical in the beginning, but the longer she lived with him, the more she had come to respect his decency and humanity. It also aroused her no end that he thought she was one of the sharpest detectives he had ever known.

But she couldn't she escape the sense of unease that twisted her insides now. The sensation of eyes watching her under a microscope.

Danger.

She had learned to listen to her intuition. Back in Vegas, there had been a stretch of weeks when she got the same feeling, that something was wrong, that she was sharing her life with a secret stalker. Later, she discovered that a predator named Tommy Luck really had been watching her all that time, and she wound up with a narrow escape.

That was then, she thought, and this is now. Tommy was history. The past was behind her.

Maybe it was simply that she couldn't escape her demons so readily. She was still haunted by memories of her teenage years in Phoenix, before she ran away to Las

Vegas. Her mother had descended into a life-stealing addiction to cocaine and begun living with a sadistic drug dealer named Blue Dog who used Serena as his personal whore. She had fought long and hard to get past the helplessness of those days and still saw a psychiatrist every month to help her cope. It was over, but it was never really over. It only took a strange, disconnected sensation of danger to reawaken the scared child.

I'm not fifteen anymore, she told herself.

Serena continued through the park to the courthouse. She took the antique elevators to the top floor, where Dan Erickson had his office as county attorney with windows overlooking the lake. She introduced herself to the receptionist, hung up her coat, and took a seat on the almond-colored sofa. Serena wore black dress slacks, heels, a burgundy blouse, and a black waistcoat with gold buttons. It was a conservative outfit but didn't hide her figure. She noted the sideways glance from the receptionist and wondered if the girl had pegged her as the next in the long line of Dan's conquests.

The inner door to Dan's office opened.

A woman in her forties appeared in the

doorway and gave the receptionist a cold smile that barely crinkled her lips. She had wheat-colored hair crisply pulled back behind her head, leaving only a few strands free to carefully graze her forehead. She was small and elegantly thin, with ruler-straight posture that would have made a Catholic nun proud. She had a Coach purse slung over her shoulder and wore a knee-length charcoal skirt and ivory jacket. Pearls dangled on inch-long gold chains from her earlobes, and a matching necklace glinted discreetly in the hollow of her neck. When her lake-blue eyes latched onto Serena in the waiting room, her brows arched into perfect twin peaks. She marched over and cocked her head.

"*You're* Serena Dial?" she asked.

"That's right."

The woman took the measure of Serena from head to toe. "Well, good for Stride. I didn't realize you were such a gorgeous creature."

"And you are?" Serena asked.

"Lauren Erickson. Dan's wife."

"Oh, sure, of course. I'm sorry, we haven't met before."

Serena recognized her now. Lauren was in the papers regularly, tangling with the city council over zoning issues on her real estate properties. She rarely lost; it helped to have the power of the county attorney quietly behind you and enough money to grease itchy palms. She was the banker and brains behind Dan's career.

"You're from Las Vegas, aren't you?" Lauren asked.

"That's right."

Lauren clucked her tongue as if Vegas belonged to a different solar system. "Duluth must be quite a disappointment for you. No Elvis impersonators. No topless chorus lines."

Serena stood up. She was nearly a foot taller than Lauren, and the other woman's small mouth puckered with annoyance as she tilted her chin upward to look at Serena.

"I was always a fan of the Liberace museum," Serena replied, smiling.

The receptionist smirked. Lauren silenced her with a glare and nestled her expensive purse against her shoulder.

"Everyone is talking about Eric's murder," Lauren said. "I took an early flight back from D.C. this morning, and Dan called me at the airport with the news." Lauren leaned in and whispered, "Of course, I always thought Maggie might blow his head off one day."

"Why would you think that?" Serena asked.

"This is a small city. People talk."

"What do they say?"

"Oh, please. We both know that Eric had a reputation."

"So do a lot of men," Serena said. *Like Dan,* she thought to herself.

"Maybe so, but I own a dress shop, and my store manager says that Eric is a regular customer."

"So?"

"So not all of the dresses he buys are in petite," she said with a wink. "Get the picture?"

Serena said nothing.

"What business do you have with Dan?" Lauren asked, giving Serena a cool smile.

"I don't know."

"That's discreet, but you can tell me. Dan and I don't keep secrets."

"I'm sure that's true, but I really don't know what he wants yet."

Lauren took a long moment to consider Serena's face and apparently decided that she was telling the truth. Serena suspected that Dan had already given his wife one story, and Lauren was trolling to see if he had told Serena the same thing.

"As it happens, I'm on my way to see Stride," Lauren continued.

"Oh?"

"Yes, there's an issue involving one of my employees. She's disappeared."

"I'm sorry."

"Well, it may be nothing, but she's a little unstable."

Serena didn't reply.

"I'll leave you to Dan," Lauren said. She added with a frozen laugh, "This is almost like wife-swapping, isn't it?"

"I'm sorry?"

"Me with your boyfriend, you with my husband. That's a Vegas kind of thing, isn't it?"

"Not for me," Serena said.

"I'm glad to hear it," Lauren told her. "It's not my thing either."

Lauren was gone when Dan Erickson invited Serena into his office.

She wondered how long it would take before he touched her. It turned out to be three seconds. As he guided her toward the red leather sofa near the window, he put a hand on her shoulder and left it there too long.

"I'm sorry to keep you waiting," he apologized. "It's been a crazy day. Everyone's calling."

"That's all right."

"Do you want some coffee?" he asked.

Serena shook her head.

"I'm addicted," Dan said. "Two pots a day."

He poured himself a cup and sat down uncomfortably close to her on the sofa. Serena slid away, putting more space between them. He noticed her maneuver and grinned. Serena didn't think she had ever seen whiter teeth, and she assumed that he treated them every night to keep them glossy.

Dan was one of those men who was every bit as handsome as he believed himself to be. She could smell his ego oozing from him like cologne. He had blond hair, heavily sprayed so that not a strand moved out of place, and a blemish-free complexion with a store-bought tan. His forehead was creeping northward, and Serena imagined him frantically applying Rogaine to stem the damage. He wore a shimmering navy suit, a gold Rolex, and a thick band on his wedding finger. He wasn't tall, no more than five feet nine, but she had no doubt that women found him attractive. Serena had seen carbon copies of him for years in Las Vegas. A predator, like a hawk. Self-absorbed. A sex addict.

"How's Stride?" Dan asked. "He must be worried about Maggie."

"Of course."

"Most people around here think she did it."

"You're getting way ahead of yourself, aren't you?"

Dan shrugged. "I've already talked to Teitscher. It doesn't look good."

"Stride says she didn't do it," Serena told him.

"He would say that, wouldn't he? Stride's not objective when it comes to Maggie."

"And you are?" Serena asked. "I know the two of you had a relationship a few years ago."

"If anything, that means I know her better than Stride. When our little affair came to an end, I saw what her temper was like."

Serena frowned. "Maybe we should talk about why you wanted to see me."

"Absolutely." Dan stood up and crossed the thick gray carpeting. He made sure the door was locked. He leaned back against the office door and studied Serena. "Before we begin, it's critical that none of this gets back to Stride, okay? This is not a police matter, and I can't have it become one."

Serena nodded. "No offense, but if it's so important that Jonny not find out, why hire me?"

"Everyone tells me you're good," Dan said.

"I am, but there are others around who are good, too, who don't happen to be sleeping with a man you hate."

Dan returned to the sofa and sat down again, even closer than before. "You think I hate Stride?"

"Don't you?"

"Stride and I have had our disagreements over the years, but that's water under the bridge. I'm moving on to bigger things."

"Okay," Serena said, but she wasn't convinced.

"What's your hourly rate?" Dan asked.

She gave him a number.

"I'll pay that plus twenty percent."

Alarm bells went off in Serena's head. "Why would you want to do that?"

Dan eased back into the leather folds of the sofa and cradled his coffee mug in both hands. "Because there may be some risk involved."

"Oh?"

"That's another reason why your background as a cop is important to me. You're used to dealing with risky situations."

"Let me hear what you have to say first," Serena told him.

Dan nodded. "I'm being blackmailed."

"Then you should call the police."

"No way," he said, shaking his head. "I can't risk this information coming to light."

"Someone blackmailing the county attorney raises all sorts of issues. You know that. You ought to be talking to Stride."

"Maybe so, but that's not an option in this case."

"What does this person have on you?" she asked.

"You don't need to know that."

"That's going to make it hard to help you," Serena said. "I don't like flying blind."

"Let's just say that it's sexual in nature. Okay?"

Serena's mind flitted to Maggie's question. *Have you two ever done anything . . . strange?*

"An affair?" she asked.

"You're not a detective anymore. Forget the interrogation. It makes no difference what I did. It's enough that I was stupid and shouldn't have done it."

"Does Lauren know?"

Dan snorted. "No, and you don't tell her a thing, okay?"

"What did you tell her about hiring me?"

"I said it was a political deal. Dirty tricks. She bought it."

"I take it you want me to find out who's blackmailing you." She wondered if he had fantasies of her conducting a hit for him.

"No, I don't care. I don't want to know. I just want to make this go away, and I need you to be my intermediary. This man has already given me a price, and I've got the money right here in cash."

Dan extracted a thick envelope from his suit pocket and deposited it on the coffee table in front of the sofa.

"He's going to call me in the next couple days about a drop," Dan continued. "I want you to make the payoff for me."

"Why not do it yourself?" Serena asked.

"And risk having the media there with cameras? No thanks. I want this all done at arm's length. Just you. No one else."

"This is a blackmailer. He won't be satisfied with one payoff. He'll be back for more."

"I'll take that risk."

Serena sighed. "Do you really need me to tell you this is a very bad idea?"

"Bad idea or not, I'm willing to pay a lot of money to have you handle this for me."

"You know there's no such thing as private investigator's privilege. If this were to wind up with the police, I'd have to tell them what I know."

"That's why I don't want it to wind up with the police."

Serena didn't like this. It smelled bad. "Do you have any idea who the blackmailer is?"

"No. He's just a voice on the phone."

"How did he get the information he has on you?"

"I don't know that either. I have some suspicions, but it doesn't matter now."

"You're sure he's not bluffing?" Serena asked.

"He told me things on the phone. It's no bluff."

Serena hesitated. There was a part of her that wanted to tell Dan to forget it, but she couldn't resist the adrenaline rush. This was the kind of hands-on street work she wanted as a PI. Something that made her feel like a cop again. The money was good, too. "Hourly rate plus thirty percent," she said.

"Now who's the blackmailer?" Dan asked. He smiled, put a hand on Serena's knee, and squeezed with his fingertips.

"Is it a deal?" she asked.

"Yes, fine."

"Good." Serena took his hand off her knee and twisted his wrist until his smile evaporated. "One other thing," she told him pleasantly. "Touch me again, and I'll snap off your fingers like the icicles on my roof."

She let go.

"Stride must have his hands full with you," Dan said, massaging away the pain.

"Call me when you know about the drop," Serena said. She picked up the envelope of cash, slid it into her pocket, and left the office.

Downstairs, she stopped again in the park near the statue of the centurion. Something about his empty granite eyes troubled her, and she felt the oppressive weight of the gray clouds overhead. She told herself again that it was nothing, but as she stood there, the feeling came back.

The same feeling that had followed her for weeks.

She was being watched.

6

He knew she could feel him staring at her, the way an antelope senses a tiger stalking from the camouflage of the bush. Invisible and deadly.

When he lifted the binoculars, her body leaped into focus, and it was as if he were standing next to her, breathing on her neck. As he watched her, she shivered. Her head wheeled in his direction, and through the binoculars, he got a chill of pleasure to have their eyes meet. His penis twitched inside his jeans, nudging its way down his leg, growing swollen and stiff.

"Ah, fuck," he murmured, relishing the

sensation. It was especially sweet since he had spent ten years watching his manhood wither away. The guards taunted him that prison would make him shrivel up like a salted slug, and they were right. The more years he spent behind bars, the more his penis shrank. Nothing aroused him. He would beat off in his cell at night, but after a while, he could barely coax a hard-on out of his cock. He'd spit on it or rub it with soap, but it would just lay there, so tiny that his giant hand couldn't even pull it out from his groin.

But his organ had risen again that night in the abandoned house in Alabama during the hurricane. As he watched the cop drown in the basement, blood had surged between his legs, making him rigid. A spontaneous erection, ripe with power.

Four months had passed since a National Guard helicopter rescued him from the roof of the farmhouse. He wore clothes he had found in an upstairs bedroom, and he had shredded his inmate's fatigues and let them float away with all the other debris in the water. By the time the storm died away, the land around the house was a lake. The squad car was gone, and so was Deet's body. He was just a trapped homeowner who hadn't evacuated soon enough.

They took him to a shelter in Birmingham along with hundreds of other refugees, but he ran away that night, stole a car, and headed north. He didn't want to take any chance that he would be found out, or that the authorities at Holman would figure out he was on the loose. As it turned out, he needn't have worried. He jacked a laptop and kept an eye on the Internet by hacking into wireless connections as he made his way out of the South. Several days later, he found an article in the Montgomery newspaper that reported the story. The squad car had been found wrapped around a tree ten miles from the farmhouse, and Deet's headless body had turned up another five miles away in a different direction. All three people in the car were presumed dead, victims of the storm.

He was a nonperson. No identity. No past.

He could have gone anywhere, but he first had to deal with the fist of rage that beat its way through his chest. Payback for ten lost years.

"You feel me, don't you?" he whispered. "You know I'm here."

He had been laying his plans for Serena ever since he arrived in Duluth. Watching her. Stalking her. He could have taken her anytime, but he wanted the experience to linger. Every hunter knew—you don't break the neck of the captured animal right away. Once it's yours, you play with it for a while.

In the meantime, he had other prey. People like Dan. Mitch. Tanjy. And the alpha girls. People with dirty secrets they were desperate to conceal.

He remembered what the little queer in Holman had told him about the art of blackmail. If you know what someone is hiding, you can do anything you want to them, and they'll never breathe a word. The danger in poking a hive, though, was getting stung. He could have let the games go on even longer, but something unexpected had popped up like a fish out of the water and made him speed up his plans.

Murder. That changed everything.

So now it was finally Serena's turn. Time to tighten the noose around her neck.

Through the binoculars, he watched her shrug and continue down the steps of the government plaza toward her car. He knew what was in her brain. She was telling herself that the fear scraping its fingernails along her spine was all in her imagination. She was wrong. Before he was done, she would be begging him to kill her.

7

City Hall was an old, drafty building, with high ceilings where the heat gathered. The floors were cold, hard marble. The chill radiated through the window in Stride's office and left frost crystals on the glass. He leaned against the window frame and stared vacantly at the traffic on First Street below him. His arms were crossed. The creases in his forehead deepened like canyons, and he felt tightness throughout his muscles.

He was wearing a suit and tie because reporters and politicians would be swarming the office as word got out about Maggie. Most of Usually time he dressed for the street, which was where he liked to spend his time. He couldn't handle a job that left him permanently chained to a desk, and he did his paperwork in odd hours when the rest of the office was dark. He preferred to be out at crime scenes, doing the real work, which was mostly hard and bitter.

He had been idealistic in his early days, which were too long ago to think about. He was like Maggie—determined to solve every crime, put away every criminal. It hadn't taken long for him to realize that there were always victims like the Enger Park Girl, with no one to speak for them and no answers to give. The burden was all his. Every murder in this city gouged a piece out of his soul, and even when they solved the case and he watched a jury bring down a guilty verdict, there was still a scar that never went away.

That was one of the reasons he lived by the lake. He didn't tell many people about that part of his soul; it had taken months for him even to share it with Serena. Stride was a hardheaded realist who had no time for anything mystical, but the lake was different. When he stood by the water at night, he sometimes felt as if he were surrounded by the dead, as if the lake were where they went to become part of the mist and vapor. He could feel his father there, who had died in the lake, and he felt communion with all of the city's dead.

There was a knock on his office door, and he saw a silhouette behind the frosted glass.

"Come in," he called without leaving the window. The vanilla oak door opened and closed with a shudder. He was surprised to see who it was. "Lauren."

"Hello, Jonathan."

He felt a chill blow into his office with Lauren's arrival.

"You're looking good," he told her.

Lauren rolled her eyes at him. She had the clothes, jewels, and laboratory-tested blond hair to match her money, and her face was as smooth as makeup and plastic surgery could make it. She was attractive, but she made no secret of the fact that Stride's charm went nowhere with her. The two of them shared an ugly history. Lauren was the only child of a father who had made millions in commercial real estate in northern Minnesota. In Stride's early days as a detective, he had exposed a City Hall bribery scheme connected to an eminent domain condemnation for a huge new shopping center. Lauren's father went to prison and died there six months later of a stroke. Lauren inherited everything, including a grudge against Stride.

He waved her into a seat. She crossed her legs and steepled her fingers on the hem of her skirt. Her blue eyes were as fierce and intelligent as ever.

"I'm sorry about Maggie," she told him.

"Sure you are."

"I just met Serena in Dan's office," she added cuttingly. "Where would she have been when you and I were in school? Playing with finger paints?"

Stride ignored the jab. "I didn't think you were speaking to me, Lauren."

"The past is the past," she replied. "We need to move on."

"Really? That wasn't your attitude last year." Stride knew that Lauren had waged a campaign with the City Council to block K-2 from hiring him back.

"I have more important things to worry about now."

"Oh?"

"You obviously haven't seen the news today."

"What did I miss?"

"Dan and I are moving to Washington," Lauren announced.

"Permanently?"

She nodded. "Dan's been invited to be special counsel in a D.C. law firm as part of its white-collar crime practice. I've been out in Washington the last couple of days, scouting homes in Georgetown."

"So Dan's becoming a defense lawyer," Stride said. "I guess it's always been about the game for him. It's easier to switch sides that way."

"Yes, I know you're only interested in truth and justice, Jonathan. Let me know when you find it."

He smiled, because she had a point. He was also pleased to think of Dan giving up his job as the county's top prosecutor. He didn't like having an enemy in that office.

"Congratulations, that's quite a coup," he told her.

"I've been pulling strings for a while," Lauren admitted. "Dan doesn't like Duluth. We only hung on here to get him into statewide office, but you erased that possibility for us, didn't you?"

"I think the voters had something to do

with it," Stride said. "When does the big move take place?"

"Next month."

"Is that why you're here? To say good-bye?"

Lauren shook her head. "Gloating is just a bonus. Actually, I have to report a crime. Or what may be a crime. I don't know."

Stride put aside their rivalry. "What's going on?"

"You know I own Silk, the dress shop on Superior."

Stride nodded. The store was another of her many tax dodges.

"One of my employees is missing," she said.

"What's her name?"

Lauren smiled maliciously. "Oh, you know her very well, Jonathan. It's Tanjy Powell."

Stride didn't mean to say it out loud, but the words slipped out as he expelled a disgusted breath. "Son of a bitch."

"I knew you'd be pleased."

He wasn't pleased at all. "Why do you think she's missing?"

"Tanjy left the shop early on Monday afternoon. She looked upset. According to Sonnie, my store manager, Tanjy didn't show up on Tuesday or Wednesday, and she didn't call. There's no answer at her home."

"Why was she upset when she left?"

"I have no idea."

"Has she ever done this before?"

"Sonnie says no."

"What about family?"

Lauren shook her head. "Her parents are dead. She lives in the bottom half of an old Victorian in the East Hillside area. I thought you'd want to check it out, in case there's some foul smell emanating from it. That's what gets your blood racing, right?"

"Give it a rest, Lauren." He added, "My first thought is that Tanjy is playing another game with us."

"Why? Because last time she made a fool of you?"

"The woman fabricated a rape charge. She had the whole city in a panic."

Lauren sighed. "I don't claim to understand what goes on in her sick little brain. I'm just the messenger."

"I hope to hell she's not wasting our time again," Stride said. "The only reason we didn't file charges was because Dan and K-2 didn't want us to look like we were beating up on a woman with psychological problems."

"My fault," Lauren admitted. "I asked them to go easy on her."

"You? I'm surprised you didn't fire her."

"I only go after people who get in my way, Jonathan. You should know that."

"Meaning you didn't want an ugly employment lawsuit."

"Meaning I felt sorry for her."

Stride didn't believe that Lauren had ever felt sorry for anyone, but it didn't matter either way. "I'll check it out," he said.

"There's something else," Lauren added.

"What?"

"Tanjy called our home on Monday night."

"After she left the shop that day? Why?"

"She wanted to talk to Dan, but he was in Saint Paul."

"What did she want?" Stride asked.

"I don't know. I called Dan from Washington on Tuesday afternoon, but he said there was no answer when he tried to call her back. Neither one of us gave it another thought until today. I took a flight back early this morning, and Sonnie told me that Tanjy was missing."

"Did Tanjy leave a message when you talked to her?"

"Yes, she gave me a message for Dan, but he didn't know what it meant."

"What was it?"

Lauren shrugged. "She simply said to tell him, 'I know who it is.'"

8

Abel Teitscher arrived home early Thursday afternoon, having spent ten hours supervising the crime scene where Eric Sorenson was killed. He sprinkled flakes of food into the large saltwater tank in his living room, which was stocked with a rainbow assortment of angels, puffers, dragonets, tetras, and gobies. On the rare evenings when he wasn't working, he would pour himself a glass of brandy, turn off the lights, and sit quietly watching his fish while they traveled the illuminated aquarium. Abel was more comfortable with fish than with people.

He lived alone in a modest house on

Ninth Street north of downtown. He had been married for twenty-seven years, until he arrived home unexpectedly on a Tuesday afternoon and found his fifty-two-year-old wife being serviced by the twenty-four-year-old unemployed son of their next-door neighbor. She had been watching too many *Desperate Housewives* episodes. They divorced six months later, and she was now living in a rented apartment in Minneapolis. The one good thing to come out of his marriage was his daughter, Anne, but she was away at graduate school in San Diego. She was studying marine biology, which Abel was happy to attribute to years as a child sitting with her father in front of the fish tank.

A few years ago, an all-nighter like the Sorenson murder would have taken a toll on him for days, but he was in better shape now than he had been in decades. Since the divorce, he had taken up running, putting on miles on the track at UMD during the warmer seasons and using a treadmill crammed in his bedroom during the winter. He had lost thirty pounds and was in training now for the marathon. At City Hall, they called him gaunt and skeletal, which infuriated him, because no one appreciated how hard he had worked to hone his body.

Abel stretched out on the sofa near the fish tank and slept for thirty minutes, which was enough to refresh him. He then spent an hour running on the treadmill. The rumble of the motor and the pounding of his feet served to clear his mind. Stride accused him of not seeing the big picture on a case, but that was crap. Abel took time early in every investigation just to think. The difference was that Stride tried to rise above the facts and get inside the heads of the victim and the killer. For Abel, the big picture was about nothing except putting the pieces of the puzzle together from what was left behind. Evidence and witnesses. Things you could touch, see, and smell.

The big picture in this case led him in only one direction—to Maggie.

He knew that having no evidence of a third party in the house didn't mean that no one had been there, but he also knew that the logical, obvious answer at most crime scenes was usually the right one. Forget the conspiracy theories, and leave them to the defense attorneys. The fact was that Oswald killed Kennedy. Alone. Deal with it.

Abel was prepared to turn over every rock. He had nothing against Maggie and no desire to pin the crime on her, but common sense told him that she was almost certainly the one who had pulled the trigger. That was how it always worked in these cases.

Like Nicole. Abel had learned with Nicole that anyone is capable of anything. Even a good cop. He hadn't wanted to believe that his partner was capable of murder, so he ignored the evidence even as it piled up. Nicole was psychologically fragile; she had just come back from paid leave after killing a mentally deranged man on the Blatnik Bridge. Nicole's husband was having an affair, and she had threatened him with violence if he didn't break it off. Two of Nicole's hairs were discovered in the apartment where her husband and his girlfriend were found naked, shot to death with her husband's gun. It was more than enough evidence to convict her.

When the jury found her guilty, Abel finally accepted the fact that Nicole had done what every other suspect did—lie to him in order to save her neck. Stride would have to learn the same lesson.

Stride probably thought that Abel was still angry about getting booted out of the lieutenant's chair. Abel was upset about that, but the truth was that he didn't miss it. K-2 was right. Abel hated supervising people and handing out assignments. He wasn't prepared to waste his time motivating cops, who were a tough breed to motivate. They hated administration on principle. They were hemmed in by paperwork and procedure and second-guessed every time they had to make a split-second judgment. He knew all that. He was that way, too, but he had a short fuse and his own way of doing things, and if he was going to be the boss, they were going to do things his way. Except no one did.

He was happier without the headaches. The only thing that bothered him was that the other cops loved Stride, and they barely tolerated Abel. He knew he was a loner and a hard case. He was crusty and closed-off, but no one made an effort with him the way they did with Stride.

Stride was human. He made mistakes. He was making a mistake this time, because Stride simply didn't understand betrayal. He had never walked in on his wife doing a reverse cowgirl on a man half her age. Hell, Abel didn't even know what the position was called until his lawyer explained it in the divorce papers. His wife had certainly never used it on him during their years of married life.

When he found his wife in bed with another man, Abel finally understood how an ordinary person could go over the edge. Like Nicole. Like Maggie. He had pulled his gun on the two of them and was ready to fire. The only thing that saved them was that, in the shocked silence as they all stared at one another, he could hear the gurgle of his fish tank coming from the living room. Something about the sound soothed him. Losing his fish would be worse than losing his wife, so he put the gun down and found a lawyer instead.

Maggie should have owned fish.

Abel shaved and showered after he was done on the treadmill and slapped cologne on his face. That was another thing the cops teased him about, that he smelled like a dapper gigolo. It wasn't a crime. He dressed in an old brown suit and shrugged on his trench coat. The coat wasn't warm enough for January, but since he had begun jogging regularly, he found he didn't mind the cold.

Time to turn over rocks.

He began with Eric's office. Eric owned a business called MedalSports, which was located in a drab manufacturing facility on a street near the airport, near businesses making medical supplies, aircraft parts, navigational equipment, and frozen foods. Small planes whined overhead as Abel pulled into the parking lot. The one-level building, painted chocolate-brown, had a series of loading docks, where several shipping trucks were backed up against the platforms. The parking lot was crowded.

He found a glass door leading into the building's office. The receptionist inside was on the phone, and he could see used tissues littering her desk. Her eyes were red-rimmed and watery. She was plump, in her late fifties, with half-glasses on a chain around her neck and gray hair peeking out from under a baseball cap. The office was chilly, and she wore a bulky red down vest. She gave him a weak smile, cupped her hand over the phone, and told him she'd be with him shortly.

The tiny waiting room was functional, with a cheap rattan sofa, a white coffeemaker sitting on a filing cabinet next to a stack of Styrofoam cups, and a veneer coffee table stocked with sports magazines. He could hear the noise of manufacturing through the door that led to the shop floor.

He examined several framed photographs hung on the wall that showed Eric at the Olympics fifteen years ago, in his Speedo with a bronze medal around his neck. He was a physically imposing man, at least six feet four, with a muscled, hairless chest and buzzed hair that was so blond it was almost white. The other photographs were more recent and showed Eric with a variety of medalists from the Winter Games, including freestyle skaters, slalom skiers, and bobsled teams. They were all displaying MedalSports equipment. Abel noted that Eric had kept himself in good shape and wore the same brilliant smile in all of the photographs. He had grown out his hair and swept it back like a long, flowing mane over his head.

"He was *very* handsome," the receptionist said, hanging up the phone.

Abel grunted.

"You're not a reporter, are you?"

Abel shook his head and introduced himself. The receptionist told him her name was Elaine.

"Is it true that his wife shot him?" she asked. "That's what the media is saying."

"We're still trying to find out what happened," Abel said. "I need you to answer a few questions for me."

Elaine sniffled. She grabbed another tissue, and her round cheeks puffed out as she blew her nose. "Of course."

"How long have you worked with Mr. Sorenson?"

"Ever since he started the company. He was a wonderful man. He treated all of us like family."

Abel sighed. Everyone was a saint once they got murdered. "He sounds a little too perfect to me. No one's perfect."

"Well, I'm sorry, but we all loved him here." Her voice rose defensively.

"How about the business? How's it going?"

"Oh, extremely well. All of the employees got year-end bonuses. Mr. Sorenson shared the profits. He wasn't selfish."

Abel nodded. "Manufacturing is a tough racket. Lots of competition. Cheap foreign labor, right? That sort of thing."

"No, no," Elaine replied, shaking her head. "MedalSports makes high-end merchandise for a very targeted audience. Everything is handcrafted. We don't compete against mass-market operations. We sell to Olympic competitors and no one else."

"Is there really enough business to support that?" Abel asked dubiously. "The Winter Games only come around every four years."

"Well, yes, but they're practicing constantly. The athletes are involved in regional and world championship competitions, too. The right equipment gives you an edge, and we customize all our materials."

"Was Mr. Sorenson the sole owner?"

"Yes, he started the business shortly after he was in the Olympics himself. He was a bronze medalist in the butterfly, you know."

"Did he have a lot of debt?"

"Well, I'm no accountant. He has a line of credit with Range Bank. I never heard Mr. Sorenson express any concerns about capital or debt payments. We had record revenues last year."

"I'll need the names of Mr. Sorenson's accountant and lawyer. Do you have those?"

Elaine nodded. "Of course."

She wrote them down, and Abel slipped

the information into his pocket. "You were pretty quick to think his wife did it. Why is that?"

Elaine frowned. "I was only repeating what I heard on television. I don't know anything."

Abel frowned back at her. "How am I supposed to solve this crime if you dish out crap like that? I never met a secretary who didn't know if her boss and his wife were having problems."

"I don't want to be a gossip," she retorted. Her cheeks bloomed red.

"You're not gossiping. Your boss was murdered."

Elaine struggled with her discretion and gave in. "Mr. Sorenson and his wife have had a difficult year," she confessed in a conspiratorial whisper. "I've heard them arguing a lot."

"When was this?"

"The worst fight was in November, a couple of months ago."

"What were they arguing about?"

Elaine shook her head. "I don't know."

"You must have heard something. Come on, it's not like these walls are six inches thick."

"It had something to do with sex," Elaine

confided, her voice dropping as she said the word *sex*.

"How do you know?"

"I heard Mrs. Sorenson shout something through the door."

"What did she say?"

Elaine flushed. "This is very embarrassing."

"Tell me."

"I don't use this kind of language, you understand. Mrs. Sorenson called him— well, she said he was a muscle-bound, yellow-headed penis."

Abel tried not to laugh. "What else did she say?"

"I couldn't hear anything more. It's not like I was listening."

Of course not, Abel thought. "Maybe he was getting ready to dump her."

"Oh, no, no," Elaine insisted. "He loved her, he really did."

"Loving her doesn't mean being faithful, though, does it?"

Elaine picked at her fingernails. "I wouldn't know about that."

"You keep his schedule, you answer his calls. No way you wouldn't know if he was cheating."

"Mr. Sorenson was a very attractive man,"

Elaine said cautiously. "In the old days, before he was married, he dated a lot. Glamorous women. Models sometimes."

"And after he was married?"

Elaine pouted as if this was no one's business. "A man like that, women come after him."

"Who? I want names."

"I don't know names. Mr. Sorenson was secretive about his personal life. I didn't pry."

"You sound like you're holding out on me again, Elaine."

"No, I'm not. Mr. Sorenson was discreet."

Abel sighed. "Did other women ever come to the office for him?"

Elaine hesitated. "Sometimes."

"Who?"

"I told you, I don't know. There's one woman who comes by every few weeks. Tall. Red hair. She's older, probably in her forties. They were very . . . friendly with each other."

"You never asked who she was?"

"Well, one time she came by, and Mr. Sorenson was on the phone. When I asked for her name, she said, 'Tell him it's his alpha girl.' She thought that was very funny."

"What the hell does that mean?"

"I have no idea."

"Were there other women, too?"

Elaine looked unhappy. "Yes."

"Did his wife know about them?"

"You'd have to ask her. I don't know how much she knew. Mr. Sorenson was gone a lot, and sometimes Mrs. Sorenson would call, wondering where he was. And, uh, who he was with."

"Did he take any personal trips recently?"

Elaine nodded. "Yes, he was in the Twin Cities over the weekend."

"Doing what?"

"He didn't talk about it. I made reservations for him at the Saint Paul Hotel. He was gone over the weekend and came back on Monday afternoon. He seemed distracted."

"Why?"

"I don't know. He talked about seeing a play at the Ordway, but other than that, he didn't say anything about his trip."

"What happened after he got back on Monday?"

"He wasn't in the office for more than a few minutes before he was gone again. Then he was in on Tuesday and Wednesday, but he had the door closed almost the whole day."

"Did he talk to his wife yesterday?"

"I don't know."

"What about his calendar? What appointments did he have?"

"He didn't have any meetings during the day, but he had me set up an appointment for yesterday evening."

"He met someone last night? After-hours?"

Elaine nodded.

"Was it a woman?"

"No. It was a psychiatrist named Tony Wells."

"Tony?" Abel asked, surprised.

"That's right."

Abel knew Tony Wells; he was the department's primary profiler on sex crimes. He also did trauma counseling for a lot of the region's cops and crime victims.

"Was Mr. Sorenson seeing Tony professionally?" Abel asked.

"Oh, no, Mr. Sorenson never saw a therapist. He was as solid as a rock. It was his wife. Mr. Sorenson told me that she had been getting counseling for months."

9

Stride lit a cigarette as he waited on the porch at Tanjy Powell's downstairs apartment. This was his first of the day, and it was already late afternoon. The wind mussed his wavy, salt-and-pepper hair with cold fingers. He glanced up at the sky, which was a bumpy mix of browns and blues. A few stray flurries floated in the air. After a few seconds, he turned back to the yellow door and pounded on it again with his fist, then listened carefully. There wasn't a breath of life inside.

According to Lauren Erickson, Tanjy hadn't come to work since she fled the dress shop on Monday afternoon. She didn't appear to be home either.

He came down off the porch and looked up at the old Victorian. The windows were shuttered; no one peeked out at him. The house was a relic in need of fresh paint and new shingles. Duluth was a city of old neighborhoods and aging beauties like this one, which reflected the money and glamour of the city in its heyday, when taconite flowed like a river and filled the coffers of the entire northern region. The mining river was a trickle now, and the houses showed it. Unlike the Twin Cities to the south, which boasted new suburbs with manicured lawns, Duluth was left with its old homes and their fading glory. Stride actually preferred it that way. He didn't mind if the floors slanted and the doors hung twisted in their frames. He hated cookie-cutter houses.

He followed the stone foundation around to the rear and wound up in a backyard no bigger than a postage stamp. The house butted up to an alley and then to the back sides of homes on the next street. They were all in disrepair. Most of the houses here were subdivided, turned into low-rent apartments for students and nurses. A summer lounge chair was half-buried in snow. A charcoal grill sat rusting. He saw animal tracks cutting across the yard. Two windows on the wall of a one-car garage were broken. He trudged over to the garage and looked inside. The shards of glass were dirty and dull. There was no car in the garage.

Back at the rear door of the house, he knocked and shouted, "Tanjy!"

He pushed hard against the door with his shoulder. It was locked. He tried to see through the white shutters, but they were closed up tight.

"Meow," said a voice at his feet. He looked down and saw a long-haired gray cat, with snow and dirt matting the ends of its fur, rubbing against his leg. Stride bent down and scratched the cat's head and was rewarded with a purr. The cat strolled away down the length of the back porch and then disappeared inside the house through one of the windows. Stride followed him, snapping on gloves. He found a jagged hole, large enough that he could reach inside and unlock the window. He pushed it up and squeezed his body through the frame. He found himself in a dark, narrow hallway leading to the kitchen. Two cat bowls were pushed against the wall, both empty.

"Police," he called out. "Anyone here?"

There was no response.

The air in the apartment was stale, as if it had been bottled up for days. Stride checked the kitchen and smelled no remnants of food. The sink was empty. He retraced his steps and followed the hallway to the living room, where he was confronted by a two-feet-high crucifix nailed to a white wall. Below the cross, he noticed stacks of Christian sheet music on a banged-up upright piano.

He saw a photograph of Tanjy with her parents on an end table made of taupe metal and glass. Her parents had died last winter on the Bong Bridge to Wisconsin, when a shroud of fog settled over the top of the span unexpectedly and caused a string of accidents. Stride picked up the frame and looked at the photo. Tanjy was in her late twenties, with long black hair and a slim body. Her father had been white, and her mother black, and the mocha-colored features of Tanjy's face were in perfect proportion. She had thin, sharply angled eyebrows that made her look wicked. Her lips made dimples at the corners of her mouth when she smiled, and she had a gleam in her brown eyes that made him think she was enjoying a secret joke. Men responded to her as if she were an erotic puzzle that they wanted to unlock. When she first came to City Hall, he watched the officers in his Detective Bureau become as flustered as tongue-tied teenagers.

Tanjy came to him with a terrible story. She had been abducted on a Wednesday night in early November from a dark parking ramp off Michigan Street. The man blindfolded and gagged her, tied her up, and drove her to Grassy Point Park, a tiny and deserted green space jutting out into Saint Louis Bay. The park was in the shadow of the arc of the Bong Bridge where her parents had died. He tied her hands and feet to the steel mesh of the barbed wire fence that separated the park from the train tracks of the seaport. When he removed her blindfold, she could see the graffiti-covered train cars and the looming black mountains of coal. He cut off her clothes until she was naked and cold, suspended on the fence, and raped her from behind. When he was done, he left her there with her car. It had all been planned out, she said; he had another car waiting for him in the park. She didn't see the car and couldn't give any description of the rapist. Eventually, she bit through the tape with her teeth and freed herself.

This all happened on Wednesday, she said. It was Friday when she came to Stride to report the rape. She was cleaned up and impeccably dressed. She didn't cry or raise her voice or show any emotion at all as she described what happened. She declined to submit to a physical examination and told them she had already visited her own clinic. It may as well have happened to someone else.

Had Stride been inside Tanjy's house back then, he would have noticed all of her religious icons and recognized the Christlike imagery of Tanjy crucified on the fence. That would have been his first clue that something was wrong.

Her rape was big news in the Duluth media. Stranger rapes were rare and terrifying in the city. Two days later, though, the daily newspaper printed an interview with a young stockbroker named Mitchell Brandt, who was Tanjy's old boyfriend. He described her obsession with rape in lurid and explicit detail—how she insisted that he pretend to rape her every time they were in bed, how she masturbated in the shower to rape fantasies every day, and how she posted erotic stories and poetry on the Internet that dealt with stranger rapes.

Within days, Tanjy became a pariah. The story went national. She became the butt of jokes by Jay Leno, *Saturday Night Live,* cable news channels, YouTube videos, and dozens of bloggers. Her support in the city evaporated. A week later, Tanjy met Stride in a coffee shop and admitted what he already suspected. She had fabricated the entire story. There was never any rape. It was a fantasy.

Stride wanted to file charges against her for filing a false police report, but he let it go under pressure from Dan and K-2, and the story disappeared from the headlines. Tanjy went underground.

Stride called her several weeks later. He was still angry with her, but he was worried that she might have suffered a breakdown under the barrage of media attention. Tanjy thanked him for his call in that silken voice of hers but declined his offer of help. In a way, he was glad of that, but he learned nothing new from the call. She was as calm and emotionless as ever. The same erotic enigma.

And now she was missing.

Nothing was disturbed inside her apartment. There was no evidence of violence or trouble. His first thought was suicide, and he kept his eyes open for a note, but wherever Tanjy had gone, she hadn't left a message behind. She also hadn't taken much with her. Her clothes were neatly hung and folded in the closet and dresser in her bedroom. Her suitcase was there, too, but he didn't find a purse, wallet, or keys.

Stride sat down on the end of her queen-sized bed, which had a red quilt neatly laid across the mattress and matching fringed pillows. He studied the books on the shelves near her bed—religion textbooks, a pile of romance novels, vegetarian cookbooks, and psychology books about rape. And, of course, *The Da Vinci Code*. The bed was prim and conservative, with another icon of Jesus hung over the headboard. He thought about Tanjy indulging in rape fantasies underneath the cross. Maybe that was part of the thrill, a forbidden mix of sacrifice and sacrilege.

He hunted on her rolltop desk for a date book or Palm Pilot and didn't find one. The desk was clean and organized, with a manila folder for bills, a neon purple folder from Byte Patrol with instructions for her laptop computer, a stack of software cases, and a collection of fashion magazines like *Elle* and *Vogue*. That fit her. Tanjy worked in a high-end dress shop, and she looked like many of the models on the pages.

Stride turned on the desk lamp and picked up a small cube of notepaper to see if he could see indentations of anything Tanjy had written. He was able to make out a phone number, but when he called it on his cell phone, he found himself connected to the local Whole Foods market.

He booted up her laptop computer. She didn't use Outlook for e-mail, which meant she probably used a Web-based service, which would make it harder to find a record of her messages. There were no appointments recorded in the online calendar. He checked her Internet favorite pages and shook his head when he found a mixture of Christian sites and hard-core pornography, including rape sites with brutal, disturbing imagery of women bound and humiliated.

When he checked her recent documents, he clicked on the first one, a Word file labeled ISLAND. The text flashed onto the screen:

The natives tied Ellen spread-eagled to stakes they had pounded in the mud. One by one, they took turns ravishing her with their pierced tongues. She begged them to stop—No! No! she cried, you can't do this!—but they were deaf to her desperate pleas. Despite herself, she felt the most intense of orgasms welling up inside her . . .

Stride closed the file and checked the other documents, which were of a similar nature. He wondered again how to reconcile the calm, quiet girl in his office with the explicit, submissive fantasies filling her brain.

He shut down the computer. Nothing here gave him any clues as to why Tanjy had disappeared, or whether she had even disappeared at all. There was nothing strange about someone getting in their car and driving away. People did it all the time. Sometimes they chose not to come back.

Stride felt the house sag and heard a sharp *pop* from somewhere in the rear of the apartment. He got to his feet and stepped lightly to the bedroom door. He listened. There were cautious footfalls near the back window where he had entered the house.

"Yo, dude!" a young male voice called. "What's up? I know you're here."

Stride emerged in the hallway and saw a young man in his twenties there, nervously brandishing a golf club like a weapon. The kid saw him and practically jumped.

"I've called the police! They'll be here any minute!"

"They're already here," Stride told him, flashing his shield. "Who are you?"

"Oh, shit. Wow, I'm sorry." He was wearing gray sweatpants, an untucked flannel shirt, huge unlaced boots, and a bulky fur hat with a turned-up flap in front and ear flaps that hung down on either side of his head as if he were a bloodhound.

I live in the land of stupid hats, Stride thought.

"What's your name?" Stride repeated.

"Sorry, I'm Duke. Duke Andrews."

Even his name sounded like a dog's. "What are you doing here?"

Duke pushed up his black-framed glasses, which were slipping down his nose. He had a wispy goatee on his chin and a string of pimples on his cheek that looked like the Big Dipper. "I live in the house next door. My bedroom looks out on the yard. I saw you go in, and I was, like, hey, could be a burglar."

"Here's a little advice, Duke. Don't try to confront burglars yourself. Let the cops handle it."

"Yeah, yeah, right, guess that was stupid." Duke tugged at the hairs on his protruding chin.

"A golf club isn't much of a match for a gun."

"I don't even golf, man. How dumb is that?"

"Do you know who lives here?" Stride asked.

Duke nodded eagerly as he bit one of his fingernails. "Oh, sure, yeah, it's that girl who was in the news, you know. The whole rape thing. Tanjy. Short for Tangerine, right? Weird name. But wow."

"Have you seen her lately?"

"Not in a couple days, no."

"Do you remember exactly when you last saw her?"

Duke didn't have to think about it. "Monday night. I saw her go out in her car right around ten o'clock."

"You sound like you keep a close eye on her."

"What?" Duke was nervous and shuffled his feet.

Stride was taller than Duke, and the kid shrank as Stride came closer. "I mean, what will I find if we go back to your place? A telescope focused on Tanjy's bedroom? That's better than binoculars for peeping, right? Leaves your hands free."

"Whoa, dude, what are you saying? No way." Duke looked at the door as if he wanted to take a running dive through it.

"Listen, you take your telescope and point it at the stars from now on, okay? I don't want to charge you as a Peeping Tom. But right now, I need to know what kinds of things you've been seeing in Tanjy's bedroom."

A small, excited grin flitted across Duke's lips. He yanked at his sweatpants. "Oh, man. It's so fresh. You wouldn't believe it."

"Try me."

"This girl, she's better than a porn star. Always sleeps in the raw. Gets herself off like every night. I should sell tickets, man. Could pay my rent and then some."

"How about visitors?"

"Nobody in the bedroom, not since I've been watching."

"Which is how long?" Stride asked.

"I moved in to my apartment in early December. Didn't take me long to realize the place had a great view."

"You have any idea where she went on Monday?"

Duke took off his hat and scratched his head. His black hair stuck up in messy wings. "No idea. I just look. I don't know her."

"Was she alone?"

"When she left? Yeah."

"Have you ever seen her with anyone else?"

"Like guys? Yeah, this one dude was over at her place around Christmas. I could see them talking on the back porch. I've seen him around a few times recently. I assume he's her new boyfriend. Lucky guy, know what I'm saying? I was hoping to catch a little bedroom action, but they must do it at his place."

"What does he look like?" Stride asked.

"Big guy. Even bigger than you. The kind of guy you expect a girl like that to go after. They don't put out for the likes of me. It messes up the gene pool. Although some of these models, they've married real ugly dudes, you know? Gives me hope. You gotta feel sorry for their kids, though. Seems like they always come out looking like the wrong half."

"Tell me more about the guy you saw." Stride had a bad feeling.

"Not much to tell," Duke replied. "Lots of muscles. Fancy dresser. Oh, and long hair, too. Long blond hair. Longer than most girls."

"And that's the guy you've seen with Tanjy?"

"That's the dude."

Stride wanted to curse out loud. Duke had just described Maggie's husband, Eric.

10

Maggie had bare feet, and her legs were pulled up to her chest with her hands laced around her knees. Her black hair was dirty. She was lost in an oversized armchair that made her look even smaller than she was. The yellow flames of the fire reflected in her eyes, which were far away and unblinking.

"You can still smell it, can't you?" she asked, whiffing the air.

Serena didn't smell anything. "What?"

"The sweat of all the cops. And the super-glue from the print box. It was two days ago, and I can still smell it."

Serena thought that Maggie was imagining things but didn't want to say so. "You hungry?" she asked.

"Not much."

"I've got smoked trout in the truck."

Maggie screwed up her face. "Yuck."

"Yuck? You were the one who turned me on to that stuff."

"I've been off it lately," Maggie said.

Serena was stretched out on a sofa in Maggie's den. It was a man's room with walnut paneling and a dead mounted head staring down from the wall with two glass eyes. The furniture was black leather. A grandfather clock ticked hypnotically in the shadows. The wood fire gave off a semicircle of heat. Serena had been here for nearly an hour, but they had spoken only sporadically.

"Jonny was sorry he couldn't come," she said.

"Yeah, I'm a leper," Maggie said. "Don't get too close to me, you might catch something."

"If there's anything he can do for you behind the scenes, he'll do it," Serena said.

"What can he do? This is the Abel Teitscher show."

Serena knew that was true. "Has Abel talked to you?"

"Oh, yeah. Three hours yesterday. He

treated me like I was no better than one of the drug dealers at First and Lake. He wants me up on his wall, like Bambi there. Shot and stuffed. This is like déjà vu for Abel, you know. His own partner Nicole was guilty of killing her husband, so I must be, too."

"Maybe you shouldn't be talking to him," Serena advised her.

"Yeah, I know, but what would you think about a suspect who shut up and hired a lawyer?"

"Guilty."

"Exactly. I didn't do it, so the truth can't hurt me, right? That's why I let Abel question me. Except I know I'm being an idiot. I called Archie Gale today, and he told me the same thing, so now I'm lawyered up and not saying another word."

"Abel's reporting directly to Dan," Serena said.

"Oh, great. More good news. That would be a nice going-away present for Dan and Lauren. My head on a plate."

"You know, if you want an investigator to run down leads for you, you've got one," Serena said.

Maggie smiled and whistled the *Charlie's Angels* theme.

"Ha-ha," Serena said.

"If you were an angel, would it be Kate, Jaclyn, or Farrah?" Maggie asked.

"Jaclyn. Cool as ice."

"Farrah," Maggie said.

"Oh, yeah, you as a blonde, that works." Maggie flashed a toothy grin.

"Seriously, is there anything I should look into?" Serena asked.

"I'll talk to Archie and let you know. It's a different world, you know, being on the other side of the case. Anything we find out about Eric may just make it worse for me."

"Okay, what about you?" Serena asked.

"What do you mean?"

"I mean old cases. People you put in prison. Could someone be out for revenge?"

Maggie wrinkled her nose. "I don't think there were any perps where it was personal between us."

"Not for you anyway. Maybe for him."

"Have you ever had a perp come after you?" Maggie asked.

Serena nodded. "A couple of times. Maybe Las Vegas killers are more prone to settling scores. It's the mob influence. There was a sack of shit that I sent up for aggravated assault because he was cutting up his girlfriend. Tommy Luck. Great Vegas name, huh? Tommy got out and tried to return the favor."

"He attacked you?"

"He never got the chance," Serena said. "He was stalking me, but he got caught running a protection racket on some local dry cleaners before he could move in for the kill. They found photos of me all over his apartment. He'd cut the eyes out of most of them. Slashed me up with a knife. Smeared my body with red paint."

"What happened to him?"

"He's rotting in prison again."

"I don't think there's a Tommy Luck in my past," Maggie said.

"Then someone else must have had a motive to kill Eric."

"I'm glad you think so. Most people think all the motives point back to me. I killed him for the money. I killed him because he was having an affair. I killed him because *I* was having an affair." Maggie ducked her head and shoved her hair off her forehead.

Serena wasn't sure how far to push her. "Look, it doesn't take a mind reader to know you two were having problems."

"I can't talk about it. My lawyer will kill me."

"This conversation never happened, you know that. Something's been bothering you for weeks. Was it Eric? Was he involved with someone else?"

Maggie rolled her eyes. "For Eric, women were like potato chips. You can't fuck just one."

"What about you? Were you having an affair?"

Maggie had her chin on her knees. She cocked her head and gave Serena a sideways glance. "Eric thought I was."

"Oh?"

"He was convinced I was sleeping with Stride."

This was delicate ground between them.

"I know how you feel about Jonny," Serena told her softly.

"I know how he feels about you, too."

There was a trace of bitterness in her voice. They had become close friends, but Serena knew that Maggie resented how quickly Jonny had overturned his life to be with her. That was something he had never chosen to do for Maggie, even after his first wife died.

Serena was jealous, too. She sometimes felt like an outsider when the three of them were together, because Maggie shared such an easy friendship with Stride with so much history between them.

"I shouldn't be saying any of this," Maggie added. "If Eric thought I was having an affair, it gives me one more motive to blow him away."

"You weren't."

"No, but if he believed it, he might just decide to leave me, right? High and dry with no money. That's what Teitscher will think."

"Was Eric planning to leave you? Was that the problem?"

Maggie snorted. "No, that's the irony in all this. Eric said he'd do anything to make things better. He loved me, he was sorry for his mistakes, he was committed to me, he'd keep it in his pants. Sweet, huh?"

"But?"

"But I was planning to leave *him*. Not by killing him, Serena. I was going to divorce the bastard. I was planning to tell him that night."

"Do you want to tell me why?"

"Let's just say there were things going on that I couldn't stomach," Maggie said.

"Like what?"

Maggie shook her head. "I'm not going there."

Serena persisted. "A few months ago, you

asked me about sex. I got the feeling that Eric wanted you to do things you weren't comfortable with."

"Just drop it, okay? Please?" Her voice rose.

"I'm sorry," Serena said. She added, "Are you getting help?"

"What makes you think I need help?"

"Come on, Maggie."

She shook her head. "No, I haven't talked to Tony since before Thanksgiving."

"Why not?"

"I dealt with the miscarriages. I'm okay. I'm past that part of my life now."

Serena was frustrated. "You're not past anything. You were so upset about something you were ready to get a divorce, and now someone just killed your husband."

"Sure, go see a shrink," Maggie said, her voice heavy with sarcasm. "That'll help. Give me another motive, Serena. I'm nuts. Maybe I can plead not guilty by reason of mental defect."

"That's not what I mean."

"I know." Maggie held up her hands in surrender. "I'm sorry for being a pain in the ass. I'll go see Tony again when I'm ready. I promise. But I can't face any of this right now."

11

Stride swung his Bronco into a parking place at the twenty-four/seven fitness club on Miller Hill on Saturday morning. The strip-mall building faced the street through a series of floor-to-ceiling windows, and he saw half a dozen twenty-something girls in sweats and sports bras, jogging on tread-mills as they listened to their iPods. The rhythm and noise of athletic machines deaf-ened him when he went inside. He saw chests heaving and smelled perspiration. Stride scanned the pink-flushed faces, look-ing for Mitchell Brandt. Brandt worked at an investment firm in downtown Duluth and made money for clients playing the stock market like a lottery. He was also Tanjy Powell's ex-boyfriend and the man who had spilled the secrets about her sexual habits to the media after she cried rape.

If Tanjy had a relationship with Eric Sorenson, Stride wanted to know more about her background, in order to figure out whether Tanjy's disappearance was somehow connected to Eric's death. Brandt probably knew Tanjy's secrets better than anyone.

Stride spotted the stockbroker at a weight training machine in the rear of the club and squeezed between the obstacle course of fitness equipment to meet him.

"Mitchell Brandt?"

Brandt continued his bench-press routine without looking at Stride. The black lead weights banged furiously as he pumped the handlebars. He was wearing a sleeveless gray T-shirt with a Minnesota Twins logo and red nylon shorts. His limbs were sculpted and strong. Sweat beaded on his skin and left a V-shaped stain at the neck of his shirt.

"Yeah, who wants to know?"

"My name is Stride. I'm with the Duluth police. We met a few months ago."

Brandt sat up, breathing heavily. He

grabbed a white towel, wiped his face, and draped it around his shoulders. He was about thirty years old, with curly brown hair cut short on his scalp and an angular, closely shaved chin. His eyes were as light as oak. He considered Stride. "Yeah, I remember. What can I do for you?"

"I'd like to ask you some questions."

Brandt's face twitched. "About what?"

"Tanjy Powell," Stride said.

"Oh." Brandt relaxed and shrugged his broad shoulders. "That's kind of old news, isn't it?"

"She's missing."

"Missing? Well, I don't see how I can help you. I haven't seen Tanjy in months."

"This won't take long."

Brandt tugged at the sweaty collar of his shirt. His jaw flapped; he was chewing gum. "Okay. There's a coffee shop next door. How about you give me ten minutes to shower, and we'll meet there."

"I appreciate it."

Brandt swung his tree-trunk legs off the machine and glided toward the men's locker room. He was tall and well-built and exuded a macho I-don't-care attitude that women obviously found magnetic. Stride saw several young girls in the club casting an eye at Brandt as he left.

Stride ordered a cup of dark coffee at the shop next door, picked up a newspaper, and found a corner table to wait. Tanjy's disappearance was on the front page, but the article was short and below the fold. Stride was quoted, asking for help from people who might have seen or talked to her in the past week. He hadn't told anyone yet, including Abel, about the possible connection between Tanjy and Eric. For the time being, he had a back door to keep his hand in the investigation of Eric's murder.

Mitchell Brandt took twenty minutes to show up. He was dressed in a black silk shirt with a snug twenty-four-karat gold chain hung around his neck. He wore Dockers and black loafers and ordered a large skim latte with an extra shot of espresso. He sported enough expensive jewelry—an Omega watch, a sapphire ring on a non-wedding finger—to send the message that he had money. Before sitting down, he shook Stride's hand firmly and gave him a stockbroker's grin.

"How are you situated for investments, Lieutenant?" Brandt asked. "I'm tracking some interesting growth companies."

"Most of my assets are in a police pension."

"Well, if you want to make some real money, call me sometime. I work with a lot of the attorneys and executives in town. My clients do very, very well. I've turned people on to some hot med-tech companies down in the Cities."

"What's your secret?" Stride asked.

"I do my homework. I worked with the Byte Patrol guys here in town to build my own research software. It helps me find out everything there is to know about a business, good, bad, and ugly. I know more about these companies than most of their C levels."

"I'll keep that in mind."

Brandt sipped his latte. "So Tanjy's missing, huh? What's the deal? She drive into a lake or something?"

"What would make you think that?"

"She's not exactly stable. Sort of a New Age choirgirl stuck in the middle of a Stephen King novel."

"Meaning what?" Stride asked.

Brandt leaned in closer and lowered his voice. "Come on, Lieutenant. You read the papers back then. This is a girl who insisted I go to church with her every night and then would have me tie her to the bed and put a knife to her throat while I banged her. She's not wired right."

"So why date her?"

Brandt chuckled and fanned himself with the sports section of the paper. "Are you kidding? I'd take her back right now if she walked in the door. She's Cleopatra meets Grace Kelly. The sex was bizarre, but it was ungodly amazing. I've never seen a girl climax like she does. You saw the Meg Ryan orgasm scene in that movie, right? Imagine that times ten. Tanjy could make the house shake."

Stride finished off his coffee. The blend was dark and smoky, and there were grounds in the last swallow. He watched the horny glow in Brandt's face and found himself getting angry. "If you thought she was making up the rape story, you could have come to the police instead of telling it to the papers," Stride told him coldly.

Brandt held up his hands. "You've got it all wrong, Lieutenant. The reporters came to me. They knew about me and Tanjy before I ever opened my mouth. I swear."

"How would they know that? Did you brag about it?"

"Sure, maybe a little, but I don't think any of my friends would have ratted me out. I figured the papers got it from Tanjy herself. That would be like her, you know, to blow the whistle on herself. That's part of the whole victim thing. Look, as soon as I heard about this rape story, I knew Tanjy was faking it. I mean, it read like a replay of our sex life. She had me do her in that very spot, down in Grassy Point Park, against the fence. For all I know, that's where she takes all of her guys. But I wasn't going to spoil her fun. The only reason I talked to the reporters is that they were going to run the story anyway, and I'd come out looking like a rapist myself. That's bad for business. If it was going to be in the news, I wanted to make damn sure everyone knew this was Tanjy's idea, not mine."

Stride had a hard time imagining Tanjy reporting a rape, then giving the media a tip to expose her as a fake. "How did you meet her?"

"Sonia introduced us at the dress shop."

"Sonia?"

"Sonia Bezac. She's the manager."

Stride felt a shiver. "Sonia Bezac runs Lauren's dress shop?"

"Sure. Do you know her?"

He had an erotic flashback. "Yes, I do."

"Don't tell me you're part of—?" Brandt stopped in mid-sentence.

"What?"

Brandt shook his head. "Nothing, never mind."

"How do you know Sonia?" Stride asked.

"She and her husband are clients. I go in the shop sometimes to talk about investments. It's just a few doors down from my office. I met Tanjy right after Sonia hired her, and we started going out."

"Was she a client, too?"

"Tanjy doesn't have any money. Her dad was a minister, and her mom stayed at home. She got a little cash after they died, but that was all going to tuition. Tanjy never has much in her wallet, but when you look like she does, it doesn't matter. Guys will buy you anything you want."

"How long did you date?"

"About five or six months. We split up over the summer. That was a couple of months before her rape story made the news."

"Why'd you break it off? Did she get too expensive?"

Brandt looked surprised. "Me break it off?

No way. She dumped me. I was having the best sex of my life, Lieutenant. Like I said, if she called me today, I'd be back over there this afternoon."

"Okay, so why did she dump you?" Stride asked.

"At the time, she said it was because I didn't want to get married."

"Why not? I thought you were hooked on the girl."

"I was, but not in a forever, roses, kids, minivan kind of way. I was happy to stay with her as long as she was greasing my pole. But marriage? No thanks. I didn't want to wake up and find her taking a cleaver to my privates someday."

"Tanjy was violent?"

"Haven't you been listening, Lieutenant? This girl was all about violence. Sex to her *was* violence. That was the only way she could enjoy it. This girl had bats in her belfry. I wasn't planning to be around if Satan suddenly told her to start slicing up her husband."

"You said you thought at the time that she dumped you because you didn't want to get married," Stride told Brandt. "Was there some other reason?"

Brandt nodded. "Oh, yeah. I'd never been

dumped before, and it was sort of a blow to my ego, know what I mean? Girls don't usually blow me off for another guy."

"Tanjy was seeing someone else?"

"Yeah. She started having conflicts on date nights. Sonia told me Tanjy would go out for long lunches. Long like two hours. So I figured she'd found a sugar daddy. Somebody richer than me."

"Did you ask her who it was?"

"No. I didn't want to find out she tossed me over for someone fat, balding, and sixty, know what I mean? I bought the whole you-won't-marry-me line, even though it was bogus."

"You're sure it was bogus?" Stride asked.

"Well, no one put a ring on her finger, did they? Besides, the way she was sneaking around had to mean one thing. Whoever she was seeing, he was already married."

Like Eric, Stride thought.

After Stride left, Mitchell Brandt watched the detective from behind his coffee cup as he climbed into an old Ford Bronco in the parking lot. Brandt had been around cops before, and he knew the games they played. They talked with you about one thing when they really wanted something else. They baited you into saying something stupid. Sometimes, if you caught them stealing a glance when they thought you weren't looking, you could see the truth in their eyes.

Stride didn't look back as he drove away.

So maybe this really was all about Tanjy and nothing else. Brandt just didn't like the coincidence of the police tracking him down at this particular moment. Not when he was waiting for the next phone call. Not when his whole life was on the line.

Brandt slid out his black RAZR and dialed a number.

A woman answered. "This is Kathy."

"Hey there, alpha girl," Brandt said.

He pictured Kathy Lassiter, cool and hard in spiked heels, cutting off balls in the boardroom, hiding her bad girl ways behind a Brooks Brothers suit. She was a bitch, but he liked that. He enjoyed their battle for control.

"Well, hey yourself," she replied, her voice turning smoky. He imagined her red lips folding into a half-smile and her nipples puckering into pink nubs.

"Are you looking forward to next week?" he asked.

"You know I am. Are you going to be first?"

"Maybe I'll make you wait, so I can watch."

"I like that."

He grinned.

"Listen, about Infloron—" he began.

"Not on the phone."

"Yeah, I know. Understood. Sorry. I was just wondering if anyone has been nosing around. Asking you questions."

The silence drew out, but Brandt could hear the measured sound of her breathing.

"Of course not. Why?"

"I'm just making sure we're safe."

"Has someone talked to you?" The erotic undercurrent in her voice was gone. She was a corporate lawyer again, as sharp as a knife edge.

He hesitated. "No."

"Then stay cool."

"Look, if someone were to start following the paper trail, they'd wind up with me, not you."

Her voice was frozen. "So?"

"So I don't like that."

"I guess you'll have to trust me," she said.

"Yeah, right."

"I'll see you next week. You can get out your frustrations then. In the meantime, don't be stupid. Okay?"

"Sure."

Brandt hung up.

He tried to decide if Kathy Lassiter was lying to him. They used each other in and out of bed, but Brandt didn't trust Kathy. Not one little bit. He couldn't afford to trust anyone now. That was how it was when you were on the hook to a blackmailer.

12

An elderly Mexican housekeeper led Abel Teitscher to the solarium at the rear of Dan Erickson's London Road estate. A silver urn with coffee waited for him, along with a warm plate of cheese Danish and croissants. Abel awkwardly filled a china cup and blew on the coffee to cool it. He ate a piece of Danish quickly without using a plate and wiped his sticky fingers on a small paper napkin, then crumpled the napkin and shoved it in his pocket. He felt foolish, trying to balance the cup between his thumb and index finger, and feeling it quiver in his hand as if he was about to drop it and cause an embarrassing mess on the white ceramic tile.

Abel could feel the chill of the floor through the bottoms of his faded leather shoes. A wall of glass, divided into geometric patterns, looked out on a broad stretch of snow-covered lawn leading down to the lake. The mansions along the coastal road were expensive and old-school, set well back from the street behind iron gates, on large open lots that did nothing except ring up dollars on a property tax bill. Abel figured that the ground itself, just the dirt, was worth many times more than his entire house. Lauren's money, not Dan's.

He noticed a reflection in the diamond-shaped windows and turned to see Dan step down into the solarium from the main house. The county attorney had summoned Abel for an update on the investigation of Eric Sorenson's murder.

"Shit, it's like an icebox out here," Dan said. "You okay on coffee, Abel? Need a warmer-upper?"

"I'm okay."

Dan poured a cup. He was dressed in a navy blue silk robe over white pajamas, with black plush slippers on his feet. Abel could see an inch or two of bare ankles. Dan's blond hair, which was normally plastered in place with half a can of hair spray, was mussed and spiky. He hadn't shaved, and there was a yellow growth of stubble across the lower half of his face.

"Sorry I'm late," Dan said. "I was on the phone until two this morning about the new job. I can't wait to move to Washington. Nothing wrong with Duluth, but I was born in Chicago, and it'll be nice to be back in a real city again. Where Chinese food doesn't mean the lunch buffet at Potsticker Palace."

Abel grunted. He ordered takeout every Monday from the Potsticker Palace and thought it was damn good.

Dan put a croissant and two cheese Danish on a plate. "Not much for small talk, are you? That's why some people think you're a prick, Abel. Think about that. You're looking even skinnier than when I last saw you. You don't have cancer or something, do you?"

Abel felt his face growing hot. "I run, okay? Everyone else in this town piles on lard to hibernate for the winter, and meanwhile, my cholesterol is one hundred and seventy-one without taking any goddamn Lipitor."

Dan laughed. "K-2 was right. You do go ballistic about that."

The man was deliberately pushing his buttons. Abel wasn't going to miss him. He hoped that Dan went to a Chinese restaurant in Washington and choked on his broccoli stir-fry.

"No offense, but why am I here?" Abel asked impatiently. "You don't usually call me in until we're ready to make an arrest."

"Well, are we?"

"No way. We won't have anything back on the forensics for a few weeks."

"All right, tell me what you've found since we last talked." Dan sat down and chewed the end of a croissant.

"I've looked at Sorenson's finances. He had a net worth in the high seven figures and a strong cash flow at his business. He did well in the market. No litigation at the company. He hasn't dismissed an employee in two years. There's nothing suspicious in his work life."

"All of his money goes to Maggie now?" Dan asked.

"Most of it. I saw his will. There are charitable provisions and some outright gifts to two sisters and a few nieces and nephews.

Nothing more than a hundred thousand dollars. The bulk of the estate winds up in his wife's hands."

"Nice nest egg for a cop. What about the happy couple?"

"Not so happy."

"What does Maggie say about their marriage?"

"She says they were fine, but she's lying. I've got reports of arguments and affairs. He wasn't sleeping in their bed. You ask me, they were headed for a divorce."

"Can we prove that?" Dan asked.

"Not at this point. I do know that Maggie was seeing a shrink. Tony Wells. Sorenson went to see Tony the night he was killed."

"Do we know why?"

"I called him. Tony says he can't say anything unless Maggie waives privilege."

"That's not likely," Dan said.

"Tony thinks Maggie is innocent, for whatever that's worth," Abel added.

"It's not worth squat. What about these affairs?"

"His secretary says Sorenson catted around. I don't have any names yet."

"What about Maggie? Is she getting any on the side?"

"I've started asking around the department, but people don't want to talk about her."

"Do you have her under surveillance?"

"Sure, that's standard M.O., but Maggie knows we're doing it. She's not stupid."

"Keep it up anyway. Twenty-four seven. I don't want anyone saying we gave her special treatment."

"K-2 already ordered it."

"If you're looking for affairs, remember that she's always had a thing for Stride," Dan reminded him.

"Everyone knows that's platonic."

"Yeah? Don't be so sure."

Abel's eyes narrowed. "Do you know something?"

"I'm just saying they spend half their lives together. Check it out."

"If you say so." Abel wasn't convinced. He didn't like Stride and didn't much like Maggie either, but that didn't mean they were heating up the sheets. Then again, he had always assumed his wife was loyal, too.

"So her husband is cheating, and she's got millions coming her way," Dan said. "Motive isn't a problem."

"Nothing's a problem. It's her gun. No one was in the house. She did it."

"You sound pretty sure. How about gun shot residue?"

"Nothing, but she's a cop. She knows how to beat that."

"Any blood spatter on her clothes?"

Abel shook his head. "We're running tests, but I didn't see anything. It was her house. She could have washed her clothes before calling us. Hell, she could have shot him in the buff and then taken a shower. Oh, and I had her take a blood test, too. She was drinking coffee, but I smelled alcohol."

"And?"

"Her blood alcohol level was point oh seven. Even if she quit drinking a few hours earlier, that's high. She must have been drunk when she did it."

"That gives Archie Gale a way to talk it down to manslaughter."

"He may be right," Abel said. "Nothing points to premeditation at this point."

"Right, the gun walked downstairs on its own, and Maggie followed to find out where it was going." Dan took a big bite out of a pastry and licked the cream cheese off his lips with his tongue. He added, "How about the conspiracy theory? Anyone get out of prison lately who might want to get back at

Maggie for putting him away? Defense attorneys like Archie Gale love to blow smoke about that kind of shit."

Abel scoffed. "There's nothing like that. I've got people running down her old cases, but so far, the violent perps she put away are all still behind bars or dead. Cases don't come much more straightforward than this. Stride's the one who wants this to be some mystery, because he can't accept the fact that Maggie did it."

Dan leaned forward. "Is Stride interfering?"

"He was at the crime scene before anyone else. I don't like that, but I don't think he actually touched anything or helped her clean up."

"If he gets in the way, or sticks his nose into this, I want to know immediately."

"You personally?"

"Damn right. I wasn't in favor of bringing him back, you know. As far as I was concerned, K-2 should have kept you in the top job, but Stride and K-2 are as thick as thieves. If Stride does anything that compromises this investigation, I will personally see that his ass gets kicked out of the lieutenant's chair."

Abel didn't know how to respond to that. "I wouldn't want it back even if K-2 offered it, and he won't."

"Never say never."

Abel didn't like game-playing. He wasn't going to be a pawn. He knew Stride was permanently on Dan's shit list because of the blown election, but if Dan was burning to take him down before he left the city, he could do it on his own.

He heard the muffled ringing of Dan's cell phone. Dan reached into the pocket of his bathrobe and retrieved it.

"Erickson," Dan said into the phone.

Abel watched Dan's eyes do a nervous dance. Dan snapped his fingers and gestured at the door, and Abel was glad to take the hint. Time to go.

Whatever the call was, it was bad news.

"Hello, Dan. Do you know who this is?"

There was a moment of dead air as Dan wrenched his way from one reality to the next. Every victim was like that.

"Yes," Dan replied, his voice forced.

"Tonight's the night. Is Serena ready to make the drop?"

"Yes."

"That's good." He added, "But you know this is just a down payment, right?"

"That's not what we discussed."

"You're right, it's not, but things have changed. A lot's happened this week, Dan. You think I don't read the papers? The price has gone up."

"That's not acceptable."

He chuckled long and low. "I love lawyers. Always negotiating. You're right, Dan, why don't we just forget about it. Hand the phone to that cop who's there with you, and I can let him know what's been going on."

He waited as Dan stewed. Targets like Dan were the easy ones. They'd chew glass rather than risk public embarrassment. Or jail.

"What did you have in mind?" Dan asked finally.

He smiled. "Let's wrap up the first deal, and then I'll check in with you again. I'd hate to see your big move to Washington get tanked."

"Give me the details," Dan snapped.

"Call Serena," he instructed. "Tell her to be at the Park Hill Cemetery off Vermillion Road at ten o'clock tonight. Alone. With the money."

"Why there?"

"Let's just say I like the idea of being surrounded by dead people." He thought about the river stench of the rising waters in Alabama and added, "The truth is, Dan, I'm a ghost."

13

Stride felt sorry for the guy from Byte Patrol, who was seated in front of the store computer at Lauren Erickson's dress shop, Silk. The store manager, Sonia Bezac, jabbed her razor-sharp nail dangerously close to his eyes and wouldn't have thought twice about digging in and gouging one out. The techie had a giant physique that made his neon purple T-shirt look as if it had shrunk in the wash, but Sonia may as well have been wearing black leather and cracking a whip.

"This is the third time in a month I've had you in here," she snapped at him. "Each time you tell me it's fixed, and each time the fucking machine freezes up again."

The tech shrugged his craggy shoulders, and his neck disappeared. "Have you tried rebooting?"

Sonia threw her hands in the air. She was tall and extremely thin, with a narrow face, prominent chin, and a slightly drooping nose. With her hands over her head, and her red hair blazing like sunshine, she looked as if she were rearing back to fire off a lightning bolt. "Rebooting? Do I look like an idiot? Don't you think I would turn the goddamn thing off and on eighteen times before calling you?"

"I have to ask," the man said.

"Don't ask. Just get busy. I need my files back."

She swung away and expelled her breath loudly as if she were spitting out a gristly piece of steak. The techie caught Stride's eye and winked at him.

Sonia stopped dead when she saw Stride standing in the middle of the dress shop, watching her. He knew he looked out of place, the way any man would, surrounded by glittering evening gowns and cocktail dresses. He could see himself reflected in half a dozen mirrors. He wasn't sure how he would feel, seeing Sonia again, and it didn't help when she immediately stalked up to him, cocked her head to one side, and kissed him on the lips.

"Soft lips," she said to him. "Thirty years later, and I still remember that."

He had dated Sonia exactly once, when he was a junior in high school. Stride was wild with grief because his father had just died, and Sonia was on a quest to rob as many teenage boys as she could of their virginity. She smuggled a bottle of Stoli out of her parents' house, and the two of them spent three hours in a parking lot near Gooseberry Falls, drinking shots until they were sick. They undressed each other through a fog of alcohol but wound up vomiting on the highway shoulder before they had sex. Neither of them was in the mood after that.

A month later, Stride met Cindy, and he never went out with Sonia again. He had bumped into her in the city off and on over the course of three decades. Sonia wound up marrying a urologist named Delmar Bezac, and Stride remembered Cindy joking about whether Delmar or Sonia had seen more penises in their days.

"It's hazy to me, Sonia," he told her. "All I remember is a cold night and warm vodka. Or was it a warm night and cold vodka?"

Sonia dabbed her lips, as if checking her lipstick to make sure she wasn't smudged. "I bet you remember more than that."

"No comment."

"You became a cop. I see you in the papers all the time. You know what they say. Cops carry big guns."

Stride ignored that. "You're working for Lauren. I'm surprised."

"What, the rich bitch and the slut?"

"I didn't say that."

"Never mind, you were thinking it. This place is just a tax write-off for Lauren. I run the store."

"How's Delmar?" Stride asked. "I understand the man is a whiz with a catheter."

Sonia giggled. "You always were fucking funny."

"Is that the way you talk to your customers? Do mothers of the bride like a girl who swears a blue streak and has a temper like a cannon?"

Sonia swept her long mane of red hair out of her eyes. "I control myself with customers, thank you very much. Except for the young girls. These new brides, they pretend to be sweet little girls for their mommies, but you should hear the stories they tell me."

"Do you have kids?"

"Two. Boys, thank God. They're both away in college."

Stride looked around at the dresses hung on the white plastic bodies of the mannequins. Sonia herself wore a glittering lilac dress that clung to her long, slender lines and would have looked stylish at a symphony ball. Her makeup minimized the tracks near her eyes and lips. In her heels, she was nearly as tall as Stride. Sonia noted his eyes and spread her arms, inviting his gaze. The dress fell low across her pale, small chest, and Stride realized he could remember vividly, even so many years later, how her breasts felt in the calloused grip of his teenage hands. Her skin didn't have the taut freshness of youth anymore, but she was still attractive, and she had smoothed some of her rough edges.

"I clean up nicely, don't I?" she asked, guessing where his mind was going. "Not bad for a girl from the wrong side of the tracks."

"I can't picture you in a place like this, Sonia."

"You mean because all my prom dresses wound up with grass stains?"

"No comment again."

"You're here, so let me give you the tour." Sonia slung an arm through Stride's elbow and steered him around the shop, which was lushly carpeted in a royal blue and had track lighting illuminating the racks. One sparkling chandelier was hung in the center of the ceiling. Sonia rattled off the names of Italian designers whom Stride had never heard of and had him run his fingers along fabrics that slid off his skin like skates on fresh ice. His hands came away with glitter.

Silk, was located on Superior Street in the heart of the brick-lined streets of downtown. Nearby, there were funky gift shops and coffeehouses offering tarot card readings designed to lure tourists out of Canal Park and New Age students from the university. For the lawyers and suits at the courthouse and in the banks, there were also jewelers and investment brokers. An upscale dress shop in downtown Duluth relied mostly on proms and weddings for its business. It was also the only place in town where the women of Duluth's small upper crust, and trendy young singles with money, could find name fashions that didn't come with a zip-out hood.

"Does Lauren plan to keep the shop after she and Dan move to Washington?" he asked.

Sonia shook her head. "I'm trying to get Delmar to buy it for me."

"Good for you."

"Yeah, except Lauren is trying to screw me on the price. The woman is fucking cold-blooded, you know?"

"You don't have to tell me," Stride said.

"Oh, yeah, I saw the papers last year. She had her knives out for you. It's lucky you're still alive."

Stride smiled and didn't reply.

"I guess you're not here just to remember the good old days," Sonia said.

Stride shook his head. "Tanjy."

"Sure. I still haven't heard from her."

"Tell me about her," Stride said.

"You probably know her better than me. I mean, because of all that craziness with the fake rape in November."

"I don't feel like I know her at all," Stride admitted. "Were you the one to hire her?"

"Yeah, she was perfect for the store. She

has those amazing mulatto features and a great eye for fashion."

"Did you know anything about her sex life?"

"Why, because sex is my specialty?" Sonia grinned in a way that led Stride to think she was still competing with Delmar for access to the private parts of Duluth males. "There's nothing wrong with a little sin from time to time, Jon. Maybe you should take a walk on the wild side."

Have you two ever done anything . . . strange?

"Meaning what?" he asked.

"Meaning not everyone is satisfied with once a week in the missionary position, you know? I may be past forty, but I'm as horny as I ever was."

"That's a scary thought."

"Why don't we have dinner, and I can tell you what I mean."

"Pass," he said.

"Well, you can't blame a girl for trying."

"Let's get back to Tanjy," Stride said. "Did you know about her rape fantasies?"

"No, around me, she's very conservative, very Christian. Maybe she has a multiple personality thing going on, who knows. Not that I'm judging what she does in bed. I sure wouldn't want to see my sex life in the papers."

"Men seem to fall for her hard."

"Oh, God, yeah. It made me a little jealous. Look, I've been with a lot of men, and I never get any complaints, you know? But no one's offered to bronze my pussy."

"Nice," Stride said.

"I'm just saying, Tanjy was in a whole other league."

"I talked to Mitchell Brandt today," Stride said. "Mitch is a friend of yours, right?"

"You could say that," Sonia said with a tiny smile.

"You introduced Tanjy and Mitch?"

"It was more like Mitch saw Tanjy in the store, and I led him over to her by his cock."

"Did he tell you about the rape stuff while they were dating?"

"Not the gory details. He just said she was an animal in bed. I was pretty surprised."

"Mitch says she dumped him for another guy."

Sonia smiled. "Poor Mitch. He's never alone for long."

"Do you know who Tanjy was seeing?"

"No, it was pretty obvious she was having a big romance, but she kept it quiet. I asked her about it a few times and got nothing."

"Any idea why?"

"I figure he was married."

"Was this before or after the rape charge?" Stride asked.

"Before."

"What happened after she admitted the story was a fake?"

Sonia caressed her chin with her fingertips as she thought about it. "I think the rape thing killed the romance. There weren't any more secret lunches. I guess the guy figured he was dating a nutcase, and he was probably worried the affair would come out."

"So she wasn't dating anyone lately?"

"Not that I know of."

Stride was surprised.

"You never saw her with anyone in the store?"

Sonia shook her head. "We don't get many men in here. Just husbands who sit and read *Esquire* while their wives try on dresses. Most of them aren't the type to catch the eye of a girl like Tanjy."

"She never talked about being stalked or followed?"

"Not to me."

"Did you know Eric Sorenson?"

Sonia's eyes narrowed into slits. "Sure. Why?"

"Did you ever see him with Tanjy?"

"No."

"Could he have been Tanjy's mystery man? The one she dumped Mitch Brandt for?"

"No." Sonia tugged on one strap of her dress and played with her hair.

"You sound pretty sure."

"I would have known if it were him, that's all."

"Why?"

Sonia shrugged and didn't reply.

"How do you know Eric?" Stride asked.

"Socially."

"Were *you* having an affair with him?"

"That's none of your business." Her red hair fell across her cheek. "What are you, a cop or a goddamn gossip columnist?"

"You think I like asking these questions?"

Sonia whirled away and planted herself in front of the store window. Her arms were folded tightly across her chest. "You don't know who I am, Jon. You've hardly seen me in thirty years. How dare you come in here making judgments about my life. You don't know anything about me."

"This isn't personal," Stride told her.

"Well, it sure as hell sounds personal."

"Look, there are only two things I want. I want to know where Tanjy Powell is and what happened to her. And I want to know who killed Eric Sorenson."

"I have nothing to say about Eric."

Stride swore under his breath. "Then tell me about Tanjy," he said.

Sonia swiveled her head to look at him. "What about her?"

"You told Lauren that she left early on Monday."

She tossed her hair back. "That's right."

"Did she say why?"

"No."

It was like coaxing drops of wine out of an empty bottle now, trying to get her to talk. "What happened that day?" he asked.

"She took a break about three o'clock. When she came back, she was upset."

"About what?"

"I have no idea."

"Did she say anything?"

"No."

Stride was frustrated. "How long was she gone?"

"Maybe half an hour."

"Do you know where she went?"

Sonia shrugged. "When she came back, she had a cup of coffee from Katrina's place down the street. Java Jelly."

"Katrina?"

"Katrina Kuli. She owns the coffee shop. Talk to her, not me. Maybe she knows what the hell happened."

14

Java Jelly, where Tanjy got her coffee on Monday afternoon before her disappearance, was three blocks down Superior Street from Silk. It was a twenty-something hangout and a haven for folk musicians on the weekends, with warped wood floors, mismatched antique tables, and black-and-white publicity photos taped on the walls. The ceiling was low, and black pipes wobbled on loose brackets overhead. He saw a few students using WI-FI on their laptops and nursing lattes. He smelled roasting beans and old sweat socks.

The woman working the counter was

heavyset, at least two hundred pounds, with brown hair bunched into two pigtails. She wore a tie-dye shirt that let three inches of her bare stomach bulge out over the belt of her jeans. Her navel was pierced, and so was her upper lip, and she had a barbed wire tattoo wound around her neck.

"Help you?" the woman asked him. Her voice was polite but cool. She was in her early thirties and older than she looked. As a university town, Duluth had its share of ex-students who never grew out of their hippy phase.

"I'd like to ask you a few questions."

"Questions go better with a muffin, don't you think?" she asked, wiping the counter.

"Sorry, I'm not hungry," Stride said. He added, "I'm with the police."

"So what? Is there some kind of no-muffin-when-I'm-on-duty rule?"

"Okay. Blueberry."

"Yah shoooor, blooooberry, the state muffin of Minnnnnnahhhsooodddaa." She grabbed a plate and snagged a muffin from the rack behind her with a pair of tongs.

Stride handed her money. "Are you Katrina?"

She nodded. "Katrina Kuli. I own the place, I run the place, I book the music, I bus the tables when my students don't show up, which is half the time."

"Cool spot," he said.

"And *you* look like an expert on cool," she told him, clucking her tongue. "What's your name? Joe Friday? Bob Thursday? Tom Monday?"

"It's Jonathan Stride."

"Well, well." Katrina folded her arms across her ample chest. "I see it, yes, I do see it."

"You've lost me."

"Maggie Sorenson is a friend of mine," she told him. "I've had to listen to a lot of stories about you."

"I'm sure none of them was flattering."

"You'd be surprised." Katrina frowned as her memory caught up with her. "How is Maggie?"

"Not good."

"I hear she's been suspended."

"She's on paid leave while we investigate this thing."

"I don't believe she could have done what they say."

Stride didn't want to go down that road. "How do you know her?"

"We met in an aerobic dance class last year."

He had a good poker face, but a twitch of his lips betrayed him, and Katrina caught it immediately.

"What, you think big girls don't dance?" she asked.

"Not at all."

"Let me tell you, big girls do *everything,* and we could teach lessons to some of those pretzel sticks in the girlie magazines. It ain't how much you got, it's what you do with it."

He held up his palms, surrendering. "You win. Can we talk?"

"Yeah, sure." Katrina waved a hand at a skinny boy with greasy black hair, who was slumped in a chair near the store's fireplace with a dog-eared copy of *Ulysses.* "Billy, watch the counter for me, okay?"

The kid grunted without looking up.

Katrina led Stride to a raised platform that doubled as a matchbox stage when bands visited the shop. The chairs wobbled as they sat down, and the table shifted unsteadily on its legs when Stride put his elbows down to lean closer to Katrina. Her breath smelled like berry tea. When he was near her face, he noticed caked-on makeup covering purplish bruises on her cheekbones and neck, and a scabbed gash poking like a worm out of the collar of her shirt.

"What happened to you?" he asked.

Katrina shrugged. "Nothing."

"That's not nothing," Stride told her.

"I slipped on the ice. Luckily, my tits broke the fall, or it would have been a lot worse."

"Did you cut yourself on the ice, too?"

"I think there was a piece of glass, yeah." She covered the gash with her hand.

"It looks like someone beat you up."

"I don't really care what it looks like."

"I'm not trying to pry. I just don't like it when husbands or boyfriends use their women as punching bags."

"Well, I don't have either one. Okay? Now what do you want?"

"Sonia Bezac at the dress shop sent me down here."

Katrina's eyes flashed with anger. "What the hell did she tell you?"

"Just that you might know something about Tanjy Powell."

"Oh." Katrina slumped.

"Do you know Tanjy?"

"Speaking of girlie pretzel sticks," Katrina replied, sticking out her tongue.

"So that's a yes."

"Sure, I'm in Silk a lot, so I see her there. Sonnie gets me decked out when I'm headed down to the Cities for a weekend of clubbing." She read Stride's expression and said, "Do I have to give you my big girls speech again?"

"No."

"Good. It's not funny, you know, the way people treat us plus sizes. And it's not just men. Women are the worst. Girls like Tanjy, they look at me like I'm some kind of freak."

"You're sure it's not the belly button ring, the tie-dye, and the tattoo?" he said.

"Okay, yeah, I may *look* like a freak sometimes. Hell, I *am* a freak and proud of it. But put me in a short skirt on the dance floor, and I can rock it out. Some women act all disgusted. Well, fuck 'em, I am who I am. I'm not going to walk around in a muumuu just because I was born with fat genes and I like to eat."

"I can see why you and Maggie get along," Stride said.

"Yeah, Maggie's got a foul little mouth on

her. I love that. For a pretzel stick, she's not half-bad."

"What about Tanjy?"

Katrina growled. "Now there's a bitch. Slinks around the shop like she's better than everyone else. Always has her face stuck in a Bible, and then you find out she likes to get tied up and nasty. Fucking hypocrite."

"Does she come in here a lot?"

"Oh, yeah, she gets a cuppa almost every day. Treats me like I'm the hired help. And what the hell is she? Like she's anything more than a salesclerk herself?"

"When did you last see her?"

Katrina took hold of her pigtails and wiggled them like antennae. "I do that when I need to think. Helps focus the brain waves." She thought for a moment and said, "I guess it was Monday."

"Was she here with anyone else?"

"No, she came in, got a cup to go, and left."

"When was that?"

"Oh, shit, I don't remember. Sometime in the afternoon."

"How did she look?"

Katrina rubbed her nose with the back of her palm. "Same as usual, I guess. Same stuck-up, bitchy attitude."

"Was she upset? Agitated?"

"Not that I could see."

Stride tried to puzzle out the time line. Tanjy left Silk to get coffee and came back half an hour later, visibly shaken. That evening, she disappeared. Why?

"Did you see where she went?"

"Nope."

"Did you see her talking to anyone?"

"Negatory."

"Did you know Maggie's husband?" he asked.

"Eric? Yeah."

"Did you ever see Eric and Tanjy together?"

"Nope." Katrina stuck a fingernail in her mouth and chewed on it.

"You look nervous," Stride said.

Katrina didn't reply.

"Was something going on with Eric?"

"How would I know?"

"That's not an answer."

Katrina fidgeted in her chair. "I don't know anything about Eric."

"When did you last see him?" he asked.

"He was in on Monday, too," Katrina told him.

Stride's face hardened. "Were Eric and Tanjy together?"

"No." She saw the disbelief in his eyes and added, "Hey, it's true. They weren't together. Eric came in about ten minutes after Tanjy left."

After leaving the coffee shop, Stride headed for the branch of Range Bank across the street and asked the head of security to queue up the tapes from the bank's ATM camera on Monday afternoon. He sat alone in a windowless office, watching the grainy tape roll. The video was in black-and-white, but Duluth in January was like a black-and-white movie anyway. He sat under the fluorescent light, not moving a muscle, watching pedestrians come and go in silence on the tape.

At five minutes after three o'clock, he watched Tanjy Powell disappear inside the door of Java Jelly. Three minutes later, she came out again with a tall cup of coffee in her hand. It was odd, seeing her again in the flesh, looking as cool and mysterious as ever. She sipped her coffee, and he could imagine the warmth of the liquid on her lips. She was dressed in a black wool coat that draped to her ankles, and she had a velvet pillbox hat nestled on her head. It was white leopard, with a matching scarf. Her raven hair flowed from under the hat and skittered across her face like streaks of chocolate skimming across the surface of espresso foam.

His view was blocked as an old man approached the ATM. His face filled the camera. Stride swore, trying to see behind him. He caught a glimpse of Tanjy turning away from the coffee shop, but in the opposite direction from Silk. He wanted to reach in and move the man out of the way.

Where was she going?

Stride fumed as nearly two minutes passed. Finally, the old man took his card and disappeared, and the camera offered an unobstructed view across Superior Street. He caught his breath. Tanjy was there, nestled against the side of a building.

Eric was with her.

He was wearing a dark suit, but no coat. His long blond hair blew wildly in the wind. The two of them were so close as to be nearly kissing. Eric spoke animatedly, clutching Tanjy's shoulder with one hand. Suddenly, she turned away, and she stared right at the camera, as if she were looking straight at Stride across the street. Her hands flew to her mouth in a look of sheer horror.

Eric pulled her back and said something more to her. Tanjy shook her head violently. She yanked away and hurried down the street away from him. He saw Eric call after her. Once, then twice. When she was gone, Eric stood there on the frigid street, alone, looking like some kind of Norse god. He shook his head and walked toward the coffee shop and went inside. He came back out again with a cup of coffee himself and headed in the opposite direction, his head down, his hair waving behind him. He walked until he vanished out of view of the camera.

Stride let the tape go. More people wandered by. Everyone was in a rush, trying to escape from the cold.

He pulled out his cell phone. His fingers hesitated over the keys, but then he dialed.

"Abel? It's Stride. We need to talk."

15

Fifteen minutes before midnight, Serena climbed from lake level up the sharp incline that twisted like a Chinese dragon through a series of tight switchbacks. She was driving Stride's Bronco, its four-wheel drive clutching at the pavement. Her high beams illuminated the neighborhood. She was in the narrow greenway of Congdon Park, one of the richest areas of the city, on a secluded street that didn't invite visitors. Grand homes lit up like monuments as her headlights swept across them, and then they vanished again into the shadows. The gated driveways were closed and locked, alarm systems on, lights extinguished.

This was a city with almost no middle class. You were rich, or you were poor, and never the twain shall meet.

She drove slowly, unsure of her directions, and almost missed the sign pointing her toward the cemetery. She followed Vermillion Road, and a few hundred yards later, the street became a rutted dirt track. The land opened up around her. Fir trees hugged the road, and beyond them, she could see slopes glowing in the moonlight and rows of silhouetted headstones. The area was primitive and empty, as if she had left the city miles behind her.

Serena slowed the Bronco to a crawl. On a stretch of straightaway, she saw a stake jutting at an angle out of the snow on the right shoulder. A white piece of cloth was tied around the stake and hung limply in the still air. She steered off the road and killed the engine, then got out and closed the door with a quiet *snick*. She stopped and listened. The night was silent, except for the rumble of a train far down in the port area below her. The clouds had passed away. Overhead, she saw a jumble of constellations and a slim moon. She took stock of the park around her. On her left was a steep hillside, and she could make out graves scattered among the trees. On her right was a tattered mesh fence mostly buried in snow. The cemetery continued beyond the fence, and she could see a plowed-out section of road where mourners could drive out to the plots.

She was dressed entirely in black: black jeans, a black turtleneck that nestled against her chin, and Stride's beat-up black leather jacket that was warm and roomy. The jacket hid the holster for the Glock secured near her left shoulder. She wasn't taking any chances. Not with a blackmailer. Not in an empty cemetery at midnight. And not with an envelope bulging with ten thousand dollars in cash inside the jacket pocket.

The snow was matted down. She climbed the shoulder of the road and then stepped over the crooked section of fence. On the other side, her feet landed in wetter, deeper snow, and some of it got into her boots. She felt cold dampness soaking through her socks. She slogged through the snow and broke free onto the plowed road, where she stopped again. The trees loomed around her like sentinels. Most were evergreens, but there were a few stripped oaks, barren of leaves. She took careful steps, trying to hush her footfalls. She slipped a flashlight out of her pocket and cast the beam around, lighting up several headstones. She read the names: Boe, Beckmann, Anderson.

Serena wasn't superstitious by nature, but a sixth sense made her jump. She wasn't alone.

"Turn off the flashlight."

Something about the voice made her body melt with fear, as if she were a frightened teenager. She thought about reaching for her gun, but she soothed herself and swallowed hard. Her mouth was dry. She switched off the light, and her eyes, accustomed to the beam, went blind again.

"Come closer."

She waited until she could see. He quickly became impatient.

"Now."

Serena saw a silhouette near one of the skeletal oak trees. She drew near him, feeling the weight of the gun on her left side comfort her. Somewhere not far away, a dog bayed like a banshee. Its howl was plaintive and scared, and the sound reminded her that the rest of the world wasn't so far away. But no one was close enough to make a difference if things went bad.

She tried to make him out and narrowed her eyes, squinting. He was standing where the ground rose above her. He had a bulky coat with a fur hood pulled up over his head. His face was invisible. His arms hung down at his side, long, like ape limbs. She realized that he held things in both hands that made his arms look as if they dropped all the way to his knees. His left hand held a heavy flashlight. His right hand held a gun.

"Seen enough?" he asked.

Meaning: had she seen the gun?

He switched on the flashlight and directed the intense beam at her face. She felt a sharp pain as the light hit her pupils, and she covered her face and backed away.

"Turn that off, you son of a bitch," she snapped.

He laughed in a low, deep rumble and switched the light off.

"Let's get this over with," Serena said. "Neither one of us wants to be out here long."

"You mean you want to get back into bed with your cop lover?"

Serena let a few seconds of cold silence

pass. "So you know who I am. Am I sup-posed to be scared?"

"I think you are."

"Big words from a blackmailer. Blackmail-ers are cowards. You can't let me see your face. You steal someone's secrets and pre-tend it makes you a big man. Stealing secrets is what little girls do."

He didn't answer right away, and then he said, "I could tell you what I do to little girls."

"What, do you dress up like them?"

"Watch your mouth," he said.

"I'm not afraid of a pissant blackmailer. Do you want the money or not?"

"Did you count it?"

"Yes."

"Ten thousand?"

"Yes."

"I hope you didn't do something stupid like mark the bills or write down the serial num-bers. Or tell your cop lover about this."

"I guess you'll have to take your chances," Serena said.

"So will you. Don't forget that."

"You're taking a big risk, blackmailing someone like Dan," she told him.

"Yeah? People like Dan pay me because they keep one face for the world and one face for all the fucking games they play when no one's watching. You don't *know* the shit that goes down in this town. You and your cop lover, you're blind."

"So it's not just Dan," Serena concluded. "Who else are you doing this to?"

"Like I said, some people around here have dirty secrets."

Serena reached inside her jacket pocket.

"Stop," he snapped, instantly raising his gun, pointing it at her head.

"I'm getting your money."

He blinded her with the flashlight again. "Slowly. Use two fingers. Don't be stupid."

She extracted the envelope and held it up. "See?"

"Put it on the headstone and back away."

She saw a stone encrusted with dead moss near her feet. It slanted backward toward the ground. The name, partly eroded by time, read BURNS. She lay the envelope on the arched summit of the marker and backed up slowly.

"That's far enough," he called when she was another fifteen feet away. "Turn around. Get on your knees."

"No way."

"Get on your knees."

"I'm not turning my back on you."

"Just do it."

She sank to her knees in the snow. The wetness soaked through her jeans. "Make it fast."

He kept the flashlight in her face. She couldn't see a thing and had to close her eyes. She heard him slide down the low slope. The snow crunched under his boots as he came closer. Her bare hands stiffened in the cold, and she fluttered her fingers to limber them up, in case she needed to dive into her coat for her gun. He was at the headstone. She heard him ruffling through the cash in the envelope.

She waited for what he would do next. She listened carefully for any footstep that meant he was walking toward her.

"See you soon," he said.

The white light disappeared behind her eyelids. She opened her eyes, blinking, seeing nothing but aftershocks of light. She heard footsteps heading away from her. He was jogging as he retreated up the hillside. When she could finally see again, she caught only a fleeting glimpse of a moving silhouette, and then it blended into darkness with the rest of the trees.

She was alone.

Serena pushed herself to her feet and brushed the snow away. She climbed back up to the fence by the road and stepped over it again. Her breathing was loud and fast. Her pulse was galloping like a Thoroughbred. Stride's Bronco had never looked so good.

Closer by, the dog howled again. It was loose. Or maybe it was a prowling wolf, not a dog at all. She didn't want to stick around and find out.

16

Serena's body was ice-cold when she slid under the fleece blanket into bed an hour later. Frosty air breathed on her face and bare shoulders through a crack in the window. The bedroom was small, like the other matchbox rooms in the old house, which had no foundation underneath it, just wooden pilings that made the floors slant like a carnival fun house. The room had a comforting, musty smell about it, a smell of age and the sea that had long ago taken up residence deep in its timbers. She often woke up to that smell and heard odd noises in the night, as if ghosts were passing from room to room.

She had spent much of the past year haunting antique shops along the North Shore to pick up cherry wood dressers, throw rugs, and old nautical equipment. She was surprised at how much she enjoyed the contrast to her condominium in Las Vegas, which was stark and modern, done in blacks and whites, with her photographs of bitterroot and landscapes of the jagged Mojave hills on the walls. It was an emotionless place, and that was how she wanted it then. Since meeting Jonny, though, she had been flooded by emotions, and she was getting better now at managing the demons from her past, letting them out without feeling that they could control her. That was one of the reasons she enjoyed the antique quality of this house. She wanted a sense of the past again, which she had blocked out for years. When she held a clock from the early 1900s in her hands, she could feel all the people who had owned it and touched it.

She molded herself against Jonny in bed. She knew from his breathing that he was awake. He hadn't said a word as she came into the bedroom, bringing the chill of the night with her, and quickly stripped. When she slid her fingers between his legs, she felt him stir.

"Do you know how cold that hand is?" he murmured.

"Sorry."

"I'm not complaining."

Serena kissed him. "I thought you'd be asleep."

"Not when you're out on a job at midnight."

"I'm okay."

"You took your gun," he said.

"It was just a precaution."

"Do you want to tell me about it?"

"I can't say anything," Serena said.

"Even in the box?"

"Not yet."

Stride turned his head toward her and opened his eyes. Serena could see he was troubled.

"What's wrong?" she asked.

He pushed himself up in bed until he was sitting. "I found out that Eric was involved with Tanjy Powell. I had to tell Abel Teitscher about it."

"So you're off the case again."

Stride nodded.

"Did Abel tell you anything about the investigation?"

"I pried a couple of things out of him," Stride said.

"Like what?"

"The most intriguing thing was that Eric went to see Tony Wells the night he died," Stride said.

Serena propped herself on one elbow and brushed her hair back out of her face. "Tony? Why?"

"Tony can't say. Privilege."

"Was Eric getting therapy?"

"Abel doesn't think so."

"But Maggie was."

"Yeah."

"Do you think Tony knows something about Eric's murder?" Serena asked.

"I do, and I think he wants to help, but he can't talk unless Maggie says it's okay."

"That's a no-brainer if it clears her of murder."

"You'd think so, but the question is, what's Maggie hiding?" Stride said. "Something's going on that she wants to keep secret."

"I have an appointment with Tony tomorrow morning. Maybe I can get something out of him."

"Not likely. Not if it involves a patient."

"Tell me about Tanjy," Serena said.

"As far as I can tell, she left her place at ten o'clock on Monday night. She took her car, and that's the last anyone saw of her."

"Did you get any hits on the car?"

"No, we've got alerts on it all over the five-state area, and the media has picked up on it, too. So far, nothing. There hasn't been any activity on her credit cards or bank accounts. Her cell phone hasn't been used since Monday night." He added, "I did find several calls to Eric over the last few weeks."

"Do you know what was going on between them?"

"Abel thinks it was an affair."

"Could Tanjy have killed Eric?"

"That was my first thought, but there isn't any evidence that she did."

"Except you say she's unstable," Serena said. "Maybe even violent."

"She's a strange girl." He waited several beats and then added, "Look, don't take this the wrong way. I'm just trying to understand who Tanjy was, so help me out here. Do women really fantasize about rape?"

Serena froze. She rolled away. "That's an ugly question."

"I know, I'm sorry."

"You know what Blue Dog and my mother did to me in Phoenix."

"I know."

She got out of bed. The frigid air raised gooseflesh on her skin. She went to the window and pushed aside the curtains that looked out toward the trees and scrub behind the cottage. She could see her own reflection dimly in the glass. "There's nothing even remotely erotic about rape. I don't understand how any woman could think so."

"I'm with you, but I've seen the bulletin boards where Tanjy was posting her stories. She wasn't the only one."

Serena didn't reply. Jonny came up behind her, laying his hands on her shoulders. Instinctively, she shrugged them away.

"I hope you don't think I ever *wanted* to do it with that bastard," she said.

"Of course not."

"The first therapist I ever went to asked me that once. He asked me if I ever had an orgasm with Blue Dog."

"Son of a bitch."

"Just to be clear, my answer was *no.* Then it was *goodbye.*"

"I wasn't trying to get you upset. I just need to get inside Tanjy's head."

Serena turned to face him. "I'm not upset."

"No?"

"I'm talking about it. A year ago, I wouldn't have been able to do that."

He put his arms around her. She knew that he expected her to cry, but she didn't have any tears inside. She was angry; she would never entirely escape the anger. But what happened to her when she a teenager was over. Her mother was dead. Blue Dog was dead, too. Her past was nothing but bad memories that would always be a part of who she was, but not the most important part, not the part that controlled her.

"Come to bed," she said.

She led him back, and she rolled over on top of him under the blanket and made love to him quickly and silently, until they were both dewy with sweat and ready to sleep. She slid off him, and she was just drifting away when Jonny mumbled something groggily into her ear.

"Put one word in the box," he said.

About Dan. About her midnight rendezvous.

She whispered back, hoping he'd still be able to sleep, "Blackmail."

17

Maggie was dreaming again.

An array of six men, naked and wearing gold masks, surrounded her bed, two on each side. They had dead eyes that reminded her of fish heads on the beach, milky skin with swollen bellies, and limp members hanging uselessly between their legs. They ogled her nude body. The two at the head of the bed parted, forming a gap in their ranks, and Eric stepped between them with her gun in his hand. He aimed it at her chest.

"I'm sorry, Nicole," he told her.

A flash of fire belched from the gun barrel.

Maggie looked down, expecting to see a burnt, gaping wound in her torso, but saw only her naked breasts. She raised her hands to touch herself, and then she realized that she had no hands, only bloody stumps unevenly hacked off, leaving nothing but bone and blood. She looked up at the mirror above her bed and realized she had no head, too. She was a limbless dead trunk, with no mouth to scream.

Maggie screamed anyway and shocked herself awake.

She was sprawled on the bed on top of the covers, taking loud, openmouthed breaths, like a fish. Slowly, the images faded to gray ash and sank back into her unconscious. She was alone and disoriented.

Maggie got out of bed and went to the bedroom door. She checked the heavy chair wedged under the doorknob, then sighed and rubbed her face with her small hands. She turned and leaned against the wall, which was papered in a forest-green Victorian floral pattern, and slid down until she was seated on the floor.

She was like a stranger to herself, acting like a victim, letting her fears win.

When you were a cop, you didn't admit to

being afraid of the dark. The dark was full of things you had to face and overcome. For weeks, though, darkness had been her enemy. She woke up every hour from nightmares. Since Eric's death, she had barricaded herself in her own room at night.

That wasn't how she wanted to live her life. She was not Abel's ex-partner Nicole, not guilty of killing her husband, not a girl who cried on the floor and cowered in corners.

"To hell with this," Maggie said aloud.

She was mad enough to fight back.

She pushed herself to her feet and ripped the chair away from the door. It toppled onto the wooden floor with a bang. She flung the bedroom door open. The hallway and the stairs to the first floor were inky-black. Without turning on a light, she squared her shoulders and felt her way to the staircase, where she grabbed the handrail and marched downstairs. A cloud of fear wrapped around her body like a fog, but she shrugged off the sensation and went to the kitchen. When she turned on the light, the monsters scattered like roaches. The white-tiled room was bright and safe.

Maggie made herself a mug of green tea

and put a salt bagel in the toaster. She sat quietly at the butcher block table, sipping the delicate liquid and crunching on the dry bagel. Her eyes were drawn to a photograph of herself and Eric pinned under a magnet on the refrigerator, and it made her lonely. They were smiling, their faces beet-red from sunburn. The picture was from a trip to Maine eighteen months ago, the last of the good times, a little sweet memory before things began to fall apart. They were in love back then, holding hands as they climbed over rocks on the beach, telling dirty jokes to each other over lobster dinners, having let-it-all-go sex that was so crazy and loud that the neighbors in the next room at the bed-and-breakfast applauded when they were done.

"Oh, Eric," she murmured to herself.

Maggie felt something wet on her cheeks, and when she touched her skin, she realized she was crying.

She didn't want to see his face in her mind, but there he was. She wished she could forget his booming laugh, but it rippled through her brain as if he were standing next to her. She could feel the solid strength of his swimmer's arms, holding her. His ghost, the fleeting spirit of the days when everything seemed perfect together, made her realize what she had lost. Not just with his death, but in the chasm that had opened up between them.

If only they could have stayed in Maine and never come back home. If only the last year had never happened.

She got pregnant on that trip. She was nearly thirty-three years old, and once she felt a baby growing inside her, she realized how much she wanted it. She was ready for a child in her life. So was Eric. He convinced her to leave the police force, and at the time, she was happy to go. Stride was in Las Vegas with Serena, and the prospect of doing her job without him weighed on her mind.

The pregnancy didn't go well. She miscarried in the third month.

That happened all the time, the doctors told her. She was anxious to try again. In the meantime, Stride came back from Vegas to take over his old job, and Maggie rejoined the force. When they were together again, she felt renewed, and when she got pregnant again in the winter, she had no intention of giving up her job or doing anything but taking a short leave and getting back on the street.

She miscarried in the second month.

That was when she started to doubt herself, started feeling like defective merchandise. Thoughts flitted in—maybe she could *never* have a baby. When you put it like that, it sounded scary. Her emotions ran away from her. In the late spring, when she got pregnant again, she spent every day worrying and wondering. Her morning sickness was intense. She was plagued by foreknowledge that she would never give birth.

She miscarried in the third month.

Something snapped in Maggie's head. She took a one-month leave and spent hours with Tony Wells, pouring out her soul, revisiting the memories of her childhood in China, and talking about Eric and Stride. When that was done, she pretended that the crisis was over. If she wasn't meant to have a baby, so be it, end of story. She was done trying to have a kid. She went back on the pill and told Eric it didn't matter. She was kidding herself.

Along the way, she and Eric grew miles apart. Their relationship had been volatile from the start. She had met Eric during a hostage crisis at his factory, and even after she talked his psycho employee into giving up his gun, they fought about it. Eric thought she took too many risks. Maggie called him a stuck-up rich son of a bitch. They slept together that first night. Six months later, they got married, but they fought whenever they weren't in bed.

She knew he had affairs. They fought about that. He was jealous of Stride and thought that she was secretly in love with him. They fought about that, too.

After the third miscarriage, and after spending a month in therapy with Tony, she tried to put things back together with Eric by throwing herself into their sexual relation-ship. She surprised herself with what she was willing to try. She was at her sexual peak; her hormones were crazy; she had nothing to lose. Why not? Even when Eric suggested things that made her skin crawl, she followed him to the wild side.

"Bring it on," she told him.

Nothing to lose. What a joke.

That was all before it happened. That was all prologue.

It was the week before Thanksgiving. Eric was out of the country. When she told him a few days later, he went crazy. He wanted to do something to make it better, but she refused all of his overtures, even when he pleaded with her and got angry and beat the walls. She screamed back and pushed him away and made him sleep downstairs, as far away from her as possible. She didn't want him to touch her, not ever again.

Now he never would.

Because someone came into their house and killed him. With her gun.

Think like a cop, she told herself. *Solve the crime.*

The caffeine in the tea wired her. She would never get back to sleep now, but she didn't want to sleep. She wanted to fight back. She had an advantage that no one, not even Stride, had in solving the case. She knew she was innocent. Everyone else had their doubts. Cops didn't trust people; they trusted facts. Facts didn't lie, dissemble, fool, mislead, imagine, pretend, or deceive. People did all of those things. She had done a lot of it herself lately.

Solve the crime.

Eric was killed with her gun. Despite the bottle of wine she had drunk near the lake, she was certain that she had left the gun on her nightstand that night as she always did. So whoever killed him had come to their bedroom first. That made sense. Whoever did this couldn't have known that she and Eric were sleeping apart. No one knew that. The gun was simply a golden opportunity. The killer must have been prepared to do it another way—his own gun, a knife, whatever. He—or she—came to the bedroom expecting to find the two of them together. Instead, Maggie was unconscious, Eric wasn't there, and the gun was an easy grab.

The killer took it, went downstairs, found Eric, shot him, and left.

Next question: Why was she still alive? She assumed that the killer couldn't risk going back upstairs after the first gunshot. If they had been in bed together, she was certain they would both be dead, but sleeping alone saved her. That meant that Eric was the target, not her, and it also meant that framing her was a crime of opportunity. No one coming into the house could have predicted the circumstances that left her in Abel's crosshairs as a suspect. That ruled out Serena's theory about a perp from Maggie's past, someone like Tommy Luck from Vegas who wound up stalking and nearly killing Serena before she put him in prison. This was all about Eric, pure and simple.

Next question: What was the motive? Something was obviously going on in Eric's life that she didn't know about. She knew she had to analyze his movements in his last few days and made a mental note to check his phone records and credit card statements to see what they revealed. Three days before the murder, for example, she knew that Eric was in the Twin Cities. Why?

Next question: What was Eric doing with Tanjy Powell, and why did Tanjy disappear? Maggie didn't think it was a coincidence that, according to Stride, Eric and Tanjy met on the street on Monday afternoon, and a few hours later, Tanjy vanished. Or that two nights later, Eric was dead. She assumed that Eric was sleeping with Tanjy, even though he had spent most of December swearing on his life that he would give up his affairs. Eric was a horndog, and Tanjy was irresistible, so maybe that was the simple answer. They were having an affair that went terribly wrong, and Tanjy killed him.

Nothing else made sense.

Unless Eric sought out Tanjy because of the rape.

Maggie thought about Eric's note to her, the one he had left for her the night he died, and wondered if she had been misreading it all along. *I know who it is.*

Last question: Why did Eric go to see Tony the night he was killed? Tony was Maggie's own therapist, and Eric detested psychiatry on principle. So what did he want with Tony? She could drive herself crazy thinking about the possibilities, and she didn't want to wait until the morning to get an answer. Maggie slid the chair back, got up, and took the cordless phone off its cradle and punched in Tony's number from memory.

He answered on the sixth ring. "Dr. Wells."

"Tony, it's Maggie."

"Maggie," he said drowsily. "It's late."

"I know. I'm sorry."

"Are you okay?"

"I'm fine," she told him. "I need to ask you a question."

"Okay."

"Why did Eric come to see you on Wednesday night?"

Tony was silent. She felt as if she had added a new weight to his fleshy shoulders. When you spent your life with cops, sexual predators, and rape victims, you could let out the stress with sick humor or carry the heavy burden like a pack mule. Tony was a carrier, but that was what made him good.

Finally, he said, "Do you really want to do this now?"

"Yeah, I do."

"I told Abel it was a privileged conversation," Tony said. "I also told him if he thought you killed anyone, he needed a psychiatrist."

"Thanks."

"Are you sure you want the truth?"

"Why wouldn't I?"

"That depends on whether you're ready to discuss it," Tony said. "Eric told me something about you—something you obviously decided not to share with me. Although I really wish that you had come to me about this."

She closed her eyes. "That fucker."

"I'm sorry. I was going to tell you tomorrow."

"What did he want?"

Maggie tensed, waiting. Eric, what the hell did you do?

"He wanted my help in figuring out how you can spot a sexual predator," Tony went on. "He was planning to see someone after our meeting."

"Someone?"

"He didn't say who."

A few hours later, Eric was dead. Now Maggie knew why.

I know who it is.

18

On Sunday morning, Serena found herself among the deserted fields and open sky in the northeastern section of the city. The urban center of Duluth was clustered in a few square miles around the lake, on terraces carved into steep hills, like a miniature replica of the roller-coaster streets of San Francisco tucked into a snow globe. On the plateau above the lake, however, the land quickly leveled off and became flat and desolate. Arrow-straight highways stretched for miles. Houses were spaced far apart, with acres of land separating neighbors.

She felt as if she would drive off the end of

the world if she ever reached the horizon line. Light snow skittered and danced on the asphalt like water in a sizzling pan. For Serena, there was something big and intimidating about this place. If the desert was like a snake—quick, sneaky, and secretive—then the north land was like a bear, lumbering and huge, full of fur, fat, and muscle. Living here felt like trespassing on land reserved for giants.

She turned left on a dirt road marked with a Dead End sign and drove another mile to the wooded lot where Tony Wells kept his home. It was a 1970s-era rambler, and Maggie liked to point out that the house, like Tony, was brown. Tony's SUV, a camel-colored Lexus LX, was parked in the gravel driveway.

She pulled in behind the truck and got out of her car. It was a bitter morning, the temperature hovering around zero. She exhaled a cloud of steam. Despite the cold, she always lingered here before going inside. Partly she could roll up her day-to-day worries into a ball and leave them on the hood of the car, to be picked up later. Partly she could enjoy the solitude of this peaceful, beautiful spot. The woods were made up of young birch trees and spindly brush, a tightly knit web with a carpet of snow underneath. There was hardly an evergreen anywhere, so she could see for a surprising distance through the trees. There was one narrow trail cut into the forest and cross-country ski tracks running through the snow. Another wrinkle in the trees was made by a tiny creek, now frozen solid.

She made her way around to the side of the house. Tony had built an addition onto the back for his office, with a glass wall looking out on the woods. You entered through a side door into a windowless waiting room, decorated with Ikea furniture and drab watercolors, and then you came through to this magnificent space with a vaulted ceiling and a view that stretched forever.

Tony kept a video camera overhead, so he could see patients coming into the waiting room from his desk. Serena waved at the camera and sat down. She could hear the beat of heavy metal beyond the office door.

"Walk this way," Steven Tyler sang.

Serena laughed. Like Maggie, Tony was a fanatic for hard rock, although no one would guess it by looking at him. He was the kind of serious collector who haunted eBay to find odd paraphernalia, like a hypodermic used by one of the bad boys of Mötley Crüe to shoot up with cocaine, or a maintenance memorandum about damage to a Philadelphia arena following a Metallica concert. Both were framed and hung over the sofa, next to his three University of Minnesota diplomas. He could rattle off the stats for every album, concert tour, and Grammy by Aerosmith and took two months off each summer to follow bands around the country. The flip side was that, the rest of the year, he kept office hours seven days a week. Many of his patients were cops and victims recovering from sexual trauma, so he saw people at all hours.

It was almost impossible to get a rise out of Tony, but Serena enjoyed the challenge and tried to come up with something new at every visit. Today, she got up and did a mock 1960s rock dance in front of the camera, shaking her head so that her hair twirled and pumping her arms like pistons in a go-go move. Ten seconds later, the music cut off, and the door to the office unlocked with a soft click.

She strolled inside. Tony was seated at his big oak desk in front of the glass wall.

The wilderness loomed behind him. He was writing on a yellow pad and didn't look up. "Funny," he said blandly.

Serena flopped down in a sofa on the opposite side of the room. "I thought so."

Tony got up from the desk and took a seat in a leather armchair near Serena. His eyes were bloodshot. "I suppose I'm going to get another lecture now about George Strait and Diamond Rio."

"A little steel guitar wouldn't kill you, Tony."

Tony harrumphed. He was about five feet ten, with a soft, well-fed physique. He and Serena were the same age, past thirty-five and on a downward slope toward forty. He had a professorial air about him, grave and concerned, which made his taste in music seem so unlikely. But you never could tell. She knew grandmothers who collected porn. Tony wore loose-fitting tan corduroys, a white dress shirt, and a chocolate-colored vest that matched his beard and his thinning crown of hair.

"You look tired, Tony."

His heavy eyelids drooped over his dark eyes more than usual. The bags under his eyes bulged like overpacked luggage. "Late-night phone call," he explained.

"Ah. Sorry."

"Coffee?" he asked.

"No thanks."

Tony went to a mahogany bureau with a mirrored bar. He had a coffeemaker plugged in on the bar, and he carefully poured from the pot into a black ceramic mug. He ripped open five sugar packets and emptied them into the mug and stirred.

"You want a little coffee with your sugar?" Serena asked.

"I like it sweet."

"Then why drink coffee? Have a Mountain Dew."

Tony sat down again and sipped his coffee. He reached inside his vest and withdrew a silver Cross pen, which he twirled between his fingers. "What do you want to talk about today?"

"Rape fantasies," Serena said.

Tony's face showed no surprise or disapproval. "That's a new topic for you."

"They're not mine."

"Oh?"

"I'm talking about Tanjy Powell."

He frowned. "I see."

"She's missing, you know."

"I know."

"I'd like to help Jonny figure out what happened to her."

Tony's face was pained. "I wish I could help you, but not this time."

"Why not?" Serena thought about it and then said, "Damn, is Tanjy a patient of yours, too?"

Tony sighed. "You know I can't say. But speaking hypothetically, if you were looking for a therapist in this city who specialized in mental issues related to sexual violence, who would you see?"

"I would see you, Tony, no one but you!" Serena gushed. She winked at him.

Tony said nothing at all, and his bearded face stared at her like a sleeping dog.

"As long as we're speaking hypothetically," she continued, "what can you tell me about a woman who fantasizes almost exclusively about rape?"

"That depends on the individual," he said.

"Let's say this woman is otherwise conservative and religious. Is that a contradiction?"

"Hypothetically?"

"Exactly." Serena smiled.

"No, that would be psychologically consistent," Tony said. "Rape fantasies are most common among women who are sexually repressed and have been taught that sex is wrong or a sin. They express themselves sexually through these fantasies because they don't have to feel guilty. The rape aspect removes their control. By being *forced* to have sex, they can enjoy it."

"That's pretty sick."

"Not really. Many professional women use these fantasies to adopt a submissive role when they have to be powerful and controlling in the rest of their lives. It can be a healthy way to relieve stress." He added, "Given your own background, of course, I understand why you would think this is abnormal."

"I can't believe men are turned on by that kind of woman."

Tony played with his pen and shook his head. "For some men, it's like the virgin and whore rolled into one. These women can be—not always, but can be—sexually explosive. They may also have a needy, vulnerable streak that appeals to some men. I don't need to tell you that men also entertain rape fantasies of their own."

"Okay, okay," Serena said, sighing. "I hear Eric came to see you on Wednesday night. What was that about?"

"Once again, I'd like to talk about it, but I can't."

"But?" Serena asked, sensing that he had more to say.

"But I'd like to get Maggie's permission to talk to the police about Eric's visit."

"Would that help her?"

"Hypothetically again, it might give them a very different idea of why Eric was killed and who killed him. And dispel this nonsense about Maggie killing him herself."

"Is Maggie reluctant to give permission for some reason?"

"Extremely reluctant."

"I'll talk to her," Serena said. "But she's stubborn, you know."

Tony finally smiled. They both knew Maggie.

"How do you feel about all this, Serena?" he asked after a pause.

"What do you mean?"

"Is it stirring up bad memories of your own past?"

Serena settled back into the sofa. She was paying for this hour; she might as well get some benefit out of it for herself. "Yeah. Jonny asked me if I ever had rape fantasies, like Tanjy, and I flew off the handle."

"What were you feeling?"

"I was pissed off. For women like Tanjy, rape is a game. For me, it was a daily ritual in Phoenix for more than a year. Blue Dog did what he wanted to me, because I was basically his slave, and mommie dearest sat there and watched, while she was as high as a kite."

"Does thinking about those experiences bring back feelings of fear? Helplessness?"

Serena thought about her midnight meeting with the blackmailer. "Sure it does."

"How have you dealt with that?"

"I tried the self-soothing technique you suggested. I literally reminded myself that those feelings came from the girl I was, not who I am today."

"Did that help?"

"It did. I was able to manage the fear."

"Good."

"I want to go back to my hypothetical fantasy girl for a minute," Serena said.

Tony was guarded. "Yes?"

"Could a woman like that be prone to violence? If she was in a sexual relationship, and her partner broke it off in a way that humiliated her, could she seek revenge?"

He rubbed his tired eyes. "You're asking me if it's possible Tanjy killed Eric?"

"I guess I am."

Tony pursed his lips and then shook his head. "I think it's unlikely Tanjy killed anyone. I'm sorry. I don't think that's what this is about."

"Do you know why she disappeared?"

"I have no idea. Truly, I don't. Obviously, I hope she's alive and well."

"So do I," Serena said. "Tanjy may be the only one who knows what really happened to Eric."

19

Sherry studied the fish house dubiously.

It was a wood-and-aluminum box not even as big as a pickup truck. She stood with her boyfriend, Josh, a hundred yards from shore in the midst of a city of dozens of similar shanties. They had walked across the lake, but plenty of people had driven cars and trucks and parked them nearby. She expected to feel the ice give under her feet, or hear the water beating at the surface to get free.

"You're sure this is safe?" she asked.

"There's probably eighteen inches of ice underneath our feet," Josh assured her.

Sherry looked out across Hell's Lake

where it broadened into a wide open space beyond the trees. "Why do they have those flags way out there?"

"Well, the ice is thinner out that way," Josh said. "You can have hot spots on any lake. You know, places where the ice isn't safe. You might have underwater currents from a stream, or warm water runoff from somewhere, or simply spots where the ice has thawed and frozen a lot, and so it's got a lot of cracks in it."

"This thing's not going to sink, is it?"

"No way. Not here. I wouldn't drive my dad's Cadillac out where the flags are, but right here, we're fine. Promise."

Sherry rolled her eyes. "Let's get inside."

It was ungodly cold. She wore a white down coat with bubble sleeves, which she hated because it made her look like the Michelin tire man, but it was her only winter coat. She wore it half-zipped and sported a pink turtleneck underneath. She had a fleece band around her head, protecting her ears from the wind, but otherwise, her blond curls blew freely. She wore Guess jeans with her initials in gold spangles on the rear pocket and Uggs that kept her feet and ankles from freezing.

She hadn't adjusted to the Minnesota weather. She was a California girl, born and raised in San Jose, and she had been appalled when her dad took a job as CFO of an airplane manufacturer in Duluth. She was eighteen years old, a senior, and instead of graduating with her friends back home, she was stuck here in the icebox of the nation, trying to fit in among a crowd of teenage rednecks.

That included Josh. He was a football player, big and slow. Even so, he was six feet three and a Scandinavian beauty, and they looked good together.

Josh undid the padlock on the fish house and let them inside. It looked like a prison cell in Siberia. No windows. Pitch-black. He turned on an oil lamp that illuminated a garage sale sofa and a couple of Sam's Club wooden chairs. Inside was just as cold as outside, and the wind blew through the aluminum siding as if it wasn't there.

"Oh, man, does it get any warmer?"

"I'll get the heater going," Josh said.

Sherry shrugged off her coat. "You just want my nips to show." She followed his eyes and glanced down at her turtleneck. "Looks like you win. The headlights are on."

She rubbed her arms vigorously and stamped her feet in the small, claustrophobic shanty. She wrinkled her nose at the fishy smell. There was a large circle cut into the ice in the center of the floor. She peered down into it and saw slushy water about a foot down. It was opaque.

"How do you cut through the ice?" she asked.

"Gas augur," Josh said. He pointed at a machine that looked like an outboard motor with two feet of black screw attached, its blades pocked with rust.

"This is like a horror movie," she said. "You're not going to cut me up, are you?"

"No!"

Sherry laughed. "It was a joke. Besides, in those movies, the girl has to get naked before she gets killed, and I am *not* getting naked in this place." Josh looked disappointed, and she added with a wink, "Okay, maybe a little naked."

The heater beat back the cold in the fish house. Sherry watched as Josh prepared the hook end of a fishing line and unwound the line deep into the cut-out section of ice. He propped the rod on an upside-down chair and reached into his pocket for a small bell, which he tied to the line with thread.

"What's that for?" she asked.

"If a fish takes the bait, the line jerks and rings the bell." He tapped it with his hand, and the bell went *ding, ding*.

"Cute."

Josh unzipped his backpack and pulled out an iPod and a set of portable speakers. He put on an album by the Black Eyed Peas, and Sherry began rolling her body to Fergie's funky beat. Josh's face lit up in a sly grin, and he reached back into the pack and came out with two frosty cans of Miller Lite.

"Let the party begin," he said.

Sherry took an open can from Josh and drank down a long swallow that she thought would freeze in her throat. Holding the can with two fingers, she danced, swiveling her hips lazily and slithering her arms and fingers up and down her body. The more she danced and drank, the warmer she felt, and the more handsome Josh got.

She crooked her finger, beckoning him to the sofa. They sat down, and his hands prowled over her back. He kissed her clumsily; his tongue felt like a wet slug exploring the roof of her mouth. She felt him tentatively cup one of her breasts, and when she didn't protest, he grabbed it as if he were diving for a fumble. A low moan purred from his throat.

She pulled away and rolled her shirt up an inch at a time, revealing her flat tummy and then her pear-shaped breasts. She left the shirt propped on top of her cleavage. His eyes were so wide she thought she could see around them into his brain. She turned her attention to his belt buckle, which she undid, and then unzipped him, exposing the white fabric of his underwear. She reached inside and pulled him out.

His eyes were closed. He was on the moon.

Ding, ding.

The fishing line fluttered. The rod rocked in the chair and tumbled to the ice.

"Shit, hang on," Josh told her, swinging his legs off the sofa.

"You have *got* to be kidding," Sherry said.

"Help me," he said, jerking on the line, his jeans around his ankles, his shaft still ready for action.

Sherry sighed. "That's what I was trying to do." She added, "Don't let your thingy get sliced off, okay?"

He battled the fish for several minutes, until it was close to the surface.

"Take the pole," he said. "Keep it pointed up."

"That's what I was—oh, never mind." She took the fishing rod and held it while Josh grabbed a pair of gloves and reached down into the hole.

"Reel in some more line," he told her.

"What am I, Supergirl? This thing is heavy."

She cranked the reel, and the line wound in slowly. It felt as if she were pulling up a boat anchor on the other end.

"Almost got it," he said.

Suddenly, Josh yelped. He unleashed a girlish scream and fell back on his ass. His erection deflated. With his hands on the ice, he scrabbled away from the hole. "Shit!"

Something black bobbed out of the ice like a gopher in a carnival whack-a-mole game. Sherry cranked the reel and inched closer, repelled but curious. When she saw it, she screamed, too.

Matted black hair danced up and down at her feet. The smell, released out of the water, was rank; she covered her face. Invisible gases fouled the air. She watched through slitted fingers and saw a human head now, snow-white and hideously swollen, peeking above the ice. More of the body was trapped below. Mud and weeds clung to its skin. Its eyes were open but cloudy, like marbles. Its mouth was slightly open, and the splashing and sucking of the water made it sound as if it were talking. As if it were alive when it was obviously dead. The head said over and over, "Let me out, let me out, let me out, let me out."

PART TWO

ALPHA GIRLS

20

Helen Danning could see her reflection in the window of the gift shop, and every few seconds, her face lit up like the glow of a wild fire as northbound traffic off the highway shot their twin beams through the glass. To Helen, the car lights were like the white tunnels of searchlights, wending back and forth across a field, hunting for her. When a car slowed and pulled off the road, she flinched. The headlights grew huge in the window as the car parked outside the shop, and Helen pushed her chair back and got up, leaving a half-drunk chai tea and her white Mac laptop open on the cast-iron table. She backed up between the oak shelves, which were stocked with Yankee candles and potpourri.

The shop door opened, and Helen felt as if the night were spilling inside. A burst of chill made her shiver. She glanced at the corridor leading to Evelyn's stockroom, where a back door butted up to frozen corn-fields. Irrationally, she wanted to run, but she saw that the people coming into the shop were harmless. A man in a Minnesota State Fair sweatshirt ordered two coffees from Evelyn at the counter, while his wife browsed the sale-priced Christmas orna-ments. Helen ducked her head and kept her face hidden.

She waited until their car was back on the highway before she sat down at the table again. When she took a sip of her sweet tea, her fingers were trembling. She closed her eyes, took a deep breath, and continued the methodical work on her lap-top, opening each of the entries in her blog and erasing them. Her slim finger hovered over the Delete key as she reread a posting about the show *Miss Saigon*. She had seen the show dozens of times, as she had seen most musicals that came through the Ord-way Center in Saint Paul. As an usher, she saw the performances night after night, and she could spot the nuances in every actor, song, costume, and set. She lived the shows almost as if they were more real than her own life. Some people became obsessed with soap operas, but Helen's obsession was *Phantom, Les Miz, Rent,* and all the other touring shows that ran over and over on the stage. Her blog was her outlet to pour out her thoughts about the characters.

She called her blog "the Lady in Me." She had come across a Shania Twain CD called *The Woman in Me* years earlier and bought it because she liked the title. The phrase became a kind of anthem to her. It summed up what she had lost in college and what she had been searching for her whole life. She even had the initials TLIM tattooed on her ankle, like a secret message she carried with her.

She didn't realize back then that she was making a mistake, that someone who wanted to find her could figure out who she was and where she worked by carefully reading the posts to her blog. She had just never dreamed that anyone would want to find her.

Helen looked up as the piano music playing overhead stopped. The gift shop went silent.

"Time to run, honeybun," Evelyn called. She was closing up the shop, cleaning out the coffeepot, toting up the register. Evelyn always seemed to do five things at once. She didn't walk. She bustled.

Helen shut down her laptop and waited. Evelyn was right. It was time to run, and that was what Helen was doing. Running.

With a flounce, Evelyn sat down in the chair opposite Helen. She had poured herself the dregs of the coffee. She took a sip and pushed her unruly, squirrel-colored curls out of her face. Under the table, she kicked off her Birkenstocks and wiggled her toes.

"How about we go home and feed Edgar?" Evelyn asked.

"Sure."

"You know, you're like my cat," she said, noticing Helen's nervous green eyes. "She's more scared of birds than the birds are of her."

"Every time someone comes in, I think it's going to be him," Helen told her.

"I understand."

"I promise I won't be in your hair too much longer."

Evelyn shrugged. "Stay as long as you like. We don't do it often enough, honeybun. What's it been? A couple years? The last few days have been like college, ordering pizza and chugging down cheap wine. Makes me forget all this gray hair."

In addition to running the gift shop, Evelyn was a painter, poet, and gardener, who lived alone in an old house on five acres near the Mississippi in rural Little Falls. They had been best friends since their days as roommates at the U of M. Several times, Evelyn had invited Helen to join her in the small central Minnesota town, but Helen was scared of open places, nervous about emptiness. She liked the anonymity of the city, where she could lose herself in crowds and live silently in the midst of the noise.

"You think I'm overreacting, don't you?" Helen asked.

Evelyn retrieved a bowl of wasabi soy nuts from the shop counter and placed it between them on the table. She took a green nut and crunched it in her mouth. "Yeah. I guess I do. But so what? You met this guy, not me."

"His name was Eric."

"Okay, Eric."

"He tracked me down, and a couple of days later, he was murdered."

"It could be a coincidence."

Helen shook her head. "He knew what happened to me."

"So?"

"So Eric was going to confront the bastard. I told you that."

Evelyn looked at her skeptically. "The papers said Eric's wife was the one who killed him."

"Well, I think they're wrong."

Evelyn sighed. "If you're so sure, honeybun, why not go to the police?"

Helen stuck out her tongue. "The police are no help. You remember last time?"

"They treated you badly."

"They told me it was *my* fault," Helen said. "I don't need to go through that again. They'd just dredge up what happened and in the end, they wouldn't do a thing. They'd say I was crazy or out for revenge."

Helen stared out the window at the highway. Evelyn reached out and covered Helen's hand. "Do you really think you're in danger?"

"I do."

"Then you need to tell someone," Evelyn insisted. "What if this guy is stalking someone else? Do you want another woman to go through what you did?"

"No."

"Okay then. You might be the only one who can stop this creep."

"I need time," Helen told her.

Evelyn smiled and stood up. "You got it, honeybun. Come on, let's go home and light a fire and crack open some Yellow Tail. The main thing is to stop worrying. No one's going to find you. You're safe here."

21

Is it Tanjy's body?" Stride asked.

Abel Teitscher nodded. His eyebrows and mustache were painted white by the snow that blew off the lake in sheets. "She's a frozen fish stick."

"Cause of death?"

"Someone caved in the back of her skull."

Stride swore and headed for the cluster of police gathered near the fish house. It was like a Gypsy city on the lake, a ragtag assortment of plywood boxes, tents, aluminum fish houses, campers, and pickup trucks. Tire and snowmobile tracks created a maze through the snow. There was litter everywhere, discarded boxes, beer bottles, tattered gloves, fish heads, and half-smoked cigars. The lake itself was huge, with spiderlike tentacles reaching around forested peninsulas, and he could see only a small slice of it from where he was. It was called Hell's Lake because of its reputation for hot spots, areas like eggshell where the ice never froze solid because of the strong current running underneath. Or maybe because lava bubbled up directly from hell and heated the water. It was a dangerous place, easy to get lost in when the mists came, easy to stray from the dense sections of ice to the fragile shelves laced with cracks. A few people went under every season; most were never rescued.

The wind across the ice was ferocious. With no trees to slow it down, it rocketed across the lake like a skate sail. Tanjy's body lay forlornly on a strip of plastic on the ice outside the fish house. Her skin's pigment had leached away. Either her killer or the current of the lake water had stripped her naked. He felt a stab of regret. Tanjy had spent her life obsessed with rape; now, like this, she really had been violated.

Stride returned to Teitscher. "You should have called me on this immediately."

Teitscher's wrinkled, weatherworn face didn't move. "We agreed I was taking over the investigation."

"You are, but I want to be in the loop."

"To me that means copying you on my paperwork," Teitscher snapped. "It doesn't mean having you second-guess me at the scene. I don't want you here, Lieutenant. Right now, I don't know which side you're on."

"Just bring me up to speed," Stride told him.

"Dan Erickson wants to know every move you make on this case," Teitscher said.

"Is that a threat?"

"Just a heads up."

"I don't care about Dan," Stride said.

Teitscher shrugged. "We found Tanjy's car. Someone drove it into the woods off a dead-end road."

"Nearby?"

"Maybe half a mile away."

"What's the scene look like?" Stride asked.

"There's blood in the trunk. We've got one set of boot prints in the deep snow leading away from the car back to the dead-end road. That's where they stop."

"So she wasn't killed where you found the car?"

"No, it looks like they killed her somewhere else and then dumped her in the trunk to drive her out onto the ice. They found an open fish house, put the body in the lake, and then ditched her car in the woods."

"They?"

"I'm thinking this would have been very difficult for one person to pull off. If she wasn't killed where her car was abandoned, whoever left it there needed another vehicle to get away. Someone else had to be driving the other car."

"What size are the boot prints?"

"Big, at least a size twelve," Teitscher said. He added, "Eric Sorenson wore a size twelve."

"Don't get ahead of yourself."

Teitscher shrugged. "He was one of the last people to see Tanjy alive, as far as we know."

"What about time of death?" Stride asked.

"She's been in the drink for several days. I don't think we'll ever know exactly how long. That should make Archie Gale happy."

"There's nothing to tie Maggie into this, is there?"

"Just that her husband was mixed up with Tanjy, and he's dead, too."

"To me, it says there might be more to Eric's death than meets the eye," Stride said.

"Yeah? You're big on theories, Lieutenant. Try this one on. Maggie and Tanjy had a big fight over her affair with Eric. Tanjy wound up dead. Maggie called Eric to help her get rid of the body. Eric had a fit of conscience and wanted to call the cops. Maggie killed him."

"You don't have a shred of evidence to back that up."

"Not yet, I don't, but I'm just saying you don't have to think real hard to tie these cases together."

Stride knew the argument was getting them nowhere. "How about the fish house? What have you got there?"

"Two kids found the body. They were screwing around when Tanjy popped up. The fish house belongs to the boy's dad, but the ev techs don't think Tanjy was dumped from there. She could have gone in anywhere around the lake and drifted up here. People leave these shanties unlocked and don't visit them for weeks."

"You'll never get a warrant to search every house on the lake," Stride said.

"I know, the best we can do is knock on doors. Maybe someone saw something."

Stride knew that without a time of death or a crime scene to mine for forensic evidence, it was going to be a tough case to solve. "If I can help you, call me. I mean that."

"Don't take this the wrong way, Lieutenant. If you want to help me, stay out of my way."

Teitscher turned into the wind and walked away. His foot slipped on the ice, and he fell to one knee. Pushing himself up, he shouted at one of the uniforms on the scene, and Stride saw the cop, who was a good kid, cringe. The only way Teitscher knew how to get things done was to bark in someone's face. He was a hard case who wasn't going to change.

Stride heard a faint buzz of music and realized his cell phone was ringing. He pulled it out of the inside pocket of his leather jacket and heard the Alabama song in his head. *I'm in a hurry and don't know why.*

He walked toward his truck as he answered. "Stride."

It was Maggie. "I need to see you. It's urgent."

"What's going on?"

"I don't want to do this over the phone," she said.

"Wherever you go, you'll have company. We can't be seen together."

"Leave that to me. I'll be alone."

Stride wasn't going to say no to her. "Let's do it late. Eleven o'clock."

"Where?"

"The high school parking lot. Up on the hill."

"Thanks, boss."

"You've left me in the dark on this," Stride told her. "You're hiding things from me."

"I know. I'm sorry." There was a long stretch of dead air, and then Maggie said, "Is it true about Tanjy? Have you found her body?"

"It's true."

Maggie expelled her breath as if she had been holding it. "There's something you need to know, but just you, not Teitscher."

"What is it?"

"Tanjy wasn't lying about the rape," Maggie told him quickly.

"What?"

"I'm telling you, it really happened."

"No way." He thought about the fantasies on Tanjy's computer and the explicit details of her sex life provided by Mitchell Brandt. "Tanjy told me flat-out that she made the whole thing up."

"I know how it sounds, boss. I didn't believe her myself, but I was wrong."

"How the hell can you be so sure?"

The silence this time was so long he thought he had lost the call. When he heard Maggie's voice, it didn't sound like Maggie at all.

"Because it happened to me, too."

22

He left the van in a deserted lot at the far end of the Point and hiked over the wooded slope to the lake. The roiled water and the thin strip of ice and sand stretched out before him toward the hazy lights of the city. When he emerged from the trees, a ferocious, twisting wind deadened his face. He pulled his wool cap down to become a mask and viewed the beach through slitted eyes. Inside his gloves and boots, he kept heat packs to keep his hands and feet limber and warm. He tucked his chin into his neck and hiked along the bumpy ice shelf, his coat doused by bitter spray as the waves assaulted the shore.

He was alone. The milelong walk to Serena's house was cold and hard. The houses were indistinguishable without the brightness of the moon and largely hidden by the skeletons of trees. He knew where to veer west off the beach when he came upon the twin pieces of driftwood he had left as a marker earlier in the day. He followed the trodden-down path up through the wild rye and picked his way to the edge of the trees, where he was only a few yards from the rear door of the cottage. He waited there, invisible. The house was dark. The concrete driveway to the street was empty.

He allowed himself a maximum of five minutes inside and set a vibrating timer in his rear pocket. He glanced at the fences on either side of the narrow lot and marched down to the rear screen door, which was open. He left his boots on the porch, where his footprints were lost in the matted snow. In his wool winter socks, he crept through the porch to the back door, shone a penlight on the lock, and let himself inside in a few seconds.

Her smell was everywhere. It was the first time he had been close enough to inhale her aroma again. He allowed himself a moment to savor it. To him, that smell was all about dry heat, sweat, and soft flesh. He felt young. He felt reborn and powerful.

His first stop was in the living room. He didn't even need thirty seconds to choose a location, secrete the bug, and test the signal strength. The next stop was their bedroom. He had hoped to plant a Web cam, but he surveyed the white walls and knew there was nowhere that the equipment wouldn't be seen. He settled for a second bug and affixed it behind the beams of their headboard.

He was outside again before the timer went off. He scouted the rear of the house and attached a signal booster behind one of the aluminum downspouts, which would give him at least two miles of transmission. From inside the van in the park a mile away, he could listen.

Back in the woods, he waited for her. The cold made him stamp his feet. It was never this cold in the South. He didn't know how people lived here. It almost made him yearn for the soul-draining humidity of Alabama. His toes grew numb as time wore on, and finally, he saw headlights sweep across the driveway as Serena pulled in and parked. His muscles tensed. He watched her climb out and go inside the house, unaware of his presence. He slipped a receiver inside his ear and heard her footsteps and the rustle of her clothes as she removed her coat. When she got close to the bug, he heard her breathing.

He half-wondered whether, at some level, she smelled him in the house, too, as he had smelled her inside, like a rumor at the back of her mind. A flashback, a memory.

He slipped out from behind the trees and made his way to her car, keeping an eye on the cottage windows. Where they were lit, she couldn't see out, but he froze when he saw her pass in front of the glass and gaze toward him. Their eyes met, as they had so many times when he was watching her. She passed into another room.

He bent down under her car and positioned the GPS transmitter, then got up and retreated to the beach without looking back. The receiver was still in his ear. He listened to her as he retraced his route toward the van. In the bedroom, he heard her humming as she undressed. He heard the jangle of the loops on her gold belt. Nearby, the water of the shower ran. He pictured her naked body, saw her skin under his hands.

His cell phone buzzed on his thigh. He was annoyed by the distraction and did a quick survey of the beach to confirm he was alone. He pulled out the phone and recognized the number. Reluctantly, he shut down the receiver in his ear.

"What?" he hissed.

"They found Tanjy's body."

"So?"

"So you told me it would take months. Maybe years."

He trudged step-by-step along the gray sheet of ice. The lake rumbled next to him. It was fucking cold.

"It's bad luck they found her, but it doesn't change anything. Don't worry, you're safe."

"You told me you'd leave the city after this was done."

"I will."

"So why are you still here?"

"I have unfinished business," he snapped.

"What business?"

"My business. This one's personal."

The silence across the night air was lethal. "Do you have *any idea* what's at stake for me?"

"That's your problem," he said.

"What other schemes are you running? Tell me."

He breathed into the phone and saw steam evaporate like a ghost in front of his face. "You don't want to know."

"What the hell does that mean?"

"I mean, Tanjy wasn't the only one. I decided to do some others, too."

He waited. It was funny how even the most arrogant, cold-blooded ego could get punctured like a fat balloon by fear.

"You're a monster."

"Yeah? What does that make you? Remember, it was your idea."

"Who were the others?"

"It doesn't matter. Alpha girls don't give up their secrets." He laughed.

"I want you gone. Is that clear? You've been well paid."

"I'll decide when I'm done, not you."

He snapped the phone shut and turned it off.

With his other hand, he switched on the receiver again and nestled it in his ear. He was back at the van. He slid inside, cranked the heat, and listened. His feet slowly thawed. He peeled off layers of clothes.

Inside Serena's house, the noise of the pipes ended. He heard her return to the bedroom and imagined her nude flesh, pink and scrubbed. Her long, wet hair. Her nipples hard and her mound glistening with moisture. With each of the others, he had imagined he was with Serena. Controlling her. Violating her. Paying her back for those ten years she had stolen from him.

It was her turn.

Soon.

23

Stride was worried. It was almost midnight, and Maggie was late.

He was parked in the lower lot of the high school, with a vantage on the lights of downtown and the black emptiness of the lake. He had gone through two cigarettes waiting for her. Snow fell in heavy sheets, blowing over the top of the hill and swirling around him like a tornado. It was hard to look straight on into the snow. His eyes squinted, and his face scrunched up, his windburnt cheeks turning pink. Ice clumped in balls on his eyebrows. The flakes streaking toward him were nothing by themselves, but together they were a relentless army. When the wind drove them home, they were like a million knives. They could blind him, freeze him, and bury him in the same storm.

Gauzy headlights appeared on the road above him and swung down into the lot. He recognized Maggie's Chevy Avalanche. Maggie drove fast, and the truck weaved on the slick, steep driveway. It was a huge truck for a tiny woman, so big that she needed wooden blocks to reach the pedals. She was a terrible driver. Stride thought she drove recklessly just to spite him, because she was worse whenever he was in the truck with her.

She parked at an angle near his Bronco and got out. She wore a leather coat that draped to her ankles and high, square-heeled boots. Her hands were shoved in her pockets. She kicked up wet snow as she came closer.

He hadn't seen her since he was at her house the night of the murder, and he realized how much he had missed her. He came closer, ready to hug her, but she pulled a hand out of her pocket and held it up to stop him.

"No," she told him. "No pity. Especially not from you."

The few feet between them may as well have been a canyon. "Come on, Mags. This is me. You don't have to prove how tough you are."

"I sure as hell do." She looked him up and down. "You ever heard of waiting inside your truck? You look like a goddamn snowman."

"I don't mind the cold."

"You mean, you don't want Serena smelling cigarette smoke inside the truck."

"Right."

"Well, I'm not standing outside. Let's get in the Avalanche."

They walked to opposite sides of her truck. Stride shook off as much snow as he could before climbing inside. The cab was warm, and he took off his gloves. Maggie didn't look at him. She sat behind the driver's seat staring at the panoramic view. He realized how strange it felt to see that she was older. There were tiny crow's-feet beside her eyes and a few strands of gray in her jet-black hair. She would always be a twenty-something kid to him, intense and smart. That was part of the problem—for him, she never grew up. It still felt like yesterday that Maggie was a young cop complaining about the Enger Park Girl murder, chewing on the rim of a Styrofoam coffee cup and insisting they had missed something, when Stride knew they hadn't missed anything at all. But that was a long, long time ago. It was as if he had put Maggie in a box in his mind, so that bad things never happened to her, but all the while she got older and bad things happened anyway.

"When?" Stride asked.

Maggie knew what he meant. She reached out and curled her fingers around the steering wheel and held on tightly. "It happened just before Thanksgiving. Eric was out of town."

Stride remembered. She had called in sick for nearly two weeks and blamed it on the flu.

"I was asleep. He had a knife." She brushed her hair back behind her ear and showed him a two-inch-long scar. "I've blocked out most of the details. I just don't remember."

"Jesus," Stride murmured.

"I said no pity, boss. Not from you. Got it?"

Stride thought that her bravado was cellophane-thick.

"You know what I did first?" she went on. "You'll love this. I laughed. It was all so fucking hilarious. This was God's big joke. I told myself I was dreaming, that I had made it all up in my head, that there was no way this could have happened to me. Then the next thing I knew, I was pounding on the floor and wailing. I sat in the dark and cried for two days."

He opened his mouth to say something and then shut it. There was nothing to say.

"You know what I did next?" Maggie continued. "I threw out all the food in the refrigerator. Nuts, huh? Everything. Right down to the bare shelves, and then I sprayed the whole thing down. Same in every room. I went through a dozen cans of Lysol. I didn't want to smell anything. The place was like a hospital."

He clenched his fists. Maggie saw him do it. "If I ever get my hands on this son of a bitch, I'll kill him," he said.

"I know you want to be a hero, boss, but this happened to me, not you. I'm only telling you this now because I don't have any choice."

"Why didn't you come to me back then?"

She turned and stared at him. Her eyes were fierce with pride. "Because this didn't happen to a cop. It happened to a woman.

Don't you get it? I didn't want you or any other man to know about this. Not then. Not ever. It was bad enough telling Eric. He wanted me to report it, and I just wanted it to go away. I still do."

"At least tell me you got help."

"Haven't you been listening? I didn't want to talk to anyone. It's killing me to talk about this now. And yeah, I know, this is rape trauma syndrome, and I was in the acute phase, and I was expressive, not controlled, and you know what? It's all psycho bullshit. Everything I've told rape victims over the years is *bullshit.* This happened to *me.* If you haven't been where I've been, you don't have a fucking clue."

He searched for the right thing to say and wound up saying the wrong thing. "I just don't understand how you of all people would not report this."

"You saw what happened to Tanjy. She was humiliated. Destroyed. I didn't want the same thing to happen to me."

"It would have been different with you," Stride insisted.

Maggie shook her head. "You can be so stupid, boss. You're a great cop, but you can be so blind sometimes that it drives me crazy.

Do you think I don't have secrets? Do you think there aren't things that I don't want out in public?"

"What things?"

"That's none of your business. The whole point is that I didn't go public because I didn't want to have my life ruined."

"How can I solve this case if you won't talk to me?" Stride asked.

Maggie dug inside the pocket of her jeans and pulled out a crumpled note. She smoothed it and handed it to Stride. There was a smeared sentence scrawled across the paper in a man's handwriting.

I know who it is.

"What the hell is this?" he asked.

"Eric left that for me the night he was killed. At first, I thought he was accusing me of having an affair, but that wasn't it at all. That wasn't what he meant."

"Tanjy left the same message for Dan Erickson the night she disappeared."

Maggie didn't look surprised. "I think Eric figured out who the rapist was. When I refused to go to the police, I think he went to see Tanjy on his own. Somehow, the two of them found something that led them to the rapist. Then this guy killed them both."

Stride recollected the chain of events in his mind. On Monday afternoon, Eric confronted Tanjy on the street in front of Java Jelly, and whatever he told her upset her deeply. Tanjy left work early, and that night, she called Lauren with a secret. *I know who it is.* Except she never got the chance to tell anyone. Someone killed her and buried her body under the ice. Two days later, Eric was killed, too.

He lowered the window on the passenger side of the truck. Snow blew in and dampened his face. He lit a cigarette, inhaled the tar into his lungs, and held it outside the window, where the smoke curled away. "Do you have any idea who Eric suspected?"

"No, but start with Tony. Eric talked to him that night. He may be able to help us."

"Maybe Eric suspected Tony was the rapist. You and Tanjy were both patients of his."

"Yeah, I thought about that, but Tony says Eric came to him about profiling a sexual predator, and that makes sense. Eric knew we worked with Tony on that kind of shit all the time."

"I'll talk to him," Stride said. "I'll go back over Tanjy's police statement, too. If she wasn't lying to us, then whoever raped her knew that Grassy Point Park was a place she took her boyfriends. At least, Mitchell Brandt says she took him there."

"Good."

"You're still hiding something, Mags," he told her. "My hands are tied if you're not completely honest with me."

"I'm sorry. I'm not just thinking about myself. Other people could be hurt by what I say."

"They could be hurt by what you *don't* say."

Their eyes connected. She knew what he meant. The rapist was still out there.

"If there's no other way, then I'll tell you why I couldn't report the rape, but as far as I know, it has nothing to do with Tanjy. There has to be a different connection."

"You know I should go to Teitscher with this. He's chasing his tail. This could take away the cloud over you, Mags."

She reached out and took his hand. It was the kind of intimate gesture she never made with him. She teased him. Winked at him. Insulted him. But she never touched him. "I'm asking you not to do that, Jonathan."

He didn't fight her. "If that's what you want. For now."

"I'm also trying to retrace Eric's steps," Maggie added. "I want to know how he found this guy."

"What have you found out?"

Maggie's eyes gleamed, looking like a cop's eyes again. "Eric was in the Twin Cities the weekend before he was killed. He came back on Monday, and that's when he went to see Tanjy. That's when everything started."

"You think he found something on his trip," Stride concluded.

"Exactly. That's why I was late. I was on the phone with people at the Saint Paul Hotel, trying to find out what Eric did while he was there. I got his invoice records from the hotel, and I checked his credit card and cell phone statements online."

"And?"

"He called and charged a ticket to a play at the Ordway Center on Saturday night. One ticket, not two."

"The Ordway is right across the park from the Saint Paul Hotel," Stride said. "He probably just wanted something to do on Saturday night."

"That's what I thought, but I checked with

the Ordway anyway and followed up with the season ticket holders who sat next to him."

"Did they remember Eric?"

"Oh, yeah. They said he almost got kicked out of the theater."

"Kicked out? Why?"

"He was bothering the ushers. Asking them a lot of questions."

"What kind of questions?"

"I don't know, but I'd like to find out."

24

On Monday morning, Serena headed down the Point toward Canal Park, using the street as her path because the plows had cleared it of snow and ice. She took long, graceful strides as she ran. She wore a Lycra bodysuit, leggings, and a down vest, with mufflers over her ears and her long hair tied back in a ponytail. She did three miles in half an hour and made it to the lift bridge that towered overhead like a gray guillotine. Serena drifted to a stop and bent over, resting her hands on her knees. She took several deep breaths and then stretched her head back and stared at the sky. She took a few awkward steps, like a peacock, kicking her legs to keep them loose. She unhitched a bottle of water she kept on a Velcro strap at her waist and squirted a stream into her mouth. It was frosty cold.

She wandered out on the sidewalk into the center of the bridge. The shipping season was over, so the bridge rarely went up at this time of year. The water in the harbor on her left was frozen over, and even the narrow canal that lapped out into Lake Superior was glazed with ice. She leaned on the steel railing, staring out at the lake.

She was alone, but the sensation that someone's eyes were on her refused to go away. The feeling even dogged her at home, where she felt as if she were sharing her life with a ghost. It reminded her of the days in Vegas when Tommy Luck was on her trail. Serena remembered being in his apartment after they arrested him and finding the wall of photographs he had secretly taken of her. Like a shrine. Some on the street. Some in her car. Some, with a telephoto, through the bedroom window of her apartment. All of them disfigured and raped, as if he was fantasizing about the real thing. She kept an eye on Tommy after that, and when he got out on parole the first time, she thought seriously about taking care of him, neat and quick, before he could nurse his obsession again. The Vegas cops would have looked the other way, but Tommy was a nobody, and she decided she didn't want his corpse on her conscience.

It wasn't the first time she had faced that temptation. When Serena was in Phoenix, living her year of hell with her mother and Blue Dog, she thought constantly about ways to kill them. She went to sleep at night drumming up the courage to take a knife and slit his throat while he slept, and then to do the same to her mother. Murder them, and disappear. No one would miss them, and no one would find her. Many times she went so far as to take a kitchen knife and stand in the bedroom doorway and watch them sleep, but she never crossed the threshold. Instead, she ran away to Las Vegas and didn't look back.

Serena wondered how her life would be different now if things had gone another way.

If she had taken the kitchen knife into her mother's bedroom.

If she had put a bullet in Tommy Luck's head.

Her cell phone rang. She slid it out of the pocket of her vest and checked the calling number, which she didn't recognize. "Serena Dial."

"My name is Nicole Castro," a woman announced. "I got your number from Archie Gale."

"Oh?"

"He told me that you and I have something in common." Her voice was ironic and tough, like a comedian who had done too many shows.

"What's that?" Serena asked.

"You're sleeping with a guy named Jonathan Stride, and my boss used to be a guy named Jonathan Stride."

Serena didn't laugh. "Exactly what do you want, Ms. Castro?"

"Call me Nicole. I want to talk with you about the murder of Eric Sorenson."

"You should talk to the police."

Nicole scoffed. "We both know that Abel already has his teeth in a suspect. Believe me, he won't listen to anything I have to say."

"Why's that?"

"He used to be my partner."

Serena stood up straight and wiped her

sleeve across her forehead. "What kind of information do you have, Nicole?"

"How about we talk face-to-face about that?"

"I don't recall Jonny mentioning you," Serena said.

"Jonny?"

"Stride."

"Oh, yeah. Well, I don't suppose he thinks much about me anymore. They all want to forget me. Look, Archie said you wanted to help out on this case. So do you want my help or not?"

"If it's a useful lead, absolutely."

"Then come see me."

"We could have lunch at Grandma's," Serena said.

Nicole's voice was bitter. "There's nothing I'd like more, believe me. Unfortunately, I don't live in Duluth anymore. I'm in the Twin Cities in a town called Shakopee."

"That's okay. I'm driving down to the Cities tomorrow anyway. Where would you like to meet?"

"You'll have to come to me. I'm in prison."

Serena exhaled steam and looked around to see if anyone was watching her. The bridge railing under her fingers was cold. "I thought you said you were a cop."

"That's right. I used to be in the Detective Bureau in Duluth. Then I was framed for my husband's murder. Just like Maggie."

Grassy Point Park was a speck of green shaped like a knife hooking into the narrow channel of St. Louis Bay. It was on a dead-end road in the heart of the city's industrial area, near ore docks and railroad tracks. The frozen harbor was on Stride's left. He could have driven onto the ice and taken a short-cut back home around the Wisconsin peninsula. On his right, where the park ended, he saw Santa Fe railcars loaded high with rock on the other side of a barbed wire fence. The wind was fierce and cold, and the morning sky overhead was a gray shroud.

This was where Tanjy said she was taken, tied to the tall fence by the rail yard, and assaulted.

He put himself in Tanjy's mind, imagining it was night in early November. The lights of the bridge to Superior glistened to the north. They were close enough to the water to hear waves slapping on the shore. Tanjy struggled, but there was a knife to her throat, and she didn't make a sound. She was tied up and stripped. The loops of the fence crushed against her naked skin.

After, she was alone. Humiliated. She didn't cry out for help. She freed herself, drove home, and washed away the shame and the evidence.

Stride shook his head. There was a piece of the puzzle that didn't fit.

When she first told Stride the story, one detail struck him as odd. After the rape, the killer left Tanjy's car behind, because he had another car waiting for him in the park. At the time, Stride wondered how the rapist could have left a car behind for himself and made his way out of the park and back into the city. When Tanjy admitted lying about the rape, he forgot about the anomaly. Now it was back in his mind.

The murder scene left him with the same suspicion. If Tanjy's murderer transported her to Hell's Lake in the trunk of her car, and then disposed of the car in the woods after dumping her body in the ice, where was his own car? He couldn't have walked far in the subzero weather. He also couldn't very well drive two cars at the same time. So how did he vacate the desolate woods where he left Tanjy's car?

Answer: There was someone else involved. Someone driving another car.

Maybe. Or maybe he and Abel were both thinking what the killer wanted them to think.

Stride gripped the fence with both hands. The more he imagined Tanjy's rape, the more he felt a jolt of anger and regret, thinking about Maggie. He had to control his rage and dole it out into his veins in doses, like adrenaline. In Las Vegas, when his partner got shot, he had felt the same fury that left him teetering on the edge of control.

He was angry with Maggie, too. Angry that she had let it go, destroyed evidence, failed to report a crime. He knew it was easy for him to make that judgment when he didn't live through it, but he was also angry that she had cut him out of her life by not sharing her pain with him, by not trusting him. The intimacy between them felt broken, even though he had no right to expect it from her.

He turned away from the fence when he heard a muffled symphony of noise and felt a thumping bass ricochet inside his chest. He saw a brown Lexus SUV pull into a parking place next to his Bronco. The engine cut off, and the music stopped. Tony Wells got out, clutching a venti cup of Starbucks coffee. He took several sips as he walked over to Stride. He wore a tan parka with a fur-lined hood and dress pants and shoes that were ill-suited to the snow heaped over the park grass.

"Good morning, Lieutenant."

"Thanks for coming down here, Tony." He gestured at the car and added, "Castrating pigs again, are you?"

"Oh, yes, another country music fan," Tony said with a faint smile. "Smashing Pumpkins won a Grammy for that song, you know."

"For what? Song most likely to make a listener conduct his own autopsy?"

Tony pulled his hood down and smoothed his thinning hair. "I read a study recently about some poor lab mice who were subjected to Toby Keith twenty-four hours a day for a month. They all developed cancer."

Stride laughed. It was an old argument between them.

He was probably one of the few cops in Duluth who had never seen Tony Wells professionally. The job did that to you—it stirred up rat holes and made you do things you never wanted to do, like drink, or hit your wife, or roll your car on a slick highway. Tony was good at taming the rats. Maggie and Serena both liked him. Stride had needed counseling himself once, but he never wanted to see a cop's shrink. He didn't like sharing stories with someone who knew everyone else's stories. After Cindy died, he found a therapist thirty miles away in Two Harbors and went there once a week for six months, which wasn't enough to prevent him from rebounding into a bad marriage.

"You know this is where Tanjy Powell said she was raped?" Stride asked.

He watched Tony take the measure of the area around him. Parks looked lonely in the winter, devoid of life.

"Yes."

"You know that she really was raped, don't you? She didn't make it up."

Tony worked his jaw as if something were caught between his teeth. "I'm in an uncomfortable position, Lieutenant. I want to help, but I'm not sure I can."

"Tanjy is dead," Stride reminded him. "You can't do her any harm by talking to me. You can only help me find out who did this to her."

"Tanjy was an intensely private person."

"I know she was, but I need your help, Tony. We go back a long way. I respect your loyalty, but your patient is dead. I think she'd want you to talk to me."

Stride could see that the choice was a genuine struggle for Tony. As a therapist with close ties to the police, Tony had seen them all—detectives, victims, and perpetrators—and he didn't always have a rule book to work around ethical conflicts.

"Yes, all right," Tony said finally. "I'd like to see you catch whoever did this. Tanjy deserves that."

"Thanks."

"What can I tell you?"

"Do you know who Tanjy was seeing at the time of the assault?"

"No, she never gave me a name. She was very discreet. It made therapy difficult sometimes, because she gave me so few details about her life." Tony hesitated.

"What is it?"

"Well, she did think she had a stalker. She told me she was being watched."

"Did she know who it was?"

"No, she said it was just a feeling."

"When was this?"

"Shortly before the rape."

"Did she give you any other details?"

"No, she didn't. Truthfully, Lieutenant, I wasn't sure the rape really happened. She told me she only recanted to you because she couldn't stand the public humiliation, but I wondered about that. The venue of the rape was too similar to her own fantasies. That's not the way it works."

"Unless that was the whole point for the rapist."

"You mean you think she was targeted *because* of her fantasies," Tony concluded.

"It's a possibility."

Tony thought about this. "I don't see how. No one knew about them."

"Her boyfriend knew. She made him act out rape fantasies during sex. She posted rape stories on the Web, too."

Tony cocked his head. "True."

"Was Grassy Point Park important to her?"

"Very."

"Do you know why?"

"I think it was because of her parents. You can see the bridge from here, where her parents were killed in the car accident. The fact that she reenacted rape fantasies at a place that's visible from the bridge is significant. I suspect she was acting out her repressed sexuality in front of her parents."

"So if she had other boyfriends, you think she would have taken them here."

"Yes, that's likely."

"Do you know who else she was seeing, other than Mitchell Brandt?"

Tony shook his head. "I'm sorry, no."

"Okay, let's talk about Eric," Stride said.

Tony shoved his free hand in his pocket and drank more coffee. The wind landed a kick across the harbor that made them both hunch their bodies against the frozen air.

"Now I'm really on thin ice," Tony said.

"I know, but I'm not asking for any privileged information. Eric talked about things that had nothing to do with Maggie, right?"

"Yes, he did," Tony acknowledged.

"What did he want to know?"

"He asked me if there were certain tells you could look for that would tip you off that someone might be a sexual predator."

"What did you tell him?"

"Not much," Tony said. "I told him you'd have to be a trained professional conducting an extended interview to make an assessment, and even then, there aren't any guarantees. Most sexual predators have spent a lifetime protecting their disguises."

"Did he tell you who he was thinking about?"

"No."

Stride watched Tony's brooding eyes. "Maybe he was thinking about you."

Tony looked back at him, steady and hard. "Me?" he said evenly.

"Right now, you're the only connection between Tanjy and Maggie. Maybe Eric thought you raped them."

"You knew them both, too, Lieutenant," Tony said. "Maybe he thought it was you."

"I'm serious."

"Yes, I know you are, so I'll be blunt. I did not rape those women. Okay? I had nothing to fear from Eric."

"Sorry, Tony, I had to ask."

Tony nodded. "I knew you would. I know how the game is played. For the record, I asked Maggie for the exact date she was raped, and then I went back and dug out my calendar from last year. I was in Seattle giving a speech that night. I can give you all the details you need to verify it."

"And Tanjy?"

"I pulled her file and cross-referenced my schedule. I had group therapy the night she was assaulted."

"Thanks. Sometimes I have to play bad cop, you know."

"I understand."

"I need to know if Eric said anything else. Did he talk about his visit to the Ordway over the weekend?"

"The Ordway?" Tony asked. "No, what does that have to do with anything?"

"I don't know yet." Stride shook his head. "I'm frustrated, Tony. Try to put aside the fact that Tanjy and Maggie were both patients. Just look at the facts of the rapes as you know them. Give me some kind of profile."

Tony scratched his beard. "I don't have nearly enough information."

"Neither do I, but you've worked with less in the past. Help me out here."

"Well, put a big asterisk next to this. I could be steering you wrong. Whoever is doing this is likely to be very intelligent and organized. He has a huge ego and a need to control his victims. He likes to play games, like a cat toying with a mouse. He researches his victims thoroughly—picks them, studies them, gets to know everything about them, before he moves in."

"You think there are other assaults we don't know about?"

"It's possible. You know as well as I do how many rapes never get reported. This perpetrator seems to choose victims who are vulnerable on sexual matters, which increases the likelihood that they won't go to the police."

"What do you mean, 'vulnerable on sexual matters'?"

Tony frowned. "I mean, like Tanjy and her rape fantasies."

"In other words, women with secrets to protect."

"That's right."

"How does he find out about their secrets?"

"I don't know. If you can find that out, you can probably identify him."

"Does he know these women? Could he have a personal relationship with them?"

"Possibly. That's not the typical profile, but the fact that he knows so much about the victims would lead me to think he has some connection to them."

"Would he be acting alone?"

Wells arched his eyebrows in surprise.

"That's an odd question. Rapists almost always act alone."

Stride knew that was true, but he still wondered about the possibility of an accomplice. "Is this man likely to strike again?"

Wells nodded. "Rapists always strike again unless they find some alternate resolution for their pathology. Some other way to address their sexual tension. I don't think that's likely here."

"Why?"

"The time line is too short between assaults. Whoever is doing this is acting quickly. I'd say he's a sociopath—no conscience, no guilt, no hesitation. Many predators *want* to stop and wage a giant internal struggle to control their violent tendencies. They can succeed for months or even years before reoffending. Not this one. He's enjoying the game. In fact, I'd have to say that this rapist is more dangerous now than ever before."

"Why?" Stride asked again.

"You said it yourself, Lieutenant. This man probably killed Tanjy and Eric. He's upped the stakes. It's not just rape now, it's murder. He may decide that killing his victims gives him an extra thrill."

25

Serena passed through a cloud of warm steam billowing out of the sewer grates as she crossed First Street downtown. The green light turned yellow, and she hurried to reach the opposite sidewalk before the five o'clock traffic roared southward. A neighborhood pizza joint was on the far corner, and she pulled open the glass door and stepped inside. The steel pizza ovens were on her left. She waved at the sweaty men in T-shirts behind the counter and took a booth for herself inside the restaurant. She unbuttoned her coat and unwound her scarf from around her neck.

She pulled her laptop computer from its case and began searching for a wireless network. A young waitress greeted her, and Serena ordered a Diet Coke. They knew her here. She and Stride had a weakness for the pizza and usually dropped in a couple of times a month. They cut the pizza in squares, and she liked to roll up each tiny piece and pop it in her mouth.

She loaded Internet Explorer on her laptop. The signal was weak. Jonny had told her about Eric's visit to the Ordway a few days before he was killed, and she searched news stories to see if there had been any recent incidents in the Rice Park area surrounding the theater. Especially sexual assaults. She found stories about road construction, the winter carnival, and Broadway musicals, but nothing that gave her any clue as to Eric's motive. The only way to find out was to go there in person, which was on her calendar for tomorrow.

She found a lot more when she searched for Nicole Castro. The murder trial of Abel's ex-partner had been big news in Duluth six years earlier. She studied the photos of Nicole and saw someone not unlike herself; a cop in her late thirties, tall, athletic. Nicole was black with dark skin. Her hair was kinky and big. She had pink, puffy lips and flared nostrils, and coal-black eyes wide with defiance. In one photo, she was on the steps of the courthouse, surrounded by cops in uniform, her mouth open as she shouted at the media.

Nicole had a little boy, twelve years old. Serena wondered what had happened to him with his father dead and his mother doing twenty-five years for his murder. He was a cute kid, pretending to be tough, but you could see his heart breaking as he clung to his mother's arm in the photo. He would be nearly nineteen now.

Serena's cell phone rang. It was Maggie.

"Hey."

"Hey yourself," Maggie said. She added after a pause, "Stride told you, right?"

"He did. I'm really sorry."

"He couldn't understand why I didn't report it."

"Men never do."

"Even telling him now made me feel so fucking dirty," Maggie said.

Serena understood. It wasn't just about telling someone. It was about Maggie telling Stride. Leaving herself naked in front of him.

"Want to join me down at Sammy's? We could talk."

Someone slid a pepperoni pizza into one of the ovens. The tangy aroma filled the restaurant, and Serena realized she was hungry.

"I don't want to talk anymore," Maggie said. "I just want to catch this son of a bitch."

"Sounds like you're sailing that Egyptian river called Denial."

Serena waited for Maggie to fire back, but she didn't. "Yeah, I know, but being angry about it is better than locking myself in my bedroom. I called to tell you I have more dirt about Eric's visit to the Ordway."

"What is it?"

"I was able to reach their floor security attendant. The reason Eric was almost kicked out of the theater is that he kept trying to find a woman who worked there. He thought she was an usher. He wouldn't say what he wanted with her, and they started getting creeped out. They told him to sit down or they'd toss him out."

"Do you know who the woman was?"

"No, Eric didn't know her name."

"All right, I'll check it out tomorrow. You sure you don't want pizza?"

"No, thanks."

Through the restaurant window, Serena saw a tall man in a tan trench coat cross the street toward her. "That's okay, your nemesis is about to join me."

"Who?"

"Abel Teitscher."

"Why are you seeing him? You're not a spy, are you?"

"I want to talk to him about Nicole Castro."

"Yeah, Archie told me she called. I think you're wasting your time. Nicole tells everyone she was framed, but we had her dead to rights."

"Like you?"

"Yeah, okay, I see your point."

"I'll talk to you when I get back. Call Tony. Get some help."

"Anyone ever tell you you're a pushy bitch?"

"Everyone."

Serena hung up and closed her laptop. Abel Teitscher entered the restaurant, and his head swiveled over his long neck, looking for her. She waved at him. He nodded back at her but didn't smile. He was earnest and bleak, like the city in January. She had met him a few times in Jonny's office at City

Hall, and although there was bad blood between Jonny and Abel, she felt sorry for him. She knew the story of his divorce and knew he kept people away with a prickly armor. He was smart, bitter, and lonely. Once upon a time, she had been the same way.

They shook hands. He had a solid grip. As he sat down, he smoothed his coat underneath him without taking it off. That sent her a message—he wasn't staying. She could see he was suspicious of what she wanted.

"Are you hungry?" she asked. "We could order something."

Abel shook his head. Serena sighed. She could smell the sausage now, blending with the pepperoni, and it was driving her crazy.

"You're a runner, aren't you?" she asked.

He nodded.

"Me, too. You've got that runner's look."

She was being kind. His face reminded her of the desert floor in Death Valley, leathery and cracked. His gray hair was trimmed to half an inch and squared off on top of his head. He looked old, but also lean and tough.

"What can I do for you?" Abel asked. "If this is about Maggie, you know I can't say a thing."

"It's not about Maggie."

"Oh?" He looked surprised.

"I was hoping you could tell me about Nicole Castro."

"Why?"

"I have to go down to the Cities tomorrow," Serena explained. "Nicole asked me to meet with her."

"She told you she was framed?"

Serena nodded.

"That's bullshit."

"You sound pretty harsh. Wasn't she your partner?"

"That's why I'm harsh. I don't like being lied to. Plus, she tells everyone that I planted evidence against her, which is a crock."

"Just give me some background," Serena said. "If it really is just bullshit, fine, but at least I'll know that going in."

Abel leaned back against the wooden wall of the booth. He worked a toothpick between his molars. "Look, Nicole was a good kid. She and I worked together for five years. She was a lot younger than me, but we got along. I'll tell you the truth, I wasn't all that keen about having a black partner. My experience is that black women assume you're going to treat them with disrespect, so you have to be careful about everything you say. I don't do a very good job of watching my mouth. You've probably figured that out."

Serena smiled.

"Nicole was just as nervous having a middle-aged white guy as a partner. We had our arguments from time to time. Having a partner is like being married, you know that. But we did okay."

"How did her problems start?" Serena asked.

"To begin with, she was married to a son of a bitch. The kind of guy that thinks the world owes him a living because he's got a good-looking face. Nicole denied it, but I know he hit her a few times."

"So what happened?"

Abel took off his glasses and stared at the ceiling. "It was just bad, bad luck. Nicole was coming back from Superior on the Blatnik Bridge on a Saturday night. There was a guy on the Minnesota side who had parked his car and was running around on the bridge deck in a winter coat. This was July. Nicole blocked off traffic and got out of her car to talk to him. He told her he had a bomb strapped to his chest, and he was going to blow up himself and the bridge."

"Oh, shit."

"She tried to talk him into keeping his hands in the air, but he wouldn't listen. He kept saying he was going to do it, he was going to set off the bomb. When he unzipped his coat and began to reach inside, Nicole shot him twice in the head."

Serena understood what Nicole had gone through in those few seconds on the bridge. She had faced the same situation in Las Vegas, when a man decided to commit suicide by cop by pointing a gun at her and Jonny. That time, she was the one to pull the trigger.

"Sounds like a good shooting," she said.

"It was, but then the second-guessing started. It turns out the guy was mentally ill. There was no bomb."

"It's not like she could take the chance."

"You know that, and I know that. But tell that to the people who weren't up on the bridge. There was more, too. A lot of people said they heard this guy shouting racial slurs at Nicole. So some politicians got the idea that she shot him because he was a racist."

"Great."

"There was an investigation. Nicole went on leave, and it was six months before they cleared her and got her back on the job. Six months. Unbelievable. She went to pieces sitting at home, watching the television stations chew her up night after night. She had a nervous breakdown."

"So what happened with her husband?"

"The son of a bitch started having an affair with a young cocktail waitress. Eighteen years old."

"Was Nicole back on the job at that point?"

Abel nodded. "Yeah, she said she was okay, but she was fragile. Therapy wasn't working. She didn't have much of a caseload, too. Stride was nervous about her getting in over her head too quickly, so she mainly pulled cold cases. He was right. She was coming apart. You'd hear her on the phone with her husband, and it was crazy, like you were listening to a stranger. Hell, I heard her threaten him myself. Nicole said she'd kill him if he didn't break off the affair."

"And?"

"I got the call. Bad smell coming out of an apartment in the Lincoln Park area. I went in and found Nicole's husband and his teenie girlfriend, both shot dead. They'd been gone at least two days. Nicole never even reported him missing."

"Was it her gun?"

"No, but it was just as bad. Her husband's gun. He kept it in the glove compartment of his car, which was parked outside the apartment building. Nicole said she was home drinking on the night of the murders, but she didn't have any witnesses to back it up. She said he sometimes went off for days on end, so she didn't think anything was wrong when he didn't come home. But she knew he was with the other girl. She also swore to me—swore to me—that she had never been inside that girl's apartment. Except we found witnesses who placed her outside the building in her car on multiple occasions. Like she was stalking them. And we found two of her hairs in the bedroom with the bodies. Perfect DNA match."

Serena whistled. "That's a lot of evidence. What did Nicole say?"

"She said she didn't do it. I believed her, too, until we found the witnesses near the apartment and got the forensics report back. Then I knew she was just like every other perp. Covering her ass."

"This was personal for you."

"Very personal. Take my advice, Serena. Save yourself a trip."

Serena shrugged. "I have to go down there anyway."

"Suit yourself." The older detective slid out of the booth. He took black leather gloves out of his pockets and put them on his hands.

"Hey, Abel," Serena said. "I know you don't want to hear it, but Maggie's not Nicole."

"I need more than faith to believe that."

He left, and Serena drummed her fingers on the table. She was discouraged. The visit to Nicole Castro smelled like a waste of time now, but she couldn't back out, even though she knew what it would be like. She hated to see a cop's life ruined. They all walked close to the line sometimes, and when one of them took a step across, you just wanted to turn your eyes away.

The waitress stopped by her table. She had tomato sauce on her shirt. "You want to order pizza?"

"Oh, yeah."

26

Stride saw a light on inside Silk, shining in a yellow triangle from the office at the rear of Lauren Erickson's dress shop. He rang the bell beside the door and heard a distant chime. As he waited, he looked up and down Superior Street, which was deserted for the night. It was almost seven thirty, and the stores were closed. A string of streetlights illuminated the slush piled in gray mounds on the curb and on the edge of the sidewalks.

Inside, he saw Lauren's petite silhouette framed in the light from the office. She crossed the store in the darkness and unlocked the door. He felt uncomfortable as he came inside. He was dressed in a dirty flannel shirt, jeans, and heavy boots, which were crusted with mud. He smelled like smoke because of an arson fire he was investigating near the airport, and there was soot in the creases of his neck. Lauren, by contrast, wore a striped dress shirt with an open collar and a gold chain around her neck, tan pleated dress slacks with a braided belt, and leather pumps. Her wheat-colored hair was loose, bobbing around her shoulders.

"Lose the boots," she told him.

He left them on the rubber mat. The blue carpet felt deep and thick under his feet. "Sorry, I'm a mess."

"Don't get anything on the dresses," she said.

She led him back to the office, where moving boxes were scattered on the floor. The bottom drawers of several filing cabinets were open and half-filled with bulging file folders. She had a bottle of pinot noir on her desk and a crystal glass filled with wine.

She held up the bottle, offering him a drink, and he shook his head.

"I know you won't believe this, but I'm

going to miss living in Duluth," she told him as he sat down.

Stride squeezed his body into a wooden chair designed for women whose trim backsides could fit in a thimble. "You're right. I don't believe it."

"I used to go hunting and fishing with my dad when I was a girl," she said. "I brought down an eight-pointer once. I had it on my bedroom wall for years."

"Don't look now, but you could be a redneck."

Lauren smiled thinly. "I'm just saying this is my home."

"You'll do okay in Georgetown," Stride said.

"I'm sure we will." She swirled her wine in the glass. "Who knows, maybe I can land Dan a job in the next administration. Something in the Justice Department."

"I always heard that 'under secretary' was the position Dan preferred," Stride said.

Lauren slapped her glass down on the desk so hard that wine sloshed over the top. Then she laughed and dabbed the crimson drops with a tissue. "Funny. You're funny. But you don't understand us."

"You're not so hard to figure out. Anything for power."

"What's wrong with ambition?" Lauren asked.

"If it means destroying people who get in your way, plenty."

"People usually get what they deserve. Look at Maggie."

"Maggie doesn't deserve what's happened to her."

"No? She's no angel. I knew that when she started an affair with Dan."

"That was years ago. Besides, I thought you looked the other way about Dan's affairs."

"Usually I do, because Dan knows who's responsible for everything he is. Me."

"So why do you still hate Maggie?"

"She asked Dan to leave me. I take that personally."

"Dan was just using her. Maggie got hurt."

"Poor angel. I hope you comforted her with your big strong arms."

Stride hated that Lauren knew how to push his buttons. "You know, there are bigger sharks than you in Washington. You may wish you were back in the small pond after a while."

"I'll take my chances. Now what do you want, Jonathan? I have a lot of work to do here."

"I want to talk about Tanjy."

"Again?"

"I need some more information."

"I heard this was Abel's case now, not yours."

"I'm not investigating Tanjy's murder."

"Oh?"

"I'm investigating her rape."

"What rape?" Lauren asked. "You said Tanjy made it up."

"No, I think it really happened."

"Why?"

"Because there's another victim," he told her.

Lauren reacted sharply. "Are you sure?"

Stride nodded.

"Who?"

"I can't say, but I think whoever raped Tanjy also killed her. And Eric."

Lauren rocked back in her chair. "That's horrible. I'm so sorry."

"Do you know who Tanjy began seeing after Mitch Brandt?" Stride asked. "I need to talk to anyone who was close to her during that time."

She shook her head. "I have no idea. Tanjy and I weren't exactly close."

"Did she ever talk about being stalked or watched?"

"Not to me. You should talk to Sonnie. She saw her every day."

"Tanjy said she was abducted going from the dress shop to her car. Do you remember seeing any suspicious individuals in the shop around that time? Or in the parking ramp?"

"In the shop? No. It's not uncommon to have vagrants in the Michigan ramp, you know that. I don't remember anyone specifically."

"Did you know about Tanjy's fascination with rape? Did she talk about it in front of you?"

"Are you kidding? No."

"How about men who came into the shop? Did anyone show an unusual interest in Tanjy?"

Lauren shrugged. "Men hit on her all the time."

"But no one special?"

"No one who was so taken with her that it seemed weird."

"All right," Stride said. Those were the answers he expected.

"Do you have any idea who the rapist is?" Lauren asked.

"Not yet."

"And are there only the two victims?"

"I don't know."

Lauren frowned and bit her lip. He could read in her face that she knew something.

"What is it?" Stride asked.

She hesitated. "Nothing."

"Come on, Lauren, I don't care what the history is between us. This is different."

"It doesn't really mean anything. It's just that I think I know who the other victim is."

"Oh?" Stride tensed, waiting to hear Maggie's name.

"She was in here a few weeks ago, talking to Sonnie. She looked like someone had beat her up."

Stride's eyes narrowed. "Who?"

"The plump girl who runs that Java Jelly coffee shop down the block. Katrina Kuli."

27

Serena arrived at the Minnesota Correctional Facility in Shakopee in the early afternoon. It was the state's only prison facility for adult women, and it housed approximately five hundred females who had been convicted of crimes ranging from fraud to murder. Visiting hours didn't begun until three thirty in the afternoon, but Stride had paved the way with the warden for a private meeting between Serena and Nicole Castro. She still had to go through the metal detector and endure a pat-down from a female guard before being shown into the visiting room.

When she had visited such rooms in the

past, they were usually crowded. Mothers visiting sons. Wives visiting husbands. Men and women getting teary as they touched the hands of children who were growing up without them. The room today was empty, and she liked it better that way, without the pain of separation and guilt that suffused these places, like cigarette smoke gathering over a blackjack table. It was an institutional room, with white walls and fluorescent lights overhead. Rows of gray plastic chairs sat facing each other on heavy-duty beige carpeting. The prisoners sat on one side, the visitors on the other. Behind a Plexiglas partition were the non-contact booths, where prisoners without personal visit privileges could talk by phone, separated by thick glass walls.

She noticed the small half-dome in the ceiling, hiding the video cameras. An eye in the sky, just like in the casinos. Everything was watched, taped, documented. There was no privacy here.

The guard pointed her to a specific, numbered chair in which she was supposed to sit. It felt like overkill, because the visiting room was empty, but Serena knew that prisons ran on rules. There were rules for everything, right down to how you trimmed your fingernails. The walls and bars kept prisoners in; the rules kept anarchy and chaos out.

She waited ten minutes before another guard showed Nicole into the visiting room. They shook hands, and Nicole sat opposite her. She was dressed in a khaki jumpsuit and tennis shoes. She squirmed in her chair and rubbed her thumb and fingers together like a nervous habit. Her foot drummed on the floor. She studied Serena with sharp, observant eyes. Detective's eyes.

"Wow," Nicole said. "Very nice. I'm surprised they didn't treat themselves to a cavity search with you."

Serena didn't smile.

"What, I'm a murderer, so I can't have a sense of humor?" Nicole asked.

"I thought the whole point was that you aren't a murderer."

"Figure of speech." She added, "So how's Stride?"

"Fine."

"What a dog. His wife dies, and he winds up with a hottie all the way from Vegas."

"Fuck you," Serena said and stood up to leave.

Nicole stood up, too. Her hostile façade

crumbled. "Hey, take it easy. I'm sorry, okay? Please don't go."

Serena sat down. She barely recognized Nicole from the photographs she had seen on the Web. Prison had aged her. Her wild hair was cropped and graying. She was thinner. Serena knew she was in her early forties, but her mottled face looked ten years older.

Nicole noticed her appraisal. "It's not exactly a spa in here."

"I know."

"I meant what I said. I'm happy for you and Stride. It must have killed him when Cindy died. Those two were the real deal."

"Yes, they were." Serena didn't add that it made her feel a little jealous sometimes.

"I made a play for him once. Did he tell you that? It was right after I joined the force. He shut me down cold."

"He was married."

"Oh, and he wasn't married when you met him? Come on, girl." She added quickly, "Not that I'm judging. Look, people do what they do, and what do I care? I haven't had good luck with men. I envy you."

"We don't have a lot of time, Nicole. Maybe you should just tell me what you wanted to tell me."

Nicole shrugged. "It's easy to tell that you used to be a cop. All business. Let me ask you this, did you get shit in Vegas because of the way you looked? I mean, did people think you couldn't do the job because you look like some kind of showgirl?"

"Sure."

"Well, now imagine being a black detective in white bread Duluth. That was me."

"You're not in here because you're black," Serena told her.

"No? Slap some shoe polish on that pretty face of yours, and live like me for a year, and then tell me that. The fact is, I was always treated differently. People were just waiting for me to fuck up. When I did, they were right there to jump on me. If it were a white cop, you don't think they would have worked harder to find out what really happened? Hell, no. I was black. I was presumed guilty."

"I know Jonny. He's not like that."

"Yeah, the lieutenant tried, but racism in a place like Duluth is like drinking water. It's as natural as breathing, girl. They're doing it when they don't even know they're doing it. Stride included. He was always busting my ass over things that white cops did all the time."

"Like what?"

"Sometimes I missed shifts. My boy was sick. For white folks, that's called a child care issue. For me, it's being a lazy-ass black cop."

"That doesn't explain your hair being found in the apartment where your husband and his lover were killed."

"No, I'm just saying you got to understand the context."

Serena leaned forward. The plastic chair was uncomfortable. "Look, I've read the newspapers. I talked to Abel. I talked to Jonny. What I understand is that you had six months of hell. You had a good shooting on the bridge, and then you had everyone on your back over it. You were questioning yourself every damn day, reliving that moment when you pulled the trigger. Believe me, I know what that's like. I've been there. Then your husband started an affair with a teenage whore, and there you are, stuck on leave and feeling guilty and ashamed, trying to raise a boy, and feeling like the whole world is against you. Do I understand the context?"

Nicole was silent. She chewed her lip and wiped her eyes with the back of her hand. "Yeah, okay. That was me."

"You were fragile."

"Yeah, but I was dealing with it. I was getting help. I was happy to be back on the job. Stride had me pull cold cases, because he didn't think I was ready to be back on the street, but that was okay. I liked it. I was on the phone and the Web ten hours a day, and I made some breaks in cases that had been stone-cold for years. It gave me my confidence back, you know?"

"What about your husband?"

"He was a prick. No other way around it. I was going to dump him."

"You didn't stalk him and his little girlfriend?"

"Okay, yeah, I did that a few times. I was wallowing in it, you know what that's like? Feeling sorry for myself. But I was done with that. I did *not* go over there that night. I did *not* kill them."

"Then who did?" Serena asked.

"Hell, I don't know. The girl was a junkie. Probably a dealer. But no one checked the drug angle."

"You said you were never in her apartment."

"I wasn't."

"How did your hair get there?"

Nicole jabbed a finger at Serena. "'Cause it was planted, that's how."

"Who do you think did that?"

"I know exactly who. Abel fucking Teitscher, that's who. He framed me."

"Why would Abel do that?"

"He never wanted me as a partner, and he thought I was guilty, and this was the only way he could make the case. You know as well as I do that cops aren't angels. You've never helped a case along when you knew you had the perp and the evidence was weak?"

"No."

"Well, that's real high-and-mighty, but here in the real world, it happens."

Serena sighed. "So what does this have to do with Maggie?"

"Are you kidding me? Two detectives from the same bureau wind up on the hook for murdering their husbands? That doesn't smell like rotten fish to you?"

"Your case was six years ago. That's a long time."

"And I'm telling you, there's got to be a connection somewhere. You've got Abel on the case again, don't you? He had it in for me then, now he's got it in for Maggie."

"That doesn't sound like Abel," Serena told her. "He's a pain in the ass, but he's a straight shooter."

"Yeah, well, a lot of my hair wound up in Abel's car, girl, but the only way it got into that apartment is because someone carried it."

"You're not suggesting that Abel killed your husband and his girlfriend. Or Maggie's husband. Are you?"

Nicole shrugged. "I'm saying anything's possible. Maybe he's got it in for chick cops."

"Come on, Nicole."

"Look, I don't know. When I was a detective, I didn't like coincidences. This is a big one. Two cops with dead husbands."

Serena got up. "If I find anything that links the two cases, I'll call you."

"Yeah, right."

She extended her hand, and Nicole took it sullenly.

"That's all I can do," Serena said.

Nicole folded her arms over her chest. "My boy is going to college now, did you know that? A state school near his grandmother in Tennessee. If I'm lucky, I see him a couple of times a year. He's eighteen now. Almost nineteen. I missed the last six years of him growing up."

"I'm sorry."

"I didn't do this. He knows that."

"Okay."

"Say hi to Stride for me."

Serena nodded. Nicole shuffled toward the door that led back to the cells. Her head was down. Serena watched her go. She left the prison and was glad to get away from the antiseptic smell and the claustrophobia of the walls. As she got into her car, she realized everyone was right. Nicole was a waste of time.

Serena hoped she would have better luck at the Ordway.

She had visited Saint Paul several times in the past year. It was an easy two-and-a-half hour drive down I-35 from Duluth, and many of her investigative jobs had roots in the Twin Cities. Minneapolis was the larger of the siblings, with steel skyscrapers, trendy restaurants, and a fast-paced corporate culture. Saint Paul was slower, quieter, and smaller, boasting only a handful of high-rises that would have been dwarfed in other towns. The dominant look in the downtown architecture was turn-of-the-century stone. The state government took up most of the office space, and life in the city revolved around two domed buildings on the hill, the cathedral and the capitol. Between the twins, Serena preferred Saint Paul.

She found a parking place at a meter in Rice Park. The park was no more than a single square city block, with a central fountain and an odd juxtaposition of statues, including F. Scott Fitzgerald and characters from the *Peanuts* comic strip. St. Paul didn't forget its favorite sons, whether they were authors or cartoonists. The Ordway Center was only a few steps away, and the other buildings on the square were classical and grave—the mammoth central library, the Landmark Center with its clock tower and green dormers, and the venerable Saint Paul Hotel.

It was late afternoon and already dark. The streetlights were on. White lights twinkled in the trees in the park, and faery ice sculptures glistened, awaiting the opening of the city's annual winter carnival. Serena made her way to the Ordway, which was getting ready for a performance of *The Producers* that night. A doorman in a cape and top hat held the door for her. She was early; the theater staff in the lobby were sweeping the floor, arranging posters and T-shirts for sale, and preparing for the rush of ticket holders.

She found a security attendant in a white shirt. He was in his fifties, short and round. He remembered talking to Maggie the previous day.

"I was hoping to get some more information from the ushers," Serena told him.

"Suit yourself," he replied pleasantly. "But you've only got half an hour. When the guests start arriving, everyone will be busy around here."

"Do you know who would have been working a week ago Saturday?"

The security guard pointed at a kid in his early twenties, who was perched beside a velvet rope leading into the waiting area outside the orchestra doors. "Start with Dave."

Serena thanked him. Dave was a talkative farm boy who was majoring in geology at the University of Minnesota and used his ushering job to watch theater performances for free. He was dressed uncomfortably in a black tuxedo, with a paisley cummerbund and a bow tie that was so twisted it looked more like an hourglass spilling sand. Serena couldn't resist straightening it for him.

"Thanks," Dave replied. He didn't look unhappy to be in the circle of Serena's perfume. "I hate wearing the monkey suit, but they insist."

"Come on, you know women can't resist a man in a tuxedo," she told him, smiling.

His cheeks turned pink. "Yeah?"

"Oh, definitely." She asked Dave if he remembered Eric from the previous weekend, and he nodded vigorously.

"That dude? Absolutely. He looked like he should be captain of a Viking ship, know what I mean? Like he just stepped off a fjord."

"You talked to him?"

"Yeah, he peppered me with questions for ten minutes. It was a little awkward, because I needed to work, you know?"

"I'm sorry to be doing the same thing."

"Oh, hey, you I don't mind."

"What did Eric want to know?"

Dave had long brown hair, and he pushed it back behind his ears with both hands. "He was talking about this blog he had found on the Web. He was trying to track down the woman who wrote it."

"A blog?

"Yeah, I guess it was one of those

MySpace things, like 'Lady in Red' or 'Dark Lady' or 'Lady in Waiting.' It was lady something."

"Did you know who the blogger was?"

"Nope. The Viking dude, he said it was probably a woman in her late thirties, but we've got lots of women like that here. So he started talking to them one by one."

"Did he say why he was looking for her?"

"No, he didn't. After he talked to a couple of the women, people started getting a little freaked-out. You know, like he might be a stalker or something. Security went to him and told him to lay off or they were going to kick him out."

"Did that stop him?"

Dave shook his head. "Not really. I saw him at intermission, and he was still talking up the women ushers. To tell you the truth, most of them didn't mind. I mean, he's a good-looking guy, you know? There was just one woman who got hot and bothered about it."

"Who was that?"

"Her name's Helen."

"Is she here tonight?"

"I haven't seen her for a while. You'd have to talk to the admin guys about her schedule. The thing is, she couldn't have been too upset, because when I left the theater that night, I saw her talking to the Viking guy in the park across the street."

"You saw Helen and Eric together?"

Dave nodded.

"You're a doll," Serena said.

Dave blushed again, and Serena retraced her steps to find the security guard hovering near the theater door. She asked him about Helen and discovered that the usher's full name was Helen Danning, single, late thirties, quiet.

"When is she next scheduled to work?" Serena asked.

The guard shook his head. "She's not."

"Why?"

"She quit last week. Called on Thursday and said she was moving out of town. No warning, no explanations, nothing."

"Did she say where she was going?"

"We don't even know where to send her last paycheck."

Serena frowned. "Do you know where she lived?"

"I think she had an apartment in Lowertown. Near the farmer's market. She told me it was nice to walk across the street on Saturday morning and get fresh tomatoes."

"And you're sure it was Thursday she called to give notice?" she asked.

"Yeah, I remember. They needed to find someone to take her place for the weekend shows."

Serena thanked him again. She checked her watch as she left the theater. It was getting late, and she still had to make the long drive back to Duluth that night. Even so, she needed to make a detour to Lowertown. She didn't like the chain of events. On Saturday, Eric was seen talking in the park with Helen Danning.

On Wednesday, Eric was murdered.

On Thursday, Helen fled the city.

28

When Katrina Kuli answered the door, Stride remembered that she had covered the bruises on her face with makeup and shrugged off the cut on her neck when he had first met her at the Java Jelly coffee shop. He wished he had put the truth together sooner. She held the door open and waited stiffly while he walked into her apartment.

"I'm glad you called me back," he said.

Katrina closed the door and locked it. "I'm not filing a police report. I don't want this to become public."

She gestured at a yellow futon by the

living-room windows, and he sat down. She made sure the blinds were closed and then lowered herself gingerly into an upholstered chair across from him. He saw her wince as she breathed.

"Are you still in a lot of pain?"

She shrugged. "A couple of cracked ribs. They don't do anything for that these days. Just grin and bear it."

"What about other injuries?"

"Bumps, cuts, bruises. I'm healing."

"I just want to make sure you're being treated."

"I am."

"What about a counselor?"

"I've got some names," Katrina said. "I haven't called anyone yet. I figured I'd be hysterical, you know, but I don't really feel anything. It's weird."

"It happens like that sometimes. I've talked to a lot of women who have been through this, Katrina. Some become very emotional, some go numb. It's normal. Just don't deal with this alone. Call one of those names, okay?"

"Yeah, okay."

Katrina was wearing a loose-fitting flannel shirt and gray sweats. Her round face was blank, and her hair lay in clumps on her fore-head. Every few seconds, she fingered the cut on her neck tenderly, as if it might have gone away since she last touched it. Her hands trembled, and the barbed wire tattoo quivered.

"When did it happen?" Stride asked.

"Last month."

"Here?"

She nodded.

"How did he get in?"

"He came up a back stairway."

"I'd like to have a forensics team go over the apartment for trace evidence."

"There's no DNA. I cleaned up."

"There could still be hair, fingerprints, residue."

"Look, he wore gloves and a stocking cap. Trust me, he didn't leave anything behind. I'd just like to move on."

"Do you have any idea who it was?"

"No, and I don't want to know."

Stride leaned forward and balanced his arms on his knees. "Why don't you want to report this?"

"Are you kidding? If a pretzel stick like Tanjy got raped all over again in the media, imagine what they'd do to a girl like me. I know exactly what kind of jokes people would tell. They're not sure if they can charge him with rape. Is having sex with a farm animal a crime?"

"No one would say that."

"Sure they would."

"Did you tell anyone after it happened?"

She nodded. "I told Sonia at the dress shop."

"Not Maggie?"

"Especially not Maggie."

"Why? You said the two of you were friends."

"She and I haven't talked in a while," Katrina said. "Plus, she's a cop."

Stride thought about what Tony Wells had said. This perpetrator picks women who are sexually vulnerable. "There's something else, isn't there?" he asked.

"What do you mean?"

"I mean, this guy doesn't choose his victims by accident. He picks women who have something to hide."

"There are other victims?" Katrina asked.

"Yes, and they learned their lesson from Tanjy, just like you did. Don't report this if you want to keep your secret."

Katrina shoved herself out of her chair.

She peeked through the blinds into the darkness and then turned back and folded her arms. She studied Stride. "If I tell you, the whole world will know."

"Not necessarily, but I can't promise you anything."

Katrina's lip bulged out in defiance. "What I do in my private life is my own damn business."

"I understand."

"You're right," she said finally. "I didn't report the assault, because there were some things about me that would have come out. Embarrassing things."

Stride waited.

"I was an alpha girl," Katrina continued.

"What's that?"

She hesitated and sat down on the other end of the futon sofa. "I'm not sure I should say anything. If you don't know what it is, it means you don't know about the club. I could cause problems for a lot of people."

"Katrina, you were raped."

"I know."

"Tell me what this is about. If it's something illegal—"

She shook her head. "It's not illegal. At least, I don't think it is. Immoral, maybe. I was part of a sex club in town. I was the alpha girl for the night."

Stride thought about his brief time in Las Vegas, which was a city that made a living on sex. Your basest desires were advertised on taxicab posters and hawked on the sidewalks. The only difference between Las Vegas and anywhere else was that Vegas didn't hide its lust. The city didn't invent sin; it imported it. All the people, all the desires, came to the desert from somewhere else. From places like Duluth.

"How did you get involved with this club?"

"Sonia recruited me."

Stride wasn't surprised that Sonia Bezac's name popped up in the middle of this. "She's a member?"

"She and Delmar started the club. It takes place at their house. There's a downstairs room she calls the temple."

"How many people are involved?"

"I'm not sure. There were a dozen or more people there when I was the alpha girl. Maybe seven or eight men and a few women, too."

"What's an alpha girl?"

Katrina squirmed on the sofa. "Look, I wasn't ashamed of it. I did it because I'm a wild chick, and I like to experiment. I'm not hung up about sex. But it's different when you have to start telling people about it."

"I'm not judging you."

"Yeah, well, we'll see about that. There's a different alpha girl each time. We're basically there to have sex with anyone who wants us. Sometimes it's men who like to do it in front of other people. Sometimes it's wives whose husbands like to see them with other women. Sometimes it's the husband and wife together at the same time. There are also couples who simply like to see public sex and make out or masturbate while they watch us."

"That all sounds like an invitation to STDs."

"Condoms are the rule. Nobody goes bareback. Even the husbands and wives who have sex with each other have to use condoms while they're there."

"I'm having trouble understanding why you would want to do this to yourself," he said, choosing his words carefully.

"But you're not judging me, right? Ha. Hey, we're swingers, so what. I told you that most people wouldn't get it. That's why it's a secret. That's why I don't advertise it, and neither does anyone else."

"It feels dehumanizing to me, not erotic."

"Well, that's you. Me, I loved it. I was never more turned on in my life than I was that night. You have no idea how a big girl like me struggles with body image. But that night, every man wanted me. A bunch of women, too. I've never felt more desirable."

Stride wanted to get the facts and get out. "When was this?"

"Last month. December."

"How often does the club meet?"

"I'm not sure. Once a month, maybe."

"Do you think the rapist knew about the club?"

"Hell, he came after me the day after the party. It's not like that could be a coincidence, right?"

"Could it have been someone who was at the sex party with you?"

"I don't know. Maybe. I doubt it."

"Who else was there?"

"I don't know."

"You mean you didn't recognize them?"

"I mean, everyone wears masks. It's part of the game. The anonymity."

"So when you go, you don't know who else is going to be there?"

"No. Other than Sonia and Delmar, of

course." She twitched and pressed her lips together. Her eyes darted to the floor.

"What is it?"

"I did know someone else who was there," she admitted.

"Who?"

"Maggie's husband. Eric. He was easy to spot. Him and his long blond hair."

Stride thought about Maggie. *Do you think I don't have secrets?*

"Did Maggie know about Eric and the club?" he asked, but he already knew what Katrina was going to say.

"Oh, yeah. She knew."

"You're sure?"

"We talked about it before I did it."

Stride shook his head. He couldn't believe any of this.

"What did she tell you?"

"She said I should do whatever I wanted, but we haven't talked since then. I called her after Eric was killed, but she never called me back. I guess I don't blame her."

"Are you telling me that Maggie was *in* the club?" Stride asked, and he could taste horror like sour wine in his mouth.

"Fasten your seat belt, Lieutenant. Maggie was the alpha girl the month before me."

29

Serena hated driving through the winter nights in Minnesota.

It was nearly eleven o'clock, and the northern highway was a long stretch of nothingness. She was an hour from Duluth, in the empty stretch where miles went by between towns. On either side of the road, the evergreens pressed in like dark towers, and the wilderness behind them was a black mass. She was afraid of deer springing out from the woods. There were carcasses on the shoulder every few miles, and when her headlights lit up the median, she could see hoof tracks cutting through the snow. The beasts were out there, tracking her.

She found a country radio station, but the signal came and went. She heard bits and pieces of songs by Miranda Lambert, Alan Jackson, and LeAnn Rimes, and she found herself singing along, making her feel less alone in the car. Country music was one of the things that she and Jonny had in common. You either got it or you didn't. Most people groaned when they heard her playing Terri Clark on the stereo, or when she told them about driving six hours to go to a Sara Evans concert in Des Moines. She didn't bother explaining. If you didn't get tears in your eyes listening to "No Place That Far," you wouldn't understand.

Her cell phone rang on the seat next to her.

"Oh, man, what are you listening to this time?" Maggie asked.

Serena laughed and switched off the radio. Maggie was like Tony Wells, a fan of hard rock and heavy metal.

"That's Garth, you heathen. Say one word against him, and I'll be forced to shave your head."

"Jeez, one innocent remark, and you

country music fans go all shotguns and hound dogs on me." She added, "Where are you?"

"I'm heading north on Thirty-five. I'm just about to Finlayson."

"Watch out for deer."

"I'm trying to."

"Have you talked to Stride?"

"Not tonight. I tried earlier, but I got his voice mail."

"He wants the three of us to get together tomorrow," Maggie told her. "He thinks he knows how some of the pieces connect."

"Do you know what he's got?"

Maggie's voice was flat. "Yeah, I did something stupid. I should have told him about it myself. I didn't think there was any connection to what happened to me, but I guess I was kidding myself."

Serena let the silent air drag on, waiting for Maggie to continue. She didn't. "You want to tell me about it?"

"I'll let him do it. I feel like enough of an idiot already."

"Whatever you want, kiddo. You want to hear what I found at the Ordway?"

"Sure."

Serena filled her in about Eric's visit to the

theater and the sudden decision by Helen Danning to skip town the day after Eric's murder. "I checked the restaurant where you said Eric had dinner. The waiter recognized Helen Danning. He saw the two of them together."

"Did he hear what they were talking about?"

"Whatever it was, Helen wasn't happy. She left halfway through the meal."

"And now she's gone."

"Seriously gone," Serena said. "No forwarding address. I sweet-talked the building manager, and he let me take a look at her apartment. She left behind her furniture, but she took everything else she could cram into her car. I swiped a coffee mug from her counter so we could run it for prints."

"You did what?"

"I swiped a coffee mug. Why?"

Maggie was silent.

"You there?" Serena asked.

"Yeah. Yeah. Something didn't feel right for a second there, like I had forgotten something important. I almost had my finger on it, but it's gone now. What was this stuff about a blog?"

"Eric apparently found Helen through

some blog she was running. Lady something. Does that ring a bell?"

"Not with me. The cops took Eric's computers, so Guppo might be able to pull a
record of sites he visited. I'll see what I can
find online."

"Any guesses on how Helen fits into this?"
Serena asked.

"I think Eric told her something that
scared the shit out of her. When he died, she
ran."

"Or maybe she told him something."

"That's a good point. I'll see you tomorrow.
Drive carefully."

Serena hung up, and she was back in the
cocoon of the quiet car. In the rearview mirror,
about a half mile behind her, she noticed
headlights. The vehicle matched her speed,
and she wondered if he was skating in her
wake. She did that herself sometimes on long
drives at night, shadowing a semi in front of
her and letting it clear a path by killing off the
deer. Right now, though, she didn't like the
idea that there were just the two of them on
the highway.

Her cell phone rang again, and she
jumped at the noise. She assumed it was
Maggie calling back. Or Jonny. It wasn't.

"Hello, Serena."

It took her a moment to recognize the voice, which awakened a shapeless fear inside her. It was the blackmailer she had met at midnight in the cemetery.

"You're out late," he told her.

"What do you want?"

She was certain it was him in the other car.

"In about a mile, you'll come to a rest stop. Take the exit and park."

"Why should I?"

"I have something for you. Something you'll find very interesting."

"What is it?"

"Take the exit and park."

He ended the call.

Serena had to make a snap decision. The exit to the rest stop was practically on top of her. She swung the wheel, braked sharply, and steered in among the trees. The rest stop was closed for the season; the road was slippery and snow-covered. She carved tracks as she went. She kept an eye on her mirror and was surprised to see the headlights of the other car pass by on the highway without stopping.

She got out of her car and stepped down into six inches of powdery snow. She reached back inside and turned off the lights, wanting it dark, not wanting to paint herself as a target. She didn't trust this man and wanted her gun in her hand. She went immediately to the trunk, opened it, and retrieved her Glock. Its heft comforted her. She walked away from the car and swung slowly around in a circle, pointing the gun in front of her. Fir trees swayed overhead, cradling snow in their outstretched branches. They looked like faceless monsters. As the wind blew, making a fearsome hiss, it sent a cold, silvery mist down from the trees into her face.

The rest stop itself was dark. There were a few other blurry tire tracks in the parking lot from drivers who had ignored the closed sign, like her, and come inside to piss or sleep. None of the tracks was fresh. She stood alone in the middle of the blanket of snow, dwarfed by the forest, feeling both invisible and exposed at the same time. The wind blinded her senses. Where was he?

Back in the car, her phone rang again. She ran for it.

"Where are you?" she asked.

"Close by."

"Are you too scared to let me see you?"

He laughed. "I know you have your gun in your hand."

Serena wheeled around and scanned the forest. She tried to find movements or shadows in the dark, but she saw only the great trees towering over her. She felt small.

"I'm leaving," she said.

She returned to her car, got in, and locked the doors behind her. She started the engine.

"I told you, I have something for you," he said.

"What is it?"

"Look in the glove compartment."

He had been in her car. "What's in there?"

"Dan's secret," he said. "Tell him I want one hundred thousand dollars this time."

"You're crazy. Nothing is worth that much."

"You'd be surprised what people will do to hide their sins."

"When do you want it?"

"Soon. I'll let you know."

She looked at her phone. She was offline.

She sped out of the rest stop, her wheels spinning in the snow. The dark highway felt like a friend compared to the cloister where she had stopped. A truck passed on the interstate, and she accelerated to catch it and fell in behind. Let it scare off the deer. Let it crush them. Even so, in the median, she saw more tracks of hoofprints, tiny and persistent, as if they were running to catch her.

She waited until she was in the heart of the city, and the woods were miles behind her, before she pulled over and looked in the glove compartment. It was after midnight. There was a slim white envelope inside that hadn't been there before. She turned on the dome light in the car and opened the envelope. A photograph was inside.

The picture was taken at night. The skin of the two people in the photograph glowed unnaturally. It took Serena a moment to figure out what she was looking at. She saw mocha-colored skin, long hair, and realized when she studied their profiles that one of the people was Tanjy Powell. She was naked. Outside, in a park. Her hands were tied to a fence, and in the blurry darkness behind her, Serena could make out railway cars. She was crying out. Or maybe she was moaning. She couldn't tell.

A man was behind Tanjy. He had a long knife poised at her throat, and his pants were at his ankles, revealing an obscene white ass. He was buried inside her. It was Dan Erickson.

30

Serena parked in Canal Park in the shadow of the lift bridge. Home was just three miles away, but she wasn't ready to go there yet. She sat for a long time, staring at the photograph and feeling trapped. Whoever the blackmailer was, he was enjoying the game. He could have put the photograph directly in Dan's hands and left Serena in the dark, but instead, he wanted her to be caught in the middle.

She needed to decide what to tell Jonny. If she kept the photo to herself, she ran the risk of derailing an investigation into rape and murder. This wasn't something she could put in the box, for Jonny to pretend he didn't know. If she told him, the only thing he could do was run with it. That would be the end of Dan's career.

Did the photograph show Dan raping Tanjy, or was this consensual sex between twisted lovers? Whatever the truth was, the question in Serena's mind was how far Dan would go to hide the secret. Would he kill Tanjy to keep her quiet? If he did, how did Eric fit into the puzzle?

Then there was Helen Danning at the Ordway. The coincidence of her leaving town the day after Eric's murder was too strong to ignore.

Serena put the photograph back in the glove compartment. She knew she couldn't involve Jonny yet. She had to confront Dan first and interrogate him.

She also thought about the man in shadows. The blackmailer who was tormenting Dan. He seemed to know all the secrets, all the things that people would do anything to protect. He pulled a string, and the city unraveled. Who was he, and how did he know so much about the private world of everyone around him?

At the rest stop, he knew she had a gun

in her hand. He had to be hiding nearby, but there was no other car around her and no way he could have positioned himself so quickly. He had to have waited somewhere else, maybe at the rest stop on the opposite side of the highway, and then walked across the road to scout out a place to watch her.

That meant he knew she was coming. He knew where she was.

She got out of the car with a sudden realization. The ground was cold and wet, but she got down on her knees and hunted under the chassis. When she couldn't see, she retrieved a flashlight from the trunk and slid beneath the frame of the car. Her skin became blackened with grease. Fifteen minutes later, she found the small box attached magnetically to the interior side of the wheel well. She yanked it off and stood up and studied it in her dirty palm. A silver antenna poked out of one corner. She recognized the unit, because she had used it herself in her own work.

It was a GPS locating device. He had been tracking her everywhere she went.

Serena took the box to the side of the

canal and dropped it into the cold, sluggish water.

Jonny was still awake when she got in. He sat in a chair in front of the fireplace with a measure of scotch poured in a shot glass. He rarely drank. Serena was an alcoholic, so they didn't keep much liquor in the house. A dusty bottle of Oban was in the back of a cabinet in the kitchen, and she had only seen him pour from it twice. Once was on the anniversary of Cindy's death. The second time was when Maggie told him about her third miscarriage.

Her clothes were wet and dirty. He eyed her as she washed the grease off her hands and then stripped down to her panties and pulled a white T-shirt over her head. She sat down on the floor beside the recliner, laid her head casually on his thigh, and watched the flames dance.

"You okay?" he asked.

"Sure."

"You're late getting back."

"I had trouble with the car."

"Uh-huh."

She knew he didn't believe her.

"What about that word you put in the box?" he continued. "Tell me more about this blackmailer."

"I can't say anything more," she said. "Not yet."

"I'd like to know what's going on with Dan."

"You know I can't tell you that."

She was glad that he didn't push her.

"You saw Nicole?" he asked.

"Yes, you were right. She's grasping at straws."

"How did she look?"

"Old."

"I'm sorry to hear it."

She told him about Helen Danning.

"I'll have Guppo run her through the system," Stride said. "Maybe she has relatives or friends who can help us find her."

"Maggie called me. She said you found something."

He nodded. "Another rape victim."

Serena lifted her head and brushed her hair back. "Who?"

"Katrina Kuli. She owns a coffee shop on Superior, not far from Silk."

"Does she have a connection to Maggie?"

"Oh, yeah."

He downed the Oban in a single shot and didn't say anything. Serena came around in front of him and leaned on his knees. "What is it?" she asked.

"Maggie was in a sex club." He recited the details without any expression on his face.

Serena sat back, and her eyes widened. "Wow."

"That's not the Maggie I know," Stride said.

"Have you talked to her about it?"

"Not yet."

"I think you should."

"I want to talk to Sonia first and find out more about this so-called club. Like whether Tanjy was involved, too. I'm betting they were all 'alpha girls,' and that's what ties the assaults together."

She heard the disappointment and disbelief rippling through his voice. "Since when do you get all judgmental on me? You always tell me you don't care what anyone else does behind closed doors."

"This is Maggie," he said.

"Okay, I know, it's like finding out your daughter's not a virgin anymore."

"Funny."

"I'm sorry. Look, sex with strangers isn't my thing, but what Maggie does with her body is her business, not mine. And not yours, either."

"I know that."

Serena frowned. "Do you? You've spent the last ten years trying to pretend that Maggie has no sexuality at all. She's a complex, pretty, erotic, troubled, funny, exasperating woman. Sometimes I get nervous that you'll wake up and realize all that and find yourself attracted to her."

"You don't have to worry about me and Maggie."

"No?" She wondered how honest she could be. "You know, when the three of us are together, I feel like I'm the third wheel sometimes, not her."

He was obviously shocked. "I had no idea you felt that way."

"Women can be tough and neurotic at the same time, Jonny."

"I thought you two were friends."

"We are, but don't think we're not rivals, too."

"There's no rivalry," he told her. "It's you and me. Period."

"I'm glad to hear you say that, but it's not that simple, is it?"

"What do you mean?"

"I mean that the only way you're going to make it through this case is to see Maggie as a woman, not as a partner. That's the only way any of this will ever make sense to you. Maybe you'll like it, maybe you won't, but everything will be different."

"I'm just trying to understand how she could do what she did," he said.

Serena stood up. "Maggie is the only one who can explain it to you. Just remember that sometimes you're better off not knowing the truth about your friends."

She went to bed and left him sitting in front of the fire.

31

Stride sat in his Bronco opposite Sonia Bezac's house. His window was open, and he was in a foul mood. He held a cigarette outside, letting the wind carry the smoke behind him. It was almost nine in the morning. The street was straight out of Norman Rockwell, with Tudor homes sitting on comfortable lots. The median was landscaped with evergreen trees spaced to break up the view from one side to the other. Snow dotted the roofs. It was a mature neighborhood of forty-something couples and families, less than a mile from Hunters Park and UMD, a quiet enclave of women who did Pilates and walked golden retrievers and men who drank brandy and pretended to be their fathers.

He wondered if the neighbors knew about the sex club. He didn't think so. The people next door probably thought Sonia and Delmar hosted elegant dinner parties behind drawn curtains and would have been appalled to find out what was really going on. Appalled. Curious. Excited. Angry that they weren't invited.

Sonia's husband Delmar, the urologist, emerged from the front door, wearing a gray suit and a dressy wool coat. He was several inches shorter than Sonia and considerably wider. The wind mussed the comb-over across his bald pate. He patted his hair down and got behind the wheel of a new, black Mercedes sedan.

Penises paid well.

Delmar roared off down the hill. Stride stubbed out his cigarette, got out of his Bronco, and crossed to the median. The front door opened again, and Sonia came out. He felt a stir of nostalgia, seeing her. It took him back to a time when his body was young and hormone-filled, like a showroom car itching for the highway. In her forties,

Sonia still carried an aura of sex. Her red hair blew like a tornado. She was tall and took quick, careful steps in her heels down the icy brick walkway. Her coat was open, and he saw a forest-green silk blouse and black skirt.

He crossed the rest of the street, and she melted, too, just a little, when she saw him. There was a softness in her face that came and went quickly. She realized he wasn't smiling.

"Hello again," she said.

"I need to talk to you, Sonia. Can we go inside?"

"I'm late. I need to open the shop. It's mine now, you know."

"This won't wait."

Sonia crossed her arms. "Maybe I watch too much television, but I don't really have to talk to you at all, do I? I can just get in my car and go."

"Sure. I'll just talk to the newspapers instead."

"About what?"

He leaned close to her and whispered. He smelled jasmine perfume. "Alpha girls."

Sonia's face, already pale, went bone-white. "All right."

She led him back to the house. Inside, she took off her coat and showed him to the living room. He took a seat on a lemon-colored sofa, which was firm and didn't give under his weight. The room was modern and expensive. An oil painting on the wall showed what looked to him like squiggles of red and blue paint. The coffee table was chrome and glass. He saw an abstract metal sculpture of a nude near the fireplace.

Sonia kicked off her heels and sat in an armchair across from him. She grabbed a pack of cigarettes. "It's okay to smoke, if you'd like." She lit one up and blew the smoke toward the ceiling fan.

"I've had my one for the morning."

"What willpower." She put a stocking-clad foot on the ottoman. Her leg was long and slender. "The club meets downstairs, if you're wondering."

"I wasn't."

"So what, do you and Serena want to join? We'd love to have you." She smiled.

"No, thanks."

"It's not a coven, for Christ's sake. Nobody gets hurt."

"I think a rapist is targeting your club."

Her smile vanished. "That's not funny."

"No, it's not. You know what happened to Katrina, don't you?"

"Yes, but what makes you think that had anything to do with the club?"

"Katrina was assaulted *one day* after the last party. Did you think that was just a coincidence?"

Sonia jabbed her cigarette at him. "I know every man who was there. It couldn't have been any of them. So yes, I thought it was just a coincidence. Or even—"

"Even what?"

"I even thought Katrina might have made it up. You know, like Tanjy did. I thought she might be feeling guilty about what she did at the club. It happens."

"It wasn't just Katrina," Stride told her. "Another alpha girl was assaulted."

Sonia closed her eyes. "Son of a bitch," she murmured. "Who?"

"I can't say."

"Are you sure she was in the club?"

"I'm sure."

"Is this going to become public?"

"Very likely."

"Shit, shit, shit." She shook her head. "Do you have any idea what this is going to do to us?"

"Try thinking about the women who were brutalized, Sonia."

"Yes, of course, I know. I just can't believe this could involve the club. We are *very* careful about who gets in."

"What about Tanjy? Was she an alpha girl?" Stride asked.

"No. I put out a couple feelers with her, but she wasn't interested."

"Tanjy had no connection at all to the club?"

"None. Are you telling me she really *was* raped? Look, that means there must be some other connection. Tanjy didn't know a thing about the club."

"Don't get carried away. Two of your alpha girls were assaulted. That's not a coincidence." He added, "Tell me how this all works, Sonia. How you get your members. How often people meet. What happens."

Sonia put her cigarette in a turquoise clamshell ashtray. "I'm not sure I should be telling you any of this."

"Every woman in the club may be in danger, Sonia. Including you."

"Even so, it might be better if I talked to a lawyer first."

"Go ahead, but then it all comes out,"

Stride said. "Do you want me to get a subpoena? Do you really want all this in a filing with the court? We're just getting started with the information I need."

Sonia leaned her head back and stared at the ceiling. Her neck was slim, like a swan's. "Just between us?" she asked.

"For now."

"All right," she said with obvious reluctance. "We have about twenty members. Mostly couples, but some singles, too. No one gets in without a personal invitation from me and Delmar. Referrals only. We do background checks on everyone before letting them in."

"Have you ever had to ask anyone to leave? Someone who behaved inappropriately?"

She nodded. "Once we had a couple who declined to wear condoms when having sex with each other at the club. I'm very, very strict about that. We didn't invite them back. Another time we had a man who slapped an alpha girl. Two of the men escorted him out immediately."

"What was his name?"

"Wilson Brunt. I don't think you'll find that he was involved, though. He was transferred out of state at least six months ago. He's in Oregon now."

Stride wrote his name down. "How long has the club been going on?"

"About a year. It was my idea."

"Big surprise."

"Oh, come on, Jonathan, don't you get bored sometimes?" Sonia waved her hand around at the living room, as if she despised her suburban surroundings. "We're in our forties. Old age is knocking on the door. You think this red hair doesn't come out of a bottle now? You think Delmar's equipment just springs to life when I take off my clothes? Tick tick tick, that's the fucking mortality clock staring us both in the face. You can go buy a convertible to deal with your midlife crisis. I wanted something else."

Stride ignored her. "How often do you meet?"

"Usually about once a month. Sometimes more."

"Does any money change hands?"

"No!"

"What about drugs or illegal substances?"

"Absolutely not. No way." Her eyes danced nervously, and he figured she was lying.

"Tell me about the alpha girls."

Sonia shrugged. "I was the first. I took on six men and three women in one night. That's still the record."

"Good for you," he said flatly. Their eyes met. Sonia knew what he thought and didn't care.

"When we started, the only alpha girls were wives of members," she continued, "but a few times, we've had women who were interested in being alpha girls for the night."

"How do they find out about it?"

"Through members. We're all very discreet. We only approach a woman if we have reason to believe she's liberated sexually, and even then, we take it slow. We don't share any details about the club itself until the woman expresses interest. An outside alpha girl never knows the names of members. It's all anonymous."

"You mean the masks?"

Sonia frowned. "You know about that?"

Stride didn't say anything.

"Yes, we wear masks. It's partly to protect identities, but frankly, we've heard from the women that they like it. There's an extra kick, an extra thrill, when they don't see the faces."

"What actually happens?"

"Why not join us and see?" Sonia asked.

"Don't be cute."

"I'm not. You're always welcome. I asked Maggie if you might be interested, but she said you'd sooner trim your nose hair with a razor blade." She realized what she had done and said, "Shit. I never use names. It's just that she—"

"Never mind. I know all about it."

"Oh my God, did something happen to Maggie?"

Stride's face was stone.

"Oh shit, I'm so sorry," Sonia said. "I can't believe this. She didn't come back after she was the alpha girl, and I just thought she was freaked-out by the experience."

"You brought it up. Tell me about Maggie and Eric."

Sonia shook her head. "This is just fucking terrible." She reclaimed her cigarette, and it wobbled between her fingers. "Eric was involved from the beginning. The first outside alpha girl was an athlete from the Czech Republic who was in town about her Olympic equipment."

"Was Maggie involved from the beginning, too?"

He realized he was holding his breath, not wanting to hear the answer.

"No, she was only here twice. The first time, she and Eric were behind the wall."

"What does that mean?"

Sonia hesitated. "One wall of the temple is all mirrors. There's a small bedroom behind the middle section where someone can watch. Eric wanted Maggie to see what the club was like."

"So no one knew they were there?"

"Just me. Afterward, Eric persuaded Maggie to be the alpha girl at the next meeting."

"I'd love to know how he did that," Stride said, half to himself.

"Maybe she saw it as payback for all of Eric's affairs. He had to stand there and watch."

"Skip the details, what happened afterward?"

"I did her, too, you know."

"I said, *skip the details*," he snapped. His voice was loud.

Sonia looked pleased to have riled him. "Maggie didn't come to the next party, but Eric did. Katrina was the alpha girl. That was the last time for Eric. He told me later he was giving it up for Maggie's sake."

"When is the next party?" he asked.

"Tomorrow."

Tomorrow, Stride thought. They didn't have much time, but they also had a new chance to lure the rapist out of his cave.

"Who's the alpha girl?"

Sonia hesitated again, and Stride said, "Just tell me, and skip the bullshit, Sonia. I have plenty of probable cause for a warrant."

"Her name is Kathy Lassiter. She's a partner with a Twin Cities law firm. She has a house on the North Shore. She's been to several parties before, but not as the alpha girl."

"Have you ever heard of a woman named Helen Danning? Was she in the club, or was she an alpha girl?"

"No, I've never heard of her."

"All right, let's talk about how this information is getting out. How could someone find out that a woman was an alpha girl in the club?"

"I don't see how they could," Sonia protested. "All the alpha girls not only sign a form releasing us from legal liability, they also sign a nondisclosure agreement."

"You're kidding."

"No way. We don't want people having an attack of the guilts and suing us, and we don't want loose lips spreading this around all over the city. Members sign similar documents, too, when they join. Plus a code of conduct."

"Good luck litigating those contracts."

Sonia smiled. "Well, I don't think we'd take anyone to court, but signing the docs makes people realize how serious we are about confidentiality and responsible behavior."

Stride tried not to laugh at the irony. "Even so, everyone who's there on a given night knows who the alpha girl is."

"Not necessarily. We don't give people a name if the alpha girl is an outsider. They'd have to know her or recognize her from outside the club."

"Or follow her."

"I suppose so."

"Do you keep records of members and who attends individual parties?"

Sonia nodded. "Absolutely. I keep that on our home computer upstairs. We don't want any legal hassles over the club, so we're fanatical about records, contracts, nondisclosure agreements, background checks, etcetera. We keep all that stuff. No one has ever challenged us, but we're ready if they do."

"How secure is your computer? Do you have a wireless network?"

"Are you kidding? Not a chance."

"How about an Internet connection?"

"Well, yes, but it's totally secure. I had Byte Patrol install the most sophisticated firewall available. It's about as hacker-proof as you can get. Believe me, no one got the information out of our computer."

"That leaves the members," Stride said.

Sonia frowned. "I told you, we vet them."

"I'm going to need names."

"Oh, shit, there's got to be another way."

"No, we have to interview them all."

"Look, you said two alpha girls were assaulted," Sonia argued. "We don't have the same members at every party. Different people come, depending on their schedules. I can get you the names of men who were at both parties with those women, and that should narrow it down."

Stride nodded. "I'll start there, but give me the whole list. All the members, and all the participants at every party. Include the alpha girls, too. I'll need to talk to all of them, because I need to find out if anyone else was assaulted." When Sonia hesitated, he added, "I'm not kidding. I'll go to court, and I'll splash this all over the papers if I have to."

Sonia got out of the chair. "It'll take me a few minutes," she said in a pinched voice.

"I've got time."

Ten minutes later, Sonia came back with a sheaf of papers in her hand.

"This is everything. Look, I'm begging you, be discreet. Delmar will kill me if this gets out."

"No promises, Sonia."

He found the lists for the two parties where Maggie and Katrina were alpha girls, and it took him only a few seconds to compare the names to see who had been at both events. Other than Sonia's husband, Delmar, there were only four men who were present both times.

Three names he didn't know.

The fourth was Tanjy's ex-boyfriend. Mitchell Brandt.

32

Serena didn't have the same feeling of being watched as she climbed the steps of the courthouse. She hoped that destroying the GPS device had given her a temporary escape from the blackmailer's prying eyes.

The photograph he had given her was now in a large manila envelope addressed to Dan Erickson, marked personal and confidential. She wasn't sure if she was doing the right thing by keeping Jonny in the dark, but she didn't see any alternatives. She couldn't destroy Dan's life if he was guilty of nothing more than kinky sex practices. The trouble was that Tanjy was dead. A photo like this would vault Dan to the top of the suspect list, if only because he would do anything to keep it hidden. Even so, Dan was a client. He was paying her. Until she knew something different, she couldn't expose him.

In Dan's office, Serena handed the envelope to the receptionist and told her to take it inside. A minute later, she came back and told Serena to go in. Serena closed the office door behind her and clicked the lock in place. Dan was standing behind his mahogany desk, with the photograph in his hand. His other fist was clenched. He took the envelopes and photo to a crosscut shredder on the wall and fed them all in. The machine whirred as it diced the evidence. He checked the bin to make sure the papers had been cut into confetti, then whirled around on Serena.

"Where the fuck did you get that? What are you trying to do to me?"

Serena held up her hands. "Blackmail is an ugly business. I told you it was going to get worse."

"*He* gave this to you?"

She nodded.

"How did he get it?"

"You'd know that better than me."

"This is a fucking disaster. You realize that, don't you? *A disaster*. What does he want?"

"One hundred thousand dollars."

"Son of a bitch." He pointed an accusing finger at her. "Are the two of you in this together? Are you gaming me?"

Serena came closer and slapped his hand away. "Don't insult me. You're lucky I didn't turn this over to Jonny instead of coming here. And I'm *going* to tell Jonny all about it unless you can convince me right now that you had nothing to do with Tanjy's murder."

"That's crazy."

"Then tell me about you and Tanjy. Is the photo legit? Is that you and her together?"

Dan shoved his hand back roughly through his blond hair. "Yeah."

"Did you rape her?"

"Hell, no. Rape was her fantasy, remember? This was just a game. We went down there in the middle of the night, and we took pictures."

"Do I have to tell you how incredibly stupid that was?"

His cheeks were tomato-red with fury. "No, I knew the risks, but Tanjy was worth it."

Serena didn't need details. "How did you and she hook up?"

"I met her in the dress shop. We had chemistry."

"Did Lauren know?"

Dan snorted. "No one knew."

"Well, someone did. You could have destroyed your career. You still might."

"That's why I broke it off. I ended it months ago."

"Despite the great sex?"

Dan went to a cabinet and opened the bottom door, revealing a small refrigerator. He extracted a bottle of Bombay gin from the freezer, filled a lowball glass with ice, and took a long drink. He extended the bottle to Serena, and she shook her head. "The whole fake rape thing was a nightmare," he said. "I couldn't afford to keep the affair going, not after all her rape fantasies came to light in the press."

"Weren't you afraid she'd go public about your affair after you dumped her?"

"Yeah, but she didn't have much credibility left. No one would have believed her."

"Except she obviously had pictures."

Dan shook his head. "I went to her place. I had a key. I deleted all the pictures from her digital camera and from the hard drive."

"Shit, Dan, do you know how easy it is to recover deleted files?"

"Not for Tanjy. She was beautiful, but she was hopeless about technology. She had to have someone show her how to do everything. Believe me, she couldn't have found those files again."

"Someone did."

Dan gestured angrily, and gin slopped over the side of the crystal. "No one knew the pictures were there! She and I were the only ones who knew about that night in the park."

Serena shook her head. "Wrong."

"What the hell are you talking about?"

"Tanjy really was raped. It happened in Grassy Point Park, just like in that photograph. Do you think that's a coincidence?"

"Oh, bullshit," Dan insisted. "The rape story was a lie. Tanjy made it up."

"Jonny already knows about two other victims. We think Eric was helping Tanjy find out who assaulted her. That's what got both of them killed."

"The rape was a *fantasy*," Dan insisted.

"Did Tanjy tell you that?"

He hesitated. "No. She always swore it really happened."

"You should have listened to her."

"I just wanted to get her away from me. I

was scared to death the media was going to find out about us."

Serena nodded. "You know that if I tell Jonny about you and Tanjy, he'll think you're good for both murders."

"I didn't kill anyone. I didn't rape anyone, either."

"Where were you on the Monday night that Tanjy disappeared?" Serena asked.

"I was in Saint Paul. I was telling the attorney general about my move to Washington. I stayed overnight."

"Where?"

"The Saint Paul Hotel."

"Do you know a woman named Helen Danning?" she asked.

"No."

"She worked at the Ordway as an usher. Right across the park from your hotel. She's disappeared. Eric saw her shortly before he was killed."

"I don't know her."

Serena watched him. He looked away and finished his gin.

"Do you have any idea who's doing this to you?" she asked.

"I wish I did. I'd kick his ass."

"I don't think this is someone you want to

mess with, Dan. When did he first contact you?"

"Last Tuesday."

"*Tuesday?* That was the day after Tanjy disappeared. You didn't think that was significant?"

"I didn't *know* she had disappeared at that point."

"You know what that means. This guy may have raped and killed Tanjy himself. And set you up to take the fall."

"This can't become public," Dan said.

"It's going to come out sooner or later."

"Are you going to tell Stride?"

Serena hesitated. She had to make a judgment about Dan's credibility, which was like guessing what was in the pockets of a magician. "Not right now."

Dan looked relieved.

"But that's only until we're sure what's going on," Serena added. "As soon as I have any hard evidence, I have to tell Jonny. If this guy really is involved in rape and murder, he's got to be stopped, even if it means the truth about you and Tanjy coming out."

"I can't believe this," he said.

"Believe it. You're in big trouble."

33

Maggie typed the e-mail on her laptop:

> HD. If this is you, we need to talk. I think you
> know what happened to my husband after
> he found you. I think that's why you left. I
> need your help. Please contact me. M.

She clicked the Send button, and the
e-mail disappeared. The handle of the blogger she had found was "The Lady in Me."
The contents of the blog had been stripped,
but Maggie had located a posting on
another blog, in which a woman who signed
herself as "The Lady in Me" mentioned see-

ing the musical *Les Miserables* at least sixty times as an usher at the Ordway Theater. It had to be Helen Danning. Before leaving town, she had wiped her past clean, deleting every posting and every response on her blog, but there was still a link to send electronic mail. Maggie didn't know if the e-mail link was live, or if Helen would ever check it, but she tried anyway.

She wore half-glasses pushed down her small nose. Her bare feet dangled off the recliner. She had a plastic bottle of Diet Coke on one side of her and a half-eaten bag of sour cream and cheddar potato chips on the other. The fingertips on her right hand were orange, and she had to lick them before she typed. She clicked through pages of search results on the name Helen Danning, but she was no closer to finding out who she was, or why Eric had gone to so much trouble to find her.

Headlights cut across the outside windows as Stride's Bronco pulled into the driveway. A couple of minutes later, she heard the door open and his heavy footsteps in the kitchen. She called out, "I'm in here."

It was his house. Maggie had a key. After Cindy died, she used Stride's house as a sort of second home, dropping in with doughnuts and coffee and bringing over movies. Sometimes Stride joined her, sometimes he didn't. That was the kind of casual relationship they had. She had pulled back during Stride's second marriage, but when he and Serena returned from Las Vegas and bought a place out on the Point again, Maggie gradually resumed her old ways. Neither of them complained about it. Most of the time, they spent evenings talking about open cases anyway, so it was easier for her to be here.

She knew that she was using his place as an escape to get away from Eric. And, despite Serena, to be close to Stride.

She didn't look up as Stride came into the living room. She was in his chair. "Chip?" she asked, holding up the bag.

"No thanks." He added, "Does Abel know you're here?"

"No, Guppo had the job of babysitting me tonight. I promised to bring him a bag of tacos when I came back, and he looked the other way."

"He's a credit to the badge," Stride said.

"Yeah. I hear that Pete McKay lost a patrol car."

Stride nodded. "He got a call up to the high school and heard some firecrackers around back. When he came back, his car was gone. Nice."

"Kids are getting smarter than the cops these days."

"Tell me about it."

"I think we should buy McKay a scooter with a siren."

"I'll tell him you said that."

Maggie smiled at their usual banter but knew it wouldn't last. Stride sat down on the brick hearth of the fireplace. He was still wearing his black leather jacket, and he smelled of cold and smoke. Maggie knew what to expect from him.

"Do I get the lecture now, Dad?" She adopted a deep voice and said, "I'm very disappointed in you, young lady."

"Come on, Mags."

"So now you know what your little girl does on weekends," she said.

"I'm not really in a mood to joke about this."

Maggie stripped off her glasses. "Hey, this is still me, okay? I joke about everything. I don't care what you think of me right now, it's still a riot to think about me playing Jenna Jameson in a sex club."

He looked at her in a way that made her feel as if he was seeing her for the first time. His face was drawn and tight.

"Please don't tell me you wore a blond wig," he said.

Maggie laughed. "And one of those cone-shaped bras, too. Like Madonna."

Stride smiled enough that she could see his white teeth showing. Relief bubbled out of her like a fountain.

"I guess you want to know why," she said.

"You don't owe me any explanations. It's your life."

"But you want one anyway."

He shrugged. "Sure, I'd like to know why you did it. I can't pretend I get it, Mags. Not from you."

"Why, because I'm not supposed to have sex? I'm not supposed to enjoy it?"

"That's not what I mean at all."

"Then spit it out. You don't have to sugar-coat things for me."

"Sex is one thing," he said. "This is women spreading their legs for strangers. With fucking gold masks."

"So what does that make me? A whore?"

"No, of course not."

"Then what?"

He looked frustrated. "I just hate the idea of *you* doing something like that."

"Tell me why."

"Because you deserve better. Okay? Because you're something special. Because I don't think a woman could do that unless, on some level, she hated herself, and I don't want to think of you feeling that way."

Maggie stared at the ceiling, not wanting to meet his eyes. "Lately, I have hated myself a little."

"You could have talked to me about it."

"About my marriage falling apart? About my husband cheating on me? About trying to rescue our sex life? I don't think so. Unless you're prepared to go all the way—and I know you're not, you don't need to say it—there are parts of my life I'm never going to share with you."

"So maybe I should just drop this. It's none of my business anyway."

"No, it's not. But since you know about it, I'll tell you anyway, because there really isn't that much to tell. I felt empty and was looking for something to fill the void. I thought it might bring Eric and me closer together, which it didn't do. And, yeah, okay, I was intrigued. For once in my life, I thought, what the hell. It was a mistake, if that's what you want to hear."

"You don't need to say that."

"Well, it's true."

He changed the subject. She was relieved to stop talking about it.

"Did Serena tell you? Katrina was assaulted, too. Right after the last party."

"Yeah, she did. I had no idea. I feel like a shit for not calling her."

"This guy is smart," Stride said. "He's making a bet that women in this sex club won't risk the humiliation of going public."

"When is Sonia's next party?"

"Tomorrow."

"Son of a bitch," Maggie said.

"Exactly. We need to move fast."

They both looked up as the back door opened. It was Serena, carrying a bag of groceries that she deposited on the kitchen counter. She kicked off her heels and joined them, taking a seat on the carpet and crossing her legs. Maggie noticed that she sat close enough to Stride that their clothes touched.

"You two okay?" Serena asked.

Stride nodded without saying anything. Maggie felt him grow colder, as if he were drawing a circle around himself and Serena to keep her out. It bothered her.

"What did I miss?" Serena asked.

"We just had sex," Maggie said. "This is afterglow."

It was a stupid joke. She felt bad when Serena's face soured with discomfort.

"I'm sorry, dumb thing to say," she added.

"Alpha girl humor," Serena murmured.

Ouch. But Maggie knew she deserved it.

She tossed the bag of chips to Serena, who flipped her hair back, took a chip out of the bag, and crunched it in her mouth. Their eyes met. The coolness melted, and they declared a silent truce between them.

"Did you get any more background on Helen Danning?" Serena asked.

Maggie told them about the empty blog page she had discovered for "The Lady in Me." Stride pulled a wrinkled sheet of paper from his jacket pocket.

"Here's what Guppo found," he said. "She's thirty-six years old, born in Florida, moved to Minnesota when she was ten. She went to the U but dropped out in the early 1990s after two years, never graduated. She's worked clerical jobs ever since. She doesn't have a sheet, and there's no record of anyone by her name filing criminal charges. She drives a blue Toyota Corolla, license NKU-167. I did a statewide ATL on it."

"Parents?"

"They retired in Arizona. I haven't been able to reach them. She's got a sister, too, but she's somewhere in Southeast Asia teaching English."

"Is there anything at all that connects her to what's going on?" Serena asked.

Stride shook his head. "Not that I can find."

"I asked Guppo to do me a favor and see if he could track down any cached pages from her blog," Maggie said. "Maybe he'll come up with something that will tell us why Eric was interested in her."

"Let's back up," Stride told them. "Let's go back to the beginning on this. The first incident in the chain, at least as far as we know right now, is Tanjy being raped, right? That was in early November, based on what she told us. I talked to a couple women who were alpha girls before that date. Nothing happened to them."

"I was assaulted about three weeks after Tanjy," Maggie said. "Eric and I argued about reporting it throughout the first two weeks in December. He kept pushing me, I kept saying no."

"Did you talk about what happened to Tanjy?" Serena asked.

"Yeah, Eric thought I should talk to her. I didn't want to do it. Later, Eric must have decided to talk to Tanjy himself. I checked his cell phone records, and he called her for the first time on a Saturday in mid-December. There were several more calls over the next few weeks."

"So we're speculating that Eric somehow found a connection that led him to the rapist," Stride said.

Maggie nodded. "We know that Eric asked Tony about the pathology of a rapist. He told Tony he was going to see someone the night he was killed. He talked to Tanjy two days earlier, and she wound up dead, too. He talked to Helen Danning over the weekend, and after Eric got killed, she left town."

"I don't understand how Helen Danning fits into the puzzle," Stride said. "But we do know there's a predator stalking women in the city, and this guy has latched on to the sex club. There's a new alpha girl, Kathy Lassiter, who's at risk starting tomorrow. If we can catch the rapist and connect the dots, then maybe we can connect him to the two murders, too."

"Except Tanjy wasn't in the sex club," Maggie pointed out.

"Yes, but Mitchell Brandt was in the club, and he was Tanjy's ex-boyfriend. Eric would have known that."

"Mitch?" Maggie asked, surprised.

"You know him?"

"Yeah, a little."

Maggie didn't tell Stride that she remembered him from the sex club. Most of the men in the club were paunchy and short, and she figured that they popped Viagra before the party to get themselves ready. Mitch was different. She remembered a gleam in his eyes and a tiny smile and strong hands and a sensation as smooth as butter. She had the uncomfortable feeling that Stride was reading her mind.

"I'm not saying Mitch is involved," Stride said, "but he connects Tanjy to the sex club."

"Is there anything in his background?" Serena asked.

"Nothing of interest. I called the SEC to see whether there were any complaints about him from clients. They were less than helpful."

"So what's our next step?" Maggie asked.

"We watch the club," Stride said. "Sonia offered to cancel the party tomorrow, but I think that's the last thing we want. This is our chance to flush this guy. We keep the alpha girl under surveillance after the party and hope he moves fast."

"Assuming this woman is willing to be used as bait," Serena said.

"I'll talk to her."

"What about Abel?" Maggie asked. "We can't mount a surveillance operation under the radar screen. He's got to be in the loop."

Stride nodded. "Yeah, it's time to see if we can get Abel on our side."

"There's something else," Serena said. "Don't you think we need someone inside the club?"

There was silence in the room.

"Are you serious?" Stride asked.

"I am. We need to see how people react to the alpha girl. If Mitchell Brandt is the guy, I want to see how he behaves."

Stride shook his head. "I can't send a cop inside something like that."

"It can't be me," Maggie said. "Not with what's going on."

"Okay then," Serena said. "I'll do it."

"No way," Stride said.

"Come on, Jonny. I won't be in the room itself. You said there was a one-way mirror on one of the walls."

Maggie frowned. "That's true."

"I still don't like it," Stride said.

"I'll be alone behind the wall. There's no risk."

"No risk? We don't know who this guy is or how he knows about the club. He could be anywhere."

"Yes, but we have an advantage," Serena said. "This guy doesn't know we're on to him. For once, we're a step ahead."

This guy doesn't know we're on to him.

Less than a mile away, he sat in the frosty solitude of the van. Listening.

Fog made the windows opaque. The shroud of darkness and the woods at the end of the Point made the van largely invisible. The wind gusted off the lake, and every few seconds, the vehicle shuddered on its tires, and the steel walls rattled. It reminded him of sitting in the rear of the patrol car while the hurricane roared closer. Back when he was a prisoner.

As he listened to them plan their stakeout around the club, he grinned at the thought of the trap they were laying. Tomorrow night, all the demons he had been hoarding would finally fly out. Tomorrow night, Serena would be the one walking into a trap.

34

Stride sat in silence in his City Hall office early the next morning. The lights in the rest of the Detective Bureau were dark as he caught up on paperwork and drank coffee. When he heard a cough, he looked up to see Abel Teitscher in his doorway. The older detective wore a brown suit with his hands jammed in his pockets and dusty black shoes. His leathery face looked like an old map of the West, tracking rivers and roads.

"Your message said you wanted to see me," he said.

"I did. Have a seat, Abel."

Teitscher closed the door and sat down in

the chair in front of Stride's desk. His long legs jutted out like a stork's. "You've been pissing in my pool."

Stride didn't bother to argue. "Yeah, you could say that."

"I'm not covering for you, Lieutenant. If you lose your job over this, don't blame me."

"I won't."

Teitscher's face burned. "You cut corners and no one ever calls you on it. If I ignored a conflict of interest the way you have, I'd be out on my ass."

"Could be."

Teitscher leaned across the desk. "What really ticks me off is that you don't show me any respect."

"That's not what I'm about, Abel."

"No? You undercut me, you sabotage me, you put the whole goddamn investigation in jeopardy. Would you do that to anyone else in the Bureau?"

"Look, Abel, it's not you. It's the case. Do you want to listen to what I have to say, or do you want to cut me a new one?"

Teitscher shrugged. He took off his glasses and cleaned them on his tie. "Go ahead."

"I know that the evidence against Maggie

is strong. You've done a good job pulling it together, and no one is ever going to thank you for it. That's the way it goes. What I'm telling you, as a detective and a colleague, is that there's another plausible motive for Eric's murder that has nothing to do with Maggie." He saw Abel about to object, and he raised his hand to stop him. "I'm not telling you to believe it. I'm telling you to keep an open mind."

"You sound like a defense lawyer," Teitscher said.

"Just hear me out."

Teitscher waved his hand and let him continue. Stride told him the whole story, laying out everything he had found. He didn't hold anything back. Maggie's rape. The sex club and the alpha girls. Helen Danning. He took the facts and told him what he now suspected, that somehow the series of rapes in the city had led directly to the murders of Tanjy and Eric.

When he was done, he saw Abel struggling to reconcile the facts with what he had already found. "A sex club?" Abel asked.

"That's right."

"You actually confirmed this? You've got proof?"

"I have names, dates, release forms, everything. It's an A-list of Duluth high society."

Teitscher bared his yellowing incisors. "What's the old expression? The rich are different? Yeah, isn't that a joke. All that money, and this is the kind of sleaze they go in for."

"I feel the same way, but that doesn't really change anything," Stride said.

"So why are you telling me all this now? Why not wait until you crack the case and make me look like a fool?"

"I need your help."

Teitscher frowned. "It doesn't look that way to me."

"The next meeting of the sex club is tonight," Stride explained. "I want your help pulling together a surveillance team. We need to watch who comes and goes, and we need to keep a twenty-four-hour team on the new alpha girl, Kathy Lassiter. If we handle this right, she might just lead us to the rapist. I'm asking you to take charge of the surveillance operation personally."

"What are you going to do?"

"I have to talk to this Lassiter woman and convince her to let us risk her life to catch this guy."

Teitscher scratched his chin. "You haven't convinced me about Maggie yet."

"I understand."

"But I'd be a lousy cop to ignore this, and I'm a damn good cop whatever the hell you think."

"I know you are."

Teitscher stood up. "Okay, I'll get the wheels rolling on the surveillance."

"Thanks, Abel. I think we should keep the details about the sex club and the rapist between you and me for now."

"You going political on me?"

"No, I don't want to tip our hand. The more people who know about this, the easier it is to have a leak."

"All right, fair enough."

Stride watched Teitscher leave. He was glad to have a truce in the war between them and to have his own role in the investigation out in the open. That was the only thing he felt good about. Otherwise, he was filled with anxiety about what lay ahead, as if he were tangled in the sheet of his parachute as the ground streaked closer. He almost wished that Kathy Lassiter would pull the plug, which would cancel the party and thwart Serena's determination to go inside the walls. He was concerned for the safety of both of them.

He was surprised when his phone rang. It was still early. The caller ID was from a 312 area code. Chicago.

"Stride."

"You're an early riser, Lieutenant. I like that."

"Who is this?" Stride asked.

"My name is Philip Proutz. I'm with the Securities and Exchange Commission at our Midwest office in Chicago. I work on compliance investigations."

"I see." Stride was on guard, and Proutz sensed it.

"If you'd like to confirm who I am, you can look up our office number on the Web and call me back through the main switchboard."

"No offense, Mr. Proutz, but I think I will do that."

They were reconnected two minutes later.

"All right, what can I do for you, Mr. Proutz?" Stride asked.

"You contacted our office yesterday, Lieutenant, making inquiries about a broker in Duluth named Mitchell Brandt. I'd be interested in knowing the reason for your request."

"I'm not really in a position to discuss that right now," Stride told him.

"You do realize that if this is in conjunction with Mr. Brandt's securities activities, then the jurisdiction is federal. It's our baby."

Stride hesitated. "It has nothing to do with that."

"Ah." Proutz sounded surprised. "What about a company called Infloron Medical?"

"I've never heard of it. Now you're making *me* curious, Mr. Proutz."

"I understand. I thought we could save each other time, you see, if we were working the same case from different ends. Infloron Medical is a public company in the Twin Cities that produces a drug called Zerax that promotes tissue regeneration in burn victims. The drug was recently approved by the FDA."

"You lost me," Stride said.

"Infloron's stock more than doubled after FDA approval of Zerax last summer. We're looking into some large stock purchases shortly before the FDA ruling was announced. We think Mitchell Brandt may have made substantial trades based on insider information."

35

Serena stood at the windows looking out from Tony's office to the birch forest behind his house. She saw more dotted lines of deer tracks in the snow. They were everywhere, leaving trails for her to follow.

"This is a beautiful spot, Tony," she murmured without looking behind her.

Tony was in his leather chair by the sofa, sipping coffee and waiting as she paced. He didn't push her to talk. He was wearing a brown suit, shined brown shoes, and a brown tie.

"I appreciate your seeing me on such short notice," she added.

"You said it was important."

Serena nodded. She figured if she actually waited here long enough, she would see the deer picking their way through the trees. It had happened before. She had seen deer, possum, rabbits, and even a fox once. The rust-colored animal with its bushy tail was much smaller than she expected.

She turned and went back to the sofa and sat down. She played with her hair. Tony was silent.

"What would happen if you wore something other than brown?" Serena asked.

"My head would explode."

Serena laughed. "Maggie jokes about it, you know."

"She's kidded me about it for ten years."

"Is it supposed to soothe your patients?"

"My patients?" Tony said. "No, it's supposed to soothe me. Brown is my armor. That's a trade secret, by the way, so don't tell anyone."

"Not even Maggie?"

"Especially not Maggie."

Serena drummed her fingers on the arm of the sofa.

"I have to do something tonight that I'm not comfortable with," she said finally.

"Okay."

"I could use some advice on how to handle it."

"Okay."

He never led her. Sometimes it infuriated her, because she wanted him to give her a direction and not feel like the burden to say where they were going was always on her shoulders. That was stupid, of course. It was her therapy session.

"Let's talk about something else first," she said. "It's about Eric."

Tony waited. When he drank coffee, the black mug covered the lower half of his face, and all she saw were his hound dog eyes.

"Did he mention seeing a woman named Helen Danning?"

"No."

"Have you ever treated a woman named Helen Danning?"

"No."

"Well, that was easy," she said. "I'm stalling, have you noticed?"

Tony didn't reply.

"Aren't you supposed to pull this stuff out of me?" she asked him.

"With what? Truth serum?"

"Yeah, yeah, I know." Serena sighed.

"Okay, I'm going to tell you about something that you may or may not already know about from other patients. I realize you wouldn't admit it even if you did. There's a sex club in town. A place where singles and couples go to have sex with each other and with women who act as 'volunteers.'"

"Okay."

"I have to watch the club tonight because of an investigation. I'm not a participant, just an observer."

"How do you feel about that?"

"Nervous," Serena admitted. "Much more so than I've told anyone. I'm afraid I could lose it. If I see a man climbing on top of a stranger, I'm afraid I'm going to have flashbacks of Blue Dog on top of me."

"Are you having them now?" he asked.

"Sometimes."

"Have you lost it yet?"

"No. I'm dealing with it."

"Then why do you think you're going to lose it tonight?"

"This is so much more explicit. It's not like a mental image I can push away. These people are going to be right in front of me."

"That makes sense," Tony said. "You're a fifteen-year-old girl. You don't have any power or choice in what's going to happen to you. You're totally helpless. Right?"

Serena rolled her eyes. "No."

"You're not fifteen? You actually have some control over your life?"

"You're a real shit, Tony."

"I gather people go to this club because they consider it an erotic outlet. Do you consider it erotic?"

"Not particularly, but I'm curious."

"So?"

"So I feel a little guilty about that."

"What makes you more uncomfortable? Your nervousness or your guilt?"

"I don't know. It's about the same."

Tony nodded. "I'm going to give you a pill that will completely remove all of your feelings and emotions about this."

She looked at him. "What kind of pill?"

"It doesn't really matter. What kind would you like? An aspirin? A chewable vitamin?"

"Funny."

Tony shrugged. "From what you've described, you're feeling exactly what I would expect you to feel about something like this. I can't help you *not* to feel anything. The only issue is how you deal with those feelings and whether you control them, or they control you. I realize that when you were fifteen you weren't in a position to control them. Fortunately—"

"I'm not fifteen anymore," she concluded.

Tony spread his hands.

"I know what you're saying," Serena said. "It's just not easy."

"I didn't say it was."

"Back in the bad days, I used to escape. There was a place in my head I called the nothingness room. I'd go there and not feel a thing. That was how I dealt with it."

"But?"

"But after a while, I couldn't get out. I was stuck there. I felt like I was spending my whole life in that empty room. It wasn't until I met Jonny that I was able to climb out, and now what scares me more than anything is the idea of going back there."

Tony leaned forward and put his elbows on his knees. "You can run from who you are, Serena, but sooner or later, you're going to come face-to-face with the past again. That's when you'll be able to decide if it's really behind you."

Stride drove along the North Shore highway that hugged the lake between Duluth and

Two Harbors. It was a gorgeous day, with a blue sky arching overhead like a cathedral dome. He'd forgotten what the sun looked like and couldn't remember when he last had to put on his sunglasses as he drove. The light cast a wide, sparkling swath over the water. It was quiet, with little traffic on the road. Except for the freezing temperature, it looked like summer outside, but at this time of year, it got even colder when the sun came out.

He found Kathy Lassiter's home about ten miles north of the city. It was several decades old, but large and solidly built, with windows on both levels looking out on the lake. The home was neatly painted in a dusty blue that shimmered in the sunlight. She had a multi-acre lot, thick with trees except for a large square of white snow surrounding the house. He parked in the dirt driveway behind her Audi. Before he could go to the front door, he saw it open and a woman came outside, dressed in a maroon-and-silver fleece track-suit with her brown hair tied in a ponytail. She wore fluorescent running shoes.

"Ms. Lassiter?" he called.

She jogged down the driveway to meet him. "Can I help you?"

Stride introduced himself, and she gave him a look of mild surprise and asked to see his identification. As she studied his shield, she asked, "What's this about? A legal matter?"

He remembered that Lassiter was a partner in a Minneapolis law firm. "No, but it is urgent. Could we go inside?"

She shook her head. "It's time for my run. I have to stretch first though. How about we go across the street and you say what you want to say?"

They crossed the highway to a small park overlooking the lake. There was a picnic bench half-buried in snow and a stone beach below them where the azure water lapped at the shore. Their feet crunched in snow. The branches of the tall evergreens around them were motionless in the still air.

Lassiter swung her left leg nimbly to the top of the bench and bent her body until her face was almost level with her foot. She gripped her muscled calf and turned her face sideways to look at him with sharp, intelligent brown eyes. She was in her forties and wasn't wearing makeup. Her cheeks were flushed red, and she had a flared nose.

"So what's up, Lieutenant?" She had a lawyer's voice, clipped and impatient.

He didn't waste time. "I know about the sex club tonight."

She kept stretching and shrugged her limber shoulders. "Yeah, so?"

"Am I correct that you're going to be what they call an 'alpha girl'?"

"That's none of your business, is it?" She put her leg down and twisted her torso to her left. "I'm not breaking any laws. When did you become the morality police?"

"I'm not, but two alpha girls have been assaulted following their—performance—at this sex club."

Lassiter stopped and folded her arms. Her breathing was even. "Are you sure?"

"Yes."

She started stretching again, but her eyes were thoughtful. "Are you suggesting that I back out?"

"I wouldn't blame you if you did."

"But you have something else in mind," she concluded.

"Yes, I do. If we cancel the party, we tip our hand to whoever is doing this. He may find other targets."

"In other words, you're hoping he'll come after me."

"We'll protect you. We'll keep you under twenty-four-hour surveillance."

"That won't be easy. I go back and forth between Duluth and the Cities twice a week. My main office is in Minneapolis."

"You're a corporate lawyer, right?" Stride asked.

"Yes, I specialize in governance issues for emerging companies."

"Long hours, but good pay."

"The pay's all right, but if you want to get really rich, don't do it by the hour," she told him.

Stride glanced across the street at her lavish home. "Four hundred thousand a year doesn't go as far as it used to?" he asked.

"Since you asked, no, it doesn't. You should see what top management of a start-up can walk away with from an IPO. But I know a lawyer isn't likely to get much sympathy from a cop on a pension."

"Don't worry, I wouldn't trade jobs with you. Anyway, the commute to the Cities isn't a problem. We'll work with the police down there, and we'll have the highway patrol with you—unmarked—every mile of the way."

"Has this guy killed anyone?" Lassiter asked.

Stride frowned. "We think he may be involved in two murders to protect his identity. He hasn't killed any of the alpha girls so far, but I won't kid you, this is risky and dangerous. I understand entirely if you want nothing to do with it."

"Do you think I'm safe if I forget about the party?"

"I don't know. We're not sure who this man is, or where he gets his information. He may already know who you are."

"So I'm damned if I do, damned if I don't."

"I'm sorry."

Lassiter stepped up and sat on top of the bench. "I'm disappointed, Lieutenant. I was looking forward to this evening. The club has always been a harmless bit of sin for me. When you spend most of your life filing 10-Ks and worrying about Sarbanes-Oxley, you don't have time for a social life, let alone a sexual life. I'm divorced. My son is in college. There aren't many outlets for a horny corporate lawyer in her forties."

"Does that mean you're going to back out?"

She shook her head. "No, I'll do it. It just

won't be what I was hoping for. Please tell me you won't have video or wiretaps or anything like that inside. I won't have to worry about showing up on the Internet because some cop sells my porn debut on the side, right?"

"No."

"Good. I also want to go over details of the surveillance. Everything has to meet with my approval. Agreed?"

"Of course. I'll send over a detective named Abel Teitscher to talk with you. Please keep this all confidential, too."

Lassiter hesitated.

"Is that a problem?" Stride asked.

"Not at all. It's just that I know the people inside the club. They're harmless."

"The man behind this may not be a part of the club at all," Stride said. "But we don't know who's talking to whom. Secrets have a way of getting out."

"Yes, they do," Lassiter said.

She climbed off the bench, headed to the shoulder of the highway, and began jogging north.

36

Stride studied the nighttime street from inside the smoked windows of a Cadillac, borrowed from a lawyer who lived a few houses down on the Point. He used it sometimes when he wanted an upscale car that blended into the neighborhood during a stakeout. Teitscher sat ramrod straight in the seat next to him, and his buzzed gray hair tickled the roof of the car. He didn't blink. Every few minutes, he used his index finger like a comb and smoothed his mustache. That was the only sign that he was nervous.

Stride was nervous, too. It was one thing to plan surveillance on a map, with pushpins to flag the cars and colored markers inking the escape routes. It was another to be here, surrounded by shadows where someone could hide. You could throw a cordon around any piece of land, and someone could always sneak through. On the ground, you couldn't see everything and be everywhere.

An hour to go.

A cop would stay inside Kathy Lassiter's house while she was at the party, and another car would keep her in constant sight on the way to and from the club. For the next several days, an unmarked car with two detectives would be within fifty yards of Lassiter's house at all times. They had installed a downstairs alarm system that would send an intruder alert both to the station and directly to the surveillance car. If someone tried to break in, they could be inside her house in less than thirty seconds.

Here at the club, they had half a dozen cars on the surrounding streets and several detectives who would patrol the streets at intervals. If the rapist was an outsider, there was a chance he would be here, where he could keep an eye on his next alpha girl coming and going.

They were parked half a block from Sonia

Bezac's house. Several homes still had their Christmas lights turned on, and multicolored strings twinkled in the trees and along the roof lines. Lumpy snowmen dotted the front yards. Looks were deceiving. There was nothing picture-postcard about this place, not with a dozen men and women about to have sex with a stranger, not with a rapist haunting the neighborhood. It made him think of driving on a lonely rural road at night and seeing lights inside a peaceful farm-house, and envying the lives the people there must have. It was just an illusion. Who-ever lived inside those places was no differ-ent than anyone else, with husbands who drank, and old people who died slow deaths, and kids who killed themselves over a bro-ken love affair. The only romance about it was in his head.

He wanted a smoke, but he couldn't have one. His fingers twitched. He couldn't escape the feeling of dread. The feeling that they had all missed something.

"What else did the SEC tell you about this insider trading scheme?" Teitscher asked.

"They got an anonymous tip, but they haven't found a connection yet between Mitchell Brandt and anyone at Infloron Medical or the FDA. They don't know yet how he got advance word of the FDA approval."

"It's a long way from insider trading to rape."

Stride nodded.

His cell phone rang. *I'm in a hurry and don't know why.* He was in a hurry tonight, feeling as if he were running in place. He wanted to skip to the end.

It was Serena.

"I'm pulling up around the corner," she said.

"You can still back out," Stride told her.

"You need me inside, Jonny."

"I know."

"Maybe I'll sign up to be the next alpha girl."

"Sonia would like that. Be careful, okay?"

"I will."

She hung up. A minute later, he saw her in his rearview mirror as she turned the corner. Serena passed the Cadillac on the sidewalk but didn't look toward the smoked windows. She wore black jeans and heels and a sleeveless down vest. Her hands were in her vest pockets. She looked casual and unconcerned, but he knew her eyes were tracking the windows and the dark spaces between the houses.

She walked up to the doorway of the

Bezac house and waited on the porch, surveying the neighborhood. The door opened, and light spilled out. He saw Sonia.

Serena disappeared inside.

Sonia greeted Serena with an uneasy smile. She let her inside and looked out into the night before closing the door behind them. The house was elegant, and the lights were dimmed. Sonia wore a Chinese silk gown tied at her slim waist. It was pink with flowers. Her feet were in heels. The two women were both tall, almost the same height.

"I don't like spies," Sonia told her.

"No one will know."

"I don't believe anyone in my club is a rapist."

"Tell that to Maggie and Katrina," Serena snapped. "Count yourself lucky that it wasn't you."

Sonia flushed. "I'll take you downstairs."

She led Serena through the upscale kitchen to a back stairway that led down to a laundry and storage room. The floor was cold cement. A musty smell came off the walls. Sonia unlocked a narrow door that looked like a gateway to a utility closet, but instead Serena found herself slipping inside a small but elegant bedroom. The wallpaper was gold with a burgundy pattern of interlaced squares. A queen-sized bed was decorated with shams and a ruffled fringe, as if it had been plucked from a showroom. There was a dressing table and mirror, a bureau, and a walk-in closet.

One wall of the bedroom was glass. It looked out on a large, plush open space, lit by candles. The temple.

Serena found her eyes drawn to the shadowy room. She felt exposed. "They can't see through the mirror, right? They won't know I'm here?"

"No, most members don't know about this space. It's kind of a VIP room."

"Is the other room wired for sound?"

Sonia nodded. "You'll hear everything."

Serena could see herself in the glass. "I hate this," she murmured.

"Give it a chance. You might be surprised."

"Not likely."

"You're a very attractive spy," Sonia said. "Jonathan has good taste."

Serena didn't reply.

"Did he tell you about him and me?"

"Yes, he did."

Serena tried to imagine Jonny as a teenager, drunk in a car with this woman thirty years ago. She herself would have been a child then, during the good days in Phoenix, before her mother became a slave to cocaine and her father walked out. Before Blue Dog.

"He's very intense," Sonia said.

"That's why he's good at what he does."

"I'm disbanding the club, you know. This will be our last party."

"Oh?"

"It's too risky now."

Serena knew she was talking about the risk to herself and Delmar and their reputations, not the risk to the alpha girls. The risk of being exposed.

"Do the members know?"

"No, I didn't think you'd want me to tell them."

"I don't."

Sonia eyed her figure. "It's a shame you won't be at the party. You could still join us on the other side."

"No thanks."

"Suit yourself. No one will know what you're doing in here. If it turns you on, there are vibrators in the bureau."

"This doesn't turn me on, Sonia."

"No? It's different when you put on the mask. It changes everything."

Sonia opened a dresser drawer and emerged with a gold mask, feminine and catlike. She slipped the band around her head and slid it down so that the elastic fell under her curly hair and nestled behind her ears. She reached around with both hands to adjust the mask gently.

Serena saw them both in the mirror, red hair next to black hair. Behind the mask, Sonia had become a stranger. Someone entirely different.

Sonia slid a warm arm around her waist, and Serena wondered if the other woman was about to kiss her. "Want to have a go with me?" Sonia asked.

"Pass."

"No one will ever know. I won't tell Jonathan if you don't."

"I'm not interested, Sonia."

"No? Women make the best lovers. I'll bet you know that."

Serena leaned into her ear and whispered with a smile, "Get the hell away from me."

Sonia's face darkened. She put on a false smile, too, as if she had brushed it on like makeup, but her eyes glinted through the mask with rage. She marched away and left Serena alone in the hideaway.

37

Maggie wanted to drive the memories of the club out of her brain, but it wasn't working. Not tonight. When she looked at her watch, she knew the party was going on. Serena was inside the secret room, and Kathy Lassiter was on the bed, as Maggie had been that night in November. She remembered exactly what it was like. The temple was open and dark, and the half-windows in the walls were blacked out with electrical tape and shrouded by curtains. She remembered thick carpet under her bare feet and hot air pouring out of the vents. The room was lit by a dozen candles flickering in glass bowls. Their aromas left an odd mix of fragrances in the air, and she caught traces of ginger and green tea, sage, lilac blossoms, and juicy orange. Soundscapes played softly from hidden speakers. She heard ocean surf, harps, and birdsong. There were wooden chairs, cocktail tables with open bottles of shiraz, and crystal glasses that reflected the numerous lights of the candles. Lush bearskin rugs. Sex toys. Condoms heaped in a bowl like candy. Subtle, shadowy erotic photographs of nudes on the walls.

The circular bed in the center of the room was draped to the floor in red silk, which was cool and slippery on her nude skin. She spent ten minutes alone before the others joined her. The alpha girl was always first, Sonia said. Do what you want. Drink wine. Listen to the music. Sleep. Touch yourself. Maggie simply squirmed on the silk and thought about running far, far away.

She had allowed Eric to pull her into this world because he said he wanted it so badly. Do this for me, let me see you like that. With other people. It was his ultimate fantasy. Looking back, she couldn't believe she had done it. Her face grew hot with humiliation.

They were so pathetic as they filed in and

shed their robes. It was like going to the beach and realizing that, underneath everyone's clothes, naked flesh was the great equalizer. Models made their money because they were so rare. The sex club was a parade of paunchy rolls, cellulite, drooping breasts, and double chins. There were beautiful bodies among them, but en masse, the impression of so much skin was nauseating and ugly. She wondered again what she was doing there and why she had ever thought this was a way to be close to Eric. Or why she thought it mattered.

Most of the time, she kept her eyes closed. She had recollections of soft lips and sweet breath from one woman, garlic and cold hands from a man, panting and sweat, sounds of moaning, none of it hers. When she opened her eyes once, she saw Eric, standing in the shadows, rapt, with his hand around his stiff member. Then she closed her eyes again and felt time drag out through more sensations of rough fingers, tongues leaving wet trails like snails on her skin, and men who came and went quickly.

She wanted to pretend that she had simply climbed aboard the roller coaster and hung on for dear life, but that was a lie. Some of the dips and valleys excited her. Sonia was surprisingly talented. So was Mitchell Brandt. For a few moments in the midst of a closed-eyed nightmare, she found herself not caring what was going on around her, because she was into what was being done to her. Enough to climb the heights and come back down. She felt guilty, but she couldn't take it back. On some level, she had enjoyed it.

That was one of the reasons she didn't report the rape when it happened a few weeks later. She knew what Serena had told her about the questions she got from men who didn't know any better. Did you enjoy what Blue Dog did to you? If she went public, the sex club would be exposed, and people would talk about what she did that night, and somewhere along the line someone would wonder. Did she enjoy it? Was she asking to be raped?

"Fuck you, Eric," she said aloud.

She was angry that he had left these memories in her brain. She couldn't separate the sex club and the rape in her mind, and she blamed Eric for both. For an instant, she was glad that he was dead, and she wished she *had* been the one to pull the trigger that night.

Maggie wanted to be out on the street,

not alone here at home, dwelling on her mistakes. She should have been in the car with Stride, not Abel Teitscher. She wanted to be there to track this bastard and catch him and see what his face really looked like. She wanted to know what Eric had found and how he had found it.

And who Helen Danning was.

She thought about Helen Danning and looked over to see her BlackBerry on the coffee table, its red light flashing. She had e-mail.

No one had sent her e-mail lately. Since the cloud of the murder began hanging over her head, she was a nonperson.

With a shiver, Maggie unwound her body from the couch, slid the PDA out of its case, and clicked over to her in box. She had one unread message, and the return address was "The Lady in Me."

Maggie opened the message and saw a single sentence:

Stop trying to find me. HD.

38

Serena watched Mitchell Brandt and knew something was very wrong. His muscles rippled with tension on his chest and down his legs. He clenched and unclenched his fists. His mask made it hard for her to see his eyes, but she could see that his head never swiveled away from Kathy Lassiter to stare at the other naked women in the room, even as some of those women caressed themselves, used vibrators, or had sex with their partners on the soft rugs spread around the floor. Brandt focused on Lassiter as if it were him and her alone in the temple.

She felt a bad vibe emanating from the

way he held himself. He looked like a race-horse, snorting and pawing at the ground, anxious to break free from the gate. Lassiter already had her limbs entwined with another man, but she stared back at Brandt, no more than six feet away, and something electric and scary passed between them.

The nudity in front of her had long ago lost its novelty. She was self-conscious at first, even hidden behind the mirror, but after a while, she became numb to it. Her unease became boredom. There was so much sex that none of it was enticing, as if she had wandered onto the set of a low-budget porn flick.

A naked man approached the mirror and stood directly in front of the glass, distracting her. She took a step backward involuntarily and held her breath. He was in his mid-forties, tall and bony, with a matte of graying hair on his chest. He sucked in his stomach and touched himself. Serena wanted to close her eyes.

Sonia came up next to the man. Her pale skin glowed with sweat. She had been the first to have sex with Kathy Lassiter, and since then, Serena had seen Sonia take turns with two other men in the room and a husband-and-wife duo at the same time. Sonia looked breathless and exhilarated. She was drinking a lot, too. So were most of the others.

"Just imagine if someone were on the other side of the mirror, watching us," Sonia told the man.

Serena watched a smile glint on the corner of Sonia's lips.

"Hell, yes," he said.

"Let's put on a show," Sonia told him.

Sonia pushed on the man's shoulders, and he didn't need further encouragement to lie on his back on the thick carpet. Sonia straddled him in front of the mirror and leered directly at Serena as she lowered herself onto his body. She moaned loudly for effect and leaned forward so that her contorted face was nearly glazing the surface of the glass.

Serena shook her head. "What a bitch," she whispered.

She wanted to pound the wall and let them all know she was there.

She tore her eyes away from the frenzied coupling in front of her. Behind Sonia, another drama was playing out, and Serena didn't like it.

Kathy Lassiter was alone on the bed now,

propped up on her elbows. Mitchell Brandt, naked and solidly built, approached and stood over her, but he made no move to climb on the bed. Lassiter turned over onto all fours, crawled across the rumpled sheets, and began performing oral sex on him. Brandt didn't react at all. His passiveness made Lassiter work harder, but she may as well have been giving her attention to a stone. He looked down at the top of her head, and the deadness in his lower face made Serena's insides lurch with unease.

What the hell was he doing?

Brandt took hold of her shoulders and separated himself from her. With both hands, he shoved Lassiter so hard that she flew upwards and backwards, landing on the far side of the bed with her hair mussed and her legs splayed. Her mask came askew, and Serena saw her eyes now, which were confused and afraid. Brandt climbed onto the bed and moved toward her on his knees. Lassiter scrabbled away from him.

Serena took two steps toward the door, trying to decide if this was a game.

Inches away, Sonia was still having sex by the mirror. The others watched her. No one noticed Brandt and Lassiter.

Brandt leaped forward like a cat and locked Lassiter's wrists in his hands. He yanked her up, her hair twirling. He took the mask, ripped it off her face, and threw it on the floor. In a single motion, he moved his hands to her hips, lifted her bodily off the bed, and crushed her against his chest. His lips moved as he whispered in her ear. Lassiter shook her head violently and struggled to get away, but Brandt held on, trapping her arms so she couldn't wrestle free. When she tried to speak, he choked her mouth with a brutal kiss.

Serena hesitated. When she saw Lassiter wriggling in Brandt's grasp, she was convinced that this was not playacting or fantasy. She couldn't let this go on.

"Stop!" Serena shouted.

The people in the room heard the muffled voice and looked up, confused and aghast. Brandt made no move to stop.

Serena bolted out of the hideaway and took the stairs two at a time. She thundered through the house and found the main stairway leading to the basement and the oak door that led to the temple. Her shoulder collided with the door, and it flew around on its hinges. She ran into the fragrant room.

A dozen naked people screamed and covered themselves with their hands. They dove to the floor. Sonia's face was screwed up with rage.

Serena focused on Brandt, who shoved Lassiter down onto her back and threw his full weight on top of her. Breath expelled from her chest like air from a popped balloon. He kept whispering, and her eyes turned moon-white. She tried to speak again, but her pleas were smothered.

"Get off her now!" Serena screamed, running to the bed.

She clawed at Brandt's shoulder, but he was deadweight. Serena delivered a backhand fist to the side of Brandt's head, her knuckles cracking sharply on his temple. Brandt reared back in pain and toppled away from Lassiter, who squirmed from under him. He cleared his head and clutched for her again, but Serena used the palm of her hand to jab directly into his forehead. His head snapped; he groaned and fell back, sliding off the slippery silk onto the floor.

Lassiter scrambled off the bed. Brandt staggered to his feet and took a few unsteady steps. The other members of the club were paralyzed, hiding by the walls and on the floor. Serena eyed Brandt and angled her body so that Lassiter was behind her. He stared at both of them, his face screwed up with rage, and then shifted his attention to the others as if he was noticing them for the first time.

"Fuck all of you," he hissed.

Brandt ran from the room. One of the men grabbed for him, but Brandt shoved him hard, and he fell back, collapsing into one of the tables and spilling wine bottles onto the floor. Shiraz flowed like blood, and sharp triangles of glass scattered on the carpet. Brandt wrenched open the temple door and slammed it behind him. His footsteps pounded upstairs.

"Are you okay?" Serena asked Lassiter.

"I'm fine," Lassiter said, her face dark. "Who the hell are you?"

"I'm a friend of Lieutenant Stride."

"Well, you shouldn't have interfered."

Serena backed up. "What?"

"You should have stayed out of it," Lassiter repeated.

"He was assaulting you," Serena protested. "He could have killed you."

"You don't know anything."

Sonia joined them. Her pale skin was

white, and her eyes were wild and on fire. "How dare you," Sonia hissed. "Get the hell out of here."

Serena ignored her. "What did he say to you?" she asked Lassiter.

"He didn't say anything."

"I saw him whispering to you."

"He didn't say anything," Lassiter insisted.

Serena put her lips close to Lassiter's ear. "I can get the police in from outside."

"No." Lassiter shook her head. "I need to get out of here. Right now."

"Let me help you," Serena said.

"I don't *need* any help."

"Are you sure you don't need a doctor?" Serena asked.

"I just need to get away from here."

Serena called after her as Lassiter broke from the others and made her way to the door that led out of the temple. "Wait, he could still be in the house."

"No, he's gone," Lassiter replied. "He's not coming back."

39

That's Mitchell Brandt," Stride said. He put his coffee cup on the dashboard of the Cadillac and leaned forward to watch.

"He's in a hurry," Teitscher said.

Brandt slammed the front door of Sonia Bezac's house and ran down the sidewalk toward the street. His open coat billowed behind him. He wore black jeans and an untucked, unbuttoned dress shirt. The shirt fell open, and they saw his bare chest. He took off across the street, dodging through the headlights of a car that blared its horn at him. He climbed into a dark Porsche.

"I don't like this," Stride said.

"Should we pick him up?"

"No, let's see where he goes."

Teitscher radioed Guppo in a tan Caprice around the corner. "Brandt is on his way. He's hauling ass. Stay on his tail, but don't make it obvious."

The Porsche shot off down the residential street and vanished, heading into the steep curves leading toward the lake. The Caprice accelerated onto the same street moments later.

"Do you want to go in?" Teitscher asked.

"Not yet."

They waited fifteen minutes. The other members of the club streamed out of the house in pockets of ones and twos, hiding their sullen faces from each other as they left. They formed a procession out of the neighborhood, and soon headlights swung past them one after another, driving fast.

Serena was among the last to leave. She took quick, tight steps from the house. Her down vest was unzipped, and her face was tense with worry. She eyed the people around her and then bent down and scrambled inside the backseat of the Cadillac. She fell back against the leather seat and whistled long and loud.

"What the hell happened in there?" Stride asked.

Serena put her elbows on the front seat between them. "Brandt freaked."

"What?"

"He attacked Kathy Lassiter right in front of everyone."

"Did someone stop him?"

Serena nodded. "I did. Lassiter says she's okay, but Brandt was out of his skull. When I broke it up, he bolted."

"We saw him. Guppo's on his tail."

Teitscher was still watching Sonia's front door. "What set Brandt off?"

"I don't know. He was on edge all night. He never took his eyes off Lassiter."

"What about you?" Stride asked. "Are you okay?"

"I'm fine, but you know what they say to do when you're nervous? Just imagine everyone naked and you'll relax? It doesn't work when they're really naked."

Stride couldn't help but laugh.

"Perverts," Teitscher snapped.

"Do you think Brandt is our man?" Stride asked. "Could he have attacked the other women?"

"I don't know. This wasn't random. It was more like he had a grudge against Lassiter."

"Did something happen between them?"

Serena shook her head. "No, that's it, nothing happened. He came into the room with a hard-on for her, if you know what I mean. It was personal."

"Personal? Like they knew each other?"

"I think so, yeah."

Teitscher glanced at Stride. "What do we know about Lassiter?"

"Not enough," Stride said. He was angry with himself.

"She's a lawyer, right?" Serena asked. "See if her law firm has a bio on their Web site."

Stride grabbed his laptop and ran a search that led him to the law firm's home page. He drilled down to the lawyer biographies and pulled up a page for Lassiter that included a photo and a summary of her practice areas and experience. He read through the narrative and then swore and slammed the cover down.

"Kathy Lassiter is outside counsel for Infloron Medical."

"You think she fed advance info on the

FDA approval to Brandt?" Serena asked. "And he used it to do inside trades?"

"Either that, or she's the one who fingered him to the SEC. Proutz in Chicago said they got an anonymous tip."

Teitscher was frowning. "What do you want to do?"

"Pick him up," Stride said. "He assaulted her. We can use that to hold him."

"We need to make sure the net around Lassiter is secure," Serena added. "Brandt may go after her again, and if he's *not* our guy, then she's got two people who may be gunning for her."

Teitscher stared at Sonia's front door. "We have a problem."

"What is it?" Stride asked.

"Lassiter never came out."

Serena leaned forward into the front seat. "What are you talking about? She should have been one of the first ones out the door."

"I've been watching everyone," Teitscher said, shaking his head. "Lassiter never left."

40

Sonia threw open the door. Her red hair was a mass of limp curls, like sleeping snakes. She wore a robe loosely tied at her waist, and her body smelled of sex. "What are you people doing here? Haven't you done enough?"

"Where's Kathy Lassiter?" Stride demanded.

Sonia shrugged. "You should know that. You're the spies."

"She's still inside," Teitscher insisted. The furrows in his forehead stretched taut, and his eyes registered disapproval, flicking over the deep V of open skin between the folds of her robe. Sonia read his expression.

"You think I have her tied to a bed some-where? Sorry, Detective. She left."

"Can we look in the house?" Serena asked.

Sonia curled her lip and shook her head at them. "You can stand out here and freeze for all I care."

"Sonia," Stride chided her.

"Oh, fuck it, all right." She held the door wider, and they poured in. Along with musk and perfume, Stride smelled alcohol on Sonia's breath. She swayed on her feet. Her nipples protruded in two bumps through the silk robe.

"I'll check upstairs," Serena said.

Teitscher stood uncomfortably in the foyer, as if he were dipping new shoes in mud. His cell phone rang, and Stride watched his face blacken as he listened to the call. He snapped his phone shut and clenched it in his fist. "That was Guppo," he told Stride. "Brandt jumped a red light down-town, and Guppo got stuck in traffic. He lost him."

"Shit," Stride swore. Things were getting out of control. Teitscher crooked a thumb at the front door, and Stride nodded. "Go, go. Get an ATL out in Duluth and Superior. Use the highway police, too, in case he's headed south on the interstate."

Teitscher left.

Stride checked the living room. The lights were low, and the room was empty.

Sonia trailed behind him. "I told you, she's not here."

"She didn't fly away," Stride snapped.

He pushed past her and headed for the opposite side of the house, but found no sign of Lassiter in any of the downstairs rooms.

"Where's Delmar?" he asked.

"Sleeping," Sonia replied.

"Alone?"

Sonia snickered. "Unless Serena wants to give him a go. He might not even need Viagra with her."

Stride felt his patience wearing down, like a bare patch of carpet that's been walked on too many times. "Show me the basement."

"All the fun's over down there."

"Just show me."

Sonia shrugged and led him to a staircase that descended to a closed oak door below him. It was heavy but unlocked. Sonia was on his heels as he crossed into the temple. He smelled smoke from the burnt-out candles, and he felt on the wall for a light switch, bathing the room in fluorescent light.

He squinted, and Sonia shielded her eyes. He sized up the room with a pit of dismay in his stomach. The sheets on the circular bed were soiled. Condom wrappers littered the floor, along with wine stains and glass. The musk of lovemaking was strong here. For an instant, he saw Maggie, draped on the bed, and felt an irrational anger.

It took him only a moment to survey the open room and see that everyone had left. When he turned around, Sonia was right there, and she laced her fingers behind his neck and drew close so he could inhale her. She leaned in to him.

"Kiss me," she murmured. "I need to be kissed."

He pried her hands away. "You've been kissed enough."

Sonia spun dreamily. "Oh, no, no, no. I've been fucked plenty, but not kissed at all. You were a great kisser."

"Shut up, Sonia. Where is Kathy Lassiter?"

"I don't know."

"You're lying."

Sonia shrugged. "Kiss me, and maybe I'll tell you."

Stride took Sonia by the shoulder and squeezed harder than he should.

"Go on, hit me," she said. "You know you want to."

He pulled his hand away as if her skin were burning him.

"This is no game, Sonia. She could be in serious danger. What the hell would you have done if Serena wasn't there? Would you all have stood around while Brandt raped her?"

"Serena misunderstood. It was sex play that got a little out of hand. Kathy told me so."

"When?"

"After."

"You talked to her," Stride said. "So you know what's going on. Tell me where she is."

Sonia ignored him and undid the bow of her robe and let it fall like a dirty towel. She was naked. "Bring back memories?"

It did. He remembered her body in vivid detail, right down to the freckle on her left breast and the appendix scar creasing her stomach. He pushed the memory out of his mind. "Tell me where Kathy Lassiter is right now, or I'll march your bare ass downtown and put you under arrest. So help me, Sonia, I'm not kidding."

Stride picked up her robe and threw it at her. She clutched it to her chest and smelled it. "We're going upstairs," he said. "Put it on."

Sonia tied the robe around her waist, letting her breasts wobble free. She grabbed for Stride's belt and sank to her knees in front of him. He wrenched away and looked down into her dilated eyes. "What are you on?"

She giggled. "A little Diet Coke and a little regular coke," she whispered.

"Son of a bitch. How much did you take? Do you need to go to a hospital?"

Sonia stuck out her tongue. "Come on, Jonathan. For old times, huh? I'm wet, and you're hard, so why the hell not?"

Stride felt the bones in his hand stiffen like a club. He hated Sonia at that second and hated that she had anything to do with his past. He jerked his hand back and knew that in the next instant he would slap her and watch her tumble backward, her cheek tattooed red with his fingerprints.

"No, Jonny."

He turned and saw Serena standing

beside him. She was unbelievably calm as she shook her head.

He swore and turned away. He watched as Serena knelt down in front of Sonia, who gave him a crooked grin. Sonia closed her eyes and rocked back.

"Where is Kathy Lassiter?" Serena asked her in a mellow voice.

"I told you, she's not here." Sonia opened her eyes and waggled a finger at Stride. "She borrowed my car. She didn't want *you* to find her."

"Where the hell was she going?" Stride demanded.

"To meet Mitchell Brandt. She said she had to stop him before he ruined everything."

41

Serena sat for a long time in the frozen silence without starting her car. She wrinkled her nose. A faint aroma of fish lingered in the leather seats, and she wrote it off to the smoked fish she had bought at Russ Kendall's last week. She opened the window, trying to dispel it, but the smell had already made its way inside her nose and lodged there. The wind whistled into the car and brought crystals of snow with it.

Jonny was gone. The alert for Mitchell Brandt and Kathy Lassiter had spread through the city, but she wasn't part of the chase. Her frustration gnawed at her. This was the time she regretted giving up her shield, when she felt cut off from the adrenaline rush as it began. She had to watch his car peel away from the curb and not follow him. She hated it.

She was worried about Jonny, too. He was surrounded by lies and secrets, and she felt guilty because some of the lies were her own. She wondered again if she was making a terrible mistake by keeping him in the dark.

Was the man in shadows just a blackmailer?

Or was he a predator whose evil went far deeper? Someone who raped. Someone who killed.

Someone who was following her.

She was uneasy, because the feeling was back. She was being watched. She didn't know where he was, but he was close to her again, and time felt short. Her unease trebled as she realized the streets were empty. All the cops were gone, and she was alone. Was that what he wanted all along?

Serena jumped as her cell phone let out a jangling ring. She thought, *It's him.*

But it was Dan Erickson.

"He wants the money tonight," Dan said. "I've got it."

"We should bring in the police right now," Serena advised him.

"I hired you because you were a homicide cop," Dan retorted, his voice hoarse with anger. "You said you could deal with this guy. Now you're telling me to throw away my life by making this public?"

"We don't know who we're dealing with."

"I don't care. I want this *over*. He says this is the final hit. He's on his way out of town."

"He's telling you what you want to hear," she said.

"You're not listening to me. We're doing this my way. If this guy so much as smells a cop, the photo of me and Tanjy goes to the papers. Do you understand what that means?"

"Completely."

"Then get down here to pick up the money."

"Where's the drop?"

"He said he'd let you know."

"I don't like this."

"This isn't about you," Dan said.

He hung up.

Serena threw the phone down and gripped the steering wheel, which felt like ice. Dan was right. This was business, and

she couldn't make it personal. She had a job
to do, period. Make the drop. Just like before.

She turned the key and started the car.
Her heart stopped.

Shattering noise exploded inside the car
like a bomb. Rap music screeched from the
speakers, so loud and painful that she felt
the beat in her chest and instinctively
pressed her palms against her ears. She
reached for the volume switch and turned it
so hard and so fast that the plastic knob
broke off in her hand.

The car fell silent. She breathed hard.

The reality sank in. He had been in her
car.

She felt as if ants were crawling inside her
clothes. Her skin rippled, and she rubbed
her palms with her fingertips. When she realized the window was still open, she quickly
closed it. She studied the front and back-
seats of the car to see what was missing, but
nothing was disturbed.

He was playing head games with her.

This isn't about you.

She drove away and kept her eyes on her
mirror, but there was no one behind her. He
had been here for a reason. When she
glanced at the glove compartment, she knew

without opening it that he had left a message for her there. Again. She had begun to think like him.

She pulled over to the curb and looked inside. Another white envelope was there, with a note in red ink:

> Under the high bridge. Bring the
> money. One hour.

42

Stride was in the Lincoln Park area, a rectangle of green climbing from the freeway that served as a hot spot for crime and drugs. Even the winter cold didn't deter buyers and sellers. He did a circuit of the park and then began a slow survey of the nearby residential streets.

He was on and off his cell phone as he drove. He connected with the detective who was waiting in the dark inside Kathy Lassiter's home, but Lassiter hadn't returned. The uniforms outside did a search of the perimeter around the house and in the woods behind, but reported no sign of Mitchell Brandt or anyone else. Stride checked with the team outside Brandt's apartment and got the same response. Throughout Duluth and Superior, squad cars were hunting for Brandt's Porsche and Sonia's Mercedes, but so far, Brandt and Lassiter had eluded them.

His cell phone rang again.

"This is Philip Proutz with the SEC, Lieutenant. My office said you were trying to reach me."

"I am," Stride said. "We have a situation here, and I could use some information."

"Does this concern Mitchell Brandt?"

"Yes, but I'm more interested in someone else. Kathy Lassiter."

Proutz took a long time to reply. "Why don't you tell me about this situation you've got?"

"I take it you know who Lassiter is," Stride said.

"Yes."

"She's primary outside counsel for Infloron Medical, isn't she? So she would be among the first to know about the status of the company's applications with the FDA."

"Of course." Proutz sounded pained. "Please don't tell me she has a relationship with Mitchell Brandt."

"We think she does. They're both part of an underground sex club here in Duluth."

"A sex club?" Proutz groaned.

"Did Lassiter know you were launching an insider trading investigation into Infloron's stock sales? Or that Brandt was a target?"

"No, we didn't know where the trail would lead us. We don't alert the company or its counsel until we've gathered more information."

"You weren't focusing on Lassiter as the source of the leak about the FDA approval?"

"Not at all. She would have been way down our list. Think what you will of lawyers, Lieutenant, it's rare for corporate counsel to be personally involved in this kind of criminal conduct. But we'd have looked at her and her law firm eventually, I assure you."

Stride didn't think they would have found the connection easily, not without access to Sonia's member lists.

"Could Lassiter have been your anonymous informant?" he asked.

"If she was, she didn't make the call herself. The phone call that alerted us to Mitchell Brandt's trading activities came from a man."

Stride tried to figure out who else could

have unearthed the connection that tied Brandt, Lassiter, and Infloron Medical together. Anyone in the sex club would have known the two of them, but he didn't see how they could have made the leap to an insider trading scheme that never made the papers.

"I've shown you mine, why don't you show me yours, Lieutenant?" Proutz asked. "What's going on?"

"Brandt and Lassiter are both missing," Stride told him.

"Do you think they've fled the area?"

"I don't know. I'm more concerned with Lassiter's safety. Brandt assaulted her earlier this evening. Could he have been tipped off to your investigation?"

"I don't see how that's possible. My staff understands that confidentiality is essential in these matters. Unless it was someone on your end, Lieutenant."

Stride counted in his head. Himself. Serena. Maggie. Teitscher. They were the only ones who knew. "That's very unlikely," he said. "Tell me something, if Lassiter disappeared, how hard would it be for you to make an insider trading case against Brandt?"

"Not impossible, but difficult," Proutz

admitted. "It depends on how well they covered their tracks. Without evidence of how the information leaked, it's hard to prove that Brandt actually had material nonpublic information when he made the trades. Usually we play one conspirator against the other by making deals."

That meant Brandt had a motive to make sure that Lassiter was never seen again.

"I'll keep you posted, Mr. Proutz."

"Please do."

Stride hung up the phone, and it rang again immediately. This time it was Teitscher.

"Are you anywhere near Enger Park?" he asked.

Stride was heading north on Lincoln Park Drive. The two parks connected near a bridge over Highway 53. "Less than five minutes," he said. "Why?"

"We got a 911 call from a motorist in the area. He heard a woman screaming near the Enger tower."

43

Two cars were parked in the snow on the shoulder of the winding road that circled around the base of the Enger Park hillside. One was Brandt's Porsche, and the other was Sonia's Mercedes.

Stride parked his Bronco behind the two cars, blocking them in. He unlocked the glove compartment, grabbed his Ruger, and got out of the truck. Overhead, a comma-shaped moon came and went behind swiftly moving clouds, silhouetting the five-story bluestone tower that crowned the summit of the hill. He smelled snow massing to the west. In the valleys of the stiff wind, he heard someone moving far away, but the sound blew around him and he struggled to pinpoint its direction.

Enger Park was the highest land in the city, serene and beautiful, and he hated it. The rolling slopes of the golf course were across the street from him, deep with snow and crisscrossed with ski tracks. But for Stride, it was never winter in Enger Park. It was always August, ten years ago, in the grip of a heat wave that made him feel as if the entire state had melted and washed down the Mississippi to spill out in the humid air of the Gulf. Even at two in the morning that summer, standing in the fairway with Maggie, his shirt was soaked with sweat. At their feet was the girl, cocoa-skinned, tattooed, butchered, and nameless. Looking at her made him angry, and his anger only grew as the months passed and the investigation froze up like the lakes. No matter how much time passed, no matter what season it was, the girl was still there, forever haunting the park. He saw her in his dreams to this day. It was the same for Maggie.

He studied the golf course long and hard, watching and listening. Brandt and Lassiter weren't there. He slipped a flashlight out of his pocket and lit up the snow around the two cars, which were parked side-by-side. The footprints told the story. Brandt came around the rear of his Porsche, using long, angry paces. Lassiter was standing by the driver's door of Sonia's car. They struggled, and the tracks became a maze. There was an oversized snow angel where one of them had fallen and cherry-red blood spots in the slush.

Her footsteps sprinted away up the hill. Brandt's shoes followed in her path. Stride led with his gun and chased the tracks along the road that twisted up toward the tower. The tamped-down snow was a mess of tire ruts and boot marks. He followed the thin beam of his flashlight, searching for the fresh prints. Stands of young trees pressed in on him from both sides. Power lines drooped overhead, and he heard electricity snapping through the lines like bacon frying.

Above him a woman's voice cried. *"No!"*

And then, *"Stop! Help!"*

Stride veered off the road and into the trees that led straight up to the summit. The snow clawed at his thighs, and he pushed his way through spindly branches that snagged his leather jacket and cut his face.

The forest was claustrophobic. He could see only the web of trees obstructing his path, and all he could hear was the crack of wood breaking and his own labored breathing. Five minutes passed as he fought his way up the hill. Then ten. He was taking too long. When he broke from the trees into a small clearing, he had to stop and balance his hands on his knees, sucking in air.

He vowed in his head that he had smoked his last cigarette.

He saw two bodies moving, running, near the tower. They were still far away. *"Help!"* the woman shouted again.

Stride pointed his gun high into the air and squeezed off a shot. The explosion was loud in his ears, and then it echoed wildly, passed back and forth around the hillside. He saw the taller shadow freeze. Stride started running again.

He found a rough trail and made faster progress as the path snaked around the bands of trees, climbing steadily higher. His boots slipped, and his knees burned, and his chest was shot through with pain, but the tower grew ever larger as he closed in on the summit. He heard trampling footfalls nearby, but when he cast the beam of his flashlight to his left, he caught a glimpse of a buck in mid-bound, antlers bone-white, fleeting gracefully toward the cover of the woods. A few yards later, the ground leveled off underneath his feet.

He stopped, waiting for his breath to come back and the dizziness to right itself in his brain, then stepped silently from the trees. He was in the hibernating gardens around the memorial tower. The stone monolith loomed sixty feet above his head, and the moon glowed on the mottled stone and dark window squares like a checkerboard. Where the slope fell away, he could see the city encircling the black lake. He turned all the way around, studying the emptiness of the park. Naked trees, picnic benches, snow-capped grills, fire pits, deer tracks and footprints. Brandt and Lassiter were nowhere to be seen. He listened for their movements and heard nothing. Lassiter wasn't screaming now. She was hiding, or silenced by Brandt's hand clapped over her mouth, or dead.

In his memory, he saw the Enger Park Girl again. Limbless and anonymous. She was silent, too.

"Don't be a fool, Brandt," he called. His

voice was picked up by the wind and whisked away. He edged closer to the base of the tower. His fingers brushed the stone. He switched off his flashlight and let his eyes adjust to the night, and then he began a slow march around the circumference, his back protected, his Ruger pointed at the trees. At each bend in the octagonal shape, he paused before taking the next quiet step.

Far below him, sirens were drawing near. Brandt had to hear them, too.

He almost tripped over Kathy Lassiter's body slumped against the rock on the north side of the tower. Her brown hair spilled messily over her face, and a dark stain of blood trickled in three streaks over her ear and along her cheek.

Stride bent down and pressed two fingers against the warm skin of her neck. She was semiconscious and alive. As he turned her over on her back, she moaned and stirred. Her limbs flailed, and her eyes fluttered open. She couldn't see him clearly, and she screamed as she saw his shadow over her and beat her fists against his chest. He clutched for her wrists, trying to calm her.

"It's okay, it's okay."

"No!"

Too late, he realized she wasn't looking at him but over his shoulder.

A cold strap wrapped itself around his neck and choked off his air. He felt himself being dragged backward, the leather biting into his skin and tightening around his windpipe. His gun dropped nose-down into the snow. When he took a breath, his lungs found nothing there, and his body seized with panic. He clutched for his neck, trying to squeeze his fingers under the edge of the belt, but Brandt had him in a death grip. His fingernails drew blood on his own throat. Part of his mind felt detached, like a spectator at his own funeral, and there was no pain at all. He found that odd. No pain.

His foot found a solid piece of ground, and he launched himself backward, colliding with Brandt's chest and tumbling them both off their heels. They landed heavily, body on top of body. He felt the grip on his neck loosen as Brandt's wrist lost its hold on the strap. When he breathed in, his chest swelled, and he clawed at the belt and ripped it away, sending it twirling like a piece of ribbon. Below him, Brandt cursed and rolled him off with a violent shove. He got to his feet, but

Stride hooked his ankle as he ran and spilled him onto his face.

Brandt was fast. Stride reached for his cuffs and Brandt's right hand at the same time, but before he could reach either one, Brandt spun and knocked him sideways. The force of the blow dizzied Stride. He grabbed a fistful of Brandt's coat and hung on as the man pushed himself to his knees.

A flash of light and sound blinded and deafened both of them. Nearby, way too close, a bullet buried itself in the earth and stirred up a cloud of wet snow. Stride and Brandt both ducked and flattened themselves into the ground. When Stride glanced back, he saw Kathy Lassiter, standing and swaying, his own gun bobbling in her unsteady hands. He followed the dancing path of the barrel with horror, and as he watched, fire burst from the gun again, and the sound wave cracked through his ears, and he could feel the heat of the next bullet as it streaked past his cheek and sparked off the metal leg of a picnic bench. A couple inches more, and it would have drilled through his eye.

"Stop shooting!" he screamed at her.

He thought she was aiming for Brandt, but he realized she might have been aiming for both of them.

She fired again. This time her aim was wild, off into the sky. She staggered two steps, and her eyes closed, and the gun slipped out of her fingers. She went down to her knees and then pitched forward. The wound on her head was bleeding profusely.

Brandt rose up, running and slipping in the slush. Stride leaped for him but missed and wound up with a cold mouthful of snow. He spit it out and gave chase, but Brandt had ten yards and ten years on him, and he watched the distance widen between them. Brandt shot into the trees and down the hill, picking up speed. The sirens were almost on top of them now, and Stride saw the lights of two patrol cars fighting through the impacted snow on the access road, winding up toward the tower. Brandt saw them, too, and changed direction, veering across the hillside, away from the cars parked below. The trees thickened. Stride held his arms ahead of him, blocking the branches that scraped at his skin, and tried to keep Brandt in view.

When Brandt broke from the woods onto a narrow trail and accelerated, Stride thought he had lost him, but suddenly, he saw Brandt become airborne, his legs cartwheeling and his body twisting and landing in the snow. Stride saw the glacial rock that had tripped Brandt and leapt it smoothly, and in another second, he closed the gap and threw himself at Brandt, who was struggling to get up. He connected solidly on the square of Brandt's back, and the man gave way underneath him, his limbs splaying. With the heel of his hand, Stride slapped Brandt's skull hard, harder than he really needed to, and then found the man's wet hands and scissored his cuffs tightly around Brandt's wrists. He slid his belt out of his jeans and secured Brandt's ankles, too.

Stride took hold of Brandt's shoulder and turned him over and saw Brandt's face twisted like a mask, so caught up with fury that he was almost unrecognizable. Stride realized that everyone in this case was wearing masks.

44

Stride climbed into the rear of the patrol car. His willpower to stop smoking had evaporated by the time he reached the bottom of the hill, and he rolled the window halfway down, lit up, and blew a cloud of smoke outside. He was wet and cold, and his body hurt. He fingered the burnt skin on his neck, which looked like a red tattoo where Brandt's belt had strangled him. Brandt sat next to him in the backseat, handcuffed, saying nothing and gazing through the glass at the outside world.

First-timers always did that as the reality dawned on them. Freedom was gone.

The circling red lights of an ambulance flashed like a strobe through the interior of the car. There were police cars and cops everywhere. Stride took another drag, then blew smoke inside the car this time, and Brandt coughed.

"Lassiter's going to be fine," Stride said.

Brandt's mouth twitched, but he was silent.

"Here's what I don't understand, Mitch. You're a hotshot broker, pulling down, what, a couple hundred thousand a year? That's a fortune in this city. Why throw it away?"

No response.

Stride sighed and leaned back into the seat. "Lassiter told me it's hard to get rich by the hour, and she was probably making twice what you were making. I guess it's never enough, is that it?"

He looked for a signal in Brandt's face, but the young broker was sullen and withdrawn.

"Or was it the thrill of the chase?" Stride asked. "Were you doing it to see if you could get away with it?" When Brandt still didn't reply, he went on. "That's okay, you don't need to tell me anything. Get lawyered up and start negotiating a plea. We already have you on assault and attempted murder, so that's at least the next six to nine years of your life gone. We'll have to jockey with the feds, of course, because they're going to want you in federal prison for the Infloron Medical deal."

Brandt's head snapped around. Stride nodded.

"Oh, yeah, we know all about the insider trading scheme. You and Lassiter. The SEC knows about it, too, but that's not news to you, is it? That's why you went after Lassiter tonight."

Stride flicked his cigarette out the window. "The SEC is going to have to stand in line, though. Once we add multiple rapes to the list of charges, your white-collar crime stuff is going to seem like cheating on an exam. Now we're talking twenty-five years to life. Hard time."

Brandt heard the word *rape,* and he finally spoke. "What the hell are you talking about?"

"Don't play dumb with me, Mitch."

"I never raped anyone."

"No? That was just a game at Sonia's house tonight?" He saw Brandt do a double take, and he added, "Yeah, we know about the sex club, too."

"You can't make that out as rape."

"What about the others?"

"What others?"

"The alpha girls," Stride said.

"What about them? News flash, that's why they come to the club. To have sex. No one got raped."

Stride shrugged. "How about Tanjy?"

"What about her?"

"You playact a rape with her in Grassy Point Park, and after she dumps you, she winds up getting raped in the same place. That's quite a coincidence. Rape stories just seem to follow you around, don't they, Mitch?"

"Tanjy made up the rape," Brandt insisted.

Stride shook his head. "No, she didn't. Was it a thrill, getting back at her like that, knowing you could expose all her fantasies, and no one would believe her? What happened then? Did you decide you liked the power that came with it? When you got away with raping Tanjy, did you realize that the alpha girls would do anything to keep their secrets? Even after you raped them, too?"

"You're talking crazy here. I do not know what the fuck you are talking about."

"I'm talking about two alpha girls getting assaulted after the parties. Just like you were doing to Kathy Lassiter tonight. And maybe you don't know this, but this case is very personal to me."

Brandt struggled with his cuffs. "No way."

"This isn't going to be a hard case to make, Mitch. We've got a dozen witnesses to the assault on Kathy Lassiter. You were one of only a handful of men who were at all of the sex club parties where the alpha girls were later raped. You've got the size and strength to pull it off. And you told me you played rape games with Tanjy every night at knife-point. That's just what you did to the other women."

"Oh, fuck it. I cannot believe this." Brandt swung his head into the window so hard that a cut opened up on his forehead and blood leaked down his face, matting at his eyebrow. A red smear stained the glass. Stride pulled a few tissues from his pocket and leaned close to Brandt, blotting the blood. The tissue turned crimson.

"The club was a secret, Mitch," Stride continued. "No one else knew about the alpha girls. What's a jury going to think? Do you honestly think they'll picture someone like Delmar Bezac as a rapist? You're the stud of the group." He leaned in toward Brandt's ear and whispered, "Eric Sorenson figured it out, didn't he? He came to you and accused you of raping his wife. So you had to stop him. And Tanjy."

Brandt was close enough that Stride could smell his sweat. With Stride's hand over one eye, and his chiseled face needing a shave, Brandt looked like a pirate.

"You don't know anything," he told Stride. "You don't know what's going on in this city."

"Then explain it to me."

"I'm being set up. Just like Maggie."

"Sure."

"Look, whatever Lassiter says, it was *her* idea. She met me in the club. She came to me with the whole scheme about Infloron Medical and the FDA approval. So when I found out she was negotiating a sweet deal with the SEC to put it all on me, I lost it."

Stride shook his head. "You've got it wrong, Mitch. The SEC didn't know a thing about Kathy Lassiter. You were the one they had in their sights, not her. They got an anonymous tip."

He watched Brandt's eyes, which changed like a chameleon.

"You're lying to me," Brandt said.

"No, someone set you up."

"Son of a bitch," Brandt retorted, air hissing between his teeth.

"You sound like you know who it is."

Brandt closed his eyes. "Fuck this, I need to talk to my lawyer. I've got something to trade, and I want to find out how much it's worth before I say another goddamn word."

"What do you have to trade?" Stride asked.

"You said you're after a rapist, right?"

Stride saw that blood had oozed out around the edges of the tissues on Brandt's forehead. He pressed on the wound hard, and Brandt jerked in pain. "Maybe I didn't make myself clear, this guy may have killed two people. Right now, I think you're good for it. If you're not, then you better tell me why and help me find him."

"I want credit if you nail this guy. Some kind of deal."

"Yeah, we'll put a plaque up for you in City Hall. Who is he?"

"I don't know."

"Then you've got nothing to trade."

"Look, I don't *know* anything about him, but he's the one you want."

Stride waited.

"I *paid* him," Brandt continued. "We had a deal, and now he blows up my life anyway. It's like a fucking game to him."

"Who are you talking about?"

"I told you, I don't know," Brandt insisted. "You said I was the only one who knew about the alpha girls, but you're wrong. He knew all about them, too."

"Who?"

"The son of a bitch who's been blackmailing me."

Stride crumpled the tissues and tossed them on the floor of the car. He backed away from Brandt and heard Serena's voice, one word, just as he was falling asleep in the wake of their making love. One word in the box.

Blackmail.

"I'm still bleeding," Brandt protested.

"You'll live. Tell me more."

"This guy knows things. I don't know where he gets it. He came to me a couple of months ago, and he knew all about Infloron and the insider trading scheme. Dates, trades, dollars. He's been bleeding me dry."

"What about the alpha girls?"

"He knew about them, too. He joked about

me and Lassiter meeting in the sex club. He *asked* me how it was with the alpha girls. He knew their names. And then last night, he called me again. He knew Lassiter was going to be the alpha girl tonight, and he told me that she'd been going behind my back with the SEC. He said I'd better take care of her. But the bastard must have called the SEC himself."

"Were you trying to stiff him?" Stride asked.

"No! The son of a bitch just decided to fuck me."

Stride got out of the patrol car and slammed the door behind him. He looked up at the outline of the tower on the hill and thought about the Enger Park Girl and then Maggie and Serena. And about rape, murder, and blackmail. He tried to sort it all out in his head and didn't like where it took him.

Mitchell Brandt was being blackmailed. If Serena meant what he thought she did, then Dan Erickson was being blackmailed, too. By someone who also knew about the sex club and the alpha girls. That made him a prime suspect in the string of rapes and in the murders of Eric and Tanjy.

He suffered a flash of anger as he wondered how much Serena knew and why she didn't tell him.

After months operating in the shadows, the blackmailer had to realize the clock was ticking. The police knew about the rapes now. It was only a matter of time before Stride put the pieces together.

That meant Dan Erickson was in the path of the hurricane. So was Serena.

45

Serena parked in an empty lot underneath the soaring span of the Blatnik Bridge leading across Superior Bay to Wisconsin. Its concrete Y-shaped supports aligned like a row of soldiers marching from the city out into the water, following a trail of white lights. Every time a car sped by overhead, the steel highway bed became a tin drum and boomed. As Serena got out of her car, the ice sheet of the harbor was on her right. On the opposite side of the road, where it circled back to the city, were the dark fields leading to the silos of the port terminal. This was where the industry of the city was done during the warmer months, bustling with dozens of ore boats loading and offloading their bellies. The port was abandoned now, locked up with ice and awaiting the spring thaw.

Snow had begun, whipping through the bridge lights like a field of shooting stars. She blinked as the flakes assaulted her eyes. She had her Glock tightly in one hand and a duct-taped shoe box under her arm, heavy with hundred dollar bills. The road, the park, the frozen water, the port buildings, and the fields leading across the railroad tracks were all deserted. She wondered where he was.

Her heels were buried in six inches of wet snow, and her feet quickly grew numb and cold. She didn't have time to change after finding the note, only time to make the pick up at Dan's house and follow the freeway back to the harbor basin. Now, she wished she had kept spare boots in the car. She found an open area near the bridge tower where the snow was matted down and waited there. She danced impatiently, stamping her feet. The chill traveled up her body.

A wave of vibration rumbled through the

concrete as a double-trailored semi streaked along the bridge out over the water directly above her. The thunder of the tin drum made her shudder, as if the bridge were falling around her.

Her cell phone rang, and she put the shoe box down in the snow so she could grab her phone with her free hand.

"Where are you?" Stride asked.

Serena took a cautious look around the empty lot. As the snow intensified, it was becoming hard to see. "I'm on a job. I can't talk."

"Is this about Dan's blackmail?"

She hesitated. "Yes."

"Get the hell out of there," he told her. "Brandt was being blackmailed, too. This guy knows all about the sex clubs and the alpha girls. He may be our perp."

"Then this is our chance to get him," Serena said.

"Not by yourself."

"I was a cop for ten years. I can take care of myself."

"You should have told me what was going on with Dan."

"I couldn't, you know that."

"Where the hell are you?"

She thought about not telling him, but she realized she was being stupid and stubborn. "I'm down in Rices Point under the bridge."

"Are you completely fucking crazy?"

"He picked the spot."

"Get out right now, he may be coming after you."

"He's coming after a box full of money. That's what he wants."

"I'm sending a car down there."

"*Don't* do that," Serena insisted. "You'll scare him off."

"Then I'll come myself."

Her phone beeped in her ear. Another call was coming in. She knew who it was.

"No, don't do that, Jonny. Not yet. Give me half an hour. If I don't call you back, send in the troops."

She hung up before he could answer. When she switched over to the other call, she heard the blackmailer's voice and realized there was something distantly familiar about it. She wished she knew why, but it was one of those memories that had to come in its own time and couldn't be rushed. The one thing she knew was that the memory carried something dark with it, and the vibration in her spine this time wasn't from the traffic on the bridge, but from a sudden fear.

"Did you have fun tonight?" he asked.

Serena was silent.

"I was picturing you inside," he went on. "Did you get naked like all the others?"

"Fuck off."

"Did all that sex make you wet? Did you play with yourself?"

"I'm leaving," Serena said. "With your money."

"No, you're not. You're staying right there.

"Watch me." Serena bent down to pick up the shoe box and hoped he could see her. She waited, wanting to see what he did next.

"Tell me what it's like," he said.

"It sounds like you know."

"Do you want to be an alpha girl?"

"No thanks."

"Too bad," he said. "You could be just like your friend Maggie. Or Katrina. They were alpha girls."

The implications of what he said made her whole body go rigid. She clutched her gun tighter and didn't reply.

"You're afraid of me now," he said.

"Why should I be?"

"You know what I did to them."

She stood there, frozen, letting the snow paint her body white. "Yes."

"I'm going to do the same thing to you. I just wanted you to know that now."

"You bastard."

"And much worse, Serena. Much, much worse."

She hung up the phone. Stumbling, falling, getting up, she began running back to her car. She peered over her shoulder, hair flying, and then spun, spying everywhere around her, certain that she would see him coming for her. The tin drum boomed again; she screamed and bit her tongue, quieting herself, and tasted blood. Snow swarmed down and followed her like bees roused from a hive.

As she ran, the box of money slipped from her grasp and tumbled away. She cursed and bent to retrieve it, and when she stood up, she was blinded by the glare of a white beacon bathing her body in light. A familiar siren shrieked and stopped. She saw twisting red lights rotating atop a Duluth city police car, and she had never been so grateful that Jonny hadn't listened to her.

Paralyzed in the light, feeling like a deer

on the highway, she also realized she was holding a gun and a box filled with cash.

The cop saw it, too. He used a loudspeaker, and she heard a Southern accent. "Throw the gun away."

She did.

"Put the box down."

She did that, too.

"Lie down and keep your arms away from you."

Serena's arms were in the air. She went down on both knees and then laid her palms flat on the snow as she stretched out her body. She craned her neck to see, but the searchlight was in her eyes. She heard the door of the squad car open, and the cop shouted to her without the microphone.

"Don't move."

She was absolutely still, holding her breath.

"It's okay, officer," she said as he came closer. "My name is Serena Dial. I'm Lieutenant Stride's partner."

"Shut up."

He was angry, and under the anger was probably fear. She didn't say anything else, not wanting to rile him. She saw a silhouette of long, muscled legs, and in his hand, by his thigh, was his gun, pointed at her. He came around behind her. She lay there, not moving; it was like having a bear sniff around you as you played dead. He retrieved her gun where she had thrown it in the snow, removed the magazine, and deposited it in his pocket.

She grimaced as his knee landed in the center of her back. He took one of her wrists roughly, twisted it behind her, and latched her wrist in the loop of his handcuffs. He took her other arm, too, and secured her. He grabbed the scruff of her neck with thick fingers. She smelled his hands.

"Get up."

He hadn't holstered his gun yet. She came up to her knees as he pulled her, and she got to her feet carefully, not making any sudden movements.

"What's in the box?" he asked.

"Money. Look, call Stride. He knows what's going on."

"Get in the car."

He landed the heel of his palm on her neck and shoved her forward. He picked up the box as they headed for the police car. She walked a couple of paces ahead of him and listened to her senses, which were saying an odd word to her.

Fish.

In her nose, a stench of fish spoiled the fresh aroma of snow, and she realized it came from the cop, where his fingers had roughly grabbed her skin. His hands smelled like fish.

That was just how her car smelled when she got back into it after the party.

Exactly like that.

Thoughts spilled through her brain, and the more they did, the more her relief blew away like ash from a fire. She thought about how odd it was that Jonny would ignore her and send a car down here anyway. She thought about how fast the car had made it here. She thought about an offhanded comment Jonny had made to her yesterday.

Pete McKay managed to get his patrol car stolen while he was on a call at the high school.

She had made a horrible mistake. The accent in his voice was a disguise. There was no cop behind her. *It was him.* He had told her what he was going to do to her, and she let him walk right up to her, disarm her, and put her in cuffs.

Serena didn't look back or change her gait, but she knew she had only a few seconds to make a move. Once they got to the car, she was trapped. Overhead, on the bridge, she saw the lights of a truck speeding away from the city, and she knew that it was about to bang the tin drum loudly. She tensed.

The highway bed boomed, and the man behind her jerked involuntarily. She could hear his clothes rustle as his instincts kicked in and he looked back over his shoulder just for a split second. Serena ran. She galloped through the snow, breaking away from him and heading for the fields and long grass that led toward the port terminal. He recovered and was after her immediately, but Serena was fast. Her shoes slipped off her feet, and she ran even faster that way, struggling to stay balanced with her arms locked behind her. She didn't look back, but heard him grunt as he fell. She reached the road, shot across it, and leaped down into the tall brush, which rose almost to her neck. When she risked a look back, she didn't see him.

Fighting through the snow was like running through deep water. The effort exhausted her, and only the blood pumping madly through her veins kept her feet from freezing. She passed under drooping telephone wires and near the concrete skeletons of a bridge that had been torn down years ago, leaving behind rubble that may as well have been the bombed-out remains of a war zone. He was back behind her again; she could hear him beating through the weeds. She emerged out of the field after a hundred yards and found herself in the middle of a field of snow-lined railroad tracks winding into the heart of the port. Rusted railway cars sat there, abandoned for the season. The struggle to run without her arms pumping at her side was wearing her down. As she followed the tracks, she pitched forward, tripping on a brick of ice. Something hard and sharp cut her face. She lost precious seconds twisting and turning and fighting back to her feet, and she saw him behind her, a violent shadow, bursting from the grassy field and steering for her, closing the gap.

She didn't know how much time had passed, and she prayed that Jonny would soon be flooding the area with police.

The tracks led her into the port, and she found herself in a world populated by sleeping giants. Cranes soared into the sky, hooks dangling on steel cables like hangmen.

Snow-covered mountains of dirt, scrap metal, and taconite dwarfed her, and concrete silos more than a hundred feet tall towered over the flat land. She tried to lose herself in the huge, silent maze, where the only noise was the hiss of the blizzard. She watched and listened for him, but he had melted into the port behind her and vanished. He could be anywhere.

She had trouble walking. Her feet trailed blood, and she could barely feel them or move her toes. Cuts and bruises stung her face, and she tasted more blood on her lips. The handcuffs rubbed her wrists raw. She couldn't move anymore. She stopped where a crevice had eroded into a pyramid of earth and forced herself inside, hating that she couldn't see out, hoping he wouldn't cross in front of her. She squatted, making herself small, but she swayed on her frostbitten feet and toppled forward, exposed. Snow continued to fall in a white rain that chilled and enveloped her. She tried to right herself, but she had no strength anymore except to lie there and hope that the giants would protect her.

Her cell phone began ringing. It was ungodly loud. Her hands were tied, and all she could do was listen to it shoot up a flare for him. She heard the slow, sure crunch of his footsteps as he found her and glimpsed his shadow looming over her, and she didn't even care. He laughed, staring down at her prone body, and dragged her by her collar off the ground. His revolver was flipped in his hand, the butt facing out. She had no more fight.

"Time for a little payback," he said.

The gun flew up, it flew down, and somewhere she saw the orange light of the sun coming closer and burning her eyes and leaving her blind.

PART THREE

HOT SPOTS

46

The second glass of shiraz made Helen Danning's head swim. She usually avoided alcohol, but a few days at Evelyn's house had relaxed her. She sat in a fraying easy chair and hummed as she listened to the soundtrack from *Damn Yankees* on the stereo. She had seen nearly every performance of the show at the Ordway, with Jerry Lewis in the role of the devil. He was a great devil.

Helen filed her fingernails to perfect crescents and swung up her legs to do the same with her toenails. She was particular about her nails, makeup, lipstick, and hair. Everything had to be clean and in place. She ironed all her clothes, even her socks and underwear, when they were fresh out of the dryer. She kept her countertops disinfected and sparkling and never left a dirty dish in the sink. Evelyn wasn't so fussy. Her friend liked mess creeping in at the edges, but she didn't complain when Helen obsessively cleaned her house.

Evelyn warbled the chorus from the show tune on the speakers. She dipped to one knee and spread both arms wide as she bounded into the living room.

Helen laughed.

"That's what I like to see," Evelyn told her. "You laughing. You with your feet up."

"I'm a little drunk," Helen said.

"Good."

Evelyn reached inside the hall closet and took out a fleece jacket covered with strips of silver reflective tape. She shrugged it on.

"You're going jogging?" Helen asked. "It's late."

"I know, I got caught up in my latest masterpiece." Evelyn wiped a smudge of paint from her cheek.

"It's slippery out there."

The windows were pasted with snow.

Evelyn shrugged. "I'm used to it. Anyway,

there's nothing but flurries now. The storm tracked north. Duluth is getting buried."

"I'm hungry," Helen said.

"I won't be long, and then we can have dinner." Evelyn sighed as her golden retriever launched a frenzy of barking in the front of the house. "That dog barks at every damn deer that wanders into the woods. Edgar! Leave Bambi alone! You know, I found him nose to nose with a moose one morning, and the moose was looking at that dog like he was nuts."

Evelyn padded over to the ottoman in her white socks, pushed Helen's legs aside, and sat down. She began putting on her tennis shoes and eyed Helen thoughtfully.

"So did you write back to that woman who sent you the e-mail? Eric's wife?"

Helen frowned. "I told her to leave me alone."

"You think that's the right thing to do?"

"She's a cop. I don't want anything to do with cops."

"She's also a woman whose husband was murdered. You might be able to help her. Don't you think you should?"

"I don't want to get in the middle of this."

"You already are."

"What do you mean?"

Evelyn dug into the pocket of her sweat pants and pulled out a scrap of paper. She handed it to Helen. It was a phone number with a 218 area code.

"Somebody called me at the shop today," Evelyn said. "He was with the Duluth police."

Helen tensed. "Oh, my God."

"They're looking for you, honeybun."

"You didn't tell him anything, did you?"

"Of course not, but he knew we were best friends. He gave me his number and said I should ask you to call him."

Helen bolted up. "I have to go."

Evelyn put a calming hand on her chest. "Whoa there, girl. Think about this. Why don't you call and talk to him? What would a phone call hurt? I know you had a bad time with the police in college, but this is different."

"Evelyn, I just want this all to go away. I want to live my life and not have anyone bother me, you know?"

"It's too late for that," Evelyn told her. "You might be the one person who can help them catch this guy."

"All I ever wanted was to put this behind me."

"I know. Look, have some more wine, and think about it, okay? We can talk about it over dinner."

"I may not be here when you come back."

"And miss my spinach spaghetti and meatless meatballs? Bite your tongue."

"I'm scared."

"Don't be. I told you before, you're safe here. Okay? Just hang on, and I'll be back in a few minutes."

"Couldn't you skip your run tonight?" Helen asked.

"I could skip it every night, but then I'd never do it. I won't be long." She jogged over to the front door. The golden retriever was still barking outside. "Edgar! You don't even like venison! Stupid dog."

When she was gone, Helen shut the music off. She put the second glass of wine down on the edge of a bookshelf. She was keyed up, and she got out of the easy chair and paced. She used the remote control to turn on the television, and she stood with her arms folded, watching an old sitcom, before she realized she wasn't even listening to the dialogue. She shut the television off, too.

Helen thought about Eric Sorenson, the

attractive man with the flowing blond hair. When he first approached her at the theater, she didn't trust him, and she didn't want to hear his story. It was only when he told her what had happened to his wife that she agreed to meet him for dinner after the show. That was a mistake. She didn't want to get involved. She had been running away from the assault in college since she was twenty years old, and the last thing she needed was this stranger bringing it all up again.

Then, three days later, it was all over the news. The man who had sat across the table from her was dead. Murdered. His wife was the suspect.

His wife, who had sent an e-mail on Helen's blog. *I need your help.*

Helen didn't want to help. She didn't want to be pulled into any of this. She had lived a long time on her own, keeping her world immaculate, losing herself in musicals every night. She wanted to be left alone, to be safe, to forget. But Evelyn was right. It was too late to do that. She was in the middle of everything, whether she liked it or not.

She retrieved her glass of wine and finished it. She sat back down in the easy chair, closed her eyes, and turned on the rest of the *Damn Yankees* soundtrack. She listened to it all the way to the end, where the devil gets outsmarted, where the good guy gets his soul back. When it was over, Helen wondered if that could happen in real life. She wondered if you could ever outrun the devil, or if he would always get you in the end.

She looked at the scrap of paper with the phone number on it.

Call the police. It sounded so simple, but Evelyn didn't know what she was asking Helen to do. And for what? She had no evidence of anything. For all she knew, Eric's wife did kill him. She had nothing to tell them, not really.

Helen picked up the phone, felt its weight in her hand, and put it down again. She was having trouble breathing. If the cop answered, she wasn't sure if she could talk. She didn't know what to say. Her mouth was dry. She walked away from the phone and stared at it from across the room. She didn't owe Eric anything. She didn't owe his wife. The only person she owed was herself.

Then do it for yourself, she thought.

Helen marched back to the phone and dialed the number before her hesitation made her freeze. She held her breath as the phone rang, and an instant later, someone picked it up.

"Hello," the voice said.

Helen was speechless with surprise. "Oh," she blurted finally. "Is this the Duluth police?"

"No, it's not."

"Well, does a policeman live there?"

"No, you've got the wrong number."

"I'm sorry," Helen said.

She hung up and repunched the buttons carefully, reciting them aloud from Evelyn's note. She waited as the phone rang.

"Hello," the same voice said.

Helen didn't say anything this time. Her brain raced. Her heart took off like a rocket.

"Who's there?" the man asked loudly. When Helen was silent, he swore and hung up on her. The dial tone buzzed in her ear.

She laid the phone gently back in its cradle. Her body went warm with sweat, and her bowels constricted. Her skin bubbled with gooseflesh.

If Evelyn were here, she'd say, *Get a grip, honeybun. So I got the number wrong.*

But Evelyn wouldn't make a mistake like that.

Where was she? She should be back by

now. Evelyn never jogged for more than half an hour in the evenings, and when Helen checked the mantel clock, she realized that an hour had slipped by while she was listening to the music.

Get a grip, honeybun. So I'm a little late.

Maybe Evelyn had sprained an ankle. Maybe she had found an injured animal by the highway and was trying to rescue it. She was always doing that.

Maybe.

Helen backed up slowly and silently until her hand grazed the north wall of the house, and then she stood motionless, studying the shadows in the hallway that led to the bedrooms. She sucked her upper lip between her teeth and bit it hard.

The dog wasn't barking anymore. Why?

Maybe the deer was gone. Maybe Edgar was asleep.

You've been drinking, she told herself. You're paranoid.

Helen followed the wall toward the rear porch that overlooked the river. When she reached the easy chair where she had been sitting, she reached behind and shut off the lamp, bathing the house in darkness. She navigated around the wicker furniture and then put a hand on the cold glass as she stared outside through the storm door. Somewhere in the night, below the garden, behind the weeping willow that brushed the ground with its dangling branches, was the Mississippi. She couldn't see a light anywhere. It reminded her again of how much she hated darkness and open spaces, how much she preferred to be cloistered where it was bright and crowded.

You need to go. Now.
He's here.

Helen cracked open the porch door and slid outside into the bitter air. The wooden deck was glazed with ice. She nearly fell as she hurriedly took two steps down to the grass, which crackled with frost.

Her car was steps away, parked beside Evelyn's old tool shed.

All she had to do was make it from here to there.

All she had to do was get in her car and drive away. She could call Evelyn from the road. Evelyn would be safe at home by then and cross at Helen for leaving. Nothing had happened to her. Helen was imagining the fog of menace around her. The presence of the devil.

She could drive to Duluth and find Eric's wife and put an end to a lifetime of running.

Twenty yards of open space, twenty yards of night, lay between her and the car. Then she would be free.

She remembered that the soundtrack to *Show Boat* was in her CD player, and she smiled at the idea of listening to it as she drove. She was thinking about that black man singing "Ol' Man River" as she ran for the car. She was thinking how scared she was of dying as she felt the hands around her throat.

47

Dan Erickson had a crystal glass of gin in his hand, and he was dressed in black slacks and a dress shirt, with a loosened tie hanging around his neck. His hair was mussed. When he saw Stride in his doorway at midnight, his mouth squeezed into a frown, and his eyes betrayed his anxiety. Stride laid two hands on Dan's chest and shoved him back into the house, where he stumbled on the wood floor, his drink and ice cubes spilling, the heavy crystal rolling away and bumping on the wall.

"What's wrong with you?" Dan demanded.

"He's *got* her, you stupid, arrogant son of

a bitch!" Stride shouted. "He's got Serena, and I want to know *who he is*!"

Dan brushed his hair out of his eyes. "I don't know what you're talking about."

"Don't play games with me. Don't even think about it. Someone put your balls in a vise, and you went and hired Serena to get you out of it."

"She told you that?"

"What, do you want a refund on your bill? It's time to come clean, Dan. I don't care if it means you lose everything. You're going to tell me what's going on."

"I don't have to tell you a thing."

Stride shook his head. "Lauren may have January lake water in her veins, but not you. I don't think it's only been about power and money with you."

"Then I guess I'm shallower than you think."

"Okay, maybe you are," Stride said. "I don't give a shit. What I'm telling you is that the life you know is *over* one way or another. It's all coming out. You can tell me right now and help me try to save Serena's life, or you can shut up and let the reporters start feeding on you tomorrow. Take your pick."

Dan leaned against the wall, exhaling like the air squealing from a tire. When he retreated down the hallway, Stride followed. A walnut door led into a dark office, where a computer screen glowed on Dan's desk. He took a seat in the reclining chair and rocked back, staring at the ceiling, his legs spread, his arms dangling. There was a photo of him and Lauren on the wall over his head, the two of them smiling and looking prosperous.

"I'm sorry about Serena."

"Sorry doesn't change anything," Stride said.

Dan sat up straight. "You know why I'm so good at putting people in prison? I understand how criminals think. I know what it's like to go after something you want and not give any thought to the consequences. I'm like a teenager getting laid and not using protection."

"You're wasting my time, Dan."

"I just want you to understand, okay? But you don't. You're too disciplined, Stride. Always in control."

"That's the last thing I am."

"Well, you've never let a woman lead you around by the cock, have you? That's my life."

Stride heard movement behind him and saw Lauren waiting in the pale light of the doorway, listening. Their eyes met. He had never seen her blue eyes so intense and bitter cold. She sauntered into the office, her hands in the pockets of stonewashed blue jeans. She wore a navy-blue flannel shirt, untucked, with the top two buttons undone, and suede boots.

"What's going on?" she asked.

Dan glared at her, and Stride saw in his expression what it was like to spend a lifetime of impotence under a rich woman's thumb. "This doesn't concern you."

"No? I heard you mention your cock, Dan. That always concerns me."

"Funny."

"It's not funny at all," Lauren said. "What have you done?"

Dan was silent. Lauren turned to Stride with a question in her eyes.

"He's being blackmailed," Stride said. "He hired Serena to be the go-between. The blackmailer kidnapped her tonight."

"Oh, my God."

"This guy is blowing up all the mines he buried, Dan," Stride told him. "Mitchell Brandt was paying off your blackmailer over an insider trading scheme, and this guy decided to fuck him. You're next. Don't you get it, Dan? Your number's up. This guy is capable of anything. We think he's already added rape and murder to his extortion racket."

"How much did you pay him?" Lauren asked her husband.

Dan didn't answer.

"How much?"

"A hundred and ten thousand dollars."

"You idiot," Lauren snapped.

"What does he have on you?" Stride asked.

Dan hesitated and looked at Lauren.

"Tell him," she said. "Tell *both* of us."

Dan shrugged. "It was Tanjy."

"Did you rape her?" Stride asked. "Did you kill her? Is that what this is all about?"

"No! We were having an affair."

Stride shook his head. "Why was that worth so much money?"

"You know what Tanjy's fantasies were like. We did things that no one would understand. He had photos of us. It would have been devastating if people found out."

"Did you kill Tanjy to keep her quiet?" Stride asked.

"No, no, that's not what happened at all."

Lauren's face was a mask of granite. "You realize what this means. This is all going to be in the papers." She looked at Stride. "Am I right?"

Stride nodded.

"Washington is gone," she told Dan. "We're ruined."

"It was never supposed to come out," Dan protested.

"Who do you think you are, JFK? Bill Clinton? You think you can get away with anything? I can't believe what you've done to me. It's all over now, Dan. Do you realize that? You just threw our lives away."

"I'm sorry," he said.

"Was it really worth it?" Lauren demanded. "Was *she* worth it?"

Dan stared at her hard, and Stride wondered if it was the first time in his life that he had told her the truth. "Yeah, she was."

Lauren stalked across the room and slapped him so hard it sounded like a rifle firing. It was an end-of-life slap. End of everything. Lauren and Dan were over the cliff. She turned and marched out of the room, and five seconds later the front door slammed so hard that the old house quivered.

"We need to find this guy," Stride repeated. "I need to know who he is."

"I have no idea."

"Then we're going to sit here and figure out how he tore apart your life, and how he tore apart Mitchell Brandt's life, and how he knew about Sonia and the goddamn sex club. And don't tell me you didn't know about the club."

"I knew about it," Dan admitted. "Look, Stride, I didn't want to tell you this, but there's something else. I don't think it will help us find him, but you should probably know about it."

"Go on."

"This guy's obsessed with Serena," Dan said. "He was obsessed with her from the very beginning."

"What do you mean?" Stride asked. He could barely breathe.

"I mean, it wasn't an accident that I hired Serena to be the go-between. That was part of the deal. Part of the price. He didn't just want money when he first approached me. He wanted Serena."

48

Stride let the silence drag out between them and grow violent. Hostility filled the room like smoke flooding from the air vents. They stared at each other. The computer on Dan's desk whirred as its fan blew. Somewhere outside, the engine of an expensive sedan raced as Lauren fled from the garage and away from the estate.

"I had no idea anything like this would happen," Dan said.

"You should have had alarm bells going off in your head, but you just didn't care. You were trying to save your ass."

Dan shrugged. "All right, maybe I was."

"If something happens to Serena, I will destroy you."

"You'll have to take a number."

"Is that all you have to say?"

"Look, I did *not* think it would go down like this. You know as well I do that most black-mailers aren't violent. They're cowards at heart. I thought maybe this guy had a crush on Serena, or hell, I thought they might be in it together. She was new in town. I had no idea who the hell she was."

Stride didn't believe him, but it didn't matter. He shoved his anger aside. "Do you have any clue who this guy is?"

"I told you, no."

"Did Serena?"

"If she did, she never told me."

"How did he contact you?"

"The first time was by phone," Dan said. "He called me at home."

"When?"

"Last Tuesday."

"What did he say?" Stride asked.

"He knew about my affair with Tanjy."

"What did he want?"

"He wanted ten thousand dollars, or he was going to tell the press and Lauren about my affair."

"Did he say why he wanted Serena involved?"

"No, he just said he knew I wasn't going to want to handle the dirty work personally, so there was someone who could be our go-between. I don't know how he knew her, or why he wanted her."

"How did he know about you and Tanjy?"

"I have no idea."

"What happened next?"

"I paid him, end of story. Serena handled the drop. A few days later, he gave Serena a very explicit photograph of me and Tanjy in Grassy Point Park. This time the price went way up."

"How did he get the photo?"

"Like I told Serena, I don't know. Tanjy took them, but I deleted them from her computer. No way this guy should have been able to find them."

"Were the photos stored anywhere else? Were they on your computer?"

"No, Tanjy took them on a digital camera, and I uploaded them to her PC for her. As far as I know, that was it. She sure as hell wouldn't have shared them with anyone else. I got rid of them back in November, after the rape charge blew up and Tanjy and I split."

"So she could have retrieved them."

"Tanjy? That girl needed a manual to turn her computer on."

"Well, someone retrieved them. Unless this guy found them *before* you deleted them."

"Then why wait to blackmail me?"

Stride nodded. He didn't understand the logic, but he also realized he was getting close to something important. The blackmailer had to have access to Tanjy's computer.

"What if this guy is a hacker?" Stride asked. "He could be intercepting e-mails, or breaking in via an Internet connection, or piggybacking on a wireless network."

Stride thought about everything else the blackmailer knew and felt his adrenaline surging. Mitchell Brandt and his insider trading scheme. *Dates, trades, dollars,* Brandt had said. The sex club and Sonia, who kept detailed records about the club on her desktop. Photos of Tanjy and Dan. Stored on Tanjy's computer.

"No way this guy got into Tanjy's machine from outside," Dan said. "It must be someone who was inside her apartment."

Stride thought about his first visit to Tanjy's

apartment and then remembered the kid from across the street who spent his days spying on Tanjy from his bedroom window. What the hell was his name? Doug? Duke? If Stride got into her place simply by unlocking a window, how many times had this kid done the same thing? What if he booted up Tanjy's computer and found a gold mine?

Stride was excited, but then he discarded the thought. Even if the kid had a connection to Tanjy, it didn't explain how he could have known what Mitchell Brandt or Sonia Bezac were hiding.

He thought about what Dan had just said. "Why are you so sure this guy didn't hack in from outside?"

"I made sure she installed a state-of-the-art firewall," Dan replied. "I knew the kind of stuff she was keeping on her system, and I didn't want anyone swiping it."

"You said she was hopeless with computers."

"Sure, she called Byte Patrol. They configured the firewall for her."

Stride stopped. Everything stopped. "Byte Patrol? Those are the guys in the purple vans, right? And the purple shirts?"

"Yeah, you see them all over town."

One by one, Stride remembered. The details broke away from the mass of facts in his head and dropped like coins plinking into the metal tray of a slot machine. The cherries lined up, and he cashed out.

He was in Tanjy's bedroom, and he saw the neon purple folder next to her computer.

He was in Sonia's living room, and she was telling him about the hacker-proof security system on her computer. Installed by Byte Patrol.

He was talking to Mitchell Brandt and hearing about the research software he used. Designed by Byte Patrol.

He was inside Silk, and Sonia was chewing out a tech in a purple shirt. The guy was like a bear, his giant paws over the keyboard. Stride tried to picture exactly what the man looked like, but all he could remember was the instant where the tech caught Stride's eye and winked.

The man from Byte Patrol knew exactly who Stride was. He was laughing at his own joke. This was the man who knew everything hidden inside the computers. This was the man who was pulling strings and selling secrets all over the city. This was the man who had raped Maggie.

Stride thought about Eric talking to Tony Wells. *How can you tell if someone ordinary could be a sexual predator?*

This was the man, Stride thought, *that Eric went to see that night.*

This was the man who had Serena.

49

Serena knew she was awake because of the pain. Her skull felt as if someone had punched it in like an eggshell. When she turned her neck, a jolt of agony shivered up her spine and made her whole body jerk. When she opened her eyes, she saw only black but felt the world spin. She tried to move her hands, but they were bound. So were her feet. She was pinned down, a butterfly captured by a collector. The mattress below her felt like burlap and scratched her skin. It smelled of mold and blood. The air carried a waft of gutted fish spilling out roe, bones, and organs. She tried to talk, shout, cry, and scream, but she was gagged, and the taste of wet cotton soured her mouth. Her throat squealed out a sound so pitiful that the wind laughed at it.

The blizzard was a monster inches away, noisy and ferocious. Steel rattled and quivered as the gales assaulted metal walls. She heard hissing, like a thousand snakes, which was the whip of snow, as furious as a tornado. Wherever she was, she may as well have been outside, because there was no protection here from the wind and cold blasting through the walls. The frozen air across her skin told her she was naked. Her bare flesh puckered. Her toes curled, and she tightened her fingers into fists. A drop of water fell on her through the ceiling, tracing an icy trail down her thigh.

She cursed herself for being so stupid. Not telling Jonny. Not watching her back. She was a prisoner now, and she didn't fool herself with hopes of rescue, and she knew it was going to be bad. The kind of bad when you realized there was no God coming for you. The kind of bad she had been through before.

He was in the room with her. Every few seconds, she heard the screech of wood and nails separating as he shifted in a rickety chair. Without seeing him, she felt his eyes. She wanted him to say something. She wanted it to begin and be over with, but long minutes passed where he let her struggle in her blind, cold world, as if he knew that the waiting was worst of all. She felt like a child in line for a scary ride, her stomach balling up into fear.

She told herself it didn't matter. It was just pain. Long ago, she had taught herself how to tunnel inside her brain to hide from pain. To switch off her emotions until she felt nothing at all. No hurt. No fury. No love. She tried to remember how she had done it, how she could follow the trail there again, how she could find that place. Even now, she found herself resisting, not wanting to go back. Nothingness was a torture all its own, a soundless room that she had spent decades trying to escape.

She struggled at her bonds, feeling the bed jostle and shake as she tried to free herself, knowing she was wasting her strength. He laughed, the first real sound he had made, and then she heard him stand up. She smelled him getting closer. She tried to wriggle backward, but there was nowhere to go. He bent over her. His breath was in her face. She wrenched her face away, but his fingers grabbed her jaw like a pincer and twisted her back.

"I've waited a long time for this," he said.

She tried to drown out his voice and the odd echoes of terror it awakened in her. She focused on the storm, imagining the burying snow on the other side of the wall, wondering if the wind would pick her up and carry her away.

He dragged something cold and sharp against her skin, starting at her neck, making a line across her throat with what she realized was the point of a knife. He pushed deep enough to make her squirm but not enough to break the skin. The knife explored her like a curious animal. It made a circle around her breasts, and then her aureoles, and then punctured one nipple in the very center, a pinprick that made her shudder and drew a wet, warm drop of blood.

Unbidden, tears streamed down her face.

The knife moved lower, scraping through her navel, detouring to her thighs, pushing up under the bones of her knees, running up the balls of her feet, climbing back up and zeroing in between her legs. He turned the knife and laid the cold flat of the blade along her mound. She tensed and hunted for the faraway place, the nothingness room, but it was lost in her brain, and she didn't know where to find it.

"I should sign my work," he said. "That way, when Stride finds you, he'll know who it was."

She threw her head back and forth violently, ignoring the pain in her skull, and thrust her body up off the bed at him. Another scream died in the wet cotton in her mouth. He waited until her resistance ran out of force, and she collapsed backward, spent, dizzy.

His big hand found the flat square of her stomach and pushed down, expelling air through her nose. He stretched the skin between his fingers until it was taut, like a canvas.

"No!" she wailed, but there was no sound coming from her, just the storm outside. The protest, the begging, the pleading, were only in her mind.

The knifepoint penetrated her. Tissue separated cell by cell. Blood oozed. He began to carve.

Somewhere in the middle, she passed out. When she awoke again, her stomach was cold and hot, stinging and frozen, all at the same time. The blood had become ice, hard like sugar candy. The storm raged on behind the wall. The smells and sounds were the same, but something was different, and she realized that the rag stuffed into her mouth was gone. She could work the muscles of her jaw and breathe stale air.

Serena screamed, and she discovered she was in a small place, because the noise rattled back and forth between the walls, unbearably loud and tinny. Outside, though, it was a murmur held up against the roar of the wind. She kept screaming until her throat was hoarse and sore, and when she stopped, nothing at all happened. No one ran to find her. The blizzard paid no attention.

"Scream if you want, but no one will hear you," he said.

She didn't answer.

"Go two feet outside, and you can't hear

anything. Believe me, you don't want to go outside now. You wouldn't last thirty seconds."

It sounded like thirty seconds of paradise to her. Thirty seconds of exposure, and then she could be warm and asleep and out of pain.

"Why me?" she asked.

"You were the one I wanted all along," he said.

"Why?" she repeated.

"Haven't you guessed?"

Something in the way he said it made her realize for the first time that this wasn't random. She hadn't crossed paths with a stalker and accidentally wound up in his sights. This was about her and him and always had been. Personal.

"Who are you?" she asked.

"I think you know."

He was right. She did know him. When she thought about it like that, she realized that there was something familiar about him, something in his voice that stirred memories. She searched her past, but there were so many names. It was like that when you were a cop—the names blurred together. Most of the time it didn't matter, because how many perps cared about being collared by a fat cop in his fifties? But when you were a woman, when you were beautiful, when you were from Las Vegas, the past somehow hung on and never let go.

Her bad luck.

Right then and there, she knew. Bad luck. *Tommy Luck.*

Tommy Luck, who scarred his girlfriend with the point of his knife. Tommy Luck, who kept that ugly wall in his apartment with dozens of secret photographs of Serena— tortured photographs with missing eyes, slashes across her neck, red paint splashed on her body, holes where he had stabbed the images repeatedly with an ice pick. Oh, God, oh, God, why hadn't she kept track? He was in for twenty years, but the more they piled people into prisons, the more they let others out.

He was out. He was back. Tommy Luck. She should have done what she thought about doing years ago, when he first got out of prison. Followed him. Killed him. She could have erased him and erased all the pain for everyone else who wound up in his path. Maggie. Tanjy. Eric. All the others.

Her fault. She should have killed him back when she had the chance.

"You know, don't you?" he asked her.

She was silent.

"I want you to see me for what comes next. I want you to look into my eyes. I'll tape them open if I need to. You're going to watch what I do to you."

She felt the knife again, on her face this time, bruising her cheekbone as he cut away the blindfold. She couldn't help herself—she opened her eyes even when her mind told her to keep them shut. There was only a single bulb lighting up the space, but it was bright anyway after so much darkness, and she squinted and turned her head. He loomed over her, huge and strong, coming between her and the light, a silhouette of evil.

50

They went through his apartment door with battering rams at two in the morning, but Stride knew he wouldn't be there, and he wasn't.

He was using the name William Deed, and the people who knew him called him Billy. Mitchell Brandt and Sonia Bezac both confirmed that Billy Deed was the Byte Patrol tech who worked on their computers, and the store owner who was now seated in front of the computer in Deed's apartment checked his records and told Stride that Deed had handled the setup and firewall for Tanjy Powell.

There was no record of William Deed in the state's criminal justice database, and the social security number he had provided on his employment application was false.

Stride ran both hands through his wavy hair and tried to hold himself in check. His adrenaline raced, coursing through his bloodstream as if he had swallowed down half a dozen cups of strong coffee. His heart was skipping beats; he could feel it stutter every minute. Along with the adrenaline was a coiled fist of dread in his stomach, churning up acid that burned a backward path up his throat. He couldn't think about Serena now. If he did, he would go crazy. He could only think about William Deed and how to find him.

Max Guppo emerged from Deed's bedroom. He was a flatulent, three hundred pound detective, fifty years old, with the worst comb-over in the upper Midwest, and he was also Stride's best evidence technician. They had worked together since Stride joined the force. No one wanted to be locked up in a van with Guppo on a stakeout, but the man was a wizard with latent prints and evidence maps and knew his way around computers as well as anyone from Byte Patrol.

"Plenty of prints," Guppo told Stride. He had a line of perspiration on his upper lip. "I raised the best of them. I'm on my way to City Hall to scan them in."

"Call the duty officer at BCA in Saint Paul, and get someone in the lab to check the database for us right now. If there's no state match, have them send it on it to the feebs and put a rush on it."

"Already done," Guppo replied. "I woke up my buddy who's the top guy in the BCA lab, and he's on his way downtown. He said he'll handle it personally."

"You're beautiful."

"Don't worry, sir, I'll get back to you in less than an hour even if I have to wake up the special agent in charge."

Guppo hustled from the apartment, and when Guppo hustled, the floor shook. Stride knew that Guppo and the rest of the team were working double-time all night on this case. They'd do it on any abduction, but this one was personal. Their loyalty was the one comfort he had right now.

Teitscher arrived at the apartment a few minutes later, and his bloodhound eyes found Stride by the window. His trench coat was wet with snow.

"Anything?" Stride asked, but when he saw Abel's face, he knew it was bad news. His heart misfired again.

Teitscher's mustache formed a frown. "We found Pete McKay's squad car in a downtown parking ramp."

"Did you check it out?"

"Yeah. Look, Lieutenant, I can't sugarcoat this. We found bloodstains in the trunk. But we're not talking about a lot of blood. No one bled out in there, okay?"

Stride needed a cigarette badly. His racing nerves made his fingers tremble. He reminded himself again not to think about Serena and not to dwell on what might be happening to her. Think about Deed. Work the case.

"So you think he switched cars," Stride said.

"Yeah. I also think Serena's alive."

Teitscher didn't explain, but Stride knew what he meant. If Serena were dead, Deed would have left her body in the trunk of the car. "Were there any cameras in the ramp?" Stride asked.

"No, but this guy has one of the purple Byte Patrol vans checked out to him. We haven't found it. We're calling everyone with an emergency ATL on the van. We've got highway patrol staking out all three of the north-south arteries—Thirty-five, Sixty-one, and One sixty-nine—in case this guy tries to head toward the Cities. The Canadian border is on alert, too."

"How about Wisconsin?"

"Yeah, we've got Wisconsin Thirty-five covered. K-2 pulled in off-shift personnel, and we're blanketing the city. The media's on it, too. I know it won't do much good until the morning news programs, but we'll have the public on the lookout tomorrow. We'll get helicopters up when it stops snowing."

Stride couldn't escape the feeling that tomorrow would be too late. "He probably has another vehicle," he said.

"Probably."

Stride shouted at the store owner, who was sifting through the material on Deed's computer. Craig was no more than thirty, wearing gray sweatpants and a red UMD sweatshirt with ratty sneakers. He looked half-asleep. He was tall and thin, with big, frizzy red hair and a lumberjack's beard. "Hey!" Stride called. "Do you know if this Deed had another car? Did you ever see him driving anything other than your van?"

Craig rubbed his eyes. "No, he kept the van overnight most of the time."

"Hiding in plain sight," Teitscher said. "Those vans are so noticeable that no one notices them."

"So maybe we'll get lucky, and he's still in it," Stride replied. "Keep me posted. Check in every half hour."

"I will. Look, Lieutenant, I know this doesn't mean shit coming from me, but I feel bad about this."

"Thanks, Abel."

"I'm also not saying I was wrong about Maggie, but this thing looks more complicated than I thought."

"You played it the way I would have done in your shoes," Stride told him.

"Maggie called and asked me if she could be part of the search. I probably shouldn't have done it, but I said okay."

Stride shrugged. "She would have done it anyway."

"I know."

"Better be careful, Abel, people will start saying you're soft."

"Yeah. That'll happen soon."

Teitscher left, and Stride continued studying Deed's apartment, looking for clues to the man. The apartment building was a drab high-rise near the pawn shops and gun stores on the far south end of Superior Street. Through his sixth-floor window, Deed looked out on a jigsaw puzzle of highway overpasses where the freeway broke apart into the city streets. It was cheap, anonymous, and seconds away from a quick escape.

Inside the one-bedroom apartment itself, there was little to distinguish the man. He ate chicken TV dinners, tacos, guacamole chips, and frozen chunks of walleye wrapped in aluminum foil. The kitchen reeked of fish. The apartment came furnished, and Deed had added little of his own other than a high-end PC. They found no magazines, no bank records, and no receipts. All they had was a description of the man: tall, heavy, strong, early forties, with black hair down below his neck, dark eyes, and a hawklike nose. He wore jeans and denim shirts when he wasn't wearing the Byte Patrol purple T-shirt.

Something about the apartment bothered Stride, but whatever it was waited like a ship in the fog and refused to show itself. The more he tried to focus his senses, the more the feeling became gauzy, as if he were imagining things. There was nothing to see here and nothing to find.

Stride pulled a kitchen chair next to the store owner, Craig, who was clicking the computer keys and staring at the screen through bleary eyes.

"What have you got?" Stride asked.

"Enough to fucking well put me out of business," Craig retorted. "This asshole put back doors and spyware into every computer he touched through the store."

"Meaning what?"

"Meaning he could use their Internet connections to log on to their systems, paw through their hard drives, and track every fucking keystroke they made. He knew everything."

"I'm going to need names."

"Yeah, sure, I'll print you a list. They're all going to sue me."

"What else?" Stride asked.

"What else am I looking for?"

"Anything that will help us find this guy. Where he goes. Where he shops. What he does. He's got to have a hideaway somewhere."

"What I've found isn't going to help you.

It's mostly hard-core porn. Disgusting stuff, lots of bondage."

"What about local sites? People, places, businesses based around Duluth? Blogs, MySpace pages, anything like that?"

"Not that I saw."

"Did he ever visit a blog called 'The Lady in Me'? Or mention a woman called Helen Danning?"

Craig tapped the keys for a few seconds. "Doesn't look like it."

"What about online bank records?"

"Nope." Craig yawned.

"Am I keeping you up here?" Stride asked.

"It's three in the morning, man. I should be asleep."

"Yeah, things are tough all over. I already woke up a judge in the middle of the night to get a search warrant, and she's not too happy with me either. It's really too bad I yanked you out of bed just because this son of a bitch you hired has kidnapped a woman and may already have raped and killed her. So keep looking and *find me something*."

"Yeah, okay, okay, sorry." Craig hunched his shoulders and went back to the keyboard.

Stride's cell phone rang, and the song taunted him. He was in a hurry and knew why. He got up and walked to the window again as he answered the call.

"Negatory on the state database," Guppo said. "He's not local."

"How about the feebs?"

"They're working on it right now. They promise it's a top priority."

"Thanks."

Stride hung up.

He straddled a chair and studied the barren apartment again. What the hell was it? There was something here, something obvious that didn't make sense, and he was missing it. He got up and checked the garbage again and looked at the scraps of food wrappers. Bacon packaging. An empty egg carton and broken eggshells. The butcher's paper from a package of ground beef, purchased at a local twenty-four-hour market. He had already sent someone to the store to see if any of the employees remembered anything about Deed. Where he went, what he drove, who he was with.

He was still missing something.

"Hey, Lieutenant," Craig called. "I think you should see this."

Stride stood over the man's shoulder. "What is it?"

"Pictures. Lots of them. Mostly of the same woman."

Craig dragged the mouse and clicked a tiny icon, and a string of thumbnail images scattered across the black screen.

"I can run them all like a slide show," Craig said.

"Do it."

The first of the pictures zoomed out to full size. Stride's heart sank. It was Serena. He recognized the area, which was downtown Saint Paul, in Rice Park near the Ordway. Another photo clicked onto the screen, and this was Serena, too. Near the Duluth court-house. He forced himself to look at the entire collection. They were almost all of Serena, more than sixty images. Secret photos, taken from a distance. Some were near their own home, on the beach, through their windows.

This guy had been planning to take Serena for a long time.

Stride pointed at an image in the middle, which was nothing more than a flash of white light. "What's that?"

"A mistake," Craig said. "The camera probably went off accidentally."

"Pull it up again."

Craig restored the image to the screen, and Stride leaned in, staring at the photo. The blob of light was obviously the camera flash firing, but he could also make out something else, which looked like brown spots and wavy dark lines.

"What's that?" Stride asked.

Craig looked closer. "I'm not sure."

"I think it's wood."

"Too smooth for that."

"Wood paneling, I mean. Cheap stuff." Stride looked around the apartment. There was no wood paneling anywhere. He checked the bedroom and the bathroom and didn't find any panels there that matched the photo.

"Do you put wood paneling inside your vans?" he asked.

Craig shook his head.

"So where was this taken?" Stride asked, but he was talking to himself. To the air. Thinking that wherever the wood paneling was, Serena was there now. This was Deed's hidey-hole.

While he was running down a mental list of places that had fake wood siding, Guppo called back.

"Tell me you got him," Stride said.

"Yeah, but there's a problem."

"What?"

"The match is perfect," Guppo told him. "He's got records in Arizona, Texas, and Alabama. Drugs, murder, extortion, and two rape charges that were dropped when the women got cold feet."

"Sounds like our guy," Stride said. "What's the problem?"

"The problem is, he's dead."

"Say what?"

"The Alabama authorities claim he's dead. He was a witness in a narcotics trial, and two officers were escorting him back to the state CF in Holman. They ran square into a hurricane, and all three died."

"Did you say a hurricane?" Stride asked, hoping that Guppo had made a mistake and knowing that he hadn't.

"Yeah."

The dread he was feeling mutated and multiplied. Stride knew where this was going. He was there when Serena got the call last fall from the Alabama police and remembered the look of relief on her face. She felt liberated. Free.

"They found the two cops," Guppo said.

"The car, too, which was a wreck. No sign of foul play, though. They figured the prisoner washed out to sea."

That was the logical conclusion, and it was wrong. He didn't wash out to sea. He escaped and headed north like a laser beam. Stride remembered how Serena described the dead man who had tortured her past. Brilliant, ruthless, charming, scheming. Exactly the kind of spider who would love to play games with his prey and then eat them. A drug dealer. A blackmailer. A rapist. A killer.

"What was his name?" Stride asked, but he already knew.

"Take your pick," Guppo told him. "William Deed, alias Billy Deed, alias B. D. Henry, alias Billy 'Dog' Ketcher, alias Blue Dog."

51

She was wrong. Terribly wrong. It wasn't Tommy Luck standing over her. It wasn't anyone from her days in Las Vegas at all. This was worse. This was a ghost from years ago, from her childhood, a ghost straight from hell.

"You're dead," Serena gasped.

Blue Dog grinned. "Yeah, I'm like the invisible man. I don't exist."

"The Alabama police called me," she insisted, although the evidence was in front of her eyes. "They said you were killed in a storm."

"You don't know the prison system down

South. They've got so many bodies crammed into a cell that one less inside is a reason to celebrate. I'm sure they figured the storm did them a favor."

Serena was flooded by memories. Images she had locked away long ago in a dark corner of her brain broke free like rats bolting from their cages. She was in Blue Dog's apartment in Phoenix again. Fifteen years old. The summer heat was an inferno, her skin so chapped it bled when she scratched it. Cockroaches watched her from the walls. So did her mother, no better than a cockroach herself, her eyes hungry and wild from the coke. Blue Dog's eyes were black and clear; he never used drugs, he just sold. He was grinning as he took her, splitting her open like a nail violating wood. The same grin he had now.

He saw her remember. "We had some good times, huh?"

"Fuck you."

"Oh, yeah, that's the plan. I've spent the last ten years thinking about you. The thought of paying you back was about the only thing that kept me alive inside."

"I've paid the price my whole life for what

you did to me," Serena told him. "That should make us even."

"Maybe, but you should have left it alone, and you didn't," Blue Dog said. "You came after me."

That was true. Serena remembered that summer ten years ago. She had to go to Phoenix to get background on a case she was working in Vegas. While she was there, her teenage memories all came back, and she wound up drinking for three days in a dive south of the city and waking up in a motel near the airport with a man she didn't know. Cockroaches were on the wall there, too. She went to a shrink who said she had unresolved issues about her mother and Blue Dog, which was like paying a hundred bucks to hear that you get wet when you walk out in the rain. That was the same therapist who asked if she ever had an orgasm with Blue Dog. The bastard.

So she did her own kind of therapy. She took a month's leave and followed Blue Dog's trail from Arizona to Texas and then to Alabama, where she found him up to his old tricks, running a crack and extortion empire in Birmingham and sleeping with a black girl who couldn't be more than sixteen. She hooked up with the Alabama police, and they watched Blue Dog blow away a street pusher who was keeping some of the product for himself. He shot him in the head, right there on camera, before they could clamber out of the stakeout vehicles and arrest him.

Serena studied him. He was older; you could see it in his face and in the gray streaks in his long hair. He was the same, though. Tall, almost six feet six, and broad like a grizzly. The same ego, too. He still had the need to control the world, the need to make women get on their knees, the need to prove he was smarter and tougher than anyone else.

That was the only advantage she had. She knew him and how he thought. He wasn't a stranger.

Her first job was to stall him. Keep him talking. Serena knew that half the city had to be on alert now, and Jonny would be looking for her everywhere. The more time she gave him to find her, the more her chances increased of escaping alive. She was a realist, though. She knew that she was probably about to die.

"Where are we?" she asked.

She could see that the small enclosure was some kind of shanty with one overhead bulb casting shadows. She saw cheap wood paneling, a sink, a minirefrigerator, and empty beer bottles littering the space. It was narrow, maybe seven feet wide and about twelve feet in length. She saw two windows on the far wall, taped over with gray duct tape. The door on her left had a diamond-shaped window, also taped over. When the wind gusted, the entire frame shuddered.

"Still hoping someone will find you? Don't count on it."

His eyes danced. He was becoming aroused by her naked body. He pulled a chair next to the bed and leaned over her and began playing with his knife on her skin again. Her flesh rippled, having him close to her. She was still freezing, and she hated that the cold kept her nipples hard, which made him leer and smile. He flicked at them with his blade and then leaned over and suckled her, licking off the blood.

Keep him talking, Serena thought.

"If this was between you and me, why did you put so many other people in the middle of it?"

Blue Dog shrugged. "Who, fuckers like

Dan Erickson and Mitch Brandt? I told you before, these people are no different than me. They all have secrets."

"How did you find out about them?"

She assessed how she was bound. She was on a low cot, no more than a foot off the ground. Her legs were spread, draped off the bed and tied with duct tape to the steel legs of the frame. Her body stretched two-thirds of the way up the length of the cot. Her arms hung down on either side of the bed, and when she pulled on them, she realized that they were tied with cloth, not tape. A stretchy fabric, like a cotton T-shirt, was wrapped around her wrists and knotted tightly, and then pulled back to the other legs of the frame about a foot behind her and knotted again. She had some play in her arms. When she put her hand down, she could rest her palm on the floor. She felt ice-cold metal.

"There was this young computer hacker in Holman," Blue Dog told her. "He was in for molesting boys, a real sick fuck."

He said this without a trace of irony.

"A guy like that's not going to last long without protection," he continued. "I made sure nobody messed with him."

"Yeah, you're a saint," Serena said.

Blue Dog laughed. "Fuck, he was going to wind up giving blow jobs anyway, so it might as well be my cock he sucked."

"I didn't realize you were queer."

Blue Dog's grin evaporated, and he turned his knife on its point and jabbed it an inch deep into the flesh of Serena's right shoulder. She screamed and jerked back. The bed frame rocked. He yanked the knife out and wiped the blood on the mattress. Waves of pain washed over her.

"You better learn to be polite, or this is going to be a long night."

"Like it's not going to be anyway."

"Yeah, that's true. But there's long and then there's long."

Serena closed her eyes. She laid her left hand down on the floor again. The bed had moved. She explored the floor with her hand, looking for anything sharp that she could use to attack the strip of fabric that connected her wrist to the frame of the bed. She felt crumbs and puddles of frigid water that had dripped through the ceiling, but nothing that could cut.

"So what did this guy do?" she asked. *Keep him talking.*

"He taught me everything he knew about computers. I realized there was a lot more money to be made online than I ever did on the street. The real money is in everything people want to keep hidden."

"Blackmail."

"Sure. I got to town, and I started keeping an eye on you. But a guy's got to make a living. I was in no hurry. I found other ways to let off steam."

"So why come after me now?"

"It's time to get out of the city," Blue Dog said. "The cops are getting too close. But you and I have unfinished business."

Out of sight, under the bed, Serena spread the fingers of her left hand and stretched them as far as she could. She brushed the very edge of a piece of metal, but it nudged out of her reach as she touched it.

Blue Dog reached around behind his back and pulled out a revolver. It was a small-frame, airweight Smith & Wesson that looked like a toy in his hands. Serena mentally took stock of the gun. Light and easy to conceal. Five rounds. She wondered if she would be alive to see the last four.

"I've thought a lot about how to do this," he told her. He put the barrel of the gun to the cap of her right knee. "You know what it feels like to get a bullet right here? Makes you want to die. I thought about doing both your knees, and then poling you after that."

Serena wriggled and tried to move the bed.

"Then I thought, you won't feel me inside you if I do that. I don't want you in so much agony that you can't feel what it's like."

He put the gun to her forehead. The barrel was warm where it had been inside his pants. "I also thought about making you suck my dick."

"You put anything in my mouth, you're not getting it back," Serena said.

Blue Dog laughed. "Yeah, I'm a practical guy."

"You'll never get away with this."

"We'll see about that. You think we're still on planet earth? Let me show you how wrong you are."

He pulled the revolver away from her head and pointed it upward at the ceiling, and without hesitating, he squeezed the trigger. Serena felt the shock waves inside her skull. Dust and paint fell in a cloud, and a stream of water dribbled over her chest like a mountain waterfall from the hole that punctured the roof. The echo screamed in her ears. Her head throbbed as if he had put two live wires to her temples.

No one came running. There were no sounds outside except the constant, whistling roar of the blizzard. Serena shivered as the falling water kept on, soaking her skin.

"See?" he said. "It's just you and me."

Blue Dog stood up. He grabbed an out-of-fashion men's tie from the floor and dangled it in her face. It was wide, with black-and-yellow slanted stripes. "Is this ugly or what? I found it in the farmhouse where I hid during the hurricane."

He strung it around Serena's neck and began to pull the ends tighter.

Blue Dog unzipped his pants. "Remember this guy?"

Serena knew she was running out of time. Her hand stretched again for the metal piece on the floor and missed it. She didn't even know what it was or whether it would help her cut through the fabric that tied her to the bed.

Blue Dog climbed onto the cot at her feet, and the springs beneath them groaned under the weight of their two bodies together. The bed moved a fraction of an inch. He lowered his weight down on her. His shirt dampened as it rubbed against her wet chest. His hands took hold of the two ends of the tie and began pulling them in opposite directions, narrowing the loop that hung around Serena's neck. Below, between her spread legs, she felt him try to invade her.

"I'm going to love watching your eyes," he said.

The sand gathered in the bottom of the hourglass.

Her fingers were flat on the floor. She reached again and this time felt the piece of metal slide under her palm, where she scooped it into her hand and prayed.

It was a fish hook. Sharp as hell.

52

Maggie grew increasingly desperate as she crisscrossed the streets of Duluth. The weather made it worse. Her windshield wipers sloughed aside snow, but the downpour was so heavy that she could see little more than a swirling sea of white powder through the beams of her headlights. She squinted to see where she was going, and the car veered and fishtailed on the unplowed streets. The glowing clock in her Avalanche told her it was nearly four in the morning. They had several hours of darkness left, and even when the sun rose, it would be behind an impenetrable blanket of black clouds. The storm would still be howling, spilling a foot of snow over the city and then billowing it into house-high drifts with a wind that swept down from the Canadian tundra and blinded everything.

No one else was out on the streets, not at this hour and not in the middle of the storm. The cars were mounds of white, pasted over with snowcaps. When she passed a van that fit the right size and shape, she had to get out of her truck and brush off enough snow with her hands to make sure that it wasn't the missing vehicle from Byte Patrol.

As she passed along the south end of Portland Square on Fourth Street, she saw windows of light in a house on the opposite side of the park and realized that it was Katrina's upstairs apartment. She must have had every light in the place turned on, and Maggie knew why. For weeks after it happened, she found herself up in the middle of the night, turning on lights and sitting in the kitchen with her gun in reach on the table. It was irrational, but that was what fear did to you.

She turned left and drove around the square to the north side and parked near Katrina's building. When she got out of the car, the gales almost knocked her over. She fought through drifts on the sidewalk and then ducked into the protection of Katrina's doorway. She rang the doorbell.

Katrina's voice crackled through the speaker. "Who is it?"

"It's Maggie."

"Oh. Hi. Come on up."

Maggie tromped upstairs, leaving wet footprints on the steps. Katrina stood in the doorway with the door open when she reached the second floor. She was wearing an extra-large Minnesota Wild T-shirt that stretched to the middle of her thighs. Her legs were bare.

"Sorry it's so late," Maggie said.

"I was up."

"Yeah, I figured."

Katrina nodded. "I was watching TV. I know what's going on with your friend Serena. Sounds bad."

"It is."

"Is it the same guy who . . . ?"

"We think so, yeah."

"You want to come in?"

"For a couple of minutes, sure."

Maggie took off her coat inside and hung it near the door. She did the same with her hat and gloves. Snow melted and dripped on the carpet. Katrina had the gas fireplace turned on, and it gave off a little heat when Maggie sat near the hearth on the yellow futon. Katrina shuffled to the opposite end, and they stared at each other.

"Look, I suppose I should say I'm sorry," Maggie said.

"Why?"

"Because I never reported what happened. Maybe we could have caught this guy before he got to you."

"It's not your fault."

"How are you? How do you feel?"

"Like an empty milk carton, nothing inside."

"It won't always be like that."

"Did you feel the same way?"

Maggie shook her head. "I was out of my skull. I couldn't stop crying."

"Tell me something. Have you had sex since it happened?"

Maggie shook her head.

"Me neither. Thinking about sex makes me nauseous. I feel like he took that away from me, the bastard."

"Give it time." Maggie's guilt showed in her face again. "I wish I'd said something."

"Let it go," Katrina told her. "You don't owe anybody but yourself."

"Stride doesn't get it," Maggie said.

"He's a man. It didn't happen to him. You can't live your life around what he thinks."

"I'm not doing that."

"No? That's a switch."

"He's my safety net. You know that. When things got bad with Eric, I found myself turning to Stride again. It's safe, because I know he's not interested in me anyway."

"Don't be so sure of that."

"Please. I'm a kid as far as he's concerned. And it's not like I can compete with someone like Serena anyway."

"So start living in the real world," Katrina told her. "What do you really want?"

"I have no idea."

"Bullshit. I think you do."

"What do you mean?"

"I mean, there's only one thing you've wanted for the last two years. And it's not Stride, and it's not Eric, either."

"A kid," Maggie said.

"Bingo."

"Well, so much for that dream. Three strikes, and I'm out."

"You don't know that."

Maggie shook her head. "No way. I'm not going through that roller coaster again. Get my hopes up and my hormones up, and then feel like my life is over when I lose it for the fourth time? No, thanks. Besides, I'm missing half the equation now. No husband."

"A husband is like an optional extra."

"It's too soon to think about it," Maggie said.

"You could adopt."

"Oh, sure, a single Chinese immigrant, a cop who was suspected in her husband's murder. I'm going to be tops on everyone's list."

"Just think about it."

"Yeah, I will."

The truth was, she had thought about it already. She had even made some calls.

"You want a drink?" Katrina asked.

"I could drink a whole bottle, but no, I can't."

"Are you working?"

Maggie nodded. "Unofficially, but yeah. We've got most of the force out trying to find this son of a bitch. We just don't know where to look."

"Well, I hope you get him. As far as I'm concerned, they can skip the trial and put him in the electric chair. I'll tell you right where they can attach the electrodes, baby."

"Yeah."

"Do you have nightmares?" Katrina asked.

Maggie nodded. "All the time."

"Me too. I keep reliving it, but it's like I'm watching a movie, you know? Like it happened to someone else."

"I've pretty much blocked it out," Maggie confessed. "Usually, I remember everything, but I've built a wall around that night and what happened."

"Lucky you." Katrina added, "Listen, I never should have done the alpha girl thing. I could tell you weren't comfortable with it."

"That was me. I wasn't going to tell you what to do."

"Yeah, but it was in your eyes, girlie. I should have known how awkward it would be. I mean, I never really figured Eric would be there, you know? Hell, I don't know what I was thinking. It was stupid."

Maggie frowned. "I never dreamed you would go through what I went through. After. When it happened to me, I never made the connection to the club. I feel like I let you paint a target on your chest."

"Big target," Katrina said.

"You know what I mean."

"Hey, the worst part for me wasn't the sex thing or having my face look like rainbow ice cream. It's losing my appetite for fish and chips." She laughed sourly.

"What are you talking about?" Maggie asked.

"Come on, I can't even walk past the fish counter in the supermarket. The smell makes it all come back."

Maggie's face was blank. "I don't get it."

Katrina's face scrunched up with surprise. "You telling me you can still eat fish after what happened?"

"Actually, no, you're right. I haven't been able to stomach it for weeks. But what does that have to do with anything?"

"Wow, you really did block it out. Well, good for you. I shouldn't have said anything. The fact is, the guy's hands smelled like fish. Even through the gloves. It was this dank, briny smell, like he was underwater. Awful."

The memory didn't even knock at the door. It smashed the lock, broke the door down, galloped into Maggie's brain, and suffocated her.

Her hands flew to her mouth. Her eyes squeezed shut. She could smell it as if it was happening to her all over again. "Oh, my God."

"Shit, I'm sorry."

Maggie clenched her fists. "No, it's okay, it's okay. This is important. Do you remember anything else?"

"Nope. It was just me and Charlie the Tuna."

Maggie yanked her cell phone out of her pocket and called Stride. He answered on the first ring. "Fish," she told him.

"What?"

"Fish. This guy's hands smell like fish. I'm in Katrina's apartment, and she reminded me that his hands stank. It's got to mean something. Maybe he has a smoker or something, or he works in a processing plant."

There was silence on the line.

"Are you there?" Maggie asked.

"Wood paneling," Stride said.

"You lost me."

"He had a photo of wood paneling on his computer. Like from a camper or something. He had fish in his freezer, too—not from a store, it was wrapped in foil. He caught it."

"He's in a *fish house*," Maggie concluded.

"Exactly right. That has to be it. He's out on one of the lakes."

"But which one?"

"Tanjy's body was found in Hell's Lake," Stride said. "It's a good chance he dumped her in the same lake where he has his shanty."

"Are you close?" Maggie asked.

"I'm chasing down warehouses near the airport. I can be out on the ice in ten minutes."

"I'll be right behind you."

53

Serena buried the fish hook in the strip of cloth that tied her hand to the bed frame, and it sank into the fabric like butter. When she yanked it down, the cloth screamed and tore. Blue Dog heard it and threw his weight toward her shoulder, but she freed her arm with a single thrust before he could pin her down. She curled her arm around his back, where he still had the gun tucked under his belt, and clawed for the butt of the revolver. It was facing the wrong way, and she fumbled it in her fingers, but then she spun it around and the butt nestled in her palm and her finger found the trigger.

She was right-handed, and the gun felt awkward in her other hand, but she found the hammer with her thumb and cocked it and fired all at once. The gun was pointed toward the muscled, hard flesh in Blue Dog's hip, but he was already moving when she got the shot off. He bellowed in pain and dove off the cot, landing heavily on the floor and scrambling backward away from her. She fired again, but the shot went wild and took out one of the rear windows in the shanty with a burst of glass. The smell of burnt metal and smoke filled the space.

He danced from wall to wall, his hand pressed against his side. A small trickle of blood oozed through his knuckles. She followed him with the gun, but didn't fire. She only had two shots left and didn't trust her aim from her left hand.

"You're good," he told her.

"If you leave now, I won't shoot," Serena said. "Just get the hell out of here."

"I don't think so."

Her head was pounding. The hot spot in her skull where the gun had landed on her temple throbbed and made her vision wobble and then refocus. She wanted to close her eyes, but she couldn't. Something warm ran on her skin, and she realized blood was leaking from her shoulder where he had stabbed her. She could see her flat stomach, too, which was a gooey mess of red streaks, and when she moved, the muscles in her abdomen howled with pain.

She swung the gun back and forth, left and right, until she was dizzy. She couldn't keep this up forever, and he knew it. He was waiting her out.

"Drop it, and I promise I'll make it quick," Blue Dog said.

"Fuck you. Come close, and watch me blow your head off."

"You're bleeding," he told her.

"So are you."

She watched his eyes as they locked onto a shelf in the middle of the shanty, and she saw her own gun there and the magazine of bullets lying next to it.

"Go for it," she said. If he got that close, she knew she could nail him.

He bent and scooped a glass beer bottle off the floor. The cap was still on; the bottle was full. He held the bottle by the neck and made circles with his wrist like he was slinging a lasso. Foam hissed and fizzed from under the cap. Serena gripped the gun tighter and aimed at the shelf, knowing that's where he wanted to go. Blue Dog zig-zagged the other way and flung the bottle underhanded at the cot. The glass shot over her head, missing her by inches, and shattered against the rear wall, cascading over her skin in a storm of beer and hail. Involuntarily, she flinched and closed her eyes. It took only a second, but the second was too long, and she heard him dive for the gun.

She had no choice. She had to fire. The gun recoiled, and her bare skin burned. The shot missed Blue Dog, but he had to hit the floor before his hand reached the shelf, and he was smart enough to know he didn't have time to try again without winding up in her sights. He skittered backward like a bug. She kept her eyes open, despite the beer leaching into her tear ducts and trickling down her face. Some of it found its way to her lips, and she lapped it with her tongue.

Sam Adams. Good stuff.

He was at the rear of the shanty again, but he was slowing down. He couldn't keep mov-ing forever, and she couldn't stay conscious forever, and sooner or later, one of them was going to slip.

"One bullet," Blue Dog told her. "You only have one bullet left."

"That's all I need."

But she knew the odds were against her. She glanced around, hunting for another weapon, and her eyes landed on the knife he had used to torture her, which was lying on the floor just beyond the reach of the cot. If she could free her right hand, she could stretch her arm out and grab it. She knew the fish hook was somewhere under her body, and it would be easy to reach around and slash the cloth that tied her down, but that would mean putting down the gun first. She couldn't do that.

He smiled at her dilemma. "You're running out of time."

"You're not looking so good yourself."

His voice was casual, as if they were two friends talking over old times. "Back in Phoenix, I knew you got into it sometimes. A man can tell."

"Yeah, I really got into it. Sure. You stupid bastard."

"Some women get off on it. Like Tanjy."

"She got off on fantasies. I guarantee you, she didn't like the real thing."

"She wasn't supposed to like it. It was supposed to be punishment."

"What?"

He made his move, surprising her. He feinted toward the gun and then jerked in the other direction and dove across the width of the shanty. His fingers clawed at the wall switch. Before she could get off a shot, he slapped the switch, fell back to the ground, and rolled away.

The light went off. She was so blind that she couldn't even see the gun in front of her, and all she could do was listen. Where was he?

The storm was loud, and the wind leaked through the tear in the tape and the broken window at the rear of the shanty. Water kept dripping and falling on her body through the ceiling. She stared into the blackness and tried to remember what it was like in the light, so she could guess where he would go and how he would attack her. She pricked her ears for every creak and groan in the metal floor, but she didn't hear a thing other than the blizzard. He was waiting somewhere. Not moving.

One bullet.

She took a huge risk. If she couldn't see him, then he couldn't see her. She put the gun down on her chest and felt around the cot silently for the fish hook. When she heard a shriek of metal, and felt the shanty sway, she grabbed the gun again and pointed at nothing. He was creeping, moving, getting closer. She didn't have much time. She tried to find the hook, but she realized it must have fallen back to the floor as she struggled with Blue Dog. With the gun on her chest again, she reached back down and skated her fingers along the metal floor and found the hook. Quickly, she slid it into her hand. She eased the gun off her body, so it didn't slide away, and then she craned her body around, trying to stretch her left arm until she could reach the strip of cloth that tied her right hand.

The frame of the cot squeaked. She hoped he didn't realized what she was doing. The distance down to her right wrist was farther than she realized, and her body strained in protest as she twisted. The cut in her shoulder sent out ripples of pain and heat. Glass pieces from the beer bottle cut her skin and sprinkled loudly on the floor. Her head spun, and the darkness turned upside down.

Somewhere, he took two hurried steps, very close by, and before she could take up the gun again, he moved away and she heard the sickening sound of the clip being shoved into the grip of her own gun.

His voice came out of the night.

"Guess what I have?"

She had to move fast. She reached out again, pulling every inch of distance out of the muscles in her back, and her fingers trembled so much that she almost dropped the fish hook. She stretched as far as she could with her right hand in the other direction until the binds pulled her back. She didn't know how far away she was, but it may as well have been a mile. She couldn't get close enough. She couldn't free herself.

Blue Dog fired. The noise rocked the shanty. The bullet missed her head by no more than six inches; she could feel its heat as it streaked by. Bits of metal ricocheted off the wall behind her. She scooped up the other gun again and aimed where she had had seen the flash of the barrel, but she could hear him moving.

"I've got plenty of bullets," he said.

He fired again, and he was gone again, before she could return fire. This time, the bullet seared across the top of her thigh before burying itself in the wall, and she gasped loudly as her leg seemed to catch fire, and the fire spread through her body. He knew where she was. There was nowhere for her to go.

The silence and the waiting stretched out. She tensed, the gun in her hand.

He fired three times more in succession, flooding the space with explosions one after another, raining down metal and snow from over her head. Before she realized he was firing in the air, distracting her, he was already diving across the short distance that separated them. He came from her right side, like a meteor, lightning-fast. His shoulder collided with her left arm, and she felt all her hopes fly away and abandon her as the gun spilled from her hand and skidded away on the floor. He crushed her, all his weight on top of her, embedding glass in her skin. His breath was in her face, and he put her own gun to her head.

"You lose."

She wasn't going to cry. "Fuck you."

She searched the floor with her hand, hoping the gun was still within reach, but she couldn't find it. She almost screamed with frustration, knowing there was a bullet chambered close by that she could drill into this sadist's head, payback for all the humiliation and pain she had suffered at his hands. Ending all the nightmares and memories. But he was right; she had lost.

Reality was too much, and she wished she could find the empty room in her mind in which to crawl for escape. Every sensation pricked away at her sanity. The heaviness and smell of him. The hot circles of pain. The dizziness. The cold, glass, metal, and ice. The blackness, as if it were all happening in midair, disconnected.

Boom, boom, boom.

She heard a deep thumping somewhere in her consciousness, and for a second, she thought it was the panicked beating of her heart, but it kept on like a hammer. This was something real, something unexpected. Blue Dog reared up in shock and spun off her.

Someone was pounding on the door. She could only imagine one person. Jonny. Coming for her.

Blue Dog crept for the door. The floor sagged with his footsteps. She knew he had her gun firmly in his hand. He waited. There was a long pause, and then the pounding continued, as if something heavy were beating on the frame.

She heard a voice. *"Billy! Open the door!"*

Her heart sank. It wasn't Jonny. The voice was familiar, but it was distant, drowned by the storm. Not a cop. Not rescue. She couldn't see Blue Dog, but she could almost feel him relax and grin. He unlocked the door and pushed it outward, and even the night was brighter than the darkness inside, and a pale triangle spilled through the opening and made him a silhouette. The wind and snow swirled through the shanty.

He started to say something, but he never finished.

Orange flame sparked and disappeared. A shotgun detonated, so loud that the storm was hushed for an instant. The smoke smelled like burnt toast. Serena felt a warm spray across her face, and she realized it wasn't snow this time. It was Blue Dog's blood.

54

Stride cannonaded down a fire road that snaked through the forest toward Hell's Lake. The wheels of his Bronco chewed at the snow. Slender birch trees hugged both sides of the road, and caps of pine trees swayed overhead, making the road like a dark tunnel. He knew he was near the lake, and then the forest opened up, as if he had bolted through the door of a church into the open air. The sky vaulted over him, angry and gray, belching out sheets of snow. His Bronco thumped off the dirt road onto the thick ice of the lake, leaving the shelter of the trees behind him. Fifty-mile-an-hour gales ambushed him and nearly upended the truck. The blizzard was a banshee here, a woman in white stretching to the sky and screaming for the dead.

The fish houses were a ghost town of shadows that appeared and disappeared in his headlights. He had to slow down to avoid piling into them. They were of all shapes and sizes, some barely larger than Dumpsters, others as large as campers, big enough for people to live in and sleep in if they wanted to escape the world entirely. Tonight, they were dark. He made circles around each one and didn't see any cars parked by the houses, because no one wanted to be caught in the tempest if a propane tank went empty or a window blew out in the wind. Stride felt tiny out here, and the world felt huge and violent.

The lake was shaped like an amoeba spread out under the microscope, with rounded fingers of land pushing into the water in wooded peninsulas and a fat, open middle where underground currents left islands of thin ice to swallow up trespassers. It stretched for miles, and from where he was, Stride could only see a fraction of its surface, and in the midst of the storm, he could see even less. He felt as if he were crawling, nudging the Bronco past each snowy hillock where a fish house was hiding.

His phone rang.

"I'm on the lake," he told Maggie. "I came in on the fire road from the southwest."

"I'm coming in from the east," she said. "I'll follow the shore and head your way."

"It's a nightmare out here. Watch out for hot spots."

"You, too. Is the cavalry coming?"

"Yeah, I've got half a dozen cars heading our way."

"Any way to narrow down the search?" Maggie asked.

"Tanjy's body popped up on the south shore, so I'm hoping she went in somewhere around there, too."

"Stay in touch."

Stride threw his phone on the passenger seat. He shot out toward the open stretch of ice, hugging the shore and following the land as it bent around toward the next inlet. The snow blinded him, but when an updraft lifted the curtain for an instant, he saw another scattering of shanties a quarter mile ahead. He steered for them, and in the midst of the blackness, he could make out a yellow diamond of light. Someone was home.

The light shone through the door of an RV, parked like a beached whale off by itself, which the owner could simply drive on and off the ice at will. Stride parked next to the RV and bailed out of his truck with his gun drawn. In an instant, he was a snowman, crusted over with a wet, white layer that clung to his hair, skin, and clothes. He jogged through the powder to the door of the camper and listened, but he couldn't hear anything inside with the wind roaring around him.

He pounded on the door with his fist. "Police!"

A few seconds later, the door slit open a crack, and he pointed his gun at the opening but quickly withdrew it when he saw an old man staring out with surprised, frightened eyes. The man wore a heavy red plaid shirt, baggy jeans, and ratty slippers. His messy gray hair flopped over his forehead. "Who the hell are you?"

"Police, sir!" Stride shouted, because that was the only way to be heard.

"I'm not leaving the lake."

"Can I come in for a minute?"

"How about showing me your badge?"

"This is a *blizzard,* sir, will you just give me a break!"

"Okay, okay, get inside. You're letting in the snow."

He pulled back the door, and Stride climbed the metal steps. The interior of the RV was littered with food cans, beer, and fishing equipment. A black-and-white television set was perched on a bookshelf, broadcasting a 1950s movie in between zigzagging lines. The air was freezing, and Stride could see his breath.

The old man was barely more than five feet tall. "I'm not coming off the lake," he grumbled. "I don't care about any storm. I've seen worse storms than this."

"I'm not here to kick you out, although you're crazy to be here on a night like this."

"Yeah, so, I'm crazy. What do you want?"

"I'm trying to find a man who may have a fish house on the lake. He's huge, around six foot six, and built like a linebacker. Very long black hair."

The old man nodded. He snorted and cleared his throat as if he were about to hack up a fur ball. "I've seen him. Hard to miss that guy."

Stride was exhilarated. "Where? Where does he keep his shanty?"

"Don't know exactly. It's not in this part of

the lake. I've seen that purple van of his heading up around the peninsula to the northeast."

"Still on the south shore?" Stride asked.

"Yeah, I assume so. Not much reason for people to be driving around down here if they're camped on the north side. It's a long way up there, unless you want to go across the belly of the lake and swim." He chuckled.

"Thanks," Stride told him. "Stay safe."

"Not like I'm going to die young."

Stride flew out of the RV and back to his Bronco. He called 911 and gave them the position off his GPS locator and told them where he was headed and asked them to scramble everyone they had. When he got the confirmation from the operator, he threw the phone back on the passenger seat and concentrated on the lake. He abandoned the rest of the fish houses in this inlet and accelerated back toward the open stretch of ice. Sheets of snow blew up from his tires in two waves, as if he were parting the sea. He tried to keep an eye on the dark blotch of land to the east, but the storm grew even worse, shrinking his universe to a few feet in front of the truck. Even so, he pushed the Bronco faster, until his foot was on the floorboard and the chassis was shimmying and wobbling on the bumpy ice. Too fast.

He lost control. The truck spun. He went round and round in a strange, graceful pirouette, and the truck came off its tires and threatened to roll. He felt himself sailing at an angle, airborne, but then the Bronco staggered back and righted itself, falling back onto its wheels with a kidney-busting jolt and drifting to a stop. He pushed the accelerator again, and the truck coughed, clamped down on the snow, and sped up.

He was lost now. He couldn't see a thing and had no idea where he was or what direction he was going. He opened the window and shoved his head out as he drove, but the wind and snow were like knives on his face. The lake, the sky, and the woods were all indistinguishable. He thought he could make out the dark stain of the next finger of land jutting out to the east, and he turned toward it, but he was disoriented by the silver, blowing swarm that was everywhere around the truck. The vision of the land vanished, as if it had been an illusion all along.

He was far out, too far out, before he realized he had gone the wrong way and strayed from the land. Something changed under his tires. What had been two feet of impenetrable ice no longer felt heavy and solid; instead, the ground trembled and moved as he drove. He knew he had to stop, turn around, get out of there. He was skating on a hot spot, trying to walk on water, and when he steered in another direction, the first sharp crack was like a rifle going off under his feet.

The ice was breaking.

The truck lurched.

Stride was thrown forward by the jolt. The nose of the truck shuddered and dipped. He fumbled with his seat belt, pushed open the door, and threw himself outside, where he hit the ice with a cold slap and rolled. He kept crawling, hearing more ice crack around and behind him. He spread his weight out and practically swam through the snow toward the safety of a thicker shelf of ice. He could see the red flags now, warning beacons that he had driven past and missed entirely in the storm.

He stood up. The ice here was strong enough to hold him.

Twenty yards away, he watched his ten-year-old Ford Bronco disappear, carrying his past and his cell phone with it. Spiderlike cracks opened up and widened into fissures. The front wheels slurped into the lake water, which freed itself from its prison like a sea monster and surrounded the truck. The Bronco flailed, fought, and floated, but not for long. Frigid water leached into its body, and steam hissed as the engine drowned. The front end dived, and the back end settled behind it, and then the truck careened to one side and made a gentle splash as it sank between the chunky plates of ice and was swallowed up and gone.

The storm raged.

He was alone in the middle of the lake.

55

Blue Dog staggered back two steps, colliding into the opposite wall. A set of metal shelves collapsed under his weight, and debris clattered to the floor around him. Someone else climbed inside the shanty with them and shut the door. For an instant, the darkness was so complete again that Serena felt as if she were wearing a mask, but then the overhead bulb lit up, and even the pale light was enough to make her close her eyes and turn away.

When she blinked, she saw Lauren Erickson with a shotgun nestled against her right shoulder, pointed at Blue Dog's head. The gun looked oversized in her small arms, but she held the barrel steady and straight.

Lauren's eyes flicked to Serena and lingered. Her mouth was tight with anger and something that might have been guilt or regret. She turned back to Blue Dog, who was clenching his wrecked shoulder with his other hand. His wound was a mess of bone, muscle, and blood.

"You stupid son of a bitch," Lauren snapped. "You had the money. You could have left the city, and everything would have been perfect."

"It was never about money." He nodded his head at Serena. "Me and her, we have a history together."

Serena interrupted them, her voice calm and firm. "Lauren, cut me loose."

Blue Dog jabbed a finger at Lauren's face. "You know you can't do that. If she walks out the door, everything comes out."

"Lauren, I don't care what you've done," Serena told her. "Look at me. *Look at me.* You could never be a part of something like this."

Lauren stared at Serena tied to the cot. Naked. Her body streaked with blood. "I'm sorry you're in the middle of this," she told her.

"It's not worth it, Lauren," Serena said. "It doesn't matter what you did. We can work it out."

Lauren shook her head. "We're way beyond that."

She shoved the twin barrels of the shotgun into the skin of Blue Dog's forehead.

"Lauren, do *not* pull that trigger," Serena insisted. "Don't do it. Once you do that, you can't go back. Just call the police. He's the one they want. You can work out a deal."

Lauren took a half-step backwards.

Blue Dog's lungs rattled as he laughed. "A deal? You think you can cut a deal? Not after you killed Tanjy."

Serena closed her eyes and swore silently to herself.

"Shut up," Lauren hissed.

"Don't you want Serena to know what an ice-cold bitch you are?" Blue Dog said. He grinned at Serena. "I told Lauren all about Dan's affair. All about Tanjy's rape fantasies. All the sick things they did together. I even had the photos. I just wanted money to keep it quiet, but Lauren here had a better idea."

"Shut up," Lauren repeated.

"She paid me to keep Dan's ass out of the

papers, and then she paid me even more. She *hired* me."

Serena saw a primal horror in Lauren's eyes. The small space swayed as the gales outside pounded the walls. It got even colder.

"To do what?" Serena asked, but she had begun to put it all together.

"*To rape Tanjy Powell,*" Blue Dog said. "She didn't just want to break up Tanjy and Dan. She wanted this bitch *destroyed*. So that's what I did."

"Oh, my God," Serena murmured.

"She was a twisted little whore," Lauren said, spitting out the words.

"Yeah, and Dan couldn't get enough of her wet, wild pussy, could he? But you fixed that." Blue Dog's grin came back. "Then Tanjy called and said she *knew* who raped her. That scared the shit out of you, didn't it? If Tanjy knew about me, then she'd find out about *you,* too."

"*Stop it!*" Lauren shouted.

"But you knew what to do, didn't you? I bet when you swung that flashlight into the back of her head, you fucking well had the biggest orgasm of your life."

Lauren was lost in what she had done, trembling, furious. The shotgun sagged in her hands. She didn't see Blue Dog moving on the floor, his right hand reaching and scrabbling on the ground behind him. Serena shouted a warning, but Lauren didn't understand and didn't see Blue Dog as his hand emerged from behind his back with Serena's gun. He grinned and fired, grinned and fired, two shots in two seconds, both in and out, one that drilled a tunnel through the flesh of Lauren's elegant neck and one that broke through her collarbone with an audible crack.

Blue Dog came off the floor, his left arm frozen, his movements slow. Lauren turned to run, but her feet were clumsy, like a clown's. He towered over her from behind. Blue Dog wrapped his forearm around Lauren's neck and lifted her bodily off the ground. She flapped like a doll, and she swung the shotgun up as she struggled to free herself. Her eyes bulged out, and she formed an O with her mouth in a silent scream of agony. Blue Dog held Lauren in an iron grip, squeezing the life out of her.

Her finger was on the trigger. Serena followed the wild gyrations of the barrel with horror and found it pointed directly at her chest. She cringed and tried to twist away, but there was nowhere to go, no way to escape. She watched Lauren's finger, which was in near constant spasm, and she could actually see the trigger begin to move. She sucked in a breath but didn't close her eyes. Then the gun was gone, pointed at the ceiling, at the walls, at the door. Lauren kicked and flailed. Blue Dog spun her around, and the gun came up again, aimed at the rear wall now, away from Serena. This time the barrel coughed up a second shell. The recoil jolted them both backward, and Lauren fell from Blue Dog's grasp. The thunder of the explosion made the cot rise up off the floor.

The shell rocketed through the space.

It blew a hole through the metal siding.

With a sharp and terrible *ping,* like a note played on a badly tuned piano, it punctured the tank of propane gas mounted behind the shanty.

Stride held up his gloved hands in front of his face but could barely see them. He was a yeti, matted with heavy snow, slogging through the drifts on the lake, fighting the headwind that bit at his skin. His long gray scarf was wrapped around his head and ears and then tied around his face and neck. Snow crusted over it and froze. Ice balls dangled from his eyelids. His leather jacket hung stiffly, like cardboard. When he stopped and listened, he heard only the incessant roar of the white banshee and wondered who she was saying would die to-night, whether it would be Serena, or him-self, or both of them.

He squinted at the horizon. Once, he thought he saw the tree-lined shore as the storm briefly lifted, but since then, he could have been walking in circles. His footsteps disappeared almost as soon as he made them. He could have been crossing the same tracks, marching himself into the ground in a kind of mobius strip that went around and around without ever ending.

He almost collided with the shanty before he saw it. When the invading snow soared upward again, he realized he was in the midst of a community towed out to the mid-dle of the inlet, within spitting distance of the forest. He looked for light and didn't see any. He wondered where Maggie was and how close she was to this spot and what she thought when she kept dialing his number and he didn't answer. His phone was at the bottom of the lake.

A rumble of thunder washed over him like a wave. But not thunder. It was a shotgun blast. He spun around, trying to ascertain where the shot originated. He looked for vehicles but made out only ivory mountains.

One hundred yards away, a fish house exploded. The night turned to day, and a willowy cloud of fire roared fifty feet into the air.

Stride ran.

56

An instant later, the tin shack became a holocaust.

Serena felt as if she had launched into space and then fell out of orbit back to earth. The explosion split the shanty in half, and the walls made a tortured noise as they cracked. The diamond-shaped windows on the rear wall blew inward, and flame spat through them like they were the mouths of dragons. Black stains bloomed across the gray metal, which sizzled and popped as it became brittle.

The shock wave split Lauren and Blue Dog apart. The shotgun banged to the floor, empty and harmless. Lauren was thrown skyward, and she slammed into the door and then through it, spilling out of the space and disappearing with a cry. The impact struck Blue Dog square in the back and swatted him to his hands and knees. He swung his head to clear his scattered brain, and his long hair fell across his face like an Afghan hound. He pushed himself up to his feet and swayed, a silhouette framed by fire behind him. His head nearly grazed the roof of the shanty. His left arm dangled at his side, useless, but he still had Serena's gun in his other hand.

Blue Dog raised her gun and pointed it at her head. She could make out the whites of his eyes and his bared teeth. Ash fell into his wound, making him twitch. "Do you want me to make it quick for you?" he asked.

"Fuck you."

The flames licked at his back. "Burning to death is a horrible way to go," he said.

Serena half-wanted him to pull the trigger.

"See you in hell," he told her, and then he turned and leaped through the doorway.

She was alone and trapped. It felt as if she were in hell already, with huge fires and the caustic smell of melting steel to torture sinners. The winter cold vanished, and she felt a superheated burn from a ferocious, merciless sun. The rear wall was almost totally ablaze, and the fire toyed with the wood veneer on the other walls, beginning to catch and streak closer. Smoke choked the enclosure. She covered her mouth and nose with her free arm, but the gray cloud made its way inside her face. She gagged, and her eyes went dry.

Serena threw her weight to her right. The cot rocked on its frame and fell back. She tried again, trying to overturn the cot, so she could get both hands on the floor and find leverage with which to push herself backward and out the door, using the mattress and frame on her back to delay the fire's assault. She rocked again, feeling the cot lift an inch off the floor before slamming down. She made a fist and shoved it against the wall, but the cot stayed rooted to the floor.

The shanty lurched. The opposite end, where the fire was, dipped at an angle, and Serena heard hissing as if she had poked a nest of snakes. She realized now that she was in an ice house out on the lake and that the hissing she heard was steam as the fire burned its way through the tough layer of ice. The shanty was beginning to sink, creating a slushy pool for her to drown in if the fire didn't get her first.

The intensity of the flames shooting through the windows diminished by degrees as the propane tank slipped into the water, but the fire fed on the fish house itself now, chewing into the wood and insulation, exploding empty bottles, surging uphill toward the cot. The first of the fire trails outlined the open door in wild orange and threw a shower of sparks that made black, smoking holes on the mattress. Some of the sparks hit her skin and ate their way inside like hungry rats. She couldn't help herself; she screamed. It was a terrible taste of the fate that awaited her, to die like that, searing away to bone and dust square inch by square inch.

She braced her left hand on the floor in a futile attempt to push herself backward from the onslaught of the fire. Her hand found something hard and cold, and she realized it was the revolver, which had slid around in the commotion and wound up back within her reach. She scooped it up and stared at it.

One bullet. It felt like a cruel joke to find the gun now, when it was useless to her.

Except for one thing.

Serena watched the flames draw closer like an inexorable army. They danced on the ceiling, and chunks of hot metal fell around her. They swirled like bright ribbons on the walls. They charred the bottoms of her feet, as if she were walking on coals. The smoke grew thick as fog and clouded around her face and blinded her. She tried to suck in air, but there was nothing to breathe but ash and fumes, nothing to see but haze, nothing to hear but the death throes of the shanty as it imploded, nothing to smell but the roasting of her own flesh.

She still had the gun in her hand. She had one bullet, and she couldn't miss.

One bullet to escape all at once from the pain, the flames, and the poison.

One bullet to help her find the nothing-ness room in the corner of her soul, where she had escaped as a child, and make a home there forever.

Serena put the gun in her mouth.

Stride sprinted toward the shanty from the west. Half of the shack was fully immersed in flames, and the lake was slowly pooling around it and drawing it back into its grasp.

He could feel the wave of heat from where he was. He had seen these gas fires before, and they were always deadly and complete, reducing metal, wood, glass, and tissue to a flat, smoldering wreck, nothing more than a black rectangle on the ground. It never took long, never more than a handful of minutes.

He shot around the corner of the shack and spied a snow-covered sedan, its door ajar, and the boxy outline of a van parked twenty yards from the shanty door. The wind had blown the snow clear, and he recognized the Byte Patrol logo. It was a caricature of a nerd dressed like a cop, with a laptop in one hand and a screwdriver in the other. The cartoon laughed at him.

Someone half-limped, half-ran toward the front of the van. He was tall and huge, and Stride saw his long hair flowing madly in the wind.

"Stop!"

The man froze and swiveled to look at him. Blue Dog's eyes gleamed with recognition across the short distance that separated them.

"Where is she?" Stride shouted.

The man gestured his head at the burning fish house and smiled. Stride ran for the door of the fish house, which was already a ring of fire. Out of the corner of his eye, he saw Blue Dog's right arm coming up, and he reacted by instinct, diving to the ground and rolling as two bullets ricocheted off the ice around him. Stride twisted in the snow, yanked his gun from his jacket, and fired back. His bullets thudded into the side of the van. Blue Dog jerked open the van door, and Stride fired again, four more times, missing the man's head by an inch and turning the window into popcorn. Blue Dog ducked, spun away from the van, and weaved as he ran through the blizzard, using the vehicle as cover as he headed for the trees.

Stride let him go. He scrambled back to his feet and pounded on the steel wall of the fish house. "Serena!"

The heat and intensity of the fire drove him back. His boots splashed in a foot of cold lake water where the ice was melting. The walls of the shanty were beginning to bow.

"Serena!"

He got on his knees and doused his head in the freezing water and lay down so that his whole body was soaked and frigid. Hypothermia was the least of his worries now; he just wanted to slow down the fire from taking hold on his skin. The wind bit at him, the heat burned, and the banshee screamed.

Stride stared into the maw of the devil.

As he prepared to jump through the doorway, he heard something that made his heart stop. Rising above the noise of the storm and the fire came the sharp crack of a single gunshot.

57

Maggie steered for the fire.

As she rounded the jagged edge of a peninsula, she saw the fish house burning like a pagan bonfire, ushering up a sacrifice to the storm god. The fire illuminated the entire inlet. She could see the twisting of windblown snow, the tin boxes of other shanties hunched against the blizzard, and the outline of birch trees like stick figures on the coast. As she navigated around the other fish houses and got closer, she could see a man outside the shanty, and even at that distance, she recognized Stride.

He was getting ready to go inside, and

Maggie could see from the monsterlike size of the fire that doing so was no better than suicide. She honked her horn frantically, trying to stop him, but if he heard her, he ignored her.

"No!" she shouted inside the car and banged her fist on the steering wheel.

As she watched helplessly from fifty yards away, Stride took three steps and dove into the center of the doorway, through the flames, disappearing inside.

Maggie didn't see Blue Dog until it was too late. She never even heard the report of the gun. A bullet ripped through her windshield and embedded itself in the headrest on her seat, so close to her head that when she reached up instinctively to cover her ear, she felt blood on her fingers. The windshield held together except for the perfect, circular round hole and a spiderweb of cracks carved into the glass. Even so, she instinctively turned over the wheel, and the truck spun, the rear end leading it around in circles as she tapped the brakes.

When she finally stopped, another bullet screamed through the far side of the windshield, which finally gave up and rained down in a shower of glass. Maggie saw a man running at the truck, right arm in the air, firing wildly. She knew what he wanted—the truck, not her—something he could use for his escape. She grabbed the keys out of the ignition and hunched down, then scooted across the seat and pushed the passenger door open. She spilled out of the Avalanche.

Maggie dropped to her chest on the ice and stared under the truck, where she could barely see Blue Dog's legs through the driving tornado of snow. He was moving carefully and silently, step-by-step, about forty feet from the driver's door. She thought about running, but she wasn't going to do that. Not from this man. Not after what he had done to her.

She needed a weapon. Her pockets were empty, and the only thing in the glove compartment was a tire pressure gauge. In the covered bed of the truck, she kept an emergency radio, a forty-pound bag of sand, a medical kit, jumper cables, bungee cords, and a shovel. The shovel was made of durable plastic, designed to push snow out of the way, and wasn't the kind of blunt object she could use to beat a man unconscious.

That was all she had.

She decided to bluff. "Stop right there!" she screamed, and she saw him freeze in his tracks, trying to pinpoint the faint sound of her voice. "Take one more step, and I'll blow you away."

A long silence followed, then he fired several more times, shattering the rest of the windows in her truck and spraying the snow with bits of glass.

"If you had a gun, I'd be dead," he shouted back.

Maggie crawled quickly to the back of the truck. She hoped he couldn't see the tailgate as she unlocked and lowered it. She reached in and gently slid out the heavy bag of sand, taking care not to rock the chassis.

She squatted down and saw that he was twenty feet away. Cursing silently, she closed the tailgate, put the bag of sand down, and scrambled back to the open passenger door of the truck. She kept low and slid back inside, hoping he couldn't see her as she replaced the keys in the ignition. She backed out carefully, retrieved the forty-pound sandbag, and positioned it on its side under the truck, directly behind the right front tire. She relied on the wail of the storm to cover any noise she made.

Maggie retreated behind the truck bed and crouched down to watch him approach. He veered wide to check the front of the truck and went all the way around to the far side. She dodged backward, staying out of view. She saw him lift one leg and kick the passenger door shut and immediately fire three bullets into the earth. One bullet hit the rear bumper with a metallic clang. She prayed he didn't see the bag of sand hidden behind the tire.

He waited. He had to know where she was—in the back, behind the truck bed. The question was whether it was worth the time for him to track her down, knowing they could circle each other as long as she wanted. She watched him retrace his steps slowly to the front of the truck and back toward the driver's door. He hesitated there.

In the distance, she heard something beautiful. Sirens. Lots of them.

He opened the driver's door and climbed in and slammed it behind him. He turned over the engine, and Maggie pushed herself off her feet and ran toward the front of the truck. She knew he could see her coming in the sideview mirror, but that was okay. She wanted him to rush. He stepped on the accelerator, and the truck ground away at the ice and leaped forward.

Ten feet later, the Avalanche jerked to a stop as the rear wheel slammed into the bag of sand. Maggie reached the driver's door at the same second. She wrenched it open, grabbed him by his hair, and slammed his skull repeatedly against the metal frame of the door. He groaned and fell out of the truck. She looked for the gun, but it wasn't in his hand; she saw it on the far end of the dashboard where he had dropped it during the impact.

She didn't bother fighting fair. When she bent over him on the ground, she realized his shoulder was bloody and torn, and she hammered her fist over and over into the wounded limb until he screamed. She jabbed her fingernails into both of his eyes. He clawed blindly for her with his other hand, and she reached out, took his wrist and twisted it, and bent his index finger back until it broke with a sickening snap. He gave a strangled, gurgling cry.

"Not like last time, is it, you sack of shit," she hissed.

His eyes closed, but she wasn't taking any chances. She reared her left fist back as if she were nailing in a spike and drove it deep into his gut. He didn't move; he didn't open his eyes; but his abdomen lurched, and he began to throw up. Vomit bubbled out of his mouth. He was a limp elephant to move, but she managed to turn him over and make sure he wasn't choking. She slid her belt out from her jeans and used it to bind his wrists together. She got up and went to the truck bed and found a bungee cord and secured his ankles.

Maggie retrieved the gun from the Avalanche and put it in her pocket.

She heard a metal crash boom across the ice, and she looked up and hated what she saw. The shanty was entirely engulfed in flames. The walls were crashing down.

58

Serena heard Jonny shout and realized he was inches away from her, on the other side of the fiery wall. At that instant, she changed her mind. If the fire wanted her, if the lake wanted her, they would have to come and get her. She also realized there was another way to use the one bullet left in the revolver, and without hesitating, she reached her left arm as far across her body as she could, stretched her right hand to the limit of the cloth that bound her, and fired. The bullet tore through the fabric. Her right arm stung with powder burns, but when she yanked her hand, it came away from the bed frame. Both arms were free.

She was dizzy as the fire and smoke choked out the oxygen from the tiny space. She braced both hands against the side of the bed frame and pushed herself up. A scorching wave of heat slapped her in the face. She leaned all the way forward until her fingers grasped her left ankle and frantically tore at the tape that bound her to the frame. She squeezed her eyes shut, unable to keep them open in the face of the heat. The torn tissue in her stomach and shoulder split further, and she felt blood dripping onto her thighs. The duct tape clung as if it were nailed to her skin. Blue Dog had wrapped it tightly, and the tape resisted when she tried to saw it with her fingernails. She couldn't believe she was this close and still imprisoned.

Her air ran out. Black, tarry poison filled her lungs. She gave up and threw herself back down, hoping there was still something to breathe in the lower section of the fish house, but the smoke had descended there, too. She heard herself gasping and wheezing, and it was as if she went outside herself and watched her labored breathing from afar. She knew she would only remain conscious for a few more seconds.

With both hands free now, she grabbed the bed frame and jerked to the right and felt the frame tilt six inches off the ground before teetering and falling back down. Expelling her last breath, grunting with the huge effort, she tried again, and this time, the cot rose straight up into the air and went tumbling over. The cot was a crushing weight on her back. Her bare skin was pressed against the floor, like a piece of raw meat tossed on the grill. Somewhere right near her lips, though, she smelled a trickle of cool air.

She clawed at the floor with her fingers and realized she was over one of the trapdoors that fishermen used to access the ice. She felt a loop of metal catch under her fingernail, and she pried the small door open and nearly sang with joy as a rush of cold air blew up from the lake water into her face. Her lungs gagged, trying to cough out the remnants of smoke and replace them with oxygen. After a few deep breaths, she felt alive again.

The flames were now circling her like wolves. She felt a singeing heat on her back that told her the cot itself was now on fire.

She began to think she had saved herself just to die in the worst way.

The shanty took a heavy jolt, and she heard a voice not even four feet away. *"Serena!"*

It was Jonny. Inside.

Stride took two steps and ripped something off the wall. The *whoosh* of compressed air exploding in a burst of foam filled the space. The nearest flames fell back and died. He sprayed until the fire extinguisher was empty, beating back the fire and creating a temporary bubble of safety around them.

He attacked the tape on her ankles. Serena saw the glint of Blue Dog's knife within reach, and she grabbed it and waved it in the air. "Jonny, use this! Hurry!"

She felt him quickly cut through the tape where it tied her to the steel legs of the cot. In seconds, her legs came free. He flung the bed frame away from her and pushed aside the mattress, which was smoldering. She tried to turn over but found she didn't have the strength to do so. Her legs were leaden. The blood flowed back to her feet slowly.

"Can you walk?" he asked.

"No." Her voice was ragged.

Jonny squatted in front of her. "Grab onto my shoulders. Hang on."

She wrapped her arms around his torso from behind and clung to him as he pushed himself off his knees. He swayed, holding her weight.

"Don't let go," he said.

Then she heard him say, *"Shit."*

As the two of them watched, half the ceiling of the shanty collapsed. A wall of fire came down like a steel curtain in front of the doorway. The fish house lurched again, a dying ship slipping under the water. The lake spread in a deepening pool across the floor. Steam and smoke mingled. There was no way out.

Stride squatted down again and eased her back onto the hot floor. She hid her face under the trapdoor. There was still fresh air blowing below the shanty, but the ice was weakening, and the pool of water was rising and threatening to flood inside. When she looked up, she saw Jonny with a wet scarf wrapped around his face. He kicked furiously at the tin wall behind them with the bottom of his boot, but the metal hung tough. Sparks landed on his clothes and started to catch fire. He spotted a gas-powered augur in the corner and lugged the three-feet steel coil to the wall. He pulled the crank cord, and the motor coughed and sputtered. The shanty swayed; it was sinking fast. The fire raced over their heads. He yanked it again, and again, and finally the whiny engine roared to life. Stride plunged it against the wall, and the metal screamed and gave way, and then he pulled it back and punched another hole and twisted his body to drill a jagged tear down to the bottom of the wall. When that was done, he brought the drill back up and cut sideways and down, until the gap in the metal formed a three-feet square.

He threw the augur down. He kicked again, and this time the wall yawed and bent, and the flap of metal pushed outward toward the open air. The rush of new oxygen fed the fire, and the flames closed in on them. He didn't need to tell her what to do; she grabbed hold of his waist, and he squirmed through the gap in the wall, dragging her behind him. He fell out of the fish house and splashed into frigid water, and he kept snaking forward until Serena spilled out behind him. She let go and fell into a foot of slushy water, but there was a sheath of ice below her.

Stride clawed out of the shallow pool and reached back and pulled her out beside him. The snow froze her wounds with an awful sting. She wanted to lay there forever, but he was already moving. He stripped off his jacket and made her put it on, then hoisted her onto his back again. Next to them, the fire spat through the hole they had made in the wall. The rest of the ceiling collapsed with a roar, and the walls caved in over the space where they had been only seconds earlier. A new tower of flame rose and fell, consuming what was left of metal and wood, until there was nothing left of the fish house.

She couldn't walk, but she knew that Jonny was near to breaking. In the distance, though, she saw rescue. Maggie ran toward them, waving madly. Behind her, only a quarter mile away, half a dozen squad cars converged on the scene.

Jonny saw them, too. He sank to his knees, unable to go any farther. She felt both of their bodies shiver and tremble, but she repeated over and over to herself that it wouldn't be long, that help was coming, that warmth and blankets and morphine were minutes away. She prayed it wasn't a mirage.

Someone else saw the police cars coming, too.

Nearby, the snow-covered Lexus sedan near Blue Dog's van came alive. Windshield wipers pushed aside the snow. Its tires spun, and it shot off away from them, away from the police, away from the wreckage of the shanty, heading straight out toward the belly of the lake, where the blizzard quickly swallowed it.

"Who the hell was that?" Jonny murmured.

Serena didn't answer. She was already unconscious, and in her dreams, the pain went away, and she was warm.

59

Lauren was in a white cloud, unseeing, with the storm blinding the night and the lake as big and open as the ocean itself. The wheels of the Lexus churned silently at a hundred miles an hour across the ice. She could have been flying.

She had no illusions of escape. She was dying. You could only lose so much blood and stay alive. Her heart kept pumping, and the red river soaked into her blue shirt and turned it purple and puddled on the leather seats of the Lexus. Dan would hate that. He could forgive almost everything else, but he'd be standing over her grave asking why she couldn't have died in the snow and spared the custom interior. That was Dan. Love was sex to him, but money was love.

It didn't matter to her to die out here. The infuriating part was that no one would understand. It was never about money or power or exposure. She didn't swing the flashlight into Tanjy's head because she was afraid of the truth coming out. She did it because Dan was in love with Tanjy.

Lauren willed the knowledge of Dan's other affairs out of her mind, because in the end, he came home to her and relied on her for everything. If he wanted to sleep with trophy girls who thought they had a chance of displacing her, she didn't care; she just didn't want to know about it. Sex was never of much interest to her, so she let Dan do what he wanted. She was the one who loved him, who created him. Their partnership was more important than anything else.

Until Tanjy.

Until that perverted, beautiful bitch destroyed their lives.

She didn't understand how Tanjy and her vile fantasies turned Dan inside out and made him forget what Lauren had done for him. People called Lauren an ice queen and made jokes about the cold face she showed everyone else, but they were so wrong. When that huge, awful blackmailer named Billy Deed showed her what was going on between Tanjy and Dan, she became obsessed with punishing Tanjy. Erasing her. Obliterating her.

It wasn't just the photographs, although she couldn't believe Dan would be so reckless. Any one of those photos would have brought their world tumbling down, ruining everything. But there was more. Blue Dog had e-mails, too. Those were the things that scared and enraged her. Dan telling Tanjy how much he loved her. How she aroused him. How he never stopped thinking about her.

How he was talking to a lawyer about divorce.

No lie. She checked his calls and his calendar. He was meeting with a divorce lawyer in the Cities. *Divorce.* To throw over someone like Lauren, who had made him everything he was, who had built her entire life around his career, for a deranged child like Tanjy Powell. Lauren wasn't going to accept that.

If Tanjy thought rape was so exciting, let her see what it was really like.

She felt like a stone watching Tanjy suffer in the park, her naked body strapped to the fence. Later, as Tanjy was crucified in the media, Dan finally broke off the affair, and Lauren was exultant. She was in control of the world again. She ramped up her efforts to land Dan a lucrative job far away from Duluth and far away from Tanjy Powell.

Everything was going perfectly until Tanjy called that night. Begging to talk to Dan. Claiming to know who raped her.

Lauren became deadly calm. She was at a crossroads. She wasn't going to let the truth come out, and she wasn't going to let Tanjy lure Dan back under her spell. She told Tanjy that Dan was at their lake house, and she knew Tanjy would drive out there that night, to talk to him, to seduce him. Lauren went to meet her instead.

To kill her. Not just to keep the secret, but to wipe her from Dan's mind once and for all. She knew she could do it.

Tanjy. That young, stupid little fool. The irony of it all was that Tanjy was *wrong,* but when she saw Billy Deed pulling up in the Byte Patrol van behind them, it was too late to go back.

So Lauren told her.

"It was me, you sick bitch."

As Tanjy turned to run, Lauren let out all her rage with one swing. Just one, that was all it took. Tanjy dropped and died. Cold-blooded? Never. She was on fire.

But there was always a price to pay. That was what her father told her. Her father knew about cutting corners, making deals with the devil. Justice always found a way to even the scales.

Like now.

At least she felt no pain. Not anymore. The doctors would say it was a rush of endorphins as the body got itself ready for death, but the peace as she drove was almost blissful.

She didn't feel anything even as the Lexus sped past the warning flags onto one of the hot spots on the lake, didn't feel anything as the nose of the car broke through the thinning ice and the car jerked and spun to a stop and the air bag deployed. Nothing.

She noticed that as the air bag deflated, it was stained burgundy, as if she had poured a bottle of red wine over it.

The Lexus settled lazily into the water. It was virtually soundproof, and she could barely hear the ice spindling into fragments, giving way. Near-freezing water seeped in at her feet, and she didn't feel that either. She knew she should open the car door, but the signals from her brain didn't travel to her limbs anymore. It occurred to her that Tanjy had come out of the lake, and now she was going into it. Balancing the scales. Body for body.

The water reached her waist. Her stomach. Her breasts. Her neck. She was floating. The car dipped below the surface, and the lake and the storm and the snow disappeared from view, and there was nothing but the cold, wet hands of the devil taking hold of her. Her lungs rebelled, as if wondering why they should die just because the rest of her was lost, but soon enough, they gave up to the inevitable, too, and she took a breath that was no breath at all.

She had a fleeting thought that the ice would close over the top of her by morning, and she wondered if anyone would ever know what happened to her. She would simply be gone.

Poor Dan. He would miss the car.

PART FOUR

THE LADY IN ME

60

The prison doctors made the police wait three days before interviewing Blue Dog. Stride himself spent a day in the hospital, treated for hypothermia and minor burns. Serena would be hospitalized for several more days, maybe weeks, as the doctors dealt with smoke inhalation and the more serious burns, mostly on her legs. She would need skin grafts where the burns were worst and for the cuts in her abdomen. It was too early to tell about the long-term pulmonary effects of the smoke. Even so, she was lucky. Lucky to be alive, lucky that the damage wasn't more severe.

Stride stared at Blue Dog through the window before going inside, feeling his muscles clench into knots. Raw hatred coursed through his veins.

Teitscher, who was standing next to him, saw his reaction. "This is personal to you. You shouldn't be in the room."

"I want to be there," Stride insisted.

He pushed the door open before Teitscher could lodge any more protests, and the two men went inside. The room was painted in institutional gray and smelled of disinfectant. The bedsheets were bleached white. Teitscher folded his arms and stood beside the bed, looking down at Blue Dog. Stride leaned against the wall and shoved his hands in his pockets.

Blue Dog's legs were manacled to the bed frame. So was his right arm, which was inked over with tattoos. The doctors had amputated his left arm when he was brought in from the lake. He had suffered too much damage from the shotgun wound to save it. He was hooked up to intravenous drips of morphine and antibiotics. His long hair had been chopped off, leaving him with a black-and-gray buzz cut. The stubble on his chin was thick, and his skin was pale under the fluorescent light. His barrel chest was naked.

"Hey," Stride called. "Wake up, asshole."

Blue Dog's bloodshot eyes blinked open, and he took note of both men in the room. He shifted, straining against his bonds, and pain shot through his body, making him grimace. He looked down at the bandaged stump on the left side of his torso.

"Hurts, huh?" Stride asked. "Good."

"Fuck off."

Teitscher removed a digital tape recorder from his pocket and set it on the table beside the bed. "We're going to tape this conversation. My name is Detective Abel Teitscher, and this is Lieutenant Jonathan Stride of the Duluth police."

"I know who you are," Blue Dog replied. He looked at Stride. "I'm just sorry you dragged that bitch out of the fish house. I would have liked to hear her scream as the fire got her."

Teitscher ignored him. "You were read your rights when you were arrested. Do you need them read to you again?"

"I know my rights."

"Do you want a lawyer?"

"For what? A lawyer won't do me any good."

"Are you willing to talk to us?"

"What's in it for me?" Blue Dog asked.

Teitscher shrugged. "We've already been in touch with the authorities in Alabama. They're anxious to get you back to Holman. You'll wind up on trial for the cops you killed in the hurricane, and then they'll stick a needle in your arm. Of course, it'll have to be your right arm."

"Fuck you," Blue Dog said.

"I'm just telling you how it is. Before you go back to that hellhole down south, where they *are* going to execute you, you have to make it through the courts up here. We're going to put you on trial for murder, attempted murder, rape, assault, blackmail, fraud, you name it."

"Maybe I don't have to go back to Alabama," Blue Dog said. "Maybe you can just keep me up here."

Teitscher shook his head. "You mean, in a state like Minnesota where we don't have capital punishment? Where we don't sleep prisoners twenty to a cell? Sorry, but the fact is, no one is too anxious for you to hang around here. But it can go fast or it can go slow. You might be back in Holman in a couple of months, or the whole process might drag out, and it could be a year or more before we get around to sending you back down there. We might even need to keep you in a private cell because of your medical condition. So where would you like to spend the next year? Minnesota or Alabama?"

Blue Dog scowled. "Yeah, so, what is it you want?"

"Tell us about Lauren Erickson and Tanjy Powell."

"Like what?"

"Did you rape Tanjy?" Teitscher asked.

"Okay, yeah. But that was Lauren's idea."

"I'll bet you put the idea in her head."

"Not me. Hey, I didn't give a shit about Tanjy. I wanted money. I knew Lauren would pay to keep the photos of Tanjy and Dan out of the papers. Lauren was the one who turned it all around and wanted me to do her."

"Why?" Teitscher asked.

"Punishment. Payback. Whatever you want to call it. Those photos made Lauren crazy."

"So what went wrong?"

"Nothing went wrong. It all worked like Lauren planned. But then Tanjy called Lauren a couple of weeks ago and said she knew who raped her. Lauren freaked and called me."

"What did you do?"

"Lauren told me to meet her at their lake house. The two of them were already going at it when I got there. Tanjy saw me pull up— she probably thought it was going to be Dan, you know? Tanjy looked like she was going to bolt, but Lauren hit her hard. Real hard. Dropped her like a bag of cement. So we put her in the trunk and took her out to the lake."

"What about Maggie and Katrina?" Stride asked from the wall. "Were you the one who assaulted them?"

"Yeah, that was me."

"Was that Lauren's idea, too?"

"No, she didn't know anything about it. Not until later."

"So why did you rape them?" Stride asked.

"Why the hell not? After I did Tanjy, I realized what a rush it was. Hell, it was like fucking Serena in my head before I got to the real thing, you know?"

Stride wished that his aim on Hell's Lake had been better, and this animal who called himself Blue Dog would already be dead.

"Plus, it was safe," Blue Dog went on. "I

knew all about the sex club from Sonia's computer. I figured these alpha girls weren't going to want the media dishing out the same treatment to them that Tanjy got. And I was right, too."

"What about Eric Sorenson?" Teitscher asked.

"What about him?"

"Did you work on his computer?"

"No."

"Did Tanjy tell him about you?"

"No."

"Then how did he find you? How did he figure out that you raped Tanjy and Maggie?"

"He didn't."

Blue Dog's words thudded like a bird against a clean window.

"What?"

"He didn't know a thing about me."

Teitscher and Stride stared at each other. Stride tried to make sense of his thoughts.

"Are you telling us you had nothing to do with Eric Sorenson's murder?" Teitscher asked.

"I found out he was killed when I saw it on TV."

"Do you know who did kill him?" Teitscher asked.

"I figured his wife popped him, like they said on the news," Blue Dog said, laughing at Stride. "Maybe once she had some lovin' from me, her husband didn't cut it anymore."

Stride lashed out. "Eric was Maggie's husband, and you raped her. Eric found out. He confronted you that night."

"I didn't know this Eric guy to spit on him," Blue Dog insisted. "You don't believe me? Check out my alibi."

"What alibi?" Teitscher asked.

"I was with my manager pulling an all-nighter on a corporate system in Hermantown when that guy was killed. You ask him."

"You already told us that Tanjy *knew* you raped her," Stride said.

Blue Dog grinned. "Tanjy was wrong."

"What?"

"Lauren told me when we were dumping the body. Tanjy thought somebody else did it. Funny, huh? She made a stupid fucking mistake, and that's what got her killed."

"Who did she think raped her?"

"Lauren never told me."

Stride ran his hands through his hair. Blue Dog had turned everything upside down. Just when he thought the investigation was over, he realized that the questions that started everything hadn't been answered yet.

Who killed Eric?

And why?

"Have you ever met a woman named Helen Danning?" Stride asked.

Blue Dog shook his head. "Never heard of her."

"You ever come across a blog called 'The Lady in Me' on any of the computers you were pawing through?"

"No."

"If you're lying to us about any of this, I'll have you back in Holman on the next flight."

"It's the truth," Blue Dog said.

Stride gestured at Teitscher, and the two men headed for the door.

"You think he's on the level about Eric?" Teitscher asked when they were alone in the corridor.

Stride wanted to say no, but he couldn't lie to himself. "I don't think he'd give us an alibi if it won't hold up."

"You know what that means," Teitscher said.

"Maggie didn't do it," Stride insisted.

"Then who did?"

"Lauren killed Tanjy. Maybe she killed Eric, too."

Teitscher shook his head. "That's not going to fly. Lauren was in Washington that night. I checked."

"So maybe Blue Dog *is* lying. Maggie beat the hell out of him. He may want her to take the fall for the murder."

"You know that's not going to happen," Teitscher said. "Look, I don't know if Maggie did it or not. I still think there's a good chance she did, but she's free and clear. We're never going to bring charges against her. There's enough reasonable doubt for Archie Gale to drive a truck through."

"She'll still have a cloud over her head if we don't find out who really killed Eric," Stride said.

"We all have clouds."

"This guy says Tanjy made a mistake," Stride said. "Eric and Tanjy thought someone else was responsible for the rapes. Whoever that was, he must have killed Eric."

Teitscher shook his head. "That doesn't make any sense, Lieutenant. If Eric was wrong, why kill him? If I accuse you of a crime you *didn't* commit, why the hell would you kill me over it?"

Stride knew that was true. He was missing something.

The two men looked up as a guard opened a door at the far end of the narrow hallway, and Max Guppo ran toward them. Guppo never ran, and by the time he reached them, he was sweating in large beads on his forehead, and his big chest was heaving up and down. He bent over and broke wind loudly, and both men involuntarily took a step backward.

"Son of a bitch, Guppo," Teitscher complained.

Stride suppressed a smile and said, "What's going on, Max?"

Guppo took several wheezing, labored breaths. He loosened his tie and tugged his belt up over his protruding stomach. "All hell is breaking loose."

"Over what?"

"Another body," Guppo told them. "We've got a body in Enger Park. Right where we found that girl ten years ago."

61

It was déjà vu all over again. Stride couldn't believe it.

The victim was placed exactly where they had found the anonymous black teenager a decade earlier. He had been over this ground so many times that he could pinpoint the growth in the trees lining the fairway and the number of footsteps it took to get here from the road. The body was on its back, arms and legs spread like a da Vinci drawing. She was in a valley that was invisible from the road and sheltered from the golfers walking the straightaway toward the green. The girl back then, who was found in August, who had haunted his dreams ever since, was found because of a doctor's errant slice.

"Two cross-country skiers came across her," Guppo said. They were calf-deep in snow, and Guppo was looking back at the slope that led to the highway as if wondering whether he would survive the climb. It was midafternoon. The snow was done, and the sun was back, but it couldn't manage more than a weak shine.

Stride nodded. His lips were thin and cold. "Any idea how long she's been here?"

"She's frozen solid, so it won't be easy to pin down," Guppo said. "But one of the skiers said he followed this path two days ago, and there was no body."

"He's sure he was in the same place?"

Guppo nodded. "He said this is his favorite route."

"Was she killed here?" Teitscher asked.

"No, not enough blood," Guppo said.

Stride studied the victim, or what was left of her. Like the girl ten years ago, this newest body was missing its head and hands. On the part of the neck that remained intact, he could see ligature marks to suggest that she had been strangled. She was naked, and he could see bruising in the pelvic area. In those respects, the murder was a carbon copy of the earlier crime.

A few details were different, though. It was summer then and winter now. The original victim was black, and this woman was white. The girl back then was young, no more than seventeen, and it was easy to tell from the condition of the skin that this victim was older, probably in her thirties or forties.

"Don't hold your breath on DNA this time," Guppo said.

Stride nodded. He had a feeling the perp was too smart to leave his calling card again. "What else have we found?"

"Not a lot. Violet's working the body for the M.E. She's up in her truck now. We're scouring the area, but like I say, I think the perp just dumped her here."

"What about footprints? He had to get her down here."

Guppo pointed at a narrow track of matted snow leading down the slope. "Yeah, looks like he dragged her. We've got blood spots and hair all along the route back to the road. I think he took a shovel and backfilled in the snow, though. Plus, we've had another inch or so in the last two days."

"Same with tire tracks?"

"Nothing on the road."

Teitscher looked up as he heard the thumping roar of a helicopter hovering over their heads. "Who the hell leaked this to the media? It's a damn circus."

"Don't blame me," Guppo snapped. "One of the skiers called his wife, and she happens to be a secretary at KBJR. They broke it first, and the others have piled on. We've got reporters from the Cities up here, too. They're all smelling a serial killer. Everyone's asking about the original Enger Park Girl case and whether there's a connection."

"More likely a copycat to throw us off the scent," Teitscher said.

Guppo shrugged. "These guys are all talking like this is something out of the next John Sandford novel."

"Well, we're not ruling anything in or out," Stride said. "It's a long time between killings if we're talking about the same perp, but you never know. If it's a copycat, he's just as bad."

"Do we have any idea at all who this woman is?" Teitscher asked. "Are there any reports of missing persons in the region that fit the profile?"

"No likely candidates except for Lauren Erickson."

Stride shook his head. "It's not her. Too tall."

He figured Lauren was somewhere at the bottom of Hell's Lake, and they would find her in the spring.

His cell phone rang, and he took a few steps away into the deeper snow to answer it. He heard Maggie's voice. "I'm watching the news," she said. "They've got you on live TV, did you know that?"

"Great."

"You've got something green on your front teeth."

"Ha-ha."

"Tell me they've got this wrong," she said. "Tell me this isn't a rerun of the Enger Park Girl."

"It's the same M.O., Mags. The scene is virtually identical."

"Shit."

Stride couldn't help but think of standing on this same ground with Maggie ten years ago on that hot August night. They had only been together for a year then. Maggie was young and smart, coming out of her shell slowly, more like a kid than a woman.

"You talk to Blue Dog?" she asked.

"Yeah."

"Did you kill him?"

"I wanted to."

"What did he tell you?"

"He says he had nothing to do with Eric's death," Stride said.

"Do you believe him?"

"Unfortunately, I do. He has an alibi."

"Meaning it's back to me."

"Come on, you're off the hook, Mags. Even Abel doesn't want to charge you."

"Because they can't convict me, or because I'm innocent?"

Stride was silent.

"I thought so," Maggie said. "Look, that's not good enough, boss, you know that. I can't come back on the job if everyone still thinks I'm a murderer."

"It's not over, Mags."

"No? Abel thinks I did it, but he can't prove it. He's not going to invest a lot of energy in solving the case."

"Give me time."

"I want back in," Maggie insisted, impatience bubbling up in her voice. "I want to be with you on the scene right now. I deserve to be on that case."

"I know."

She sighed over the phone. "Look, I'm

sorry, I know this isn't your fault. You've got work to do. I'm going over to see Serena, okay?"

"Thanks."

"She's probably watching you on TV, too, so why don't you moon the camera?"

"Goodbye, Mags."

He hung up the phone and rejoined Guppo and Teitscher, who were standing stiffly a few feet apart from each other. There was no love lost between them. Guppo had been among the loudest to complain during Teitscher's short tenure as lieutenant, and Teitscher knew it. It didn't help that Guppo also had a long and close relationship with Stride.

"I want to review the original case file on the Enger Park Girl," Stride said. "Who's got it now?"

Teitscher blanched. "I think it's in my desk."

"What's up with it?"

"What's up? Nothing's up. You know how it is with cold cases, Lieutenant. Every few months, you pull it out of the drawer and rifle through it to see if you get a new idea. It's not like I've got the time to work a ten-year-old file."

"Especially if the victim's just a black teenager, huh?" Guppo asked.

"Now just one goddamned minute," Teitscher exploded. "That is bullshit, and you know it."

Stride held up his hands. "Both of you, knock it off. We're not going to do this now."

"This is *not* about black or white," Teitscher insisted, jabbing his finger at Guppo. "This is about a case that's *ice-cold*."

"You're right," Stride said. "It's a cold case, and I never said it wasn't. Both of you drop it, and move on. Who was the last person to really touch the case?"

"Other than you and Maggie?" Guppo said. "It was Nicole."

Stride looked at him in surprise. "Nicole?"

"Sure, when she came back after the shooting on the bridge, you gave her half a dozen cold cases rather than put her right back on the street. The Enger Park case was one of them."

"I don't recall seeing any of Nicole's notes in the case file," Teitscher complained.

"That's a surprise?" Guppo said. "Nicole was always months behind in her paperwork."

"Well, if she was working it, we should find out if she latched onto something we've missed," Stride said. "Abel, I want you to go down and talk to her."

Teitscher's brow knitted into a maze of angry lines. "You're shitting me."

"No. Do it tomorrow. We need to move fast."

"It was six years ago. What the hell is she going to remember?"

"You won't know until you ask her."

"I'm the last person she's going to talk to," Teitscher said. "Send Guppo. He and Nicole were as thick as thieves."

"We need Guppo working the evidence here. I need you to do this, Abel, so suck it up."

Abel shook his head fiercely. "This is unfuckingbelievable."

He turned and stalked away from them, climbing back up the deep snow of the hillside toward Hank Jensen Road. His trench coat flew up behind him as if he might become airborne, and each of his strides was long and hard.

"I'd give good money to see him and Nicole together," Guppo said.

Stride smiled. "Yeah." He and Guppo looked up as the medical examiner investigator on the scene waved to them.

"Hey, detectives!"

Violet Gabor was a short, squat woman in

her early thirties with a baseball cap turned the wrong way on her head. She was bent over the corpse, with a magnifying glass focused on the victim's ankle.

"We got something here," she told them.

Stride bent down. His knees were quickly wet with snow. He squinted where Violet was pointing. "I can't see, what is it?"

"Man, you're old," she told him.

"I'm seasoned, Vi."

"Roasts are seasoned," she replied. "You're just old. It's a tattoo, a small one, on the back of her ankle."

Stride saw it now. The tattoo was nestled in the skin of the victim's ankle and appeared to be a series of letters crafted in an old-fashioned font, the kind of typeface he would expect to see written on parchment. The tiny brand was easy to miss if you weren't looking for it or didn't know it was there. "What does it say?"

"Near as I can tell, it says TLIM," Violet told him. "Whatever the hell that means."

"TLIM? Are you sure?"

"Yeah, it's in purple ink, and the script is a little hard to read, but I'm sure that's what it says. Why, does that mean something to you?"

"Yeah, it does." Stride got to his feet and brushed off the snow. He added in a hushed voice, "Damn."

He felt as if they had killed her themselves by dragging her name into it. By not finding her sooner while she was out there, unprotected, a target. His only salvation was that this time around, the killer had made a mistake. Not catching the tattoo. Not knowing the victim had a secret identity.

Stride knew whose mutilated body was lying in the snow, and it meant this wasn't a random slaying at all. It was somehow connected to Eric's death.

TLIM.

The Lady in Me.

It was Helen Danning.

62

Maggie found Serena in her hospital bed, vacantly staring at the television suspended from the ceiling. When she saw Maggie, she clicked off the screen with the remote control and offered up a weak smile. Her shoulder was bandaged. A clear tube looped around her ears and stretched across her pale, pretty face, delivering oxygen to her lungs. Her black hair was pulled back and tied behind her head. A blanket covered her body, but Maggie could see her bare arms, which were patchy with cherry-red burns.

Serena saw her looking. "Those are the minor ones," she said.

"I know." Maggie pulled a chair next to the bed and sat down. She sucked her upper lip between her teeth and clamped down on it. The room was uncomfortably warm. Her eyes wandered to the amber fluid in the IV bag and then to the watercolor print of Canal Park that hung on the soothing baby-blue wall. "I'm not sure what to say. Everything sounds so stupid. How are you. Are you okay. That kind of thing."

Serena eyed the pink box in Maggie's lap. "That for me?"

Maggie looked down. "Oh, yeah. I almost forgot. Doughnuts. You want one? I've got old-fashioneds, crullers, and a couple of the cream-filled ones that go splurt when you bite them."

Serena laughed and paid for it with jabs of pain. "Old-fashioned, please."

"You want me to feed it to you?"

"No, my left arm isn't so bad. I can do it."

Maggie opened the box by slitting the tape with her fingernail and handed her a doughnut. Serena wolfed it down in three bites and brushed the crumbs from her lips. Maggie took a chocolate cruller for herself and put the rest of the box on the table beside Serena's bed.

"Why no morphine drip?" Maggie asked.

"I told them to take it away."

"Why? Burns are the worst."

"They set it up so you can push a button and get a shot when you need it," Serena said. "You know me. Addictive personality. I don't want to walk out of here hooked on painkillers."

"You need to manage the pain," Maggie told her.

"When it gets so bad I want to cut off my legs, then I call the nurse and get a shot."

"When did you have your last one?"

"Too long ago," Serena admitted.

"Don't be a martyr."

Serena glanced at the nurse's call button, which dangled near her right hand, but she didn't reach for it. "I saw the news," she said. "The Enger Park thing."

"Stride thinks the body is Helen Danning."

Serena arched her eyebrows. "So there's a tie-in to Eric's murder?"

"Could be."

"That's good for you."

Maggie shrugged and nibbled on the doughnut. She licked chocolate from her fingers. "Just as long as they don't think I did it. Beheading isn't my style, though. I hate all that blood. I prefer a quick tap to the forehead."

"Nice," Serena said.

"I hate thinking about the Enger Park case all over again. I've carried that one around for a long time."

"We all have cases like that."

Maggie knew that was true, but the Enger Park Girl was different. There was something heartbreaking and lonely about the black girl out in the wet grass, not even a girl at all anymore, just a mutilated thing left there to decay. One final humiliation on top of the agony, rape, and death. She wished she could have given the girl a name and a little justice to make her human again. She also didn't tell Serena that it was on that case that her feelings for Stride became something else, because suddenly working with him wasn't just solving crimes, it was suffering emotionally together at the failures.

"Thanks for nailing Blue Dog," Serena said. "I'm not sure I could deal with any of this if he was still out there."

"It was payback for me, too," Maggie reminded her. "He won't bother any of us again."

"That's what I thought before."

"I think even Alabama can manage to keep a one-armed murderer behind bars," Maggie said.

Serena's face was far away, and Maggie didn't know where she was.

"Did he . . . ?" Maggie asked softly. She added, "You don't have to tell me."

"He never got the chance," Serena said.

"That's a relief. I mean, it's one less thing to deal with."

Serena bit her lip. "Sure."

"Are you all right?"

"I just want this to be over. I want to get out of here."

"Don't push it. You need to heal. At least you're going to be okay."

"Yeah. That's what they say."

Maggie watched vulnerability bloom in Serena's face. Her voice cracked, her chin trembled, and her eyes turned watery and scared.

"Hey," Maggie murmured. She leaned close and stroked Serena's hair.

"I'm sorry," Serena said. "Real tough, huh?"

"You're entitled."

"I should be grateful. I'm here, I'm going to make it. Then I cough, and my lungs feel like they're burning up, and I wonder if I'll ever be able to take a breath again without remembering. I wonder if I'll ever run again. Hell, I wonder if I'll ever walk again."

The tears flowed out of her eyes now. Maggie felt angry and helpless.

"I looked at my body, too," Serena went on. "They told me not to, but I did. Oh my God, Maggie. Oh, my God."

"Don't do this to yourself."

"It's so stupid and vain, but I don't want Jonny ever to see me again. Not like this."

"You'll heal. You'll get through this."

Serena shook her head.

Maggie whispered. "Come on, it's not just your body that needs time. It's your head, too. Remember what you told me? You were right. I was in denial. I need help, and so do you. I'm going to see Tony again tomorrow. You'll do the same thing. Anytime you need someone, I'm there for you. Stride will be, too. You know that."

"It hurts," Serena told her. "It hurts so much. When I think about it, it hurts even more. I don't think it will ever stop."

Maggie reached over and pressed the call button. Serena didn't protest. Her mouth had fallen open in agony. Her skin tensed, making it worse, and her legs jerked under the blanket. Maggie watched Serena's long fingers curl into fists.

"Nothing will ever be the same," Serena murmured. "Nothing will ever be okay."

"Shhh. Don't talk."

"Tell Jonny not to come. Tell him not to come."

The nurse ran in. She already had a hypodermic of morphine in her hand; she knew what Serena needed when the bell rang and knew that she needed it quickly. Maggie watched her swab Serena's left shoulder and then insert the needle and squeeze the plunger. The narcotic began to work almost immediately. Serena's eyes blurred and relaxed. Her body settled gently back into the mattress. Her mouth worked, but she didn't say anything.

Maggie and the nurse stayed until Serena was asleep and out of pain.

"How is she, really?" Maggie asked.

"This is the worst time," the nurse replied. "The pain makes you very emotional. Don't worry, her skin is already starting to heal. Her lungs are clearer today, and her breathing is stronger. You won't believe how much better she is in a few days."

At least on the outside, Maggie thought.

The ward was dark when Stride arrived at the hospital. It was after midnight. The lights were dimmed in the rooms he passed, and he saw patients stretched out on their beds and saw a few weary caregivers sipping coffee. He smelled the harsh cleansers that were used to scrub the floors. There were kids and adults here, men and women. Some were getting better, and some were getting worse. Living and dying. It was a struggle to remind himself that Serena was going to be fine, because this was the same hospital where Cindy had finally yielded to the cancer. Being inside this place, walking these corridors again, made the memories almost too vivid to bear.

He found Serena's room and stood at the end of the bed, watching as her chest rose calmly up and down in her sleep. He did what he had done many times years ago, take off his leather jacket, drape it over the back of the chair, and sit in the semidarkness watching the woman in his life. Back then, each day, Cindy was a little worse, and he felt as if a rat were gnawing out more of his heart whenever he saw her. He couldn't believe then that the woman in that bed was his vibrant, beautiful wife, that she had once been the seventeen-year-old girl who had changed his life in the course of one amazing summer.

She was gone too soon, and nothing was as he planned it.

He couldn't believe now that he had been given a second chance, and he did something he couldn't remember doing in years. He let himself pray. He had prayed back then, too, and when God ignored his pleas, he turned his heart away and decided that there was no point ever wishing for anything again. Until now. Until this woman came into his life, someone he would literally walk through fire to save. He was grateful that she was alive and desperate for her to recover.

As he sat there, Stride reached out and softly laced his fingers with Serena's hand on the bed. He tried not to wake her, but he felt her squeeze back with a weak touch. Her eyes blinked slowly, as if opening them were like lifting weights. She was groggy and drugged. When she saw him, her faced warmed, and he did his best not to break down. Cindy did that, too, lit up like a Christmas tree when she saw him, even when her time was short.

Serena mumbled something, and he couldn't hear her. When she said it again, it sounded intense and important.

"Couldn't go there," she told him.

He leaned toward her, but he didn't understand. "What?"

"Tried to," she murmured in a cottony voice. "Couldn't go there."

Stride smiled as if he knew what she was trying to tell him.

"'Cause of you," she said.

"Don't talk," he said. "Let yourself sleep."

"Still here," she said, and her eyes closed.

Stride watched her for a while longer, until the weights on his own eyes felt like lead sinkers pulling them closed, and he slept and dreamed of a long-ago summer on the Point.

63

Abel Teitscher sat stiffly in the private meeting room in the women's prison in Shakopee. He held a white Styrofoam cup with both hands and stared at the black coffee without drinking it. He was wearing a pressed gray suit, the kind of outfit he would wear to church if he ever went there. His trench coat was neatly folded on the chair next to him. His black shoes were shined. He made it a point to dress well when he visited correctional facilities, as if the suit and tie were another set of bars between him and the prisoners incarcerated there.

He hadn't seen Nicole Castro in six years,

not since she was led out of the St. Louis County courtroom after she was convicted. She had shot him daggers then with her eyes, and he looked back at her and saw a stranger. There was no morbid curiosity in his mind about what she looked like now, no desire to do anything but forget her. He never wanted to see her again, and it killed him to be here, hat in hand, coming to her for information. He knew what kind of reaction to expect.

The door unlocked loudly. A guard led her in. Abel didn't look up, but he felt her eyes as she saw him, and the warm, stale air in the room turned frigid. She didn't spit or scream, but she turned back to the guard and said calmly, "Get me the fuck out of here."

"Be nice," the guard retorted in a bass voice that boomed in the small space. He filled most of the doorway.

"I don't want to see him. Take me back."

"He's a police officer, so be polite and sit your ass down and hear what he has to say."

Nicole slouched to the chair on the opposite side of the wooden conference table and slumped down. She eyed Abel as if he were a spider and picked at the grooves in the wood with her fingernail. He didn't look up from his coffee. The guard closed the door, locking them in. The room was absolutely silent, and they sat alone for two or three minutes without saying anything. Her contempt radiated across the table, and he sat there and stewed, letting it wash over him and wishing he could walk out.

"You look like shit," Nicole said finally. "Tell me you're dying or something."

Abel's eyes drifted away from the smoky pool of coffee and drank her in. She wasn't the young cop he remembered. "Look who's talking."

"I hear you got divorced. Found your wife humping some stud."

"You heard right."

"So what do you do now? Sit on that old sofa of yours and stare at your fish all night?"

Abel hated the fact that she was right. "I run."

"Yeah? You got a lot to run from, Abel. A whole trainload. Word is you washed out as lieutenant, too. People hated you so much they had to bring Stride back, or everyone was going to take a hike."

Abel shrugged. "You done yet?"

"I'm not even getting started."

"You can blame me all you want, but I'm

not the reason you're in here. You fucked up, Nicole. I couldn't help you."

"Oh, yeah, like your help is worth shit. You helped me right into a twenty-year sentence. My son had to grow up without his momma."

"I didn't kill those people. You did."

"You know that ain't true."

Abel shook his head. It was the same song. "Please."

"Don't you sit there and shake your head at me. Not after you messed with the crime scene to lay it on me."

"Is that still the best you can come up with? I framed you? I thought after six years you'd try a new story."

"Fuck you, I'm out of here."

Nicole got up and pounded on the locked door. The guard's square face loomed behind the window, and he ignored Nicole and looked questioningly at Abel, who shook his head. The door stayed locked. Nicole swore in frustration and sat back down heavily and folded her arms.

"What the fuck do you want anyway?" she asked. "Why are you here?"

"I'm here because Stride asked me to talk to you."

"Yeah? About what?"

"About the Enger Park Girl case."

Nicole's head bobbed in surprise. "Say what?"

"You heard me."

"You want my help with a case? Are you kidding me?"

"I want to know if you found anything when you were working it as a cold case. There's nothing in the file."

"Yeah, well, paperwork was never my thing."

"So meanwhile, the case sits in my desk gathering dust."

"It's not like you ever asked me. No one did. Six years, and no one ever asked me about it. I had a good angle, too."

Nicole was always pretending she was a supercop. Most of the time, her trails were dead ends. "I'm asking now," he said grudgingly.

"Well, why should I tell you a fucking thing now? Do your own research. I'm not exactly on the job anymore."

"Another woman was murdered and dumped in the park," Abel told her.

Nicole was quiet. She drummed her legs nervously under the table. "Same M.O.? Chopped off the head and hands?"

Abel nodded.

"Damn. Another kid?"

"No, she was older. We think her name was Helen Danning. You ever come across that name?"

Nicole shook her head. She was subdued. "No."

"What was your angle?"

"You think it's the same perp?" Nicole asked. "After all this time?"

"Maybe, or maybe it's a copycat. Either way, we're trying to find out if there are any connections between the murders. If you know something, it would really help us out." He got the words out as quickly as he could, before he choked on them.

"Why'd Stride send you?"

"It wasn't my choice," Abel admitted.

"So what? You're like some virgin sacrifice Stride's giving me? Give me a chance to rag on you, and in return, I tell you what I know?"

"Something like that. The cold case is technically mine now."

"Technically, meaning you're not doing shit with it."

"Okay, sure, you're right. I don't have time to waste on cases that aren't going anywhere, because I've got plenty of new files laid on my desk every day."

"Cases where the victims are white, you mean."

"Don't put that bullshit on me. We've been down that road. You've got Guppo believing I'm a damn racist, and you know that isn't true."

"Oh, yeah, like you were so surprised when your black partner got arrested for murder. Dem colored apples don't fall far from the tree, do they?"

"Look, I didn't give up on you because you were black. I gave up on you because you were guilty."

"That's the same thing in your book, Abel. The same damn thing."

"Are you going to help me? Or am I wasting my time here?"

"What makes you think I even remember a fucking thing about the case after six years?"

Abel had said the same thing to Stride, but looking in her eyes now, he knew she did. She remembered everything. Somewhere deep down, she was still a cop. "Because you've got a kid," he said. "And you wouldn't want him ending up like that girl in the park."

Nicole's anger dwindled to ashes. "Yeah."

"How's your boy?" Abel asked quietly.

"Far away. He's far away, and good for him. He's in college down south now."

"That's good."

Nicole studied her calloused hands as if they belonged to someone else. "Aerosmith," she told him. "That was my angle."

"What?"

"The Enger Park Girl had a bunch of video game and heavy metal tattoos, remember?"

"Stride and Maggie covered that lead. They talked to the bands. It didn't go anywhere."

Nicole smiled. "Yeah, but that was before all the Web shit, okay? And chat rooms and crap like that. I spent hours hanging out in chat rooms with fans of the bands. Bon Jovi, Barenaked Ladies, Aerosmith. I thought if the girl was a big fan, someone might remember her, like she was a groupie who stopped showing up after the summer of '97."

"That's a needle in a haystack. Teens come and go around the bands all the time."

"Well, it's not like I had much else to do, you know?"

"So what did you find?"

Nicole leaned forward. She was excited again, forgetting where she was. "A girl in Chicago told me about this black girl she hung out with at a bunch of Aerosmith concerts during their Nine Lives tour in the summer of '97. The black girl's name was Teena."

"Who was this girl in Chicago?"

"She never told me her name. When I told her I was a cop looking into a murder, she got freaked-out, signed off, and I never found her again."

"So?"

"So she said she was supposed to meet Teena again at their concert in Chicago, but she never showed."

Abel frowned. "That's not exactly a hot lead."

"No, but get this. This girl saw Teena for the last time at the band's Kansas City concert on August 26, 1997. She saw her getting into a car with an older white guy. She never ran into the girl again."

"August 26?" Abel asked. He saw the connection now.

"Exactly. That was two days before we found the Enger Park Girl. Okay, sure, maybe it's nothing, but it's a hell of a lot more than we ever had before. I was going to go down to Kansas City and start getting records of the ticket purchases from back then, see if I could find Teena, or see if I could find any buyers with connections to Duluth or with sheets. I was also going to start tracking down people who had been to the concert and see if anyone else could tell me about the girl or the guy she left with."

"That's a lot of legwork."

"Yeah, well, it's not like I had much else to do, and I had some things to prove to a lot of people."

Abel rocked back in his chair. "So why did you quit?"

Nicole frowned at him and gestured at the walls. "I got busy, you know?"

"Oh. Sorry."

"I'm telling you, though, I think this Teena was the Enger Park Girl, and some guy picked her up at the concert, raped and killed her, and dumped her in Duluth."

"I wish you'd told someone about this back then," Abel said.

"Like I said, I wound up with a few problems of my own."

"I'm not sure how any of this ties in to the murder of Helen Danning."

"Maybe she was an Aerosmith fan, too."

Abel shook his head. "This woman was an usher for Broadway musicals. She doesn't sound like a hard rock fan."

"Look, you know what you've got on this new case," Nicole said. "Maybe there's no connection. But do me a favor, okay? Don't let this drop. I mean, maybe you can still find something in Kansas City. Or you can track down this girl in Chicago again."

"Yeah, I spend a lot of time in heavy metal chat rooms," Abel said. "I'll fit right in."

"These fans are die-hard. If she was into Aerosmith in 1997, she's still into them now."

"So how did you find this girl six years ago?"

"I talked to my shrink," Nicole said.

Abel stared at her. "What?"

"You know Tony Wells, don't you? He's the ultimate Aerosmith fan. He gave me a bunch of Web sites. That was how I found this girl."

"You were seeing Tony," Abel repeated.

"Yeah, so? I was messed up. You know that."

It was probably nothing. Abel knew that. Nothing at all. Tony Wells saw half the detectives on the force. That was his job.

Except he knew it was everything. For a

man who didn't trust anything he couldn't see, touch, and smell, Abel suddenly found himself taking a leap of faith. Seeing the big picture. He stared at Nicole and felt a well of regret so deep that he could drop into the hole for a mile and never splash into the cold water.

"Did Tony know why you wanted the information?" he asked her.

"Not at first. I told him later, when I found the lead about Teena."

"What exactly did you tell him?"

Nicole studied his furrowed face, and her eyes grew curious and hard. "Just what I told you, that I thought I had made a break in the Enger Park case. He became a consultant for us on that case, you know. He did the profile."

"Yeah," Abel said. "I remember."

"Lieutenant, you better see this," Guppo called.

Stride popped the top on a red can of Coke, which opened with a fizzy hiss. "I'm coming."

They were in the basement of City Hall at seven o'clock at night. Half the overhead fluorescent lights were dark. Guppo was in a tiny cubicle with walls that looked like gray burlap, with three computers glowing in front of him. One was a standard city-issue unit belonging to the Detective Bureau; the other two were computers taken from Eric's home and office.

Stride waited in the doorway of the cube, looking down at Guppo, who overflowed out of a small rolling chair. He didn't get any closer. Guppo was munching guacamole chips and salsa, which for him constituted a lethal weapon.

"You got something?" Stride asked.

"Oh, yeah."

Stride rubbed his eyes and watched Guppo's fat fingers tap the keyboard on the high-end laptop they had taken from Eric's company headquarters. The musty smell of the basement was in his nose. He felt strangely at home among the evening shadows.

"I was looking for 'The Lady in Me,'" Guppo said. "That was pretty much a dead end. She wiped her blog clean, and I couldn't find any cached pages that told us a thing. But the tattoo clued me in, and I went back over the sites that Eric had been visiting, looking for the TLIM acronym."

"And?"

"Voy-la," Guppo said. He clicked on a blog entry and maximized the window on the screen.

"Is this Helen's site?" Stride asked.

Guppo shook his head and crunched a handful of chips in his mouth. "It's a recovery site for Midwest rape victims," he said, spitting out mushy emerald crumbs as he talked. "You need a password to get in."

"So how did you access it?"

"I found Eric's password," Guppo said.

"How did Eric get in?"

"Looks like he joined. Family members of victims can be part of the community. His handle was Swimmer. Not tough to figure out."

"So what did you find?"

"A thread from about eighteen months ago. A college student was date raped at the University of Minnesota, and she talked about it online. Then a woman chimed in with a response and told her own story from the early 1990s."

"TLIM?"

Guppo nodded. "Right. Helen Danning."

"What did she say?" Stride asked.

"See for yourself."

Stride leaned in next to Guppo and smelled onions and peppers on the detective's warm breath. He read the blog posting on the screen:

Same date rape thing happened to me at the U in the early '90s. I went out with a grad student, and I had way too much to drink. It didn't seem like a lot at the time, and it wasn't until much, much later that I realized he probably put something in my drink. Girls, you HAVE to watch out for that kind of crap. There are PREDATORS out there. This guy was going to KILL ME, but thank God, a security guard found us in the park. The police told me it was my fault (!!!!) because of the alcohol. They never even charged this animal. TLIM.

"The time line fits," Stride said, "but there's no way that was enough for Eric to make a connection."

"There's more," Guppo went on. "This is just the beginning of the thread. Helen talks about dropping out, how she bounced around in dead-end jobs. She never got over it. Then the other girl asks her about counseling. Check this out."

He clicked through several more entries and leaned back for Stride to see.

> Counseling? Yeah, right. The real kicker is that the bastard who did this to me is now in the business of counseling rape victims! He's some shrink up in Duluth! TLIM.

"Damn it to hell," Stride murmured. "Abel was right about Tony. All this time, he's been advising *us* about sexual pathology."

"Yeah, he's an expert," Guppo said sourly.

"Can we prove that Eric ever saw this?"

"Oh, he saw it," Guppo said. He clicked on a new posting.

> TLIM. I think this guy may still be at it. I think he raped my wife. What's his name? Swimmer.

"What was Helen's reply?" Stride asked.

Guppo shook his head. "There was no reply. TLIM didn't post anything else."

"So Eric went to find her," Stride said.

At which point, he knew, all the dominoes began to fall.

64

Tony hadn't changed.

Maggie hadn't seen him in almost two months, but his routines were always the same, no matter how much time passed. He was always in the leather armchair when she arrived, with his head down in his notes, his double chin bulging like a blowfish under his beard. He always had his black mug of coffee in one hand and a silver Cross pen in the other, which he rubbed nervously between his fingers. His eyes brooded like a sleepy dog's stare, and his trimmed eyebrows were the only part of his face that ever moved. He was so predictably bland that he had no personality of his own. He was a watcher. A mask.

Except for Aerosmith.

That was the only clue she ever had as to who Tony was. He was always playing heavy metal when she arrived, and they usually spent the first few minutes of their hour together talking about music and bands. Sometimes Mötley Crüe. Sometimes Guns N' Roses. Mostly Aerosmith. She knew it was a way to relax her enough to share the wolves that were in her brain. Today, he was playing their last big single, "Jaded," and something about the song felt nostalgic to her, as if Tony were taking a rare walk down memory lane. It was about yesterday's child. Things that were lost and not coming back.

He clicked the song off as she sat down on the sofa, and the silence felt loud. It was night, and the wall of glass overlooking the wilderness behind him was a dark mirror. The office looked like the end of the world, and where the carpet ended at the windows, you could step off and fall into the sucking gravity of a black hole.

Maggie squirmed to get comfortable. Her feet dangled above the floor, making her feel like a teenager. Tony didn't look up. He never looked up until she spoke. He just sat there, sipping his coffee, sometimes stirring it up in his mug as if there might be grounds resting on the bottom that could float around and flavor it.

"Long time," Maggie said.

Tony put the black mug to his lips and took a quiet sip. "Yes."

He deigned to look at her then, with the mug in front of his face like a muzzle.

"You heard about everything that's happened?" she asked.

He nodded, and the overhead light danced on the smooth, high scalp of his forehead. "How is Serena?"

"She'll be okay, but she'll need help."

"Of course."

He didn't push her, didn't ask questions. How are you. What are you feeling. What's on your mind. Sometimes they spent a long time not saying anything at all. He just studied her from behind his coffee mug, and she felt like a lab rat.

"I should have come to you after I was raped," Maggie said.

"Why didn't you?" Tony asked.

"I thought if I didn't tell anyone, I could

make it go away. Block it out. I'm good at that."

"But not good enough."

"No," she admitted. "No one's that good."

"You caught the rapist, I hear."

"Yeah."

"Does that help?" he asked.

"I thought it would, but to be honest, it doesn't. Not really. Don't get me wrong, I'm glad the shithead is out of circulation. But it's like having your house burn down and then putting out the fire."

"I understand. So what are you going to do about that?"

"What do you mean?"

"Well, you can't change what happened. It's already done."

"I was hoping I could mope around and feel sorry for myself for a while," Maggie said. "Eat Doritos. Watch the soaps."

Tony didn't smile.

"Actually, I'm thinking of adopting a kid," she admitted. She wondered why she was telling him that. Old habits died hard.

"Ah."

"What, ah?"

"Nothing. Go on."

"You think it's too soon?"

"What do you think?" Tony asked.

"I think it would be nice to get an answer once and a while for all the money I'm paying."

"How did you come to this decision?" he asked.

"It's not a decision. It's something I'm thinking about. I feel like that's what I'm missing in my life. Being a mother. All the bad things began to happen after the miscarriages. That's when the universe went out of whack."

"So if you become a mother, the stars will be aligned again."

"Something like that."

"You sound like you're looking for approval or disapproval."

"I am."

"From me?" Tony asked.

"No, not from you," she said. Too quickly. "I guess I'm looking for approval from myself."

"And?"

"I'm not ready to give it yet."

"Why is that?"

"I still haven't found my way out."

Tony raised his eyebrows. "What do you mean?"

Maggie sighed. "Have you ever watched a

spider on a screen? He gets in through a crack in the mesh, and then he's trapped inside, and he walks around and around and around and around trying to find that same little seam where he can get out. He can do it for days. The question is, can he find it before he starves to death?"

"So what's your crack in the screen, Maggie?"

"Isn't it obvious? Eric was murdered."

Tony stopped twirling his pen and froze with his coffee mug halfway to his face. Their eyes met. "Of course."

"I need to find out who did it. I can't go on until I do."

"I thought this rapist, this escaped prisoner, was the murderer."

Maggie shook her head. "He has an alibi."

"Surely no one still thinks *you* did it."

"A lot of people do. They can't prove it, but it will always be out there. You can't be a cop suspected of murder."

Tony's upper lip disappeared under his mustache. "We both know that murders don't always get solved, and it's no one's fault. You can't take them all on."

"No, but this one is my river, Tony. I cross this one, or I'm stuck where I am forever. I get past it, and I can get on with my life. Anything else is like drowning."

"You seem to think I can help you."

"You were the last person to see Eric that night," she told him.

"I've already told you everything I know."

"Humor me," Maggie said. "Tell me again."

Tony drank from his black coffee mug and studied her face. "Eric told me you had been raped. He thought he knew who did it. He wanted advice from me on how to figure out if he was right. He wanted to know what kinds of questions to ask to determine if someone could be a sexual predator."

"But he didn't give you a name."

"No, I don't know who he suspected," Tony said.

"Eric didn't talk to Blue Dog," Maggie said. "That means he thought someone else assaulted me, and he was wrong. The trouble is, I still think whoever he suspected was the one who killed him. Crazy, huh?"

Tony frowned. "If Eric was wrong, why would anyone have a reason to kill him?"

"Maybe because that person had something else to hide."

The words floated like dead leaves blown in the air and never touching ground.

"We've known each other a long time, Tony," Maggie said softly. "Ever since the Enger Park case."

"Yes, that's right."

She remembered how young they all were back then. They spent hours together—Stride, Tony, and Maggie—going over evidence, looking for a pattern, building a picture of the killer. Tony was the profiler. *You're dealing with a serial killer*, he had told them. *He's going to do this again. He's a male, probably married, probably in his forties. He has a teenage daughter, and he either abuses her or fantasizes about abusing her. I don't think cutting off the head and hands is about obscuring the victim's identity. It's about the killer's anger and guilt. He needs to erase this girl.*

The profile made perfect sense, and it got them nowhere.

"The Enger Park case is back in the news," she added.

"I know."

"What's your gut say, Tony? Could we be looking at the same perp?"

"After ten years? That's a long time between crimes."

"But it does happen. I mean, serial killers sometimes wait that long."

Tony shrugged. "Yes, it depends on whether they can find some other way to resolve their pathology. Something that provides a similar sense of power or release."

"How would a rapist and murderer *resolve* his pathology?" she asked. "I've always wondered about that."

Tony got up and went to the mahogany bar where he kept his coffee press and poured another cup. His paunch made a bump in his sweater. He made a face as he drank. The coffee was cold. He stood in front of the glass wall, and all Maggie could see were reflections and nothing but darkness framed behind him.

"There are many ways," he told her. "It depends on the individual. The perpetrator needs to find a substitute for his deviant behavior, something that satisfies his underlying need for power and control. The BTK killer in Wichita wound up as a leader in his church, and the social status he had in that role was apparently enough to keep him from committing more murders for many years."

"That sounds too easy."

"No, it's not easy at all. Keep in mind that most of these killers *want* to control their violence. They live a constant, mortal struggle between good and evil. Some control their impulses all their lives. Others fail. The lucky ones find a way to cage the beast."

"What about being sort of a sexual voyeur?" Maggie suggested. "You know, being involved in rape cases, working with rape victims, that sort of thing. Could that do it?"

Tony narrowed his eyes. "Maybe."

"So being a cop could actually work, I suppose."

"It's possible."

"Or working with cops. That would do it, too."

"Like I said, anything's possible."

Maggie nodded. "You remember Nicole Castro, don't you?"

Tony took a seat behind his desk on the other side of the room. He reclined backward in his Aeron chair. "Yes."

"I didn't realize you treated her," Maggie said.

"I work with lots of cops, but I can't talk about patients."

"Right, privilege, I know."

Tony sipped his cold coffee.

"Stride came to see me this evening," Maggie went on. "Abel Teitscher was in the Cities this afternoon talking to Nicole about the Enger Park case."

"Oh?"

"It turns out Nicole thought she was close to a breakthrough on the case right before she was arrested. She said you were a big help."

"Me? I don't recall."

"She says you pointed her in the right direction. Told her to *walk this way*. Get it? Aerosmith? Pretty funny, huh?"

"You've lost me."

"Well, you helped her find out a lot about Aerosmith fan sites and chat rooms, and wouldn't you know, she thinks she found out who the Enger Park Girl was. She thinks it was a girl who got picked up by a bad, bad guy at an Aerosmith concert in Kansas City in 1997. That was a couple days before we found the body in the park. So Nicole figures the murderer was at the concert, too."

"Sounds like a pretty big haystack in which to find a needle," Tony said.

Maggie rolled her eyes. "Yeah, that's for

sure. Nicole was optimistic. Those concerts are zoos, right? Tens of thousands of people there. But I don't need to tell *you* that."

"No."

Maggie turned around and squinted up at the diplomas hung on the wall behind her. "I need glasses. It kills me. Say, I'm right, you went to the University of Minnesota, didn't you? You were there in the early '90s?"

"Yes. I got my B.A. and then did my graduate work there, too."

"We were probably both there around the same time, but we never ran into each other."

"The U is like a city," Tony said.

"It sure is. Thousands of students, and you never meet more than a fraction of them. You never hear their stories. Like Helen Danning, she went to the U at the same time we did, but she dropped out and never went back to school. Too bad."

"Who's Helen Danning?" Tony asked blandly.

"She's the second Enger Park Girl," Maggie told him. "The woman we just found yesterday."

Tony stroked his beard and briefly closed his eyes. When they opened again, Maggie stared at him without blinking. Her eyes were bright and cold. She was talking to him silently. Telling him the truth. Daring him. It was as if they were connected by an invisible tether, a waxy string tied to the bottom of two foam cups, and she was whispering in his ear.

"I didn't hear that you had identified the body," Tony said.

"No, they haven't released that to the press, but it's her. The killer made a big mistake. He missed a small tattoo on her ankle."

"Oh?"

"The tattoo said TLIM. Helen kept a blog. The Lady in Me. The blog was how Eric traced her to the Ordway in St. Paul."

"Eric?"

"That's right. Eric went to see Helen Danning just before he was killed. Helen disappeared the next day. You see, we're still putting the pieces together, but we think Eric found her because of a story she posted on the Web about being sexually assaulted while she was at the U."

Tony shrugged. "Why would Eric want to talk to her about that?"

"Yeah, that's the real question, isn't it? What would lead Eric to believe that a girl named Helen Danning getting raped in college would have anything to do with *me* being raped fifteen years later?"

"I assume you're going to tell me."

Maggie reached inside the pocket of her jacket and slipped out a single sheet of paper. "Here's the part of the blog that Stride and I found really interesting," she said. "This is what Helen wrote. 'The real kicker is that the bastard who did this to me is now in the business of counseling rape victims! He's some shrink up in Duluth!'"

Tony stared at the glossy surface of his desk as if it were a mirror.

"So let me know where I go wrong on this, Tony," Maggie said. "Eric was trying to find out who assaulted me and Tanjy, and he wound up on this Web site for rape victims. He saw what Helen wrote, and alarm bells started going off in his head, because he knew that Tanjy and I had one thing in common. Our shrink. So Eric went to see Helen Danning to confirm exactly who she meant, exactly who this Duluth psychiatrist was who raped her back in college. But he knew what she was going to say. She told him it was you, Tony. That's why Eric came to see you the night he was killed. He wasn't there to find out how someone ordinary could be a rapist. He didn't tell you he was going to see someone else after he left. He was there to accuse *you* of raping me and Tanjy."

Tony looked up from his desk. "The problem with your little story is that I didn't rape you, Maggie. Or Tanjy. Even if Eric suspected something ridiculous like that, why would I care? I was innocent."

"Sure, you may have been innocent of raping me and Tanjy. But what about your DNA?"

"What are you talking about?"

"I'm talking about the Enger Park Girl. Teena. The girl you met at the Aerosmith concert in Kansas City. The girl you raped, killed, and dismembered. You left semen inside her, Tony. You didn't think about that back then, did you? But if we ran your DNA now, it would lead us right back to the Enger Park case. That's why you killed Eric. To make sure that didn't happen."

"Please, Maggie, I've been around the block," Tony said. "I know the standards a court would apply in granting a motion to take a DNA sample. Rumors and innuendo like that wouldn't constitute probable cause."

Maggie pointed a finger like a gun at

Tony's right hand, where he was cradling his coffee mug. "But Eric didn't care about that. He just *took* a sample for himself. You know, I forgot all about the coffee mug. When I came back home the night Eric was killed, I was so drunk. Eric left me a note, and he put it on the counter under a black coffee mug. I didn't think twice about it. The damn thing disappeared, and I never realized it. I didn't even put it together until I saw you holding that coffee cup of yours. Same as always. Like you were daring me to notice. Eric took it from you that night, didn't he? He was going to get *me* to run your DNA. So you had to get that mug back."

Tony laughed. It sounded odd, laughter bubbling out of the man who never even smiled. He stared at the mug, shook his head as if it were the funniest thing in the world, and then flipped it across the room. The mug twisted in the air, and coffee streamed and splattered on the carpet, leaving a dark trail of stains. When the mug hit the floor, it bounced and rolled to a stop near the far wall.

Tony slid open the middle drawer of his desk.

"Don't," Maggie said. She knew what he was reaching for.

Tony drew out a black Glock from the drawer and cradled it in his hand.

"Take a look at the camera," she said.

He glanced at the monitor that kept an eye on his waiting room. Stride was there, his own gun in his hand, staring back up at the camera as if he knew that Tony was watching him and deciding whether to run.

"And the door," Maggie added.

Tony turned and studied the glass door that led out of the office into the field of birch trees, and Abel Teitscher was there, tall and windswept, looking back at Tony with his grizzled face. He had a gun in his hand, too.

"There are more," Maggie said. "The place is surrounded. You're not going anywhere, Tony. So just put down the gun, and let's go."

Tony held the Glock as if he were measuring its heft and how solid and heavy it felt in his hand. "You know, I was planning to kill you, too, Maggie. That night. But I didn't."

"Instead you used my gun to kill my husband and frame me," she snapped.

"Don't pretend it was such a loss. You didn't love him."

"Fuck you, that's not the point."

"Once I killed Eric, I couldn't risk going back upstairs," Tony said. "Kicking your husband out of your bed kept you alive. That's rather ironic."

"What about Nicole?" Maggie asked. "You framed her, too, didn't you?"

Tony slipped his finger around the trigger of the Glock. "Yes, we had a session together, and she told me about tracking down the girl from the concert in Kansas City. I was stunned. I knew if she looked hard enough, she'd find me."

"So why not just kill her?"

"If Nicole were killed, people would wonder why, but if she wound up in jail for murder, it would all just go away. I knew Nicole. She never wrote anything down. She was always forgetting our appointments because she didn't keep a calendar."

"So you killed her husband and his girlfriend and planted evidence against her."

"She was always leaving hair behind on that couch," Tony said. "It was actually pretty easy. It all went underground again for years until Eric started nosing around. He was raving about me raping you, raping Tanjy, about what a monster I was, about who I'd raped in the past. Can you imagine the horror? All these years, I've kept the secret, I've beat my demons down into a box. Now this fool was going to expose me over something I *didn't do.*"

"What happened?"

"I went over there and waited until you were both home. You're right. I needed to get that mug back."

"Why wait for me?"

"This time, I wanted to kill you both," Tony explained. "I wanted the focus to be on *you,* not Eric. But like I say, you weren't in bed together. And the frame-up worked with Nicole, so I figured I could make it work again."

"What about Helen Danning?"

Tony shrugged. "Loose ends."

"You bastard."

"If anyone found her, the arrow was going to point straight to me. She had to go. And you know what? It was *such a thrill* doing it again. To stop fighting the desire and finally give in after all these years. It was like reliving my greatest triumph to lay another body out in Enger Park. It was like yelling it to you and Stride and the whole world. I'm back, baby, I'm back. I told Serena there comes a time when you have to look your past in the eye and decide who you really are. I know who I am, Maggie."

Maggie's skin shivered. She stood up. "Let's go, Tony."

"No, I don't think so."

"There's no way out." She stepped closer to the desk.

"Actually, there is. I've always known the way out. I knew one day the monster would come back, and I would have to exterminate him. I was kidding myself to think I could hold out forever."

"Tony," she said, her voice a warning.

"It's okay, Maggie. I'm a psychiatrist. I know how these things work. You know the trick to committing suicide? Speed. Hesitation is the enemy. If you put the gun in your mouth and think about it, well, you won't do it. I've had lots of people sit on my couch and tell me about it, and the fact is, if you don't pull the trigger immediately, you never will."

"Put the gun down."

"I want you to remember something, Maggie."

She didn't take her eyes off the gun. Her whole body was still, as taut as a cable spanning the towers of a bridge. She was measuring how fast she could run, how far she could jump.

"Cops like you and Stride think you can

spot the monster," Tony went on. "You think if you look in someone's eyes, you can see what's in their heart. The fact is, you don't have a clue. You really don't. Everyone wears a mask."

Maggie jumped. She shouted as she took two steps and leaped across the desk, her arms outstretched like the talons of a hawk as it drops toward the earth, her fingers curled, clawing for the gun. She wasn't nearly fast enough. Tony swallowed the black barrel of the Glock and pulled the trigger, just like that, without a millisecond of hesitation, and he was already dead as she came across the desk. The explosion jangled her brain like a marble rolling around an empty bowl. She kept coming anyway, momentum carrying her, and her body spilled into Tony's as they both tumbled head over heels and landed together, and his blood, tissue, and shards of bone spattered across her skin and clothes.

Stride kicked in one door. Teitscher kicked in the other. They both thundered in, guns leveled.

"I'm okay!" Maggie screamed. She shoved Tony's fleshy corpse away from her own small body, and she stood up, spitting his blood out of her mouth and wiping her face with the back of her arm. She wobbled on her feet, but she stood over him, unable to tear her eyes away. "I'm okay."

Ten years of her life came and went with the man lying on the floor. She heard Stride say something, but didn't hear what it was. The gunshot was still roaring in her head, making her deaf. She had a vision of Eric on the floor, remembering the sprawl of his naked body, and she still didn't feel anything at all. When she finally looked up, she stared into the crazy reflections of the dark glass, and somewhere out there, she thought she saw the Enger Park Girl in the woods, not desecrated and alone, but alive and dancing. The beat she was following was an Aerosmith song. That was the way it was supposed to be, the way it should have been, with that girl out there paying no attention to her at all.

She felt Stride's arm around her.

"I'm okay," she said again.

65

Abel Teitscher stabbed a shrimp from a greasy paper plate, where it was swimming in a candy-red sauce. It was rubbery as he chewed, but his tongue relished the sweet-and-sour tang, even though it tasted burnt. He took a forkful of fried rice, too, and then washed it all down with a sip of green tea. He leaned back against the stiff frame of his old sofa and watched a school of lemon tetras race around his fish tank in streaks of shining blue.

Sinatra was singing softly on the stereo. Ring-a-ding-ding.

It was a Monday like any other Monday,

and like lots of Tuesdays and Wednesdays, as well. Potsticker Palace. Old music. Bubbles whooshing in the tank. "Dad, you've got to get out more," his daughter told him when she called from San Diego, but it was easy to say that when you were living in California.

She was right, though. He was lonely. It wasn't warm enough yet for the spring crime wave to wash over the city, so he didn't have to spend his evenings closeted away in his cubicle in City Hall. Sometimes that was easier than being home.

His doorbell rang, surprising him. He twisted around and looked out the living room window and saw a dirty Ford Taurus under the streetlight that he didn't recognize. He got up, noticing the wrinkles in his untucked white dress shirt. His gray slacks were baggy, because his waist had shrunk by a couple inches in the past year, and he hadn't bothered buying new clothes. He just cinched his belt tighter.

He opened the door.

"Hello, Abel," Nicole Castro said.

They stared at each other across the threshold. He felt self-conscious standing there, wondering if he had Chinese sauce on his mouth. He wiped his face. "Hi."

"Can I come in? It's okay, I'm not going to kill you."

"Funny."

He pulled the door wide, and Nicole wandered into the living room. She was dressed in a Minnesota Vikings jersey and jeans, with a new pair of Nikes. Her gray hair was still short, a prison cut. Her hands were in her pockets. She looked as uncomfortable as he felt.

"I heard you got out," he said. "I'm happy for you."

"Yeah. Free bird, that's me."

She stood in the middle of the room, biting her lower lip.

"You want some Chinese?" he said.

"No, that's okay. It looks like cherry barf, Abel."

"Yeah, it's only so-so, but it's kind of a routine for me."

"Uh-huh."

He rubbed his own flattop steel hair and tried to think of something to say. "Look, I'm sorry, Nicole. I don't know what else I can tell you. I didn't trust you, and I was wrong."

"Actually, I came here to apologize to you."

"What the hell for?"

"For thinking you set me up all these years."

"I would never do that," Abel said.

"Yeah, well, I know that now. I guess I needed someone to blame, you know. You were a big 'ol white target."

Abel sat down on the sofa and put his hands on his knees. "I didn't see the big picture. I saw the evidence, and that was it. The evidence said you were guilty, so you were. Same thing with Maggie."

"Not like you were the only one."

"You want to sit down?" he asked.

Nicole shook her head. "I can't stay. I'm driving south. My son and my momma are in Knoxville, and I'm moving down there."

"You going to join the force?"

"No way, not for me. Forget that. I don't want to put anyone in prison ever again, know what I mean? I couldn't do it. I couldn't stand the idea of being wrong. No, momma's got a restaurant, I'll probably work there."

"What kind of restaurant? Chinese?"

Nicole laughed. "That's a good one. I forgot you could be funny."

"I guess I did, too."

She looked around the living room and frowned. "What the hell are you still doing here, Abel? Ain't it about time you got your-self a life? That whore you were married to is long gone, so why hang around?"

He winced, but she was right. His ex-wife had sucker punched him, and he was still sitting here gasping for air. "I wound up in a ditch, and I was stuck for so long I figured I must like it there," he said.

"Well, go down to the pancake breakfast at church and get yourself a chicky."

Abel snorted. "I forgot how to date about forty years ago."

"I'm not talking about dating, I'm talking about getting yourself some." She grinned. Her teeth were yellowed. She was ten years younger than he was, but they could have passed for the same age. He felt responsible.

"You won't believe this, but I miss having you as a partner," Abel said.

"That's 'cause I was the only one who would put up with your shit."

He nodded. "Yeah, you're right about that."

"What say you dump that Chinese barf, and you and I go to dinner someplace, huh? Before I leave town. For old times."

"My treat," he said.

"Damn right it's your treat."

* * *

Maggie tilted a bottle of imported lager to her lips and drained the last third, then tossed it into the pile of empties on the sand. "You know what I would have paid good money to see?" she said.

Stride and Serena both looked up, and the orange glow of the bonfire reflected on their skin.

"What?" Stride asked.

Maggie began giggling. "I would have loved to see your face when your beloved Bronco sank to the bottom of that lake."

Serena laughed, too.

"Hey," Stride said. "That's not funny."

The two women laughed so hard they had to hold onto each other to avoid spilling backward off the driftwood.

"Are you kidding?" Maggie said. "I can't believe you didn't dive in after it."

"That truck was a classic."

"Oh, Jonny, it was a piece of junk," Serena said. "It had like six hundred thousand miles on it."

"It was only a hundred and seventy-five," Stride said. He finished his own beer and retrieved the bratwurst that was blackening on a skewer and dripping fat with a rich sizzle onto the circle of flames. He blew on it and bit off its head and sighed. "Oh, man, that's good."

It was the middle of the night. The three of them had stayed on the beach behind Stride's house for hours, stoking the fire pit, watching the stars, and listening to the slap of lake waves a few yards away. The March night was cool, and snow lingered in patches on the sand, but winter had loosened its grip, giving sea-blue color back to the gray sky. The sweetness in the air tasted like spring. It was the time of year when every Minnesotan in the north knew that they weren't yet safe from a late fist of icy anger descending on the arrowhead, but time was on their side.

"I haven't shown you my new trick," Serena told Maggie.

"Go for it."

Serena breathed in slowly through her nose, swelling her chest until her lungs were completely filled with air. For weeks, she had been unable to take a deep breath without a fit of coughing. Now, she held it for fifteen seconds, then thirty, then forty-five.

"Honey, that's great," Maggie said. She added, "How are the legs?"

Stride saw Serena catch his eye before responding. It was sensitive ground. He was so used to thinking of Serena as tough that it brought him up short to find her breaking into tears over how she looked. He told her over and over to be patient and that, however it worked out, it didn't matter to him at all. That got him nowhere. It mattered to her.

"I'm not going to be modeling any swimsuits this summer," Serena said, and her voice had an edge. Stride thought the thin ice holding her up might give away again, but she took another deep breath. "But I'm doing better. It stings when I walk since the last surgery, but that only lasts a few days. It doesn't feel like alligator skin anymore."

The day before, she had lingered in front of a mirror. She hadn't done that in a long time.

"What about you?" Serena asked.

"Don't you worry about me," Maggie said, lifting her arms over her head. "It's spring. My favorite time of year. The lakes melt, the rivers melt, and the bodies all come drifting ashore. I feel like a catcher in the rye."

"You're just happy to be back," Stride said. "And you're drunk."

"I am. I'm a little drunk, I'm back on the job, and I'm rich enough to buy and sell you both, so be nice to me."

"Do we want to know just how money you've got now?" Serena asked.

"You don't. You really don't. But don't complain, because I bought the bats. I mean, I brought the brats. Whatever."

"Yeah, but I bought the beer," Stride said. "And you're on your fifth beer."

Maggie laughed again, a happy, drunken laugh, a laugh that forgot everything else in the world.

"Speaking of the spring thaw," Stride said quietly.

He was drunk, too, but when he was drunk, he brooded. He had been dwelling on the bad news all day, and now it bubbled out of him. He could never entirely escape. It was like living on the Point, in the shadow of the lake. There were long, gorgeous summer days, cool spring breezes, a watercolor pallet of fall leaves, and winter mornings where each twig on each bare tree was sheathed in a silver wrap of ice. Every moment was beautiful and fleeting, but lurking behind all of them was the mass of the lake, which took lives and didn't give them back, which was like the foggy shroud of evil that was always gathering behind him. It was impossible to outrun.

Serena, who wasn't drinking anything harder than mineral water, recognized the sadness in his tone. "What happened?"

"Tony left a calling card," he said.

"Oh, man," Maggie murmured. "What did he do?"

"I got a call from the police in Hassman," Stride said. "When the snow melted on the highway shoulder this week, they found a woman's body."

Maggie and Serena absorbed the information in silence. The wind took that moment to gust off the water.

"Do they know who it is?" Serena asked.

"They think so. A woman named Evelyn Kozlak has been missing for several weeks out of Little Falls. Turned out she was Helen Danning's college roommate and best friend. That's how Tony tracked Helen down. He knew them both at the U."

"Shit," Maggie said. She added, "And you know what really sucks? I actually liked him. I have a hard time getting past that."

"Me, too," Serena said. "He helped both of us."

"You helped yourselves," Stride told them. "Tony just happened to be in the room."

"Helen's the one I really feel bad about,"

Maggie said. "She wasn't part of any of this. She just wanted to live her life and be left alone. Instead, she and her friend got sucked into a hurricane. Makes me feel pretty helpless."

"We're not in prevention," Stride told her. "We're in cleanup."

Maggie stood up and brushed sand off her jeans. "On that cheery note, boys and girls, I'm going to go home and sleep for a couple hours. You two can do whatever it is you do in that bed of yours."

"You shouldn't drive," Serena told her. "Sleep in our spare bedroom."

"Thanks, but I've done that too much lately. I've got my own home, you know. At least until I sell that stinking mausoleum and get my own place. Besides, I'm not as buzzed as I look. Talking about dead bodies sobers me up. Don't worry, I'll go slow."

"I'll walk you out," Stride said.

As they left the ring of fire, Stride felt the remnants of winter chill creep back in under his clothes. Maggie seemed unaffected. She dangled her red leather jacket over her shoulder. The top two buttons on her pink blouse were undone. Stride had a flashlight, and the beam guided them along the trail through the woods. He walked with her past his house, past the used and dusty black Ford Expedition in his driveway, and out to Minnesota Avenue. The road cutting through the Point was deserted. Maggie's gleaming new Avalanche, painted in shocking yellow, was parked at the curb.

"It's good to have you back, Mags," he said, as they leaned against her truck. His fingers itched for a cigarette, but he had given them up again, and hopefully for good. Serena couldn't handle the smoke now.

"Thanks."

"You don't need the money anymore," he said. "Why come back to a job like this?"

Maggie shrugged. "It's what I do."

"You come to any decision about adopting a kid?"

"I'm still thinking about it," she admitted. "I've got to get my life put back together, and then we'll see. One step at a time."

"That would be one lucky kid," Stride said.

Maggie got up on tiptoes, ran her fingers through his wavy hair, and pulled his head down and kissed him. Her lips were soft as they moved on his mouth, and he wrapped his arms around her back and pulled her close. The kiss went on, a deep kiss, the kind of kiss he never imagined he would share with her.

She broke it off and smirked at him.

"No offense, but I've decided to stop loving you."

"Okay." As if anything was that easy.

"I have other things to do with my life, and you're in love with Serena. But it was nice to know I had a shot for a second there." She gave him one of the sarcastic, know-it-all, infuriating looks she had given him for ten years. "I did have a shot just now, didn't I?"

"Yeah, you did," he said, surprising himself.

"Leave them wanting more, that's my motto."

"Go away."

"I'll see you tomorrow, boss."

Maggie tossed her keys in her hand as she strolled around to the driver's door. He heard her whistling. He stayed where he was for a long while, because he could still feel the touch of her lips and smell her perfume, and it disoriented him. When he followed the snowy trail back to the lake and sat down in front of the fire next to Serena, he was quiet. He felt guilty.

Serena glanced at him, suppressed a grin, and stared off at the lake.

"So she kissed you, huh?" she asked.

"Are you a mind reader?"

"No, but that's not your shade of lipstick."

Stride cursed and wiped his face. "Sorry."

"It's okay."

They watched the bonfire dance. Knotty pine crackled and spit.

"Just so we're clear," Serena added, "if you ever do it again, I'll be forced to kill you both."

"Don't worry, you're my alpha girl."

"Better believe it."

Serena sidled across the sand and sat so that their legs were touching. He put his hand carefully on her thigh and caressed her skin through the loose fabric of her sweatpants, not touching too hard. She didn't stop him. Her body didn't cringe in pain, and her soul didn't pull away. When he looked at her, her eyes were closed, and she was smiling.

"This is okay?" he asked her.

"This is great."

They sat there in silence while the fire worked itself down to ash, and when it was nothing but a faint auburn glow on the ribbon of sand, they buried it with snow and hiked back over the grassy slope to their home.

ACKNOWLEDGMENTS

Much of this novel was conceived and researched in a rental cottage on Park Point in Duluth that bears suspicious similarity to the home now owned by Stride and Serena. You can actually stay there yourself, or you can tour the home at *www.cottageonthepoint .com.* Many thanks to Pat Burns for her hospitality.

As in the past, I am in debt to several people who have done so much to advance my career and who help me turn a manuscript into a novel each year: my agents Ali Gunn, Deborah Schneider, and Diana Mackay; my editors Jennifer Weis and Marion Donaldson; and my wife Marcia (to whom I owe so many other debts, too).

I would be remiss if I didn't mention several others in the industry who have been wonderful friends and supporters: Peter Newsom; Kim McArthur; Beth Goehring; Carole Baron; Markus Wilhelm; Sally Richardson; Gary Jansen; Silvia Sese; Iris Graedler; Matthew Shear; Carrie Hamilton-Jones; Kate Cooper; Carol Jackson; Gunilla Sondell; Genevieve Waldmann; Frank van de Stadt; and a host of editors and publishing colleagues in the United States and around the world.

In the past three years, I have built relationships with many, many booksellers and readers. Thanks to all of you for your enthusiasm and support. Special thanks to Gail F.; Eric S.; Paul P.; Shelly G.; Jean N.; Ron F.; Bonnie B.; Mike O.; and Jim H.

Finally, I hope you'll all visit my Web site at *www.bfreemanbooks.com* and continue to send me e-mails at *brian@bfreemanbooks .com.* One of the great pleasures of my life as an author is the opportunity to chat with readers.

Thanks, Mom and Dad. You made everything possible.